IS IT

It has to be a dream.

But he can't remember what real life is.

The head moves again, swinging against the blackness, twisting as though some giant hand has tangled in the matted curls of black hair and is raising it aloft... The madness of it all makes itself known to Jack Callaghan, a rational man, a policeman, he remembers, who has no time for the impossible in his life. The mouth moves, lips twitching around the voice that pours forth. White bone shines through ragged flesh and sinew hanging from where it has been severed at the neck. Jack isn't afraid of the ghostly head...why should he be? This is just a dream...

The eyes rove, rage burning behind them. They bulge in their sockets. The voice roars. Jack can feel the voice resonating with the blood as it roars through his body. And slowly, one by one, each unknown syllable starts to fall in time with his heartbeat.

There is heat, but this time it is inside him. It feels as though his blood is coming to a boil in his veins.

Fire threatens to consume him.

IS IT ALL A DREAM?

A

FIREBORN™
NOVEL

EACH EMBER'S GHOST

BY STEVEN SAVILE

Fantasy Flight Publishing, Inc.

This one's for Steve Lockley—cowriter, good friend,
with me every step of the way on this one.
It couldn't have happened without you, fella. Enjoy.

Cover illustration by Mathias Kollros.

This is a work of fiction. The characters, incidents, and dialogue are
drawn from the author's imagination and are not to be construed as real.
Any resemblance to actual events or persons, living or dead, is entirely coincidental.

ISBN: 978-1-61661-432-4

Fantasy Flight Publishing, Inc.
1975 West County Road B2
Roseville, MN 55113
USA

Find out more about Fantasy Flight Games
and our many exciting worlds at

www.FantasyFlightGames.com

EACH EMBER'S GHOST

CHAPTER 1

THE HEIST

Alice Ho slipped through the darkness like a razor blade cutting into a vein. Silence was a virtue in certain walks of life. In Alice's it was the stuff of life and death itself. She pressed herself up against the wall, feeling the thrill of cold stone on her back. She offered as little of her profile as was physically possible to the surveillance cameras. It was impossible to hide from all of them. The cameras covered every inch of the corridor, a miniaturized version of the world outside: once upon a time, London had been the most spied upon city in the world—there were still eyes everywhere. Alice was pragmatic. She wanted to make life as difficult as possible for the authorities, and yet still taunt them with the hope that they might *just* be able to identify her. It was all about angles and light and shadow, and the fact that she just loved to tease. It didn't hurt that she enjoyed being three steps ahead of the people chasing her, twice as intelligent as them, and better looking.

Alice barely suppressed a chuckle at that.

Sometimes when she was on the job her thoughts would ramble so she didn't obsess about what she was doing. Obsessives invariably made mistakes and became OCD about stupid superstitions when they were on the job. More often than not in her line of work the obsessing needed to come before the heist; during the job itself *instincts* were far more important.

She edged toward the great, grey metal door at the far end of the corridor, and then turned, just for a second, and flashed a killer smile at the camera; she could imagine their consternation at that. That made her smile all the more.

Two small, circular metal plates on either side of the huge brass handle shielded the old-fashioned keyholes. The entire mechanism was an echo of a bygone age. It never ceased to amaze her that so many banks were reluctant to let go of that simpler time. Instead of replacing the vault's door with a hi-tech electromagnetic locking mechanism, optical reader, biometric scanner, or other foolproof layer of protection, they had simply added an electronic alarm. It wasn't even a sophisticated one. She could disarm it with a four-digit code punched into the keypad beside the door. There was an arrogance in the fact that they hadn't taken measures to protect the vault adequately; it was as though they didn't think anyone would have the balls to rob them. Some jobs didn't need the proverbial testicles, they just needed a ruthless woman like Alice Ho.

She traced her fingers over the metal. The contact sent an involuntary shudder of pleasure through her body. A sudden surge of heat through her fingertips distracted her for a moment. Alice took a deep breath, and then moved her fingers again, feeling out the intricacies of the mechanism that lay sheathed within the layers of thick steel. Her smile spread with the heat as, on a molecular level, the steel grew more and more agitated by her touch. The heat intensified, almost burning now, as it ran through her fingers, through her hand, and crept up her arm. The metal began to weaken at her touch, softening around her fingers until Alice felt the levers beneath begin to move. One by one they eased themselves into alignment, matching the precise position they would have fallen into if she had pushed the right code into the keypad, and then they moved again, as though keys had been inserted and turned. A sudden sharp burst of static charge coursed through her body as the final pieces fell into place.

Alice grasped the great brass handle and with one confident twist of downward pressure pulled back the six solid steel bolts that held the door closed.

She was in.

Alice let out a breath she hadn't realized she'd been holding as the heavy door swung open. The sheer weight of the thing created its own momentum. A light came on inside the vault as though it were a giant refrigerator.

For the sliding moment of silence between heartbeats Alice was tempted to let the door slowly swing all the way back until it thumped up against the raised rubber stopper that had been screwed into the floor. There were chunks of plaster missing from where the door had chipped away at the wall for years before the stopper had been screwed into place. She didn't, though; she caught it before it could. There was a second metal door—this one no more imposing than a metal-mesh gate—that separated row upon row of safe deposit boxes from the shelves of files and other things that needed to be kept in the safest part of the bank. Alice laid her palm flat against the lock plate. It only took the briefest surge of heat to pop the lock. The gate slipped open and she slid through the gap even as it was still opening. Inside the vault proper she played her fingers along the rows of boxes.

Which ones? Which ones? she thought, using her gift to feel out the contents of the vaults. It wasn't that she could "see" what was in them, or actually even "feel" the contents, but certain things vibrated at different frequencies, so she could sense a difference between paper and gemstone, for instance, meaning she could methodically work her way along the line feeling out which box held jewels and which held cash, but she couldn't know which box held dusty old documents or bearer bonds, because they were essentially the same. Likewise, a work of art was indecipherable from a last will and testament. Her touch wasn't that precise, but that was all part of the fun. Life would have been *oh so dull* without a few surprises along the way.

The security was laughably poor, to the extent that it took a lot of fun out of the job. There was nothing here to test herself against. She could have beaten this system with one hand tied behind her back when she was barely into her teens. Now it was an insult to her skills.

The individual safety deposit boxes only needed the box holder's single key; there was no counter-key measure for the bank itself. There wouldn't be any spares; it wasn't that kind of bank. This was the kind of bank where anonymity was a better protection than any key code or combination lock could ever be. It was the kind of bank where the police would need a court order and a drill to gain entry, and even then the client would be tipped off to remove their belongings long before the drill could breach the lock.

But Alice Ho was one of a kind.

She walked slowly along the line, letting her fingertips trail across the doors of the boxes one after another, then another, and another, each time feeling the satisfying soft *snick, snack* of the locks on each of them open and close again.

There were no cameras within the vault itself. The bank's clientele were the sort of people who demanded absolute privacy. There was no telling what lost treasures were stashed away down here, Alice realized. She knew for sure she could make herself rich beyond her wildest dreams in less than two minutes flat, such was the wealth stashed in the vault, but this job wasn't about personal gain. There was a lot more to it than that. On the simplest level, she was doing it out of gratitude for one person and to gain the favor of another, but even that didn't come close to scratching beneath the surface motivation.

She had memorized the numbers of the boxes she needed to open. Writing things down in her line of work wasn't just a mistake, it was a potentially fatal one. The people she did jobs for didn't want their involvement known. Discretion was a priceless commodity. If pieces could be put together in such a way as to make a trail, measures would always have to be made to be sure it was a cold one, meaning a dead end. Literally. Alice had no intention of ending up as one of those. So she didn't write things down. Ever. Her mind was a steel trap when it came to the intricacies of a job. She worked alone. She controlled the variables. All of them. Indeed, she thought ahead through so many possible permutations that she actually welcomed the discovery of the theft from one of the boxes. It was a vital part of the disguise she was building to hide what else she had planned.

Alice moved quickly and efficiently, opening the two boxes she wanted and leaving the rest alone. She only took two things. From one box she removed a necklace and with the blade of a penknife she pried a single gem from the setting, then tucked it away safely before returning the rest of the necklace to the box. From the other she took a small velvet pouch, feeling the weight in her hand before adding it to the jewel in her zip-pocket at her hip. She replaced one of the boxes carefully, making sure that no one would be able to tell she had been anywhere near it, and left the other sitting wide open on the table in the middle of the room.

It was time to go.

The CCTV cameras were still watching as she left.

Alice flashed one a single smile, knowing that it would never be seen by anyone.

CHAPTER 2

FIRE BURN WITHIN ME

Jack Callaghan is in darkness so black that the world seems brighter when he closes his eyes.

There are voices here, and deeper in the darkness, the sounds of battle.

The words are unfamiliar...wrong...but the screams and cries of the dying and the smells of death are not. They're very familiar. Intimately. They are all around him. Jack has no idea what this place is, where it is—or was—and yet there is something naggingly familiar about it. It is as though he has been here before, but now it feels like a long-forgotten dream.

And a bad one at that.

There is heat in the air, and the unmistakeable odor of sulfur.

Jack is torn. He wants to call out to whoever is lurking out there in the darkness, but he doesn't dare to draw attention to himself. Fear knots itself in the pit of his stomach, screaming for him to make himself small.

The afterimage of a face drifts in and out of focus, like a ghost slipping across his mind. It's not just a face...it's a head. There are ragged wounds of blood and gristle around its neck where it has been hacked clear of its body. Its wild eyes stare at him. Into him. Its mouth moves, sounds bellowing out. They're words he

12

can't understand and yet, they exhort him to rise up, to battle, to fight, to rage... The words don't matter, it's what they do to him that does. They banish the fear that had wrapped itself around his soul. Even though he cannot understand a single word, they give him courage. They set his pulse to racing. They drive his blood pounding through his veins and drumming against his ears until that maddening dub-dub dub-dub *is all that he can hear.*

He longs to scream a battle cry and charge into the fray. Battle is calling him. But this can't be real. It has to be a dream.

But he can't remember what real life is.

The head moves again, swinging against the blackness, twisting as though some giant hand has tangled in the matted curls of black hair and is raising it aloft... The madness of it all makes itself known to Jack Callaghan, a rational man, a policeman, *he remembers, who has no time for the impossible in his life. The mouth moves, lips twitching around the voice that pours forth. White bone shines through ragged flesh and sinew hanging from where it has been severed at the neck. Jack isn't afraid of the ghostly head...why should he be? This is just a dream...*

The eyes rove, rage burning behind them. They bulge in their sockets. The voice roars. Jack can feel the voice resonating with the blood as it roars through his body. And slowly, one by one, each unknown syllable starts to fall in time with his heartbeat.

There is heat, but this time it is inside him. It feels as though his blood is coming to a boil in his veins.

Fire threatens to consume him.

CHAPTER 3

BLACKBIRD

Curzon Street was deserted when Alice Ho stepped out into the brisk morning air. She'd slept in the townhouse rather than her work place out on the Isle of Dogs. The townhouse was an indulgence from a rich ex. Rich men liked to shower her with trinkets and toys, and the richer the man, the more extravagant his gifts became. It was as though they were trying to disprove the old adage *money can't buy love*. Alice didn't love them, but she was rather partial to their generosity, so she smiled and pretended when it suited her. It was just another form of theft, really. A long grift. And like any theft, there was an art to it. And Alice was *good* at what she did.

The street was strewn with litter. Not so long ago this had been one of the most prized addresses in the city, home to the rich and famous, the richer and the even more famous. Times had changed. Now they couldn't even get a street cleaner to work at night around here. There were too many terrors lurking in the shadows, too many strange things stalking the side streets and alleyways for anyone to put themselves in harm's way. It was all primal, in-stinctual. They didn't know what was happening around them, but some long-buried danger-sense flared up and they *had* to listen to it. Street cleaners worked from sunrise to sunset and not a minute longer. If the clean up couldn't be finished before sundown, the garbage sacks could stack up, the cardboard burger boxes and the sheets of yesterday's news could line the gutter.

The last orange glow of streetlights would soon fade away as the sky gradually grew lighter, heralding the relative safety of dawn.

Alice was not afraid of the dark; if anything she welcomed it as part of her natural habitat. She was a night walker. A creature of the moon. She rarely needed sleep, and when she did, she was just as happy to close her eyes when the sun was at its highest and the streets crowded. Crowded was a relative term. It was a long time since London had genuinely been choked with people. The dark skies had put an end to that.

Still, for all that, the houses along the old curved street almost smelled of wealth. The richest and safest homes were still to be found in this part of London, replete with their high security protection, surveillance cameras, and guards. Some of the more regal old buildings still had doormen standing like sentries in their crisply ironed red uniforms. The only difference was that now they carried concealed weapons to give the residents the peace of mind they paid so richly for.

Alice saw changes everywhere she went. The sad thing was that she'd long since stopped paying attention to them; *plus ça change, plus c'est la même chose*, as the saying went. The world had changed, and she had changed with it. That was just the way it had to be. It was either a case of becoming part of the new order or becoming a relic of the old. She was no one's relic. What she was was a thief, and a damned good one at that.

She closed the red door behind her. She didn't need to lock it. She had all sorts of security in place that made something as banal as keys redundant. No one would break in to the townhouse. She started to walk. She needed to clear her head. The last dregs of adrenaline still buzzed through her system, though the high that had got her through the night was long since gone. Now she was itchy. She needed to be moving. Doing something.

She ended up going to the café on the corner. It was blissfully quiet. No one had slumped down into the deep faux-leather seats for hours. She loved those chairs, with their foam poking through to offer a lesson in the secret anatomy of upholstery. And she loved this time of day. The coffee shop was quiet apart from the gentle rattle and clatter as Franco set up for the day, the occasional gurgle of the espresso machine, the tamping of the coffee press, the slice of the carving knife on the breadboard—all of those small comforting sounds that said she wasn't alone in the world after all.

Alice had been coming into Franco's for coffee since she had moved into the townhouse. The café wasn't actually called *Franco's*, it was called *Brasco's*, after an old movie mob character, but it would always be Franco's to her. Franco was well into his fifties, with that olive skin and dark stubble of a second generation Italian, and dark, smoldering eyes that could have melt the panties off an unsuspecting woman at one hundred paces. He was ruthlessly charming, and an incorrigible flirt. They had a good thing going on; he smiled and tried out his lines on her, and in return she got the best coffee in the city. She never felt dirty or threatened by anything he said, unlike some of the jokers she met on the underground club scene. With Franco the "Hey, pretty lady, you're looking especially lovely this morning" always felt like an honest compliment, and that made her feel good. It never came across as a prelude to something more, which made a pleasant change of pace.

Franco brought over her espresso and a plate of biscotti.

Alice liked to imagine that he had an elderly mother who got up at the crack of dawn to make them especially for her. She didn't need to know about the wholesaler who lurked behind the curtain or the factory conveyor belt of sugar rush he presided over. Reality was always so much more boring than the fantasy. Besides, thinking there was a secret family recipe and a little old lady slaving over them made the biscotti taste so much better.

"So, tell me again how it can be that a pretty girl like you is in here drinking coffee on her own at this godforsaken hour? I'm beginning to think you've got a thing for me," Franco said, offering her a cheeky grin. That was the way it was.

"I want you for your caffeine, darling, what can I say?"

He went back to the counter and changed the music. A moment later a rich, sad-voiced man started singing about *Lips Like Ether*. Alice listened to the lyrics. She was never one for the melody;

the real beauty was always in the words. She sipped at her coffee. This had to be one of the saddest songs she'd ever heard. The man was obviously in pain, singing about the kind of lost love only the luckiest ever really knew. The song changed after a few minutes, the same sad voice saying he *prayed for love to the martyr in his blood*. "And they say women are the soppy ones," Alice said, but Franco didn't hear her.

Through the window she could see the line of tall trees that screened the residents' garden. The gates were locked, but the iron railings were no more than waist high, so it wasn't like they were really serious about keeping people out. Alice liked to sit in the garden and watch the people. She loved that London was still so full of green places.

A row of street-side tables stood empty outside. It was too early in the morning for people to want to take the weight off their feet and refuel on caffeine. The morning chill lingered in the air. Give it an hour or so and it would be different.

In the height of summer this was one of her favorite spots from which to watch the world go by.

A shadow passed across the tables for a moment, like a ghostly walker, and then they were bathing in sunlight once more.

Those same base instincts she relied upon when she went to work bristled now: something was wrong. Unnatural. She had no idea what or why. That didn't matter. She'd learned to trust her instincts.

Alice got up from her seat, catching the edge of the table with her hip and sending a splash of coffee across the pristine white tablecloth like arterial spray. Franco looked up from his work as her chair scraped on the wooden floor and smiled without a word. She shrugged an apology and moved to the window. Alice looked out through the glass as a great black mass moved across the sky. She peered up at it as its shape shifted, constantly changing as it moved over the houses until it finally became a great bird—a great black bird. Its shadowy wings beat in a slow, fluid motion as it stretched and swelled, growing until it utterly blotted out what little sun the pall allowed through, and plunged the city into darkness. She pressed her hands flat against the glass, looking up, and counted two full minutes of pitch black before the shadow-bird shrank back. It circled behind the Hilton Tower hotel, out of view for a moment, before reappearing. This time she could see it for what it really was: a murmuration of starlings. Their flocking pattern was both perfectly coordinated and an amazing thing to behold.

"Hey, Franco, have you seen anything like that before?" she asked, even though he couldn't possibly have seen the birds within the shadow-bird from where he was standing. He was already walking toward her, tea towel in one hand, coffee mug in the other.

"Too late," she said. "It's gone."

"What was it?"

"Birds. Starlings. Flying in formation."

"Was it a face?"

"No," Alice said. "A bird. A huge bird. Have you seen them make a face?"

"A couple of times," he told her. "And you know the weird thing?"

"What, weirder than birds making faces in the sky?"

He chuckled at that. "I'm sure that it was the same face both times."

"Okay, I'll give you that. On a one-to-ten scale of weird, that's weird factor seven."

"A bird is not good," Franco said. "Birds are creatures of omen."

"Omens? What of?" She knew the answer before she'd finished asking the question. She didn't wait for the reply. Alice gathered up her coat.

"Death," he said as she closed the door.

* * *

The sky was clear when she stepped out of the café.

That in itself was a surprise. It wasn't blue. It had been a long time since it had been blue. But there wasn't a single bird up there despite the mass that had banked and rolled across the clouds only a few moments before.

Alice slipped her jacket on as she walked. She had no idea

where she was heading. It was purely about movement. The streets were still quiet, but the first few signs of life had begun to stir in some of the glass buildings and concrete towers—people leaving for work, people arriving at work. At night they hid behind locked doors and barred windows, but in daylight they found short-lived courage. Alice couldn't imagine living her life like that; she needed the danger, the adrenaline rush that came with being in places that she had no right to be. She lived by defying convention and ignoring the risk. Only then was she *truly* alive.

There were times when her mind wandered, when her thoughts left her and her body moved of its own volition. She became a living ghost. The sight of the great bird had sent her mind reeling so much so that the previous night's activities had slipped into the status of half-forgotten dream. She replayed the flight of the bird over and over again, picturing it in her head until it was burned there. She would never forget it, not how it looked, or how it moved.

It wasn't some miraculous sight or some incredible sound that dragged her back to the here-and-now; it wasn't even something *strange* that intruded on her thoughts. It was one of the few things that had remained constant despite the flood of changes and the uncertainty that had enveloped London. She had walked past this point so many times, once or twice a day at least, but she had never stopped to listen before. She did today. It was almost hypnotic.

Speaker's Corner was one of those weird places that exists in various shapes or forms in just about every city across the world; a place where anyone can stand and address whatever crowd will gather and is prepared to listen, or heckle. The patch of ground in the northeast corner of Hyde Park had always been held in special regard even though there had never been any laws passed to protect it; it was a place where anyone could stand and speak out about injustice, justice, burning needs, pressing problems, or even just The Lord. Few bothered to stop and listen anymore. Fewer still wanted to stand on their soapbox and speak. It was just one more sign that the old days were slipping away. Marx and Lenin had both spoken here in their time. She realized, somewhat sadly, that if they'd stood there today no one would be there to listen to their call for change, and what a sorry state of affairs that was.

Today a single man had stopped to listen to the current speaker—an elderly man in a long raincoat. His small dog tugged on its lead impatiently.

Alice stopped for a moment and listened, doubling the size of his audience.

"Listen to me, London! You need to hear me! The day is coming. Soon the last of the ravens will leave the Tower. You know what that means, don't you?"

At least it made a change from the usual array of religious fundamentalists and nut-jobs of all persuasions that predicted the end of the world on a daily basis, even if it wasn't a pleasant one. There was something about this shabbily dressed man that kept her listening, though. Actually, she realized, looking at him properly, the speaker was well-dressed, though it looked as though he had been sleeping in the suit for several days. His face had not seen a razor for a month or more, which added to the wild-eyed effect of his rant.

"You!" he said, pointing straight at Alice. "You know what it means when the last raven leaves, don't you? You know what will happen to this once great country of ours, don't you, my friend?" She found herself nodding without thinking about it. "I don't know what's going on in there. You don't. None of us know. We don't know what abominations lurk in there now, but you must believe me, you must… I've seen things. Bad things. It won't be long before the last of the birds is dead and gone."

Ravens. That was what the great bird had been; all those hundreds, maybe even thousands of starlings had taken the shape of a raven, not just any old black bird. Alice suppressed a shudder. What would Franco have made of an omen like that, she wondered.

The man became more agitated, his gaze constantly flicking up to the sky as though he expected to see the great raven of birds return. There was nothing to see but the high-lying smog.

Nothing to be afraid of.

A couple of passersby barely gave him a second glance. A few moments later the dog pulled its master away in the search of something more interesting and she was the only one left to listen to his rambling imprecations.

She didn't have to believe what he was saying; it was abundantly clear that he believed enough for both of them.

He believed enough for the whole city.

CHAPTER 4

THEN I SAW HER FACE, NOW I'M A BELIEVER

It was another day in hell for Jack Callaghan.

The detective squad room was littered with the night shift's mess: screwed up balls of file paper and scrubbed out report pages, a couple of well-read red-top newspapers, and a precarious sculpture of plastic cups with the dried up dregs of hours-old coffee crusting in the bottoms of them. Like everywhere else in the city, the cleaning teams arrived well into the hours of daylight rather than risking the night, even though all was quiet. It was easier to work around office workers than it was to run the night streets.

Callaghan had worked the night shift before; he knew the kind of man it took to survive, and more than that, he knew the kind of cop it demanded: a loner, a nonconformist, someone who swam against the effulgence of life without opening his mouth and swallowing mouthful after mouthful of crap. Calls that came in that weren't considered urgent were left until the morning. That was just the way it was. He didn't miss it. He still wound up working through the night sometimes, but every now and again he got to sleep in his own bed.

He was the first of day watch to report for duty. He'd been the last to sign out the night before. Descartes had it wrong, it wasn't thinking that made someone, it was working: Jack Callaghan worked, therefore he was. Of course, he was ready to leave the moment he arrived. The handover consisted of a brief handshake, the rundown of the night's incident reports, and a signature on one of the forms on the night sergeant's clipboard. There were half a dozen sheets of paper on the desk. Anything interesting on them would have already been logged into the antiquated computer system. The actual paperwork was the Met's equivalent of a backup. In reality it *barely* passed for a paper trail, but it would be just enough to ensure that blame was avoided.

Callaghan fed a pound coin into the vending machine and punched in the two-digit code for his poison and waited as the machine rumbled and grumbled into life. A plastic cup dropped into position a second before the steaming hot liquid began to pour. He'd summoned coffee but suspected it really didn't matter what combination of keys he'd pressed, the same vile liquid would gurgle down the spout. He held the cup carefully and went back to his desk. He read through the pages of scribbled notes. It was always the same kinds of comments that appeared day-in day-out, and more often than not some of the same names made guest appearances. It was all a bit pointless really. Nosy neighbor sightings of people moving through back alleys in the middle of the night. Reports of strange noises from neighboring houses and apartments that were supposed to be empty.

The most serious event of the night appeared to have been a minor disturbance outside The World's End. Callaghan knew the pub by reputation. It wasn't the kind of place a man like him would ever be welcome. It *was* the kind of place that attracted the strange and the unusual to it, drawing outsiders and misfits like flies because they didn't fit anywhere else. But most of all it attracted the kind of people who were not afraid to go out at night. The goth scene was an entire subculture he didn't understand with its bondage affectations, studded dog collars, and stark, painted faces, but he didn't need to understand them to appreciate the fact that they *lived*, which was a damned sight more than could be said for a lot of the denizens of the city these days. The brief note said that all was quiet, at least outside the pub, when a patrol car drove past to check on the disturbance. No surprise there. It was also the kind of place where they sorted out their own problems.

Callaghan raised the cup to his lips but the nuclear fallout heat steaming off it was enough to make sure that he kept the plastic cup well away from his mouth. It was a miracle it didn't melt the plastic. The coffee had a strange metallic smell that no matter how much he smelled it, he simply couldn't come to terms with. Coffee shouldn't taste like Uranium-235. He put the cup down on his desk knowing he wouldn't pick it up again for at least three half-lives.

The squad room door swung open and slammed shut.

"Morning, Guv," Jenny Lawson said, bright and breezy as she bustled into the office. She put a decent store-bought cappuccino on the desk in front of him.

"My hero," Callaghan said, dumping the still decaying grey-brown liquid he had wasted good money on in the wastepaper basket.

"Doesn't take much to impress you, does it?" she said. Lawson picked up the reports in her free hand, hitched her bag higher up her shoulder, and doing that balancing act women seemed to manage effortlessly, hands full, bag swinging on hip, sashayed between the desks as she made her way to her own seat. It was the same every morning; they were always the first in. It didn't matter if he tried to get a head start and rolled in half an hour earlier to catch up, she *always* walked through the squad room doors a few minutes later. A paranoid man would have thought she was stalking him.

"Anything interesting?"

Callaghan shook his head. He took the first sweet sip of ambrosia that was the proper coffee she'd brought in. It could have brought a dying man back from the brink, it was that good. "Nothing to write home about. Which will have pleased the boys on the snore shift." They both knew that at least one of the guys on duty last night would have been asleep at any given time—two if it was a really quiet night—it was just a perk of the job.

The phone rang.

Callaghan knew it would be the first of many calls that would come through over the next couple of hours: all of those people who had wanted to report incidents or strange happenings in the night but had been afraid to call in at the time. These were the kinds of people who thought that the authorities should know about things, but the thing Jack Callaghan could never quite wrap his mind around was why they always assumed that the police were the right authorities to inform, or the fact that they felt compelled to call in, but didn't actually want to have their nice cozy evening by the fireside disturbed by a knock at the door from the police responding to their call. It came down to the fact that they didn't want to get involved, but somehow managed to absolve their conscience by making a call, pretending to be good citizens, even though the horse had well and truly bolted by the time they picked up the receiver.

Lawson took the call.

Callaghan tried to work out the gist of the conversation from her side, but it wasn't easy. She scribbled a few words on a pad as she listened, then put the phone down, a smile spreading Cheshire Cat-like across her face. It was obvious that she thought this was something rather than nothing.

He raised an eyebrow.

"You'll never guess what, Guv?"

"Probably not, so how about you take pity on the old guy and put me out of my misery?"

"We've got ourselves a good old-fashioned honest-to-God bank job."

"You're right, I never would have guessed in a month of Sundays." And that was true; it wouldn't have even made his top five guesses. Top ten at a push, coming in behind a granny battering, some petty shoplifting, a twoccer (taken without owner's consent), ram-raid, and oh so many other not-so-grand larcenies. The Flying Squad was made up of crime solvers, thief takers, but all too often these days they had to pick up the slack and deal with petty crimes that should have been handled downstairs. He knew that they were far more likely to get asked to deal with shrinkage—the theft of materials from factories or raids on bonded warehouses— than they were to be asked to get their hands dirty with something like this: a good old-fashioned bank robbery. He couldn't help but smile. This was the *right* way to start the day. This was what he'd signed up for. He took the piece of paper from her and grabbed his jacket from the back of his chair.

Callaghan was halfway out the door before he asked, "You okay to hold the fort?" It was a stupid question; Lawson was more than capable of running the show on her own, but it never hurt to ask, even if it was just an afterthought. She waved him away.

"Have fun, Guv."

"I always do."

* * *

Uniforms were already standing vigil outside the Sidney Street Bank. The Force had changed a lot over the years—from Bow Street and its Runners to the Peelers, all the way up to the modern Metropolitan Police and Scotland Yard—with professionals taking the place of criminals on the hunt. The old logic had always been that it took a thief to catch a thief. There was still an aspect of Callaghan's job that demanded he think like a thief, like a killer, a thug, a gangster, a bully boy, or any other more common varieties of villain, but now more often than not he had to think like a well-educated, devious, white-collar crook.

The bank itself was a fairly inconspicuous building that looked solid but unimposing. Discreet. This wasn't just another High Street branch of one of the major banks—there was no glass or chrome in sight. This was old school banking. He knew it was going to be a nightmare before he walked through the front door. It was a private facility hidden in plain sight, the kind of place whose clientele demanded a certain anonymity in return for their business. There wasn't going to be a nice database of accounts for him to browse through, no inventory of contents for him to check off. Everything beyond those doors was a closely guarded secret—even from the staff working there. *Oh joy*, Callaghan thought bitterly. There were laws about cash transactions, about reporting the movement of money for the purpose of tracking money laundering and the like. The safety deposit boxes were another beast entirely; there was no regulation covering them— anything could be down in the vault, stowed away safely until it was forgotten about. This was one of the places where blind eyes were turned. Jack Callaghan had been to a place like this before. It hadn't ended well that time. He was hoping for better luck this time.

The sight of the security guard dressed in a morning suit, including top hat, came as no surprise. This was the way things had been done in the world of old money for generations, and they liked it that way. Traditions were maintained more often than not purely because they kept the *nouveau riche* on the outside.

He saw a familiar face as soon as he stepped inside: Harry Peters, a dour Scot who thought everything about life was better over the border, but stayed down here in civilization all the same. He liked Harry. He was as good a scene-of-crime officer, or SOCO, as the Met had, even if he was a gruff, abrasive, tell-it-like-it-is kind of soul. As far as Callaghan was concerned, the world needed more of those anyway. Harry had been working crime scenes for as long as Callaghan could remember. He couldn't recall the last time he'd seen him when he wasn't suited up in his white coveralls. He was dusting for prints on the outside of the huge vault door. He didn't look happy. Two of his technicians were inside, bagging and tagging and taking photographs.

"All right, Harry? Anything interesting?"

"Jack." Harry peered up from the capstan handle on the vault door. The lower half of his face twisted into something that wasn't quite a grimace, but wasn't a smile either. He looked perturbed. "Comes down to your definition of interesting, I should think. This lock, for instance, is well and truly knackered. And I don't just mean broken. This vault wasn't cracked, least not in any traditional way. Take a look for yourself."

Callaghan moved closer, leaning in to get a better look at what Harry was talking about. There was no sign of the door having been forced; no telltale signs of acid having been poured into the lock, no great tear in the metal. He crouched down to peer up at the mechanism from a different angle. Then looked up at Harry who was only too happy to offer up his wisdom.

"As you can see, there's no sign of force having been used," Harry said, kicking off a game of State the Bleeding Obvious.

"Key?" Callaghan suggested, joining in.

Harry produced one from one of the pockets of his white suit. Without a word he slid it into the keyhole and turned it first one way then another. "You try it." He did; there was no resistance at all. Callaghan turned the key again. There was nothing to suggest that there was even a mechanism inside. "As I said, knackered. That's the technical term, you understand," Harry said.

Callaghan tried to think about what that lack of resistance entailed: Could someone have opened the whole door up, removed the lock, and put the plates back in place without anyone noticing? Meaning whoever locked it last night didn't realize that it wasn't actually secure before they went home to bed? That was one elaborate inside job, if so. And improbable, if not impossible. He made a note to ask if anyone had been carrying out any maintenance work down here over the last day or so, and as a second thought, whether the alarm system was sophisticated enough to detect if the lock mechanism was actually in place, or if it just relied upon the contact on the lock plate completing the circuit.

He'd worked with some idiots in his time, but was it really possible that someone could be stupid enough *not* to test the handle and make sure the door was locked before setting the alarm?

It was only then that he saw the smile beginning to play across Harry's lips. The Scot didn't have a face made for smug grins.

"Okay, what gives?"

"In my role as police psychic, I predict you are thinking about the practicalities of stripping the mechanism out of the door, am I right? Of course I am," he went on before Callaghan could confirm or deny it. "Well, my imaginatively challenged friend, I would think that taking one of these babies apart and putting it back together again would take all the king's horses and all the king's men at *least* a day. Maybe two. Now, I can't imagine anyone apart from the Invisible Man being able to do that without being noticed, can you?"

Callaghan felt more than a little stupid.

"It's still early in the morning," he said, meaning that his brain wasn't quite in gear. "I'm at least two cups of coffee from doing anything clever."

"Only two? Feeling a tad optimistic this morning, are we?"

"Shut it."

The SOCO chuckled. "It's gonna take a wee while to get someone down here to take a look at the problem, but I've got a portable X-ray machine on the way. I'm hoping that will help me see how they got in."

"Any prints?"

"Plenty, as you'd expect, and I'm sure they'll ping like crazy on the database, but that door hasn't been wiped down in forever. Ronnie and Reggie Kray's prints are probably still on the damned thing," Henry grumbled, referring to the long-dead East End gangsters. Callaghan wasn't about to argue. This place was every bit as much a relic of the bad old days as it was the good ones.

He looked around. From what he could see from out here, the vault was old-fashioned in its simplicity and lack of sophistication. Security deposit boxes lined the walls. There was a table in the middle. And that, to all intents and purposes, was it. There was a CCTV camera outside the vault, but as far as he could see, nothing inside. "I hope to God that thing works," he said, looking up at the eye in the ceiling.

"If you'll accompany me," a small, balding man said, appearing at the far end of the corridor. Callaghan exchanged glances with Henry. People who could do that whole appearing out of thin air trick gave him the creeps.

"My mother always told me not to talk to strangers," Callaghan said.

"Sorry, sorry. My name is Malcolm Hannon. I am the manager. I made the call to your station."

"Hannon," Callaghan made a note of the name. His little black book filled up pretty quickly, unfortunately not with the kind of names that made good dating material.

The balding man began offering more information than Callaghan needed right then. The devil might be in the details, but if you started focusing on the minutiae before you had a sense of the big picture you were going to miss the blindingly obvious stuff. Hannon started in on the small details, about to spill the life story of each and every member of staff under him. Callaghan held up his hand to stop him before he got started. He needed to get a feel for the lay of the land and work out what exactly he was dealing with first. The rest could wait. "Any idea how much has been taken?"

The little man shrugged. It was an eloquent expression that spoke volumes for how little he actually knew about what went on inside his dominion. "Impossible to say until we've contacted the owner and, err, even then…" He turned his palms up as though to say, *Your guess is as good as mine.* "This vault only holds the safety deposit boxes. What little cash and bearer bonds we keep on the premises are held in a separate strongroom."

"Right. And?"

"Only one box has been opened, but we have no idea what the contents would have been. So we can't tell if anything was actually stolen."

"Whose box was it?"

"I'm sorry, I'm sure you can understand the situation: we have a strict policy of client confidentiality. You'll have to get a court order for that kind of information."

"A court order? Is that right?" Callaghan said. He had dealt with officious little pricks like this before. He leaned in a little closer than necessary, his own body language every bit as eloquent as the bank manager's had been. It said: *I could break you in two if I wanted to. Go ahead, make my day.* "I am sure your client would want us to do everything we possibly could do to recover his property."

Hannon shuffled his feet and looked at the floor without saying another word. He was intimidated, but he wasn't going to spill his guts. Which meant that the threat of the box holder was a scarier proposition than the physical presence of Callaghan. That in itself was interesting. Very few men were that frightening.

Callaghan looked past Hannon into the vault. There was always more than one way to skin a cat. He wasn't averse to applying a little pressure as an incentive, but it might well be easier to do it later, when it was time to really shake the tree and see what fell out. He could wait. As clichéd as it sounded, patience really was a virtue.

Two of Harry's technicians were in the vault itself, dusting for prints and bagging up what little forensic evidence they could find.

He was itching to get inside and take a look for himself, but he knew he'd only get in the way. He was better off letting them do their thing. They'd let him know when it was okay for him to go in with his size elevens and trample all over the crime scene.

"So let's take a look at this CCTV footage shall we?"

* * *

Callaghan stared at the screen.

He wasn't sure what he'd expected to see on the tape, but not this: a woman made her way along the corridor that lead to the vault. She was so slight she could have passed for a young girl.

He must have been staring at the image for more than a minute before he realized that he hadn't so much as blinked.

Callaghan forced himself to close his eyes for a moment. His dry corneas stung as his eyelids closed. He felt a protective wash of tears film over them.

He had been on his own for far too long.

The woman reached the door and, as she did, turned to look toward the camera. He held his finger poised above the pause button, ready to capture her *in flagrante delecto*.

She looked up, right at him.

Callaghan froze the frame.

It was always going to be too much to hope that he would be able to recognize her, and close the case in a matter of hours.

But for all that life liked to batter him, Jack Callaghan lived in hope.

He looked at her. She looked back at him. Straight at him. He was sure that she was smiling, but her features were blurred beyond any hope of recognition.

"What's wrong with this?" He tapped the screen, then wiped at it. He knew that there was nothing wrong; the rest of the picture was sharp and in perfect focus, it was only her face that was in any way distorted. So much for hope.

Hannon leaned forward and hit the rewind button, making the woman on the screen dance backward erratically to his tune until she was back, pressed up against the wall.

Callaghan stared intently at the spot on the screen where her face was; it remained in focus the entire time, so it wasn't some fault with the pixels. He hit the play button again and she moved forward again. As she reached the great metal door, he froze the frame again. Every single hair was in perfect focus then, between one frame and the next, yet as she started to turn toward the camera, it blurred again.

There was nothing wrong with the camera.

Whatever was happening here, she was causing it.

"I'll get one of our guys to take a look at it, see if they can clean up the image," Callaghan said, but he knew full well that even though they were miracle workers, there was very likely nothing they could do with it. He let the image play on, curious as to how she actually went about opening the door. She shielded whatever it was she was doing with her body, but as best as he could make out there was no sign of a key, no sign of acid being poured into the lock, and no explosive charge, which would have been his best guess, despite the lack of charge residue on the lock plates.

Actually, the more he studied the image, the more it looked as though the only thing she did was place her hands on the cold metal plate and wait until the door sprang open of its own volition.

The picture flooded with light as the door swung open on the vault. She stepped, or rather skipped, inside, as if the whole thing was no more than a game she was happily playing.

She moved out of view of the camera, but he could still see her shadow moving across the screen as she worked her way around the room, looking for the box she wanted. Callaghan watched it intently, matching her movements to the shadow in his head until she came back into view with a safety deposit box in her hands.

* * *

The safety deposit box lay on the table in the center of the room. The remaining contents had already been placed into individual evidence bags and tagged by the SOCOs. Callaghan ran a finger over the items, until he came across an official document that declared that it was the *Last Will and Testament of John Doughty, written by mine own hand on this day of the Twelfth of October 1584 in the commonwealth of Leicester.*

The first lines recorded what the man believed to be the brutal murder of his brother Thomas, accused by Sir Francis Drake of being a conjurer and seditious person, and beheaded for mutiny and treason. The rest of it was a division of assets and property down the family tree. Several pieces of jewelry within the box, it seemed, were a part of that division, though one piece of particular mention by John was the acquisition of a gem from Drake, the inference being it was stolen by Thomas, one last thumbing of the nose to his one-time friend. The will offered some names, some parishes, but very little else. It was a curious document to find in a bank vault, and almost certainly worth very little beyond curiosity value, even if it offered some irrefutable evidence in a five-centuries-old cold case.

"Well, well," Callaghan said, making much of folding up the will and putting it on the table to be bagged and tagged and taken back to the station as material evidence. "I guess we'll be able to trace the owners without your help, *Mister* Hannon." He labored over the *Mister*, stressing it. It was a little dig at the propriety of the man. Sometimes little victories were sweeter than the big ones. Well, they were when he was feeling petty. Right now he felt exceedingly petty. He gambled that the bank manager hadn't read the line that dated the will as originating in 1584. "After all, who keeps someone else's will in their safety deposit box?"

"You can't take that out of here," the little man stammered. His nose twitched like a weasel's snout. It looked for a moment as though he was about to stamp his feet. "That belongs to our client."

"Right now it's also evidence," Callaghan said, enjoying himself now. "We won't be able to tell without running a lot of forensic tests on it, obviously, but there's every chance that the thief left fingerprints on it, or some other residue. We have to exhaust every avenue. I'm sure you understand. I know your client would."

With that, there were no objections left that Hannon could reasonably make, and he knew it. The bank manager had played his one roll of the dice, and had come up short.

Apart from that, the box held a number of interesting, and, quite likely, exceptionally expensive pieces of jewelry. Some of them were in presentation boxes, which he couldn't open without removing them from their evidence bags, but there were plenty of loose pieces. There was, quite literally, a king's ransom in the box. And the thief had left it behind.

That didn't make sense.

He tried to think it through.

The woman had basically perpetrated what could easily be considered the perfect bank job only to leave the spoils behind? He remembered the slight skip as she'd entered the vault and the impression of it all being a big game to her.

Out of all the boxes available to her, she'd only opened the one, and she had done it seemingly without any effort. Why stop at one? Why this box? And then why not take all of the contents when there was so much obvious wealth to be had? Why leave so much behind? There were so many questions, all of them utterly reasonable to him, but there were no answers that sprung readily to mind that were even half as reasonable.

No, he realized, that wasn't quite true. There was one reasonable explanation: she had broken in for one particular thing, and having got it, she wasn't interested in anything else. Which meant it wasn't about money. It was about that one thing. And without knowing what was in the box, basically, they were screwed.

He sighed.

He hated the whole sleazy nature of this almost-underworld. He preferred it when crooks were crooks and wore black and white uniforms with arrows on them, making it easy to tell who was the bad guy.

Callaghan sifted through the evidence bags, then picked up the last of them, taking a closer look at a necklace. It really didn't make sense that something so obviously valuable had been set aside as not being worth taking.

He turned the piece over in his hand, examining it more closely. He noticed immediately that one of the gemstones was missing from the setting. He wondered if that was why the necklace was buried away down here instead of around someone's neck?

He held it up to the stark white light of the bare bulb in the ceiling and saw that the gold of the setting was just that little bit brighter where the jewel had been in comparison to the rest of it, meaning the gold hadn't been subjected to years of wear and cleaning. There was a small build up of polish where the stone had met the gold. Which, Callaghan realized, meant the stone must have been removed fairly recently.

So the thief had taken it. That added another layer of curiosity to the theft, but didn't explain why none of the other stones had been taken, or why the thief hadn't just lifted the entire necklace… He was frustrated. If the thief had stolen the complete piece he could have put out the word, got the right people looking for it. He had plenty of friends in low places. But a single stone could be recut and disappear forever.

The best he could hope for was that it would make its way to a cutter who had a bit of integrity. That was a slim hope that lurked right beside no hope at all.

He turned the plastic bag over in his hands again, feeling out the slight protrusions and indentations in the back of the metal setting. The mount was sharp. As he pressed it with his finger the metal punctured the plastic membrane and caught the skin of his finger. He pulled his hand away as a bubble of blood smeared the clear plastic.

His vision blurred, and for a moment the intense light from the naked bulb burned weird shapes onto the backs of his eyes, even with his eyelids closed. The air tasted stale in his mouth and nose as his breathing became just a little more urgent, a little more labored, and he knew that he had to get out of there. He was having some sort of weird panic attack. Heat surged through him. He dropped the bag and reached out for the table to steady himself as the strength drained from his legs. Even as his legs began to buckle beneath him, a raw, intense energy surged through him. In that moment he felt as though his skin was struggling to contain something so much bigger than him and he thought for one sickening moment it was about to tear open.

He staggered outside. He head swam. His balance betrayed him, he felt himself falling, and as he hit the ground, looking up at the sky, he saw fire.

* * *

The sky is ablaze; fire and flame fill the air, but even in the constantly changing light he can still see colors shifting, filming over, as though sparkling beneath the skin of water. Clusters of rubies and emeralds, sapphires and diamonds catch the light of flames as the fire rages higher. The fire dances within the stones as though they are alive. Some, he sees, are rough and uncut, as though they have come straight from the ground, while others have been cut and faceted to show off their light and quality. They are pure. Beautiful. He reaches out for them, reaching up into the water—or is it the sky? He doesn't know anymore—and hears the notes of a perfect, haunting elegy call to him. The song swells within his mind. His mind? Who is he? Callaghan? Jack? That doesn't feel right. His heart sings the song of the stones. He needs to hold them. To own them. To possess them.

But he is no thief...

CHAPTER 5

THE WORLD'S END

Alice checked her watch. It was still early morning. She had been up for hours, but London was a later riser these days. It was still too early to do some of the things she needed to do.

There were far too many places across the city where it was far too easy to attract attention these days, even if only because so few people would be out and about when places were only just beginning to open for the day. Habits changed. When her father was her age he'd told her about arriving more than thirty minutes before his shift began every single day of the week, meaning he was in the old family restaurant on Gerrard Street three and a half hours a week longer than he had to be. It was the same with her grandfather and everyone else from that side of her family.

It was the Chinese work ethic, she supposed. They had come over on the boats as refugees and always seemed so glad just to be allowed to stay, forgetting the hardships of the journey with the boat people and everything they'd left behind just to be allowed to work like slaves in a foreign land. She had never felt the same debt to this country. She was a third generation immigrant; she carried a British passport, had voted in the elections and protested against political idiocy when she was a student just like any other British kid angry at the establishment. She had raged against the

machine. She had made out in back alleys, and stood on the ter-
races with her dad watching the Spurs and cheering her young
lungs out like everyone else. When she bled it was red, white,
and blue.

But she was still an immigrant. They still called her names
when she walked down the wrong streets. It was the kind of subtle
racism that was just permanently ingrained into the culture of certain parts of town. She lived with it. She *had* noticed, though, that
the older she got the more sexual in nature the heckling grew. She
assumed this meant the bigots were struggling with some issues
of their own, and did her best not to let it get to her.

Eventually she needed to visit the British Library, which meant
taking the backstreets to Piccadilly, heading up Shaftesbury Avenue and across the corner of Covent Garden, up to New Oxford
Street and into Bloomsbury. They were still "safe" parts of the
city. But she knew that she would be more noticeable once she
was on the other side of Covent Garden and into the business
district. Once inside the library itself, she'd stick out like a sore
thumb. It was one of the curses of being a strikingly attractive
woman in a place frequented mainly by dusty old men who spent
their lives among books. It was difficult to go unnoticed, and she
couldn't just blur her face for them. That little guise only worked
effectively with electronics, anyway. To pull it off in a crowd it
would need to be woven around every one of the onlookers. It
wasn't her face that was blurred, but rather their eyes that failed
to *see*. It was a neat trick, though, and had its uses.

Later in the day the huge old building would still be far from
full, but it would at least come alive with research students and in-
dividuals in pursuit of knowledge for their own reasons, meaning
it wouldn't just be dusty old dons hunched over the manuscript
archives. Alice would be a little less noticeable at least. There
were other things she could do to disguise her appearance, but
they only lasted for short periods of time and took a tremendous
amount of strength to weave and willpower to sustain. And for the
moment at least, anything like that was beyond her.

It would have been so much easier for her to go unnoticed back
when the Reading Room had been part of the British Museum itself—the artifacts stolen from older civilizations scattered across

the globe and brought back here to be hoarded away held much greater appeal to the visitors than the books hidden away in the stacks did, which would have meant less attention paid to what she was after. The things she was looking for would have been found in the deepest, darkest corners of the basement stacks, and very rarely taken down from the shelf, never mind opened. But that was no longer true.

So, instead, she'd make another visit first, and then visit the library later, even if that meant venturing into streets that were decidedly less "safe."

Alice rested a hand on the velvet pouch that nestled against her breastbone to reassure herself that it was still safely in place. It was.

* * *

There was one place in London where she knew she would be made welcome, no questions asked. It was the one place in the city she felt like she belonged. Unlike in Chinatown, she was made to feel like she was part of the family. The World's End was quite unlike any other pub. It was more than just a watering hole. Much more than that. It was more than just a club where like-minded souls went to let their hair down—though it was that, too. The most intense, industrial, hardcore, and gothic tunes pounded out through the speaker systems. The lights were low, but pulsed epileptically in time with the beats the DJ laid down, capturing them all in freeze-frame gyrations like a zombie *danse macabre* playing out across the dance floor.

The World's End wasn't one of those places where last orders was called and people were shown the door just because the pub had closed and the music had stopped. If the revelers needed to crash after partying too hard through the night, then it was a good night, and they were welcome to sleep it off without being hassled. It catered to a very unique subculture of party people. Leather, lace, pale faces, painted masks, bondage chains, dog collars, and the most unique jewelry was on display beside intricate tattoos and affectations of blood and sex and the cult of death. Here the clothes made the men, the lack of clothes made the women. They were like peacocks preening, all the darkly beautiful tortured souls lost in the underground.

There were plenty of other pubs in the city where revelers could drink and dance and all else until dawn, even when the vast majority preferred to stay hidden behind their own closed doors between sunset and sunrise, but there was nowhere quite like The World's End. And that was why she liked it. Because, as far as she was concerned, there was no one quite like Alice Ho, so they were made for each other.

She had other reasons for feeling at home there. One of the "better" ones was a man. If someone put a gun to her head and forced Alice to choose the one person in the world she could trust, the one man she could count on completely, she would have said Joseph Pennington, the man who owned The World's End.

But trust was a double-edged thing. And, oddly, Joseph was the one man who had taught her one of the hardest lessons of all: You don't have to like someone to trust them, or, more pointedly, you don't have to trust someone you like. They had a past. The risk, she knew, as she reached out for the door, was that if she needed to ask a favor from Joseph, he was the one man who would know just how much that favor was worth, and would price it accordingly. That wasn't the problem. She expected that. It kept things clean. The problem was that she was prepared to enter into a bargain like that. Again.

Alice pushed the door open and peered inside the dimly lit pub.

It smelled of stale alcohol and staler sweat, but beneath that there was the desperation of want, need, and the whole heady fusion of pheromones still lingering in the air with the twists of lemon and lime rind, and the sickly sweet musk of the joints that had been smuggled in and toked in the darkest corners while the girls squatted across the guys' laps and they swapped saliva.

The small spotlights above the mirrors behind the bar were still on but they barely touched the rest of the room. The green illuminated sign that indicated the fire exit was the only light in the place.

More likely than not a few party animals would be curled up somewhere in the back or sprawled out on one of the leather banquettes, but the chances were that there would be no one at this end of the bar. They were like vampires: they liked the dark places. No, they didn't just *like* them—they needed them.

A red glow punctured the darkness. Like so many other things that had fallen on the way, the smoking ban was pretty much ignored everywhere; the police had far too much to be worrying about without getting their knickers in a twist about minor misdemeanors like smoking in a pub.

Joseph Pennington made people welcome, that was his gift; no matter who they were, what walk of life they were from, they came to The World's End as equals. But he was no innocent. He dealt with trouble in whatever form it came. And come it always did.

"Well, well, well," said a familiar voice. It came out of the darkness. Alice didn't jump, but the sound of it made her bones want to crawl out of her skin. "Would you look at what the cat's dragged in?"

CHAPTER 6

THERE IS NO PAIN,
HE IS RECEDING

An intense sunburst of light and flame blinds him.

He tries to shield his eyes, but it makes no difference.

The light scorches the back of his eyes, leaving behind a kaleidoscopic afterimage that detonates over and over like sunspots across his brain.

Through it all, though, he sees something shining... It's so much brighter than the yellow light, and so very hard to focus upon. It's a single pinprick of brilliant white. Intense. Like it could sear all the way through his retinas into his brain behind his eyes. He is lost. He has no idea where he is. He has no idea who he is. Not anymore. There is nothing and this is everything. There's nothing in the residual images burned into his mind to give any indication; only the light.

Is this Hell?

Is he dead?

He buries his face in his hands and tries to blink—nothing more than that. Just to blink. His eyes swim with tears. There is movement but he can't focus on anything. The world is a yellow light. It sparkles through his tears.

And he remembers the song of the stones calling to him, lost in the roar that fills the air.

The song.

The elegy.

He reaches out, the notes swelling within him once more. He is powerless to resist them. It is everything. It is the world. It is the blood in his veins and the soul beneath his skin. It is all this and more. It is him. And it consumes him. Completely.

As his fingers break the surface of the water he feels a thrill of unexpected warmth. The water is hot. Before he can pull his hand away or plunge it deeper, the air is filled with a roar so mighty it makes the very stuff of the air vibrate and the skin of the water churn. It is the only sound that he can hear, louder than his own heartbeat. Louder than the drumming that echoes inside his head.

There is nothing else.

There is only the sound, the roar, and then it stops, replaced by a single word that he feels shiver through the marrow in his bones.

THIEF!

Smoke fills the air all around him.

Another wave of heat washes over him, making it harder to breathe. He struggles to catch a breath, to hold it, only to break out into a huge raking cough that has him doubled over as he chokes. His mouth fills with the acrid taste of sulfur and bile. Is this Hell? Am I dead? His body is wracked again and again with the urge to vomit. It is all he can do to hold it down. His stomach convulses. His throat closes. He gags on the acid taste at the back of his mouth.

And it only gets worse.

The next wave of heat brings a scream with it, and the overpowering sickly sweet smell of scorching flesh.

It takes a moment for him to realize that the screaming is his own.

And that he is not dead at all.

That would be a mercy.

CHAPTER 7

SHADOW WALK WITH ME

Jack Callaghan felt the sheen of sweat film his body. It made his clothes cling to every inch of his skin. It wasn't anywhere near warm enough to have him so sweaty. The dog days of summer were already over. The leaves were starting to fall now. In a few weeks there would be snow. That was the wonder of global warming. London lived in a perpetual state of climate change. So, while it was barely ten degrees outside, Callaghan was roasting like a pig. His lips were cracked and dry, his tongue stuck to the roof of his mouth. He used the wall to steady himself. He'd barely made it outside before the world had started spinning. It was the second time he'd lost it in the last twenty-four hours. He didn't know what was happening to him. It had been three years since a drop of alcohol had crossed his lips, so it wasn't drink-inspired, whatever it was. No pink elephants. But that didn't explain what was happening to him. He took a deep breath, held it, counting to eleven before he let it go.

The count of eleven was a superstition. He'd read a book years ago where a man was obsessed by numbers, letting them rule his life to the point that he'd roll dice to make decisions so he could lay all the blame for every bad thing he did at the foot of Fate and the universe. Eleven was an interesting number. It was the first that couldn't be counted on the hands. It was the smallest positive integer requiring three syllables to say it. It was the largest prime number with a single morpheme name. It was the atomic number of sodium. In chemistry, Group 11 included the three coinage metals—copper, silver, and gold—known from antiquity. It was the number of space-time dimensions in M-theory. It was the number of disciples after Judas was cast out. It was all that and more. It just *felt* better than ten.

Callaghan could still feel the residual heat fermenting beneath his skin despite the firm breeze blowing down the quiet street. He leaned against the railings for a full five minutes, gathering his wits and his bearings before heading back down to the vault. He was frightened. He really didn't understand what was happening to him.

"You okay?"

It took Callaghan a moment to realize that Harry was talking to him.

The SOCO had paused mid-dusting, his fingerprint brush in midair, about to make its next stroke. "Because you look like crap, if you don't mind me saying."

Callaghan fumbled for the right word, but his mind seemed intent on hiding the majority of his vocabulary just to be spiteful.

He realized distantly that he could see each and every bristle of the brush with startling clarity, right down to the single grain of powder about to fall from one of them.

This was all *wrong*.

He felt like a stranger in his own skin. A passenger.

"I'm fine," he said at last, even though he was anything but. "Must be something I ate," he said, knowing that it would be enough to placate the technician. People said things like "Are you okay?" out of politeness, not genuine concern. All they wanted to hear was that yes, you were fine, and then they could carry on doing whatever it was they had been doing. He continued on down the stairs to the cramped little room where Hannon was fussing over the security tape. The air tasted strangely stale, as though it had already been breathed a hundred times and carried the traces of its past.

The bank manager looked more like a stunted goblin suspiciously hunched over the console as Callaghan opened the door.

"I'll need that."

"Yes, yes, of course. I'll just burn you a copy. It's all stored digitally, you understand. It'll just take a second." Hannon popped a disc into the player and started the burning process. True to his word it only took a minute. He handed it over without any objection, no grumblings about client confidentiality or anything else.

Callaghan knew all too well why: the disc was useless.

* * *

Back at the station, Callaghan watched the CCTV footage again.

Lawson leaned over his shoulder as he flicked backward frame by frame, then forward again, then back, watching the woman creep backward through the shadows to press up against the wall, freeze framing it in that moment where she gazed directly at the camera, and each time hoping that it would reveal something he had missed before. It never did. He could have watched her skip in and out of the vault all day and still not recognized the thief if she skipped up to him on Oxford Street and planted a big wet smacker on his lips.

Callaghan rolled the image back again.

And again.

"I'm not seeing something," he said. "It's right there in front of me and I'm missing it. I know I am." He pinched the bridge of his nose between thumb and forefinger. He was bone tired. He hadn't been sleeping well for nights now. Bad dreams. Not to mention whatever that had been outside the bank.

More of that rancid brew the Station's quartermaster tried to pass off as coffee was going cold on the desk beside him. It didn't taste any worse tepid than it did hot.

He reached for it, and then changed his mind. There were better ways to poison yourself slowly to death.

Jenny Lawson tapped one of the screen's lower quadrants. "There," she said. He watched the thief again, still not seeing it. "Don't look at the woman, Guv. Watch her shadow."

He did as he was told.

It was hard not to watch the woman. Her body commanded his attention, and that, of course, was why he'd missed it. The libido could have a shocking impact on common sense sometimes. This time he watched her shadow. And only her shadow.

Lawson was right: the shadow was the key.

It was right under his nose. Or eyes, to be more exact. The shadows were probably the only thing not actually lying to them. He watched the short loop of film again, paying close attention to the shadow's erratic movement around the vault. It wasn't easy to follow because of the angle, but from what he could tell it lingered twice, not once. Meaning *two* boxes had been interfered with, the second replaced without any of them realizing it had been disturbed. It was so quick he wasn't surprised he'd missed it, but he was in no doubt now that there was more going on here than met the eye. Much more.

"So, what do you reckon? Box number two's the real target, and all the stuff she's left on the table is just window dressing to send us off in the wrong direction?"

"That's where the smart money would be," Callaghan agreed. "But I'm not sure knowing that helps us all that much. When you get down to brass tacks, all it means is that we've got two boxes, and no idea who either of them belong to. Five minutes ago we had one."

"A problem doubled," Lawson agreed. "And from what you've said, I can't imagine the bank will be too happy with the idea of calling a bunch of their account holders and saying their deposit boxes may or may not have been interfered with."

"Yeah, hardly inspires confidence, and I'm thinking their clientele are not the kind of guys you want to be upsetting."

"Back to square one then."

"Maybe not. I've got an idea. It might not be a *good* idea. But it's an idea. And beggars can't be choosers."

CHAPTER 8

EVEN STRANGER TIDES

Certain sounds, and more specifically certain voices, are hard-coded into the brain, and like Pavlov's dog invoke a certain reaction. When it comes to sounds, there's the report of a gun. Nothing else sounds quite like it; for all that some sounds are similar, a car backfiring cannot stir that same primal fear the way hearing a single gunshot split the night can. Each person's life is built up around a select core of auditory cues and preprogrammed responses. Just the sound of them is enough to trigger a visceral reaction.

The man's voice was one of them.

Alice Ho stopped dead, rooted to the spot.

Her pulse quickened.

Her lips parted as her breath hitched.

Her mouth dried up.

Her fingernails dug into her palm as her fist clenched.

It wasn't Joseph Pennington cloaked in shadow. She knew this voice so much more intimately. Just hearing it now, so unexpectedly, sent a shiver of dread walking one bone at a time down the ladder of her spine all the way to the root of her being, and for one terrible moment she wasn't sure if she should stay, or turn around and run.

"You haven't changed in the slightest, Alice," Rufus Shadwell said. It wasn't what he said so much as the way he said it. His words were full of that insufferable arrogance of the man. No one ever denied Shadwell. Ever. He was not the kind of man who allowed that to happen. And yet he was her former lover; the relationship had been one of mutual convenience—she'd used him as much as he'd used her—and when it came to ending it, the how, where, what, and why had been Alice's choice. He hadn't fought her. He'd simply walked out. He hadn't taken a single thing with him. It wasn't dramatic. He hadn't offered any grand speeches. There was no fond farewell in the doorway, no heartbreak or tears or theatrics. He had snatched his coat up from the back of the chair, shrugged it on, and walked out of the door without a word. But that was Rufus Shadwell, a man of very few words. He didn't need them, he had something far more potent: charisma. The man radiated raw sex.

But given what had happened between him and Joseph, Rufus was the last man she ever thought she'd meet at The World's End. In fact, the last time she'd listened to it, the word on the street was pretty insistent that Joseph was still very much gunning for his old friend.

"You really do like playing with fire, don't you, Rufus?"

And like that it was as though he'd never been away. She chewed at her top lip, biting it nervously. Everything came back to her, all of that unfinished business between them. Emotions she had thought she'd come to terms with were cracked wide open with a single line: "It's been a while, Alice."

"I expected you to say not long enough."

"Ah, sweet Alice. Always so quick with the put-downs. You wound me. I missed you."

"And if I believe that, you've got a bridge to sell me, right?"

Assuming he'd made his peace with Pennington, this was exactly the kind of place where Rufus Shadwell's sort congregated; and by that she meant those half-damned souls locked in a never-ending search for pleasure and new experiences who couldn't seem to find satisfaction or peace no matter how desperately they needed it. Shadwell was an emotional butterfly. He flitted from one obsession to another, never settling for long. That made any sort of meaningful relationship a kind of hell.

She touched the tip of her tongue to her lips. She could taste him on the air. She inhaled. Exhaled. She felt his heartbeat up against her breastbone as though they were bound, bodies falling into a single all-consuming rhythm. The red glow of his cigarette grew brighter again as he drew on it. The lambent glow was *almost* enough to light his face. She saw him in the shadows. And she saw the shadows in him.

Alice closed the distance between them.

"I'm looking for Joseph," she said.

"Of course you are. Why else would you be here? Certainly not looking for me. Don't worry, I'm not offended. I should be, but I'm not," Shadwell said. He turned on a small art deco lamp on the table beside his chair. "Or? No, you wouldn't be here looking for me now would you?"

He spoke with that same all-knowing certainty, and yet again Alice found herself wondering if he could look inside her heart with those damned dark eyes of his, sure she could feel his presence in there, picking over innermost thoughts. "Of course not," she said without conviction. He had unnerved her. She didn't like it.

"Funny, then, that you have something for me, don't you think?"

She didn't understand. "For you?" Alice shook her head. "I have nothing for you."

Rufus smiled. It was horribly smug. He sat back, lacing his fingers behind his head. "Of course you do, Alice. Don't be so naïve. I couldn't exactly ask you to fetch it for me, now could I? I'm not going to apologize. I used you. I'm a bad man. I think we've already established that, haven't we? It was just so much easier if you thought you were getting it for Joseph." He shrugged. "What can I say? You were working for me all along. Sue me."

Thieves worked on instincts and tells; one of the best inventions in the known world for a pickpocket, for instance, was the "Beware: Pickpockets Working in the Area" sign. Whenever someone saw it, their hand instinctively went to check that their own wallet was still there, letting the pickpocket know exactly where their light fingers needed to go to work. It was psychological. And the moment Rufus mentioned her having something for him, every neuron in her brain was sending messages to her hand to check on the pouch, but she resisted, concentrating on the feel of the velvet between her shallow breasts.

The jewel wasn't for him, and, quite simply he could never know that she had it.

She didn't dare move a muscle until the impulse had passed.

He looked at her, tilting his head slightly to the left. His smile spread slowly. It didn't reach all the way to his eyes. That was the fundamental difference between Joseph Pennington and Rufus Shadwell right there. She would trust Joseph with her life, she could only trust Shadwell about as far as she could throw him, and if her pockets were weighed down with anything valuable, only half that far. The two men were so very similar and yet so utterly different. Shadwell was the yin to Pennington's yang. They were different sides of the same coin. Different halves of the same twin soul, light and dark. But then, the pair of them *were* Seelie fae, reawakened, aware.

"I know you've got something for me, Alice, it's written all over that beautiful face of yours," he said. "Why don't you just hand it over and be done with it? It's so much easier than all of these games you like to play." His eyes didn't waver from hers, not even for a split second. He was so utterly sure he was right. She wanted to prove him wrong and turn out empty pockets. But of course, her pockets weren't empty.

Shadwell ran his tongue across his lips and his nostrils flared, savoring the taste and smell of her. He breathed her in. He waited for her to lie to him again. He breathed her out.

"I have nothing for you," she said.

"Please, Alice. Enough lies. Of course you have something for me. You wouldn't have come all this way without something to give dear old Joseph, would you? And like I said, you were working for me, not him, so time to pay the piper. Hand them over, there's a good girl." He held out his hand. "I've waited so long for this moment, let's not spoil it by playing hard to get. The coins. Give them to me."

The two coins she'd lifted from the second deposit box.

No matter what Rufus said, she knew she'd done that of her own accord when she'd felt out the metal. Or so she'd thought…

When her fingers had brushed over them and felt the unexpected thrill from the residual energies of their last owner, she'd responded automatically, like the mark checking their pockets when they saw the "Beware: Pickpockets Operating in this Area" sign.

But, the fact remained, Rufus wanted them. And she was the kind of girl who liked having people owe her favors. What surprised her was the fact that she had all but forgotten about them because they had meant so little to her compared with the gemstone.

Alice reached inside her pocket and palmed the two coins she had taken from the vault. Who knew how many hands they had fallen into and out of? How many times had these two coins been lost and found, stolen and taken again?

And yet it was obvious that Shadwell recognized them, and not just as some treasure, but as though each of them was precious beyond words to him, each as individual and identifiable from its brother as he was from Joseph Pennington.

"Ah, hello my old friend," Rufus said, lifting one of the coins from her palm and closing his hand around it. When he opened his hand it was still there. "It's almost as good to see you again as it is to see the beautiful woman who brought you back to me." Alice had half expected him to make it disappear with a flourish. Instead, he held it up to the light, examining it carefully, and then ran it across the back of his knuckles like a conjuror. Alice watched, mesmerized by his sleight of hand. The coin traveled one way and then back the other, rolling over Shadwell's knuckles and barely seeming to touch them. He was completely in command of the coin, making it dance to his tune just like everything else he came into contact with. It didn't once lose momentum, even as he reversed it and sent it back the way it had come. It was a trick. Nothing more than that, but Alice couldn't help but appreciate the sheer control he had over the coin, and how the slightest shift in his fingers seemed to make it dance.

"You have my eternal gratitude, Miss Ho. If there is ever anything I can do in return, do not hesitate to ask. I may still say no, but at least this has bought you the right to ask the question, which is so much more than you had before you walked through the door. And whatever you may think, I am still a good friend to have in your corner."

She wasn't about to argue with that. She knew exactly what he was capable of.

"Tell me, my dear, I'm curious, do you even know their provenance? You must have recognized something in them, but are you aware of what that something was? Do you even know where they come from?"

"Of course I do," she said, still mesmerized by the coin and only too aware that he had not looked up at her since he had taken possession of it. Or rather, she realized, since the coin had taken possession of him. "I'm the one who stole them, remember."

"Oh, my dear, sometimes you really annoy the hell out of me. You're so…literal. I don't mean where you stole them from, or whose little stash they were part of. I mean where they *come* from. First and foremost. I mean where they originated, which forge saw them shaped, which treasury disbursed them, who first held them, who eventually held them. These coins have history."

"I'm sure you're going to tell me all about it," Alice said, barely managing to keep the sarcasm out of her tone.

"I am, but only because you asked so nicely, dear. These coins…" He opened his palm, both coins lying flat on it. She hadn't noticed him claim the second one from her. "…were once part of one of the most incredible hordes of coins ever assembled. They brushed faces with treasures from the purse of Caligula, of Claudius and Nero, even Gaius Julius himself. They nestled beside the currency of Heraklion, touched by Minos himself and used to pay for the commission of the labyrinth. Within this horde there was a single coin of electrum from Lydia, in Asia Minor, that had once belonged to the scholar Herodotus, but what made that coin so special was not, for once, the scholar, but rather the water that washed over it during its shaping. It was cooled in the Pactolus River beside the slopes of Mount Tmolus, which I am sure means nothing to you, doesn't it?" He didn't wait for her to confirm or deny her ignorance. "The river was where King Midas of the nearby Phrygia bathed to wash away the curse of his golden touch. There were coins minted in Hellas and Phoenicia, coins once close to the skin of Cadmus, the man who created the *phoinikeia grammata* and introduced those Phoenician letters to the Greeks, giving us the alphabet. There were coins from the coffers of Agamemnon himself, used to finance the war with Troy. And the pick of the bunch, one of the most rare coins of all, lifted from the death purse of the man of Kerioth, Judas. One of the thirty *tetradrachms* of Tyre, the silver pieces that the betrayer could not spend. They were all there. And these coins were among the pick of the bunch."

Alice wasn't sure what he was talking about; for all that it sounded impressive, what could be so important about these coins just because they'd come into contact with other relics of antiquity? There wasn't some sort of magic that rubbed off from one to the other like contact poison. They were still just coins. They were old, barely even recognizable as coins when they were put up against their modern equivalent, and more like tiny, worn down works of art than anything else.

He flicked his wrist, and with a flourish of fingers meant to mask the actual disappearance, the coins were gone.

"These two coins were part of King Henry VIII's treasure, sweet, slightly ignorant, Alice. The man was a hoarder. A glutton for things of beauty and the trappings of power. There was a reason he grew so obese, and it wasn't just the juices of boar and stag dribbling down his pitted chin. He needed to *possess* things. In many ways he was a typical man, you might say—when it came to beauty he needed to own it. Own it and hide it away, or own it and flaunt it, depending on his mood. These two were on the *Mary Rose* when Henry's naval flagship sank on her maiden voyage, and then spent so many lifetimes at the bottom of the sea. But, for all that, it doesn't mean that they *belonged* to him. This gold wasn't his to do with as he wanted." He looked up at her then, and she saw something in his eyes: rage. Black and intense.

"Are you sure these are the same coins? I mean—"

"Of course I'm sure," he cut her off. "Don't you think I *know* them? We go back, a long, long way. And believe me, they know me every bit as well as I know them. Did you not see how they responded to my touch? They are mine. They always have been, and I am theirs. I always will be. That is our nature, and we will do anything and everything in our power to find our way back to one another. It's like love. You remember that, don't you, Alice?" Love, the most painful four-letter word known to man. Yes, she knew it for the bitter backstabbing bitch that it was. That was why she shared her life with two cats and a barista named Franco, and kept real people at a safe distance. "Actually, I suppose you could say they're like old lovers: I know their bodies by touch, intimately, even if I haven't held them for a long time. Like you. It might be a long time since we touched, but I remember every contour and curve, I remember the play of light on your hip in the morning as you lay there on your side, watching me pretend to be asleep, and I remember the way you used to hide your belly button like it was the most intimate part of your body. I remember you. I remember them. It's no different. Just like you and your cats. They fill a hole in your life, don't they? The hole where I once lived."

Alice had forgotten just how completely and utterly she had let this man into her life, and just how deeply he had insinuated himself into it, worming his way into every fiber of her being.

It wasn't just that he knew the names of her cats, or the fact that he was familiar with what she ate for breakfast and what brand of toothpaste she used, it was the fact that she could never have secrets from him.

And that had always been the main reason she could not bear to have him in her life. There could be no secrets. Not from him. Not ever.

CHAPTER 9

A GIRL'S BEST FRIEND

Two hours later, she stood amid dusty stacks of unloved books in the heart of the British Library, counting both her sorrows and her blessings. The encounter with Shadwell had shaken her.

She traced her fingers across the bindings, feeling the cloth and beneath it the forgotten and unvalued knowledge of the books, most of which hadn't been moved since they had been shelved. Judging by the tramlines cut through the patina of dust that had accumulated on the metal stacks, there were a few that had been taken down from the shelves. Even so, no more than a dozen out of the thousands in the stacks had been taken out to read in years. There was something infinitely sad about that.

Once upon a time this would have been a controlled environment; now cleaners didn't even venture this far down into the archives because of the limited hours they were prepared to work. The only time another human being had been down here in the last month had been to collect their cleaning equipment from the cupboards in the corridor outside. They hadn't given a moment's thought for these lost shelves.

Needs must as the devil drives, though... Wasn't that what they said? Security around the British Library had become lax; money was tight, people were edgy, and these days there just wasn't the commitment to the past that there had been. There wasn't that much interest in the future, either, truth be told. For once it was all about the now.

Fiscal cuts had savaged all aspects of public services, from streetlights to policing and hospitals, with library funding being hit the hardest. Once North Sea Oil revenues had run dry that was that; the government was writing checks the Treasury couldn't possibly cash. Where once librarians would have scurried to locate requested volumes, delighting in the diversity of readers' interests and holding interesting conversations about the authors or the subjects at hand, visitors were now given the freedom to track down whatever it was they were looking for and deliver them to the desks or simply leave them to be cleared away at the end of the day.

It all worked on trust, and that worked because there was still some sort of mythical protection around the hallowed halls that meant people just didn't steal, even though some of the texts they handled were quite literally priceless and most certainly irreplaceable. The scholars who came here were just pleased that the library was still being maintained as a viable institution and they could tap into the accumulated wisdom of centuries upon centuries of thought.

There were benefits to the cutbacks, of course, including the new freedom of movement they afforded her, so she wasn't about to look this particular gift horse in the mouth. Alice moved through the stacks unobserved and undisturbed, grateful that she didn't need to rush and risk drawing unnecessary attention to her presence.

Of course, not everything was as easily accessible as she might have wished, but then beggars really couldn't be choosers. Sometimes they just needed to improvise and be thieves instead. And, unsurprisingly, the current object of her affections was very much off limits, locked away with the interdicted texts and esoteric tomes of the various inquisitions and purges of the past. But not so long ago what she was looking for would have been available to anyone with a Reading Card instead of being hidden away along with the heretical texts and medieval studies of witchcraft, books of devilry, satanic worship, and bestiaries that had been accumulated over the centuries. The shelves she walked along now were cluttered with all manner of macabre and grotesque fantasies that by dint of being buried away so far below ground were essentially out of sight and out of mind of the general population.

You'd have been forgiven for thinking all of the banished texts were mysteries and plumbed the depths of the supernatural, but the truth was far from this. They counted among their number some of the most banal documents of the city, going right the way back to the laying of the foundation stone, long before the Romans came and built their wall around the settlement.

Anyone looking to study that sort of lost lore was more likely to find their curiosity satisfied in some of the old monasteries or down in the cathedral vaults than they were here, whilst the more modern city plans could be found in council offices if the buildings were new enough. All of those places at least conjured the illusion of safety, even when the strangest things were happening just outside their front door, and in the case of the monasteries, cathedrals, and seminaries, the cloak of faith was far more powerful than any mundane surveillance or security measure could ever be. After all, they had the Big Fella on their side, and no security firm could offer that.

A lot of obstacles could lurk within just a few feet. A lot of safeguards, depending on just how desperately someone wanted to keep their secrets. In this case, the only barrier was a locked door, which for a woman of Alice's unique talents was no obstacle at all. On the other side of that door were the royal records. These were copies of every important familial document from 1714 and the inauguration of George the First to the accession of the Hanover line, who had ruled over Great Britain ever since, despite marriage into the Saxe-Coburg and Gotha lineage with Victoria and Albert's son, Edward taking his father's name and thus inaugurating a new house, and wars with Germany forcing the adoption of Windsor as the family name. The originals had been stored in Windsor Castle, with no copies, until fire threatened not only to destroy one of the finest royal residencies in the land, but wipe out all trace of those irreplaceable histories, so replicas had been produced and deposited in the vaults of the British Library for safekeeping.

In amongst these papers were the blueprints and floor plans of Windsor Castle and Balmoral, of Edinburgh Castle and Buckingham Palace, and both of the houses of the Palace of Westminster. These drawings showed in perfect and precise detail the paths the water and sewage pipes followed, the gas pipes and electricity cables, and were marked with everything from water table depths and rock type for the foundation stones as well as countless other essential information for anyone undertaking any repair or restoration work: the thickness of walls, the material used in the construction, which wasn't all locally sourced but shipped in from far and wide, and tiny little details like the depth of tread on staircases to save them being measured when a new carpet needed to be laid. Everything was recorded on these plans or in the appendices that accompanied them—*everything*, and because of that they were quite rightly protected as a matter of national security; that was just the world they had inherited. It was impossible to look at them without questions being asked.

That same room held other secrets, though nowadays they were far less incendiary than they might once have been: the private diaries of monarchs listing affairs of state and affairs of the heart—and more than once affairs of the extramarital kind—the names of inactive spies and sleeper agents, details of military activities that had failed gloriously or ingloriously, or had simply never come to pass. All of the secrets of a State long since gone, the papers put back into the public domain; they were all here, and there had been a time when some of these revelations could have started or ended careers, lives, and begun wars, though now they were utterly insignificant. It was funny how things changed, and there was something really quite wonderful about it, too—a lesson about secrets the world could do with relearning.

Since the return of karma, the weight of importance placed upon the mundane had shifted; it was a subtle shift, but to the kinds of people who moved in the right—or wrong—circles, it was an obvious one. Alice saw it, but only from the periphery. She wasn't one for walking down the corridors of power in Whitehall or through Parliament. She was much more likely to be seen sneaking across the rooftops of both, picked out by the moon, or through the sewers beneath, keeping company with the natural rats, not the human kind. Had she been taken with the notions of gunpowder, treason, and plot, Alice Ho could have been a very dangerous woman, but instead she let those boys have their petty squabbles and very self-ishly concentrated on having fun.

She was, however, a woman with a very peculiar definition of fun.

A window set high in the wall allowed dust-streaked light to creep into the room.

A thin crack ran the length of the glass, breaking it clean in two, top to bottom.

It wasn't the first time she'd seen that broken pane of glass.

For a moment she let herself be transported back to the first time she had noticed it. It was her first visit to the library. She couldn't have been more than five or six years old at the time, walking hand-in-hand with the latest in a long line of nannies. She fumbled for a name—Linda, Lisa, something like that? Like that, but neither of those. The name floated to the front of her mind: Lucy.

She could remember her clearly now: a teenage girl much more interested in meeting her boyfriend whenever they went out on a trip than making sure Alice either had fun or learned something. It could have been worse. It had been worse, in fact. Much worse. At least Lucy didn't lock her in the cupboard when she was naughty. It was hardly surprising she'd grown up with an intense dislike of confined spaces and a fear of being locked, alone, in the dark.

Alice tried to think, shaking off the memory of the stiflingly hot cupboard and the nanny's fingernails dragging down the wooden door, pretending to be some witch looking for a little girl to boil her bones and make sweeties. She shivered at the memory.

What had been in here?

Oh yes. Of course. She smiled, realizing that to all intents and purposes this was where it had all begun, and now it had returned, full circle. Back then this room had housed an exhibition about the history of the Tower of London. She had been fascinated by the old plans and the 3D cutaway diorama that had been part of the display. There were replica jewels, the ceremonial costumes of the Beefeaters, even copies of the keys held by the Keeper. There had been a stuffed raven on top of one of the glass display cases.

Alice remembered its dead eyes.

She had been to the White Tower, too, but that had been a different time, and a different nanny. Again, not the one who used to delight in locking a little girl in the dark, though this one had her own cruel and unusual punishments she meted out when the fancy took her. Whoever said your childhood was the best days of your life had never been unwanted, handed off to nannies, and brought up kicking and screaming without so much as a kiss on the forehead from a "loving" parent.

That was why she recalled the good days so clearly, like the day they went to the Tower. There were so many snippets that had stuck in her mind even now: listening to the ghost story of the Princes in the Tower; hearing for the first time the legend of the Welsh king, Bran the Blessed and his head that was supposedly buried beneath the White Tower; seeing the Crown Jewels, Mary Modena's three crowns, the Sceptre of the Cross with the 530 carat Cullinan I diamond at its heart, the Sword of Spiritual Justice, the Sword of Temporal Justice, and the Sword of Mercy, and so many other treasures secure in the Jewel Room.

And watching the ravens.

Especially the ravens.

Part of her was sure she would remember her way in the Tower, even after all these years. It was so deeply ingrained on her psyche. That one room in the Tower had made her who she was today, after all. But the thief in Alice's nature hadn't remained at liberty for this long by listening to those reckless voices. She planned meticulously, down to the very last detail. There was no room for unnecessary risks, not when chance still played such a pivotal role in the success of any job. The best she could do was eliminate as many of the risks as she could, and hopefully weighting those she couldn't control in her favor in the process.

If she really was going to do this, steal the one thing that had entranced her since childhood, she was going to have to take every damned precaution in the book, and then some. She wasn't stupid. She'd noticed that all of the strange things happening in the city seemed to gravitate toward the Tower. It was just unfortunate that the one thing she *really* wanted, a single gem amongst the many, just happened to be locked away inside it: the *Koh-i-Noor* diamond.

And that was why she was here.

Despite all of the upheaval, despite all of the paranoia, or even perhaps *because* of it, there was no way those plans would have been destroyed. Those duplicates were somewhere in the adjacent room.

Now all she had to do was liberate them.

But that, of course, was all part of the fun.

It would have been so much more boring to just walk up to a librarian and *ask* for them.

CHAPTER 10

THE STONECUTTER

Jack Callaghan let rip with a curse and slammed his fist against the metal door in frustration.

He really shouldn't have been surprised.

Actually, it would have been more surprising if the lift was working.

The joys of an East End council flat meant that there were two certainties that could always be relied upon. The first, that the lobby would always have the faint odor of urine somewhere not far enough beneath the pungent smell of disinfectant. Second, that the lift would be out of order. Those two truths were part of the immutable laws of the universe. He didn't know why. It wasn't his place to worry about it. It had always been so, and always would be. It was just one of those things, right along with the eternal "shit happens" that guided so much of the day-to-day workings of the world he lived in.

For once, though, Callaghan fervently wished this could have been the exception that proved both rules, rather than just another instance of them sticking two fingers up at him. He was out of luck. There was an addendum to the laws, of course, unproven but prophetically accurate in this instance, which posited that the higher the story of the flat that needed to be visited, the less likely it was that the lift would be working. Art Mortimer lived on the fifteenth floor. He'd never had a chance.

The smell of urine, some other ammoniac, and disinfectant wasn't restricted solely to the lobby. It permeated up the staircase. All the way up the staircase. It was as though something had crawled into the stairwell to die. And die again and again. The lack of ventilation made the climb all the more arduous. Not being able to breathe without retching didn't help.

Each landing was strewn with litter, chip wrappers, cans of Coke, and signs of more dangerous games being played—strips of tin foil, a twisted lemon rind, and a blackened spoon sat on one of the steps beneath walls covered with inventive graffiti. It was hard to imagine how people could live in conditions like this. Callaghan was inured to the squalor. It came with the turf, but even so, he got to go home and wash it off when he was done. The residents of The Gaitskell had no such luck. It was hard to credit just how far Morty had fallen. He had been so much better than this, but like Icarus with his burned wax wings, Morty had climbed too high, and had had so much further to fall for it.

Callaghan paused for a moment on the next landing.

A broken window allowed something approaching fresh air to seep into the stairwell. He leaned against the windowsill and sucked it in greedily.

It was a long way down.

It was still a long way up.

There was a half bottle of scotch in his jacket pocket, a sweetener for Morty, who was more than a little partial to a nice single malt. It was smart to know your informers inside out. Callaghan had known the old man for a lot of years now. He didn't know stuff like his birthday, his shoe size, or his wife's name, or if he had even ever been married for that matter. He limited it to useful stuff like chosen brands of malt, favorite greyhound tracks, and that he supported the Hammers. So, call it a bribe or a thank you in advance, it didn't really matter as far as Callaghan was concerned, so long as it did what it was meant to do: lubricate the wheels of justice.

For a moment, though, he was tempted to crack open the screw top and take a quick slug.

He kicked a burger carton as he stepped back from the window, revealing a discarded syringe. He nudged it with his toecap into the corner, out of immediate harm's way. By rights he should call it in, get someone out to clear the mess away, but that kind of thing only happened in a perfect world. In this one it wasn't his problem, and he wasn't about to make it his problem. He had no intention of explaining his presence here either. The Gaitskell wasn't exactly on his manor. There were blocks like The Gaitskell all over London. Soulless. Hopeless. Some of them had been taken into private ownership and had security systems now to keep out the very people they had been built for. Others had been left to fall into disrepair. Named after the old Labor Party Leader, Hugh Gaitskell, the tower block had been built to provide housing and, in no small part, hope for the people who lived there, but now it only represented misery.

He reached the fifteenth floor.

The glass in Morty's front door had been replaced with a piece of plywood. Next to slurs like *kike, yid,* and *Jewboy* someone had daubed a swastika. They'd got it the wrong way 'round, but then you couldn't expect morons to know the difference. It wasn't as though they went to Racist Bigot School to learn this sort of stuff. They just had to pick it up as they went along. And there was so much stuff worthy of their hatred. It sickened Callaghan. It wasn't that he was particularly enlightened. He wasn't. It just made his job so much more difficult, and people like Morty, for all their sins, they were good people and didn't deserve to be crapped on in their own home. The doorbell hung on by a wire, having come loose from the doorframe. It had been like that for as long as Callaghan could remember.

He knocked on the sheet of wood. It bowed beneath his fist, rattling against the frame with each strike. On the third knock he heard a shuffling movement from inside. Then labored, emphysemic breathing. He waited for Morty to open the door, but instead of the chain rattling and the old man fumbling with the Yale lock, the old guy barked, "Sod off, will you! Go on, get out of it! Leave me in peace to die in this shithole alone. I'll be dead soon enough, then you can bang on the damn door all you want."

Callaghan smirked to himself, glad that the world hadn't quite broken Morty's spirit just yet.

"Morty? It's me? Jack Callaghan."

"Go away."

"Come on, Morty, open up. I've got a little something for you. You know you want it." He felt like a pusher trying to cajole a junkie into taking another hit. *Just one more. Go on. You know you like it.*

This time he heard the old man shuffle all the way to the door and eventually the sound of a chain rattling as he fumbled with it before he opened the door a crack.

"Mr. C?"

"Yes, you daft old bugger, it's me. Now open the door and let me in will you?"

The door closed again and Morty struggled with the chain before it swung back open again.

Callaghan stepped inside to see the old man's back, Morty already halfway back to the living room and his favorite armchair. He followed him, closing the door behind him.

The flat lay in semidarkness; the ragged curtains were still drawn, and the air was heavy with the fug of the stale cigarette smoke of a forty-a-day roll-your-own man. *No wonder the old bastard wheezes like an asthmatic donkey,* Callaghan thought. Half a dozen ashtrays were dotted around the living room, and each one of them was filled to overflowing with cigarette butts and jaundiced filter tips. It was impossible to guess how long the dog ends had been there. They could have all been that morning's ash, or Morty could have become lazy in his old age and not emptied the ashtrays for days. Callaghan took a look around. Judging by the sheer filth that coated the rest of the flat it was almost certainly the latter. The grime was ingrained into the faux-grain of the Formica counter tops, the once white melamine stained nicotine yellow. The chip pan on the gas stove was full of fat, the fat in turn full of battered curls of potato that had cooked a dozen times. There was a cup on the windowsill with a tube of denture cream beside it. Callaghan wasn't about to check to see if Morty had his teeth in. The old man could use some help, but he wouldn't thank Callaghan for making the call to Social Services. He was a stubborn old codger at the best of times, and these clearly weren't the best of times.

"How are you doing then, Morty?" Callaghan said, looking at the old man properly. There was a kid's nursery rhyme about a crooked man who walked a crooked mile. That was Art Mortimer. He had thin hair, thin features, and thin skin draped across thin bones. He looked, Callaghan realized rather bleakly, like an Auschwitz survivor.

"Just dandy, Mr. C. Can't you tell? The new digs are positively palatial."

New was obviously a relative term. The old jeweler had been one of The Gaitskell's inmates for nearly a decade now. It was either that, or a sign that the old guy was living in the past.

"That they are, my friend. And your health? Keeping up? Eating okay?"

"Can't complain." Morty gave a nervous laugh. "Well, I can, obviously, but being as the NHS has gone to crap these days, and the Social are about as much use as waterproof teabags, no bugger listens when I do."

Callaghan laughed. It sounded a little forced to his own ears, but it seemed to make the old man feel more at ease.

"You're an easy audience, Mr. C."

"I don't get out much," Callaghan said.

"I can tell. Don't see you around here much nowadays…" It wasn't an accusation. It wasn't Callaghan's job to police the estate anymore. He hadn't been a beat copper for the best part of a decade. Life had changed in innumerable ways since he'd transferred to the Flying Squad, and not all of them for the good. Once upon a crime he'd been happy, or as happy as he could remember being. And then the job had consumed him, his relationships, and everything else that passed for his life. He couldn't remember actually being happy for a long time. Now his pleasures were simple. Selfish. And more often than not self-destructive. Better to burn out than fade away. Or sit in a dark corner and drink yourself to death. Just the thought of drink had him reaching for the half bottle in his pocket.

"Sorry about that, Morty. Life's got a way of kicking you in the nuts then laughing when you double up in pain. You know how it is."

"Indeed I do, Mr. C. Indeed I bloody do. Sit yourself down.

Take a load off. Tea?" Morty held up a chipped mug with *World's Greatest Nobody* written on it, and wiggled it vaguely in his general direction. "Only the best teabags here." Callaghan had seen the kitchen on the way in. It was no cleaner than the living room. He declined, politely, trying not to show the reason why.

"Sorry, Morty, can't stay too long. There's a lot on at the moment. You know how it is. People to do. Places to see."

"Won't take a minute, Mr. C. The kettle's already on. It's like I'm cyclic," the old man joked.

It was hard to say no a second time without seeming ungrateful, and given he'd come cap in hand looking for the old man's help, that was the last thing he wanted to do. So he nodded and said, "Then thanks very much, I'd love a brew."

He took the opportunity to take a better look around the room while Morty was rattling around in the kitchen.

There was a jam jar on the mantlepiece filled with used bus ticket stubs. There was another handful of them piled up next to it. Callaghan picked one up, surprised at the weight, and when he unfolded it, discovered twelve pence carefully hidden inside it. He refolded the little parcel and put it back on the mantlepiece. The next one held exactly the same twelve pence wrapped inside the used ticket. He checked the price of the fare: 88p. Which meant Morty always paid with a pound coin. Which in turn meant that every single folded up ticket stub was loaded down with 12p. It wasn't a fortune, but it would add up quickly, and Morty didn't look like he was living the kind of life where those 12p's didn't matter.

Callaghan realized too late that Morty was watching him from the doorway.

He felt like he'd been caught with his hand in the cookie jar... or in this case the quite literal jam jar. It was sloppy. He wasn't in the habit of making sloppy mistakes.

"Sorry, Morty," he said. "You know what it's like, incurable curiosity."

Morty said nothing, but he looked as though he'd just taken a knife to the base of the spine as he shuffled back into the kitchen. Callaghan found this silent, wounded act far more disconcerting than it would have been if Morty had gone off at him. The old man returned a moment later with two mugs of brown sludge that would have put the Station's vending machine to shame.

"Sit, sit."

Callaghan looked around for a space on one of the chairs that wasn't covered with piles of old newspapers, or stacks of dirty plates abandoned for a moment and forgotten about, or heaps of dirty laundry. There weren't a lot of options.

"Sorry about the mess, Mr. C," Morty said. For all that the words were self-conscious, there wasn't any sign of embarrassment in the old man's voice. He wasn't sorry at all; he was just playing out the whole social etiquette thing, saying what he was supposed to say. "I've been so busy I've not had time to tidy up. No time to stop. Not even for a minute. Just so much to do. On and on. Things to do, things to do." He sounded slightly manic, his hands fluttering like butterflies. He was agitated. Jittery. *Like a man with something to hide,* Callaghan thought. "If I'd known you were coming…"

"You'd have baked a cake, right?" Callaghan grinned. That was what his gran always used to say when they turned up unannounced. *If I knew you were coming, I'd have baked a cake.* It was an old Gracie Fields song from the Fifties.

Callaghan perched himself on the arm of the settee, leaving the one empty chair, where Morty spent most of his life, to its rightful occupant. It was like the Siege Perilous, though that would have made The Gaitskell Camelot, and all the crap Morty had buried his life under Knights of the Round Table stuff.

"So what brings you here, Mr. C? Not that I'm not grateful for the company, but like I said, we don't see you 'round here much any more." There was an edge of suspicion to the old man's voice now that hadn't been there before. Callaghan cursed himself for a fool. He couldn't believe he'd been so clumsy.

He had no choice but to fall on his sword and try unsugared honesty.

"Okay, no beating around the bush. I need help, Morty. I need the kind of help only someone with your background can offer."

"I'm not sure what sort of help a drunken recluse can offer, Mr. C. Not sure I want to know, neither. It might look like crap to you, but I kinda like my life now. It's uncomplicated. I'm just sitting here waiting to die."

"It's clutching at straws a bit, but you're the only person I can think of who might hear if anyone's being asked to cut a diamond. A big one. So I'm hoping you'll keep your ear to the ground. There's a drink in it," Callaghan said, fishing out the half bottle and putting it on the table between them. He really did feel like a pusher peddling crack now.

Morty shifted uncomfortably in his seat. His eyes darted about almost as though he suspected they were being watched.

"I'm not involved in anything like that any more, Mr. C. You know that. Conditions of my release. All ties severed. No contact with anyone from my old life. I don't really want to go back there. Not unless I have to. And by have to I mean it's the difference between life and death. Mine. And even then I reckon I'd think twice, 'cause I'm not sure dead is such a bad way to be." He broke off into a wheezing cough, punctuating the last statement with a very graphic example of just how likely an outcome that was. And sooner rather than later.

Callaghan raised a hand to reassure the man. "I know you're not, Morty. Like I said, it's clutching at straws, but you know my motto: leave no stone unturned. So, just in case. You know, if you hear anything…"

"I don't get out much, Mr. C," Morty said again.

The truth of that was all around them. He could imagine Morty's ghost still sitting in that armchair in one hundred years' time. Just sitting. The bus tickets represented a weekly trip to the shops to stock up on groceries. The local pubs weren't the kinds of places where someone like Morty would feel at home anymore. They weren't the friendly boozers with their snugs and old timers propping up the bar with back-in-my-day wisdom. They'd been taken over by gangs, skinheads, firms of West Ham supporters, and, working out of the toilets, drug dealers. They weren't the kind of place that a lonely old man would go for a quiet pint and a little company. That was just another way the city had changed. Not so long ago people had come out with platitudes like: *The East End? Salt of the Earth, those people.* Now the word was *scum,* not *salt.*

"That's okay Morty, I'm not asking for you to put yourself out there, or put yourself in harm's way, but I know how easy it is to bump into someone in the queue at the Post Office."

"Ain't no Post Office 'round here no more. Last one closed down a few years back. Kept getting robbed on Pension Day."

"I'm speaking figuratively, Morty. You know what I mean. People who used to share a trade like to gossip like little girls when they get together. If you happen to bump into the old crew, I'd appreciate a tip off, that's all. And there's a very nice single malt in it for you. *Quid pro quo.*"

Morty took the half bottle of twenty-one-year-old single malt off the table, cracked the screw top off, and took a deep swallow, smacking his lips and letting out a sigh that would have been contented under any other circumstances, before setting the bottle back down.

"If I hear anything I'll be sure to give you a call. Best I can do."

"That's all I'm asking. How about we make this tea Irish?" He reached over to hand Morty his proffered mug, and for a brief moment their fingers touched. It was no more than that. A touch. A spark seemed to leap between them. Morty snatched his hand away, letting go of the mug just as Callaghan let go.

The mug fell.

It hit the carpet and rolled, splashing hot brown tea all over Callaghan's trousers.

He felt the searing heat through the material, but there was no pain. It should have scalded his legs and left him screaming.

He reached for the mug, which had rolled just out of his reach.

Morty was staring at him.

"I think you should go, Mr. C. Now. Please." Morty backed away, putting his own mug on the mantlepiece. There wasn't quite room for it so the mug balanced precariously beside the jar of bus tickets, the weight of the tea all that kept it from falling.

"It's okay, Morty, no harm done."

"You need to go. Now. Please," Morty repeated. The level of politeness was almost comical. Only it wasn't. It wasn't funny at all. The tea soaked through Callaghan's trousers. He could see the steam wreathing up from them but couldn't feel a thing. Not hot. Not cold.

"Honestly, Morty, it's fine. I promise. I guess I got lucky, it must've missed the skin."

"It's not that, Mr. C... It's just..." The old man fumbled for the right words, but it was abundantly clear that he was too distressed to find them. He looked at Callaghan helplessly. "It's just better if you leave," he said at last.

"Come on, Morty. It's me. Jack. We're friends. Mates. What's a little spilt tea between mates? Is everything okay? You can tell me. You know that, right? Nothing we can't share. We've known each other a long time. If something's bothering you, you can tell me." It was obvious that everything was far from okay. Even in the dim light he could see that the old man had turned an alarming shade of grey, and that he was trembling. Callaghan's first thought was that it was something to do with the piece of plywood that had been used to replace the glass in the door to the flat—either that he was afraid of someone who might have seen Callaghan arrive, or that Morty expected the morons who'd decided his faith was objectionable to pay a visit—but he was dead wrong.

"Please. Something's happened to you, Mr. C. If you don't mind me observin'. You've changed. I'll let you know if I hear anything about the stone, I swear, but I don't want you coming here any more. We aren't friends. We never have been. I've been your grass for the best part of a decade. That ain't friendship. Least no sort of friendship I want a part of. I hope you understand."

Callaghan shook his head. He didn't. He really didn't. But there was obviously nothing he could do to calm the old man down now that he'd worked himself up. "Okay, Morty. Sorry you feel that way. Keep the whisky. Call it a pay-off then if you don't think we're friends. But believe me, I'd much rather we raised a glass together like the old days."

Callaghan got up. Living alone for so long in a place like this couldn't be good for the soul. It was a shocking glimpse of what his future entailed. The only difference between them was that once upon a time Art Mortimer had been a well-respected member of the criminal fraternity rather than a copper. They were on opposite sides of the thin blue line, but there had always been a mutual respect between these old school criminals and "the filth" as they liked to call the police. Morty was a relic. His associates were all gone now: dead and buried, or in the Scrubs and unlikely to be released from Her Majesty's pleasure for the foreseeable future. He was the last of that dying breed, the gentleman crook. Oddly, Callaghan was going to miss the old guy.

"The old days are gone forever, Mr. C."

CHAPTER 11

I Love the Smell of Death In the Morning

The underpass stank. It was the sickening fusion of bodily functions and desperation unique to any big city, but especially redolent in London these days. The desperation was far stronger than the urine and vomit for once. A kid sat hunched up against the wall, head down, with a mangy old dog curled up beside him. He had a handwritten cardboard sign by his feet that told his life story up until the moment he'd been eaten by London. *What is it with the homeless and dogs?* Thomas Sabine thought.

The kid didn't look up as Sabine dropped a couple of coins in his hat.

Above him Hyde Park Corner only had the occasional rumble of cars. It was a haven of tranquillity compared with how it had been before. The irregular sound filled the tunnel with the music of chance. And that was all that kept them apart. Chance. But for the grace of song on the radio or a cell phone ringing at just the wrong moment. Sabine didn't like to think about it. He couldn't control chance, but the rest of the variables, well, those he liked to believe he could influence if not control. And life was all about control.

He whistled as he walked the length of the underpass. He remembered hearing how Bob Dylan's granddad begged down here, but figured that was just one more of the apocryphal tales of the city, Dylan being American and his father needing to be about two hundred years old for the story to work. He emerged from the underpass and breathed in deeply. It was a stretch of the imagination to call the lingering exhaust fumes fresh, but compared to the muck of the tunnel, it was the stuff of life itself.

Sabine took a copy of the *Standard Lite* from a vendor outside the park. If he closed his eyes he was sure he would be able to feel the history of the place seep into his bones. It was *that* rich. And *that* bloody. If ghosts were trace memories captured by the earth and stone, this particular spot ought to have been the most haunted acre in London with all of the dead that had swung from the gallows at Tyburn coming back. Now there was a multiplex cinema, a pub that served "brown" food, a fast food joint, and, of course, in the middle of it all, Marble Arch.

He folded the paper under his arm and walked into the park. He liked to sit in the park and watch people. It was one of the few places in the city where people were happy to be themselves, but now all too often it was all but deserted. Still, there were a few people who weren't rushing to be somewhere. They were kicking a ball about, tossing a Frisbee, playing touch rugby, running laps, or just sitting on blankets and picnicking and trying to pretend they weren't desperately into the person sitting across from them. Mothers and nannies walked with strollers. He could always tell the difference just from looking at them. He had a good eye for detail, and the truth was always hidden in the smallest details. There was one woman with her security detail walking five steps behind her, not exactly inconspicuously. She was a nanny, and the kid was obviously one of the chosen few, either the heir to big money or a fancy title.

But he wasn't here to look at the women.

He settled down on one of the park benches just along from Speaker's Corner, close enough to hear the mad ravings of any and every lunatic who took it upon themselves to stand up on their soapbox and rant. Every weekend there was the usual array of doom merchants predicting the Rapture and a dozen other End of Days scenarios, but there was one man who interested him, because hidden away in his monologue were things he shouldn't know. The speaker had seen things he shouldn't have seen.

That was why Sabine was here: threat assessment.

Back in the office they called them *Carrion*: creatures formed from dead and decaying flesh, golems animated from once living tissue. He had seen one before, on the railway lines near the disused Brompton Lane station, but the spark had already left that one and the dissolution had begun to settle in, breaking it down into its constituent parts. He could still remember the smell. It was unerringly similar to the stench of the underpass with its fusion of fecal matter, rot, and despair.

No one listened to the speaker. "They're here," he said, spreading his arms wide in Christ-like benediction. "They're rising up like Lazarus, coming out of the darkness. Their flesh is rancid. Their bones and joints are broken and dislocated, meat and muscle and sinew pulled together without skin. They walk among us. They are here, now, if you know *how* to look! OPEN YOUR EYES! They dart between the cars and disappear down dark alleyways, always lurking just on the edge of sight. But you can *feel* them. I have seen them with my own eyes. They are hunters crawled all the way out of Hell. And we are their prey. Listen to me. I am begging you. OPEN YOUR EYES!"

It was easy for one man to be dismissed as a lunatic, Sabine knew, the risk came if more people started to listen, and believe. Enough belief and panic would come. That was the way it worked. It was all down to crowd dynamics. He watched the crowd, taking its temperature. It was cold. No one was paying the speaker a blind bit of notice. They were far more interested in a top-heavy girl who had planted her own soapbox down twenty feet away and was lobbying loudly for the rights of women to get cosmetic surgery on the NHS whilst pulling at her blouse to provide visual aids. Up against her obvious benefits, the speaker didn't have a prayer. He wasn't the right sort of nutter for the crowd, but he railed on valiantly for another ten minutes before he gave up and stepped down from his soapbox.

Sermon over, he picked up the crate and hurried away.

Sabine left his newspaper on the bench and followed him.

The man was obviously distressed. He pushed through the tidal swell of people coming in through the park gate, then, out on Park

Lane, he ran along the side of the bus queues until he saw a break in the traffic big enough for him to dodge between the cars rather than wait for the lights.

Cursing the guy's death wish, Sabine took off after him.

By the time he finished playing Frogger and re-established eye contact with the speaker, he was already shuffling down one of the narrow streets behind the Hilton Tower, mumbling to himself and looking back over his shoulder every few feet, terrified that he was being followed. And obviously sure that he was. Sometimes even paranoids were right. But the speaker was looking for Carrion on his heels, not a decidedly unremarkable man who didn't stand out in any crowd, so Sabine made no attempt to hide his presence. He followed the speaker onto Down Street. Almost a hundred years ago this had been a stop on the Piccadilly Line. Like the Strand and Dover Street and other ghost stations, Down Street had closed down so long ago it had never appeared on the iconic Underground map. The speaker made the sign of the cross and threw another petrified backward glance as he passed the red-glazed tiles of the abandoned station. It was boarded up, but some of those boards had been worked loose.

Thomas Sabine stopped.

He could smell it.

The smell of death.

The Carrion *were* coming.

The speaker was right to be afraid.

Sabine tugged at his collar to make sure that the wire picked up his voice clearly despite the background noise. "Alpha, we may have a problem."

CHAPTER 12

BREAKING AND RE-ENTERING

Alice couldn't believe quite how simple it had been. It unnerved her. Nine times out of ten, breaking into a building was simple and straightforward once there was a plan in place. Plans circumvented stupid mistakes, and with a little extra thought—and a little extra time—could overcome most obstacles. Alarms could be dealt with—there wasn't a single one that couldn't be beaten once you understood how it worked. CCTV almost always had blind spots—the area of coverage could be worked out and a path plotted that left the scene looking as though it had been hit by a ghost. And if there wasn't a way through, there was at least a critical path that could be walked which would minimize the amount of times she would need to use one of her special gifts.

But tonight, she could have gone in blindfolded and with one hand tied behind her back and a big neon sign saying, "I'm here to rob you," and it wouldn't have mattered. It was too easy. So much so she started to wonder if she was being set up…but that was impossible.

No one knew she was coming here.

She wondered for a moment if Shadwell could have sold her out, but he had no reason to suspect she intended to hit the library. Thinking like that was just dangerous. It started to assign motives where there weren't any, and turned shadows into threats.

The daytime visit had been a simple reconnaissance mission with one objective: to find a place where she would be able to hide and remain undiscovered until the last of the staff had gone and the building was closed up for the night.

Alice was fairly confident that the building would not be patrolled at night, but even if it was, it was so huge that finding her would be like looking for a needle in a haystack. The usual procedure in these places was a pair of security guards in the control room monitoring the CCTV as camera feeds moved from feed to feed, covering the whole building in a constantly repeating circuit. She knew the mentality of security guards; like everything else, it was just simple psychology. They wouldn't expect someone to already be inside, so their attention would be focused on cameras covering the various entry points.

Internal surveillance was always going to be weak and the rooms were unlikely to be checked once the building was locked up for the night. Even if the guards did rounds, it'd take them an hour to cover each floor, and given they weren't protecting state secrets or huge piles of gold bullion, she reasoned they weren't exactly going to be thorough. Sloppiness, in these circumstances, was part of the human condition. She traded on it.

Alice had found a number of places that would have sufficed, but each had carried with it a small amount of risk. The best place would almost certainly have been the locked room down among the restricted texts, which, of course was the very place she needed to be. It wouldn't have been too difficult to slip into the room and lock the door behind her, but there was no way she could guarantee that it wouldn't be checked as part of the closing routine. A book cupboard, on the other hand, would not be looked into; it just wouldn't, no matter how thorough the security guard. More likely than not, the guy wouldn't even have a key for it.

There were any number of them scattered throughout the building. She settled on one that currently housed a collection of children's books. At a time when parents were more likely to take their kids out of the city for a day's distractions, a book cupboard full of Enid Blyton and Beatrix Potter first editions was a pretty safe bet when it came to being undisturbed; it was a sorry state of affairs, but that didn't make it any less true. Another thing in the book cupboard's favor was that it had no CCTV coverage inside it—after all, who spied on books?

The choice meant that she would have to descend two flights of stairs and find her way through corridors in darkness. It could have been worse. She'd walked the route four times that morning, counting the steps in her head each time, measuring the length of her stride and then doing it a fifth time with her eyes closed to be sure she had memorized every turn and would be able to find her way in total darkness if that was what it was going to take.

She had counted out sixteen cameras around the building, concentrating on the entrances and emergency exits, anywhere the staff would interact with the public in case of an altercation, and on the stairwells. The stairwells could have been a problem but for the fact that the lights in the basement stairwell were off, leaving it dark. The cameras each had a small red light beside the lens—she could see the two red lights covering the lower stairs—confirming that they were live, but she doubted very much the library had installed infrared lenses, meaning it really didn't matter if the cameras were on or off, they'd only be recording darkness. That made life a lot easier.

Alice had been inside for an hour before closing. Trying to slip in any later would have increased the chances of someone realizing she hadn't left. An hour was long enough for them to forget about her. The first thing she had done was walk the route once more, just to make absolutely certain it was still firmly fixed in her mind, and then she had set off to hide in the cupboard and to wait with the smell of the neglected books filling up what little space there was around her. She tried not to move too much in case a foot or an elbow or a knee nudged into something it shouldn't and sent a stack of books bumping and tumbling. Anything that made a noise was bad.

But now she was in here, the door closed, the light out, the air thick and oppressive, and all she could do was think. She wished she'd picked anywhere but a cramped cupboard. So many bad memories waited in the dark. Memories intrinsically linked with cramped cupboards of her childhood. Memories she could have lived without revisiting. She felt beads of sweat break out and crawl from the nape of her neck down the vertebrae of her spine one bone at a time, slowly at first, and then running faster as her breathing hitched in her throat. She clenched her fists, digging her fingernails into her palms until it hurt. It didn't help. She was breathing hard in a matter of minutes. Her mouth bone dry. Her tongue cleaved to her palette.

She could have killed for a torch.

And it only got worse when Alice heard footsteps just outside the door.

She had made a mistake. Not only were there night guards, they were patrolling the halls.

Every inch of her skin crawled.

Suddenly the cupboard felt tiny, pressing in on her on all sides.

A minute felt like forever in the dark.

Two felt like the end of everything.

Spots of color detonated behind her eyes as panic began to take hold.

The footsteps weren't receding.

How long did it take to check a room was clear?

Did they know she was here?

Did they suspect?

No.

No they couldn't.

That was impossible.

Alice pressed her hand flat against the wood, fighting every instinct in her body to scratch at it and beg to be let out, beg and beg and beg... No one knew she was there. She wasn't trapped.

But it didn't matter. Her breathing grew faster and faster as panic threatened to take hold. She could feel herself on the verge of hyperventilating, sucking in old book smell, almost choking on the dust she inhaled and giving away her presence.

Go, she urged the man on the other side of the door. Go!

She could hear him pacing slowly, each footstep clear and agonizingly loud in the darkness. He was walking back and forth in front of the cupboard.

Prowling.

Alice bit down on her lower lip, drawing blood.

On the other side of the door the pacing seemed to quicken, as though the guard had scented the blood.

Her skin *crawled*.

All she could hear in the darkness was the *in-out* rasp of her own breathing. It sounded so desperately loud in her own ears. How could the guard not hear it?

And then she could hear *his* breathing.

It was wrong.

Animalistic.

Alice's mind started racing. What was out there? Not who. *What*?

The sound moved back and forth, back and forth, more animalistic than ever. With stone cold dread certainty she knew the guard could *smell* her.

She wanted to scream.

And it was so much worse because of the dark.

She hated the dark.

She always had.

All manner of *things* lurked in the dark places.

She listened for anything, any noise, any hint that the guard was still out there.

Nothing.

Silence.

She slowly mastered her breathing. She had no idea how long it took her to regulate it, seconds, minutes, hours, time had lost all meaning in the dark.

Alice couldn't help but wonder how much of it had been in her head, triggered by the darkness. That creeping doubt didn't help. She waited for a full five minutes more before risking opening the cupboard door an inch.

It was dark on the other side.

There was no sign of the guard.

She breathed a sigh of relief.

The light switch was in reach, but there was no way she was about to light the place up like November 5th before she was absolutely sure that the guards had finished their rounds. By now, hopefully, the guy was settling down with a mug of tea and the evening paper, ready for his nap. But she wasn't about to take that for granted, she'd already been wrong once tonight.

There was nothing to be gained by waiting now. The clock was ticking. She'd come here to do a job, with time to do it, and get out before the guards came back on a second check, assuming the worst and that their rounds were hourly occurrences. Alice rushed out of the room, down the hall, down the two flights of stairs, and then made her way carefully from door to door down the narrow corridor until she reached the one she was looking for.

She pressed her hands to the cold metal of the lock, feeling the mechanism inside, letting it take shape in her mind's eye, aligning the tumblers in her head and applying a gentle blush of heat to agitate the metal on a molecular level, causing it to spring open.

It was a far simpler process than the vault door down in the private bank had been. That door was six-inch thick steel, lined with lead; this was cheap wooden panels she could have put her foot through if noise wasn't an issue, and a hardware store lock. There was little more to it than turning a handle.

She walked into the dark room. The room in which she had been earlier that day.

She hated the darkness with all of her being, but she refused to be intimidated by it.

Yet, still she found herself hearing things in it…the *in-out in-out* rasp of animalistic panting. A wolf?

No.

She clenched her fist, mastering the momentary surge of fear.

She was alone in the dark.

Alone.

It wasn't completely black—the glow of a street light outside the narrow window with the cracked pane of glass gave her just enough light to see by.

She approached the other door. It was better protected than the first. But still not much better.

Alice had had plenty of time to think about different possible places the plans might be and in the absence of finding them within the Royal Collection, or in any of the folios, she had whittled it down to the secure room. She'd know once and for all when she was on the other side of the second door.

The moment of truth, she thought, licking her lips. She looked for the telltale red light, hoping that her hunch about the lack of CCTV coverage in the room would prove to be on the money.

Worst case, she could disguise her features for the benefit of the camera, but she really didn't want to have to maintain the glamour for any longer than was absolutely necessary. It took concentration and strength and both of those things took attention away from the job at hand—getting the plans and getting out. It was more than just not getting caught, too. She didn't want anyone knowing *what* was missing until after she'd hit the White Tower, if ever. Never was better.

Entrance to the secondary room was by means of a keypad. She'd studied it during her reconnaissance that afternoon. It was mechanical rather than digital, but only a little more technical than the flimsy lock that had provided security for the outer room. It wasn't much of an obstacle. The problem was that she wouldn't be able to lock it after her when she left, meaning the chance of someone noticing she'd been in there increased exponentially. It could not be helped. She would be long gone before anyone would notice. Again, she just had to hope the whole affair would be over before the authorities worked out *why* she'd been in there.

Her fingers danced over the keypad, caressing the steel. She felt the spark that heated the metal inside, and smiled. She still relished the thrill when the mechanism fell into place. There was nothing in the world quite as satisfying. It didn't matter how small the challenge. Overcoming it felt good. It was all about the little victories.

The metal melted and merged to create the pattern that unlocked the door and with a smile she turned the doorknob. It swung open with the slightest push. Alice waited a moment, listening for a distant alarm or any indication that she might have tripped some sort of warning system, but no siren sounded, no lights flashed, of course it could have been wired with a silent alarm, but she'd cross that bridge if she ever came to it. She waited a minute listening for heavy footfalls echoing through the building.

Nothing.

She knew that she was safe. At least for the time being, and that was safe enough.

Alice peered into the darkness. Again there was no red light to betray the presence of a camera.

She stepped into the room and closed the door behind her,

covering her tracks. Now that she was in, it was very unlikely there would be any security measures left for her to bypass. It wasn't impossible, but given the fact that the collection was already locked away behind the keypad that immediately restricted access, it wasn't likely. The room wasn't hermetically sealed. The impurities weren't filtered out of the air. In reality it was little more than a fancy "chained library" filled with restricted knowledge and books so valuable because of their scarcity. In fact it probably afforded less. She cursed herself that she had not tried simply pressing buttons two and four together and then three. It was the standard factory override for so many of these locks, and it never ceased to amaze her how many places never thought to either change the combination, or clean-start the system to kill the backdoor. For a start, that would have meant she could have locked the door behind her. Well, no use crying over fused metal circuit boards.

The room was bigger than she'd expected. There were a dozen aisles, each stacked high, not just with books as she'd imagined, but long-term storage boxes as well. There were no windows, which meant she could turn the lights on without fear of discovery.

Few of the shelves were labeled.

No doubt the librarians knew where everything was inside the room.

That didn't help her.

Alice ignored the row upon row of volumes of books stacked side-by-side and end-upon-end and jammed in dangerously tightly. They were all studies of the supernatural, books on alchemy, and bookending them were several local history offerings about supposed hauntings and strange goings-on. Those brought a smile to her lips. This was taking things into the realms of paranoia. It was hard to imagine how these old ghost stories could possibly fall within the remit of the new legislation restricting access to esoteric material.

She was probably within touching distance of some of the most valuable old texts in the world, and they were just gathering dust.

Somewhere in this lot she was sure all of the material relating to the White Tower would have been boxed and stashed away and forgotten about.

Alice wasn't stupid. She had eyes in her head. She had ears. She watched, she listened. She knew *some* of what was happening in the world. There were a *lot* of ancient landmarks in London, but of all of them it was the White Tower that had become the focus of so many peculiar and just plain strange phenomena. That fact alone—it had to be beyond coincidence—was going to be enough to get anything about the old Tower labeled as subversive material and moved out of general circulation. More likely than not it'd be boxed to keep it all together. Librarians lived for order.

She walked the stacks, trailing her fingers across the spines of the old books and labels of the piled up boxes, reading through them. Most of the material seemed to be recorded in some sort of code. It wasn't Dewey Decimal, but it wasn't straightforward either. She read off a sequence of numbers: 1.00.11.2.93/7. It could quite literally have meant anything. It meant *nothing* to her. It was more like an IP address than a filing system.

Alice rubbed at her jawline, thinking. She couldn't very well go through every single damned box in the place or she'd be there all night. She needed to be methodical. Apply reason. Think. There were ways this worked. She had to think in an orderly fashion. The room would fill up from the front because people are inherently lazy and would rather not have to carry heavy boxes all the way to the back of a shelving system if they didn't have to, so anything shelved pre the huge dark cloud over the city was likely to be nearer the doors; anything likely to have come down here later would be nearer to the back. All she had to do was decide where on the scale the weirdness of the White Tower of London lay. It didn't take a lot of thinking. She headed to the back of the room, as far away from the doors as possible, and started to work her way back.

She found what she was looking for, but didn't steal it straight away. It was all about subterfuge. Sleight of hand. Her primary target hung on the wall, neatly framed. Before she took it down, Alice looked for three more sets of plans, these to Hampton Court, the Maritime Museum, and the Imperial War Museum. Two shelves in, surprisingly clearly labeled, she found the first of what she was looking for: detailed plans of the Maritime Museum, not building schematics, unfortunately, but, of all things, a map within a tourist brochure. Further along she found the remaining two plans.

This was all about killing multiple birds with one stone. She went for her primary target on the wall—the White Tower.

It only took her seconds to lift the frame down, cut out the back, roll up the drawing and replace it with the plans of another building, not quite as old, but no less historic. No one giving it more than a cursory glance would be any the wiser. The switched-out plans would more likely than not hang for years without the change being noticed. She didn't expect it to last, but even a few days of them *thinking* the White Tower plans were still on the wall would be enough.

She had deliberately picked the third set of plans just to screw with anyone trying to follow in her footsteps: the schematics were for the Imperial War Museum. She had no intention of visiting the place, but if the filth were *good*—an unlikely occurrence—and somehow managed to track her this far—an even more unlikely occurrence—then hopefully this little added layer of subterfuge would send them off on a wild goose chase. That was the art of misdirection: make the rube think they knew what they were seeing. With luck, the authorities wouldn't even realize that the missing Imperial War Museum plans were actually staring them in the face, and that the *real* missing plans were for the Tower.

She only needed the illusion to hold for three days—that would be enough to do the job and get the hell out of London. Anything beyond that was a bonus.

Alice carefully stowed everything in the small rucksack she'd brought in with her, and started to make her way toward the door when something made her stop; not a sound but a feeling, an echo of something from the past that called to her. She didn't move. What? She tried to reach out with her mind, feeling self-conscious even as she did. There was something here, and it *wanted* to be found by her, just as the two *Mary Rose* coins had wanted to be found. Whatever it was wasn't from her *own* past.

She closed her eyes and reached out with a trembling hand, hoping that it would somehow be guided to whatever it was.

The familiarity physically hurt her.

It was there.

She could *feel* it.

She inhaled slowly through her nose, holding on to the breath, and then let it leak slowly out of her mouth. She felt herself beginning to drift slightly, her balance undermined by the sudden surge of dizziness that threatened to overwhelm her. She grabbed at a shelf to steady herself, and as her hand came into contact with the metal she felt the thing crying out to be lifted down, to be held, but she couldn't make the connection. She couldn't understand what it was, or why it wanted her.

And then she knew.

She didn't know how, but she knew for sure that this thing here was linked to the jewel she had stolen from the vault.

But how?

How were they linked?

And the question beyond that: What did it have to do with her?

"Come to me," she whispered. They were the first words she'd said in hours. Her voice cracked slightly around them. Brittle. Dry.

She broke contact with the shelf and the frisson-thrill passed. She touched it again, and there it was, stronger than ever. She worked her way along the shelf, feeling the heat in the metal. This time it wasn't her doing. She wasn't the one agitating the molecular structure. She felt her way, moving toward the heat, as though playing a child's game, getting warmer, getting warmer, and then her hands closed on a small box file and she could have screamed from the sudden surge of heat.

Alice could barely hold it as she lifted it down from the shelf.

The copperplate handwriting was faded but she could just make out the name: *Doughty*.

CHAPTER 13

THE GREAT ESCAPE

Dawn was only an hour away by the time Alice stood outside the National Maritime Museum at Greenwich. There had not been a single vehicle on the road as she had gunned her motorcycle through the center of the city, down Gray's Inn Road, skirting Bloomsbury, into Holborn, through the old diamond district of Hatton Garden, before bringing the bike up to 90 mph and crossing the river to the South Bank at Blackfriars. It was out of her way and she was desperate not to lose time, but not desperate enough to take one of the tunnels. She really didn't want to be under all of that water in the dark. She skirted Southwark, taking Druid Street and Crucifix Lane instead of the wider, more traveled Old Kent Road, onto Jamaica Road into Deptford and finally to Greenwich. It wasn't far, but it was so much more circuitous than it needed to be. The Thames had plenty of bridges, but none of them on the Isle of Dogs, which, while not an island at all, was the fastest route between the library up at St. Pancras and the National Maritime Museum in Greenwich as the crow flew. The roads were good, though. No one was out at this time of night. She savored the adrenaline rush, the wind in her hair and on her face, and the closest thing to fresh air London ever had to offer, but the journey took her from old time industry, the huge temples of the railway stations and museums, down through regal white granite wealth into poverty, pure and simple, showing her the best and worst the city had to offer in a matter of minutes.

What happened now was all about timing. Alice needed to be in place to pull off the next stage of her plan before the world woke up. If she wasn't clear before the city started to wake, it wouldn't take much for everything to begin unraveling. It was as simple as that for stuff to fall apart now. Failure was not an option.

Because of the delays inside the British Library, time was shorter than she would have liked, but then two jobs so far across town in one night was always going to be a big task. Like it or not, she was going to have to take a few shortcuts, and that meant risks. The biggest of all was going to be involving someone else. She was a loner. There was no Team Ho. She knew burglars who liked to work in teams, but she had never played well with others. It went against everything she'd been taught, but for the second time that night, the old aphorism about the devil driving dictated how things had to happen.

She parked the bike outside the museum and walked down toward the riverbank. There were small enclaves of tramps down by the water still. They congregated around braziers and built their cardboard cities beneath the overhangs where centuries before the mudlarks used to scavenge. She wasn't about to walk into the middle of one of these clusters. Instead, she walked quietly along the waterline, keeping out of sight while she looked for one man huddled off a little way from the main group. There was always one who wasn't welcome, even by the underclass, one who was an outsider amid the outsiders. A genuine outcast.

She found the man she was looking for curled up between the huge wooden ties of a decommissioned warship. He was using stones for a pillow. She smelled him before she saw him, which, given the proximity of the other vagrants gathered down by the river, spoke volumes about his hygiene. She moved carefully, not wanting to startle the man. This was a dangerous place at the best of times, and dollars to donuts he was going to be armed with a shiv of some sort, and more than happy to use it.

Alice stood just out of reach and kicked the sole of the tramp's foot, startling him away.

He lashed out wildly, swinging with his left arm as he scrambled to his feet.

Alice didn't move.

She came bearing gifts: vodka—the favored tipple of the serious alcoholic. That would change things. He'd go from violent and defensive to needy and wheedling at the sight of the two bottles. It had taken her forever to find an all-night garage that served as an off-license too. There were benefits to working with drunks, the primary one being just how unreliable they were as witnesses. Even if he could describe her to anyone, they'd not take him seriously. Homeless drunks weren't credible witnesses down at the Old Bailey.

Alice dangled one of the bottles of vodka in front of him, swinging it by the neck between finger and thumb.

"Leave me alone. Ain't done you no harm."

"You want this, don't you?"

"No."

"You're a liar. I like that."

"What do you want?" But the way he said it, it sounded like he'd said, "*Wachuwan?*"

One hand snaked out as he tried to snatch the bottles from her, but Alice kept them just tantalizingly out of reach.

"You have to earn it. You don't get anything in life for free. You should know that better than anyone," she said, using the same tone and intonation she would have used talking to a small child.

The man struggled to free himself from his bedding, releasing the stale but sickly smell of his rancid body odor. He kicked at the tangle of old newspapers that lined his nest. It wasn't a bed. Not even remotely. Alice could have hurled the bottles into the water and he would have chased after them. She had him completely. The power of addiction. She looked at him, wondering what he'd been in that other life before this. She'd heard plenty of stories of stockbrokers and investment bankers ending up down by the river— those too frightened to end their own lives after the crashes. Could he have been one of them? There was no way of knowing. There wasn't even the spark of intelligence left behind his eyes. Alcohol and desperation made the man. He was exactly what she wanted.

"I want it."

"I know you do. And it's yours. I promise. But I need you to do a little job for me," she said, and started to walk away, knowing without looking back that he would be following her. "Nothing dangerous. You're not going to get hurt, but you'd be doing me a big favor, and I like to reward people who do me favors. So, can we work together for a few minutes?" She heard him stumbling in her wake, slipping and sliding and lurching over the loose stones. He was still behind her when she paused by the Prime Meridian and the great compass there. And he was still there when she stood finally beneath the steps of the Maritime Museum.

He was like a stray dog.

Alice gave him his instructions softly but insistently. He nodded eagerly, desperate to prove his worth, because as far as he was concerned that worth could be measured out in ounces of vodka. He would do what he was told, she was sure of that, assuming he managed to stay awake long enough.

"I'm trusting you now," she said, handing over the two bottles of vodka. "I don't mind if you open them now, but it's imperative you do exactly what I told you. Can you do that?"

He nodded.

She didn't trust him, but she didn't exactly have a choice.

"There's more where this came from. Don't let me down."

"I won't," he said. "I used to be someone else. Someone people trusted…before…before…all this. I'll be him again, just for you, just for tonight. You can count on me. I swear on my mother's life." No doubt his mother had been six feet under for a decade but she wasn't about to put a damper on his enthusiasm. It was important that he believed in himself, if only for twenty minutes, and if that meant she had to believe in him then so be it. She could manage twenty minutes.

Alice left the drunk sitting on the damp grass, leaning against a wall of the Maritime Museum guzzling greedily from the bottle and smacking his lips.

She hoped that he would not drink it *too* quickly, but that was why she'd invested in the second bottle. Better to be safe than sorry, even if safe in this case meant being left with an accomplice in an alcohol-induced stupor.

There was no point wasting time wishing things were different. She might have preferred to have the plans in her possession sooner, but if wishes were fishes she'd never go hungry. This part of the sequence had fallen into place late in the day. There was nothing that could be done about that. She just had to make the best of it. Daybreak was less than an hour away. She didn't have the time to worrying about making it pretty. She needed to get in and out and far, far away from here. Anything approaching finesse would be a bonus.

She had only had a few minutes with the plans, but that had been long enough to know that her prize was housed on the upper floor. Unfortunately, that was pretty much the sum of her knowledge.

She hadn't had the time to so much as think out a route, never mind walk through it. It really was unlike her. She was so much more methodical in everything she did. Always. It wasn't just that she liked it that way, she *needed* it that way. This seat-of-the-pants living was for fools. But like it or not, it was too late to be worrying about working out a route now. She might as well just smash a window and run, following the signs like a tourist.

From across the river she heard the sound of a siren spiraling into the night. It could have been the police responding to her breaking into the British Library already, or more accurately breaking *out*. She actually hoped that it was. Not that she expected the police to descend on the building. It'd be the fire department first, and then when they worked out the place wasn't burning to the ground, they'd wonder about the broken glass around the alarm housing, and then maybe, just maybe, make the logical leap that someone had been inside, but the second leap, that'd they'd stolen something, could be a long time coming. She half-expected them to write it off as a glitch in the system and just brush the broken glass under the proverbial carpet. Really, all she wanted was their eyes turned that way, because if they were looking at the library, they weren't looking at the Maritime Museum.

More sirens joined the first, adding a layer of confusion to the song of the city. Alice Ho smiled, feeling for the first time in hours as though she might just get away with it. The more confusing those notes became, the easier it was going to be for her to use it to her benefit.

She leaned back against the wall. It had been a long time since it had last been repointed. In places the mortar was loose and crumbling, as though the walls themselves were mourning the sorry state the city found itself in. Again, this managed disrepair was going to work to her favor, so she wasn't about to complain about it. Sometimes the gods of entropy were kind.

Without a second thought for equipment or safety, Alice found a toehold in the weeping brickwork, and boosted herself up, reaching for the thinnest of crevices above her head. She worked her fingertips into the crack, and let them take her weight as she brought her feet in beneath her. She may have only been a few feet off the ground, but she hung there on four fingers while her free foot tried to find some sort of purchase.

It wasn't a huge climb, but any climb was difficult in the dark, especially freestyle. But Alice had more than one gift that made a life of crime more than one of convenience. You worked with the tools the Good Lord gave you, as one of the many nannies with a more fervent religious persuasion had liked to say. Alice had always had sticky fingers, both metaphorically and quite literally. The darkness stripped away the distractions and allowed her to concentrate completely on the movement of each muscle, every sinew, until she felt one with the stone.

A bead of sweat formed between her shoulders and moved slowly down her spine, breaking as she gave every once of strength to the climb.

The window was still twenty feet above her head.

She hung there a moment, the toes of her right foot taking all of her weight as she looked up above her for the next handhold. The beauty of climbing a wall like this over a rock face was its regularity. She knew she'd be able to find another hold without having to overextend herself and risk falling, and the higher she climbed, the greater a comfort that became. She made the climb patiently, hand-over-hand, keeping her body close to the wall. The secret was to minimize the amount of time she leaned back by plotting the climb in her mind five and six handholds ahead like a chess player.

She made it to the window, and climbed up onto the narrow sill and waited.

First she heard the roar, and then she heard the distinct sound of a stone clattering against glass. She smiled. Her conscripted drunk had impeccable timing. He'd finished the first bottle at the precise moment she needed him to, and now he was very loudly providing the diversion she'd bought with her booze.

She didn't expect him to break the glass. Hell, she was surprised that he had even managed to *hit* the window. All she needed from him was to provide a distraction. She hadn't had time to scope out the security arrangements here, but it was reasonable to assume they'd be every bit as lax as they had been at the British Library. It was only going to play out one of two ways: either he would be ignored, or his little stone throwing antics would draw a guard from the building. Somewhere in the middle was the likelihood that they'd draw someone to the window he was throwing stones at. That was all she wanted.

Alice pressed one hand flat against the glass, surprised as always at how cold and unresponsive it was to her touch.

She concentrated on the glass, feeling her way through the sluggish, unresponsive molecules until she could feel the heat of the metal lock through the barriers of glass and the wood. The heat built quickly, and conducted by the glass, she began to feel the familiar vibrations of the metal responding to her gift.

A light went on somewhere below her.

The sudden change distracted Alice momentarily, causing her hand to break contact with the glass, and in turn break the connection with the metal hasp. The lock was already open, though. The window started to swing open; like so many of the old windows, it swung away from the building, not into it.

Alice lost her balance as the window began to swing out, and barely managed to shift her position, hanging precariously by her fingertips with thirty feet of nothing between her and the ground for a lot longer than she would have liked, until she managed to kick back from the window ledge and haul herself inside.

As her feet hit the floor, her first panicked thought was for pressure sensors, but it was too late to worry about that.

It was all or nothing.

She looked around quickly, getting her bearings. She was in the right room, that much was obvious because of the dozens of display cases and stands and pictures of the great explorer himself, but given that the room was huge, and there were perhaps fifty display cabinets, any one of which could have contained what she'd come here for, it could still be a case of looking for a needle in a very fancy haystack. Only this particular needle was the prize of the collection, which ought to mean it'd be in pride of place in the middle of the room.

She grabbed the torch she'd kept in a bag on the back of her motorcycle and transferred to her belt. She clicked it on.

Speed was more important than caution.

Its beam was precise, but it was still strong enough to light the whole room up. She ignored the glass cases around the walls, and instead played the light across those in the middle of the room. She didn't let the light linger for longer than a heartbeat. The third cabinet along offered up her prize: the Drake Jewel.

She knew a little of the jewel's history, being a gift from Elizabeth I to Sir Francis Drake in commemoration of his circumnavigation of the globe. She looked at the jewel through the glass: it was an unusual piece in many ways, a jewel that wasn't really a jewel at all, but a sardonyx cameo with a portrait of the queen by the miniaturist Nicholas Hilliard on one side and on the other, double portrait busts of a regal woman and an African male. It wasn't particularly spectacular, or even remotely beautiful. It was only considered a jewel because it was so rare for royalty to bestow a gift bearing their likeness upon a commoner like Drake, and people tended to forget that in return Drake had given the queen an incredible stone worth far more in comparison. Still, it was important to her benefactor: he had wanted it and that was all that had mattered. If he said he had to have it, he had to have it. It was as simple as that.

She heard a commotion, and as much as she wanted to believe it was her very enthusiastic tramp, she knew better than that: it came from inside the building.

She'd almost certainly tripped a silent alarm.

It could not be helped.

It just meant she had to move. Fast. Meaning niceties went

out of the window. She grabbed a fire extinguisher from its wall-mount and pounded the glass once, causing it to crack, twice, causing it to spider web, and three times, finally causing it to smash. Shards of glass sprayed in every direction. A sliver struck her face high on her cheekbone. She left it. She didn't have time to worry about picking it out. She could take care of it later. Every second counted. Alice threw the fire extinguisher aside. She thrust her hand into the cabinet, her fist closing around the jewel as the door burst open.

She snatched the prize from the cabinet.

Two guards charged into the exhibition room.

Alice realized immediately there was something terribly *wrong* about the way they moved. Their gait was more animal than human.

The semidarkness made it impossible to make their features out clearly.

She shone her torch in their faces.

They threw their hands up in front, shielding their eyes from the sudden, blinding glare.

In the split second before they covered them completely, Alice saw the black fur, snarling fangs, and spittle-flecked jowls of wolves. She stood frozen, rooted to the spot as they came for her. Details screamed through her mind: torn, ragged uniforms, the weird jointing of their legs and arms as they moved awkwardly on two legs instead of four, the slack jowls and the black, ebon eyes. They came forward, breaking to block off any escape. They were herding her, driving her back toward the wall and giving her nowhere to run. Alice wasn't about to let them trap her. "Good doggies," she said. They didn't laugh. It didn't matter, she hadn't done it for them, she'd used the sound to break her own paralysis. She backed off a step, then another, her fist tight around the Drake Jewel. Their tongues lolled out of their mouths. She saw more tears in the guard uniforms and realized they must have transformed on their way to get her. She should have been flattered.

The silver bullet kept as a lucky charm around her neck felt anything but lucky now.

Maybe she could throw it at them?

"Well, boys, it's been…fantastic. You know how to make a girl feel real welcome, but if you'll excuse me, I've got to make like a shepherd."

They didn't say anything.

They moved closer.

She saw their claws.

"Man, you're a tough crowd. Make like a shepherd, you know, get the flock out of here!"

They read her meaning and sprang, rushing at her.

Alice bolted for the window.

She couldn't allow herself to think about how far down it was, or what would happen if she landed badly… She covered the gap in three quick strides and without a backward glance threw herself out the open window.

CHAPTER 14

CARRION

Thomas Sabine kept his distance. The last thing he wanted to do was get too close to the speaker. The man had been ranting and raving openly about things that really should not have been out there. The public didn't need to know everything. It was much safer for everyone if they didn't. And that was his job: keeping people safe. There was the old British motto: *Keep calm and carry on*. Thomas Sabine was a vital part of making sure that was exactly what happened. Generally, the less people knew, the calmer they were. If they had any concept of the things crawling around in the sewers beneath them—not just the nine million rats down there—they would have run screaming for the proverbial hills.

He checked his watch.

Backup was on the way.

The clean-up team would be here soon. In the meantime, the best that he could do was observe and hope to learn as much as he could in the process. As callous as it was, it was not his job to keep the man from harm. If he put himself at risk, so be it. It wasn't his job to pick up the pieces, either. Some would probably call him a misanthrope. He cared about the job, and the job was keeping London clean. If innocent people died, well, they were probably guilty of something, sometime. No one was truly innocent in his experience. And if thoughts like that made him a misanthrope, then, well, there were worse things to be. It got the job done.

Something moved in the shadows.

He couldn't be sure what it was.

He was half-tempted to move closer, hoping to catch a glimpse of whatever was in there, but only half-tempted.

A couple walking toward him hand-in-hand skirted instinctively away from *something* without ever actually looking in its direction. They just naturally moved as far away from the creature in the shadows as possible. They hadn't seen the tainted *thing*, and yet they had instinctively known to avoid it. He watched the woman. If she had smelled it, her expression would have changed. It didn't. They had not stopped talking for a moment.

Sabine was observant. That was another thing that made him special. It was one of the reasons LN-7 had sought him out. He saw things that were out of the comfort zones and comfortable lives of normal people, and knew what they meant. A look wasn't always as simple as a look, a gesture wasn't always as natural and honest a thing as a simple gesture. Sometimes other things guided these little quirks. Like lovers letting go of each other's hands in an empty street, or in this case skirting the shadows. It also meant that the man he was following could be like him. *That* interested Sabine. If he was, maybe they could use him.

Maybe.

There had been times, usually in the small hours of the night, when he had wondered if this had always been the case. Was it possible that these things had always moved amongst us? Was the only difference now that since the explosion of karma some people had discovered the ability—he stopped short of calling it a gift—to see them? His mind ran to other times when people had claimed to see things, and instead of nurturing those talents they had been shunned and treated as mad, or worse, witches. The hellish asylums like Bedlam could actually have been full of the few people who actually knew what the world was really like. Sabine suppressed a shudder. It wasn't worth thinking about.

The speaker was walking faster now, shuffling along the street and constantly looking back over his shoulder. Sabine saw the look of panic etched on his face. He knew that the man wasn't looking at him; he was completely unaware that he was being followed by something as prosaic as a man on foot. No, he kept staring into the shadows. They were the cause of his agitation.

And then the Carrion creature stepped out of the shadows, just for a moment, but that was all that Sabine needed to be sure of what it was. Unlike the one he'd seen near the Brompton Lane station, this one had the spark of "life," or whatever you'd call it. It was a grey mass of moving, writhing, churning, dead flesh. Meat that constantly changed shape as he blinked. It reeked. The speaker had seen it too. He started to run, stumbling over his own feet in his haste.

The dead Carrion creature wasn't alone.

Another followed and another.

Three of them. Awkward, ungainly, and impossible creatures, like dogs of dead, raw meat, moving on all fours, sniffing at the air. They moved with alarming speed, the sound of wet meat slapping the road as they bounded after the speaker.

He was a dead man running.

And not fast enough.

Sabine watched the man duck into an alleyway. He shook his head. The poor bastard thought that he would be able to outrun these things? It didn't matter how fast he ran, or how far, they would keep pace with him and outdistance him. They showed no signs of tiring. But then, how would dead meat look tired?

The first Carrion rose up onto its hind legs, sniffing the air. Posed like this it looked almost human—in so much that it had two arms and two legs, but its head was distinctly lupine, bloated and rotten, and seemed to be attached directly to its body with nothing even remotely resembling a neck. It moved stiffly, turning to look back at Sabine. Dead nostrils flared as it marked his scent. And then the thing bolted after the speaker. Its gait was disjointed and unnatural, but it didn't slow the Carrion down in any way.

The two others followed.

Sabine stopped at the entrance of the alleyway. He wasn't about to follow the Carrion down there.

He spoke into the wire. "Alpha, we've got three of them, heading east on Shepherd Street. They're chasing our boy."

"Roger that, Four-Five. The clean-up team are two minutes away."

Sabine pulled a gun from inside his jacket. He had no idea how effective it would be against these things. Could you kill the dead with a bullet? Two minutes was a long time in the maze of alleyways around Mayfair. He followed them down the alleyway.

Within a dozen paces it narrowed until it was barely wide enough for two men to stand side by side, offering a choice of exits, left into Shepherd's Market, straight on to an even narrower path that curled around to Curzon Street, or right down toward Piccadilly. There was a fourth choice but it went nowhere, really, dead-ending at the gates of the Japanese Embassy. He followed the Carrion at a distance, and took the right toward Piccadilly just a few seconds after they did. Again there were choices. This time they turned toward what Sabine knew was a dead end at the back of one of the area's many five star hotels.

Huge metal drum bins were lined up along the wall to catch the kitchen waste as it poured down the chutes from inside. Farther along he saw a small cluster of old green plastic dustbins. The speaker, trapped in the dead end, backed up against them as the Carrion gathered around him, moving forward slowly. There was nothing rushed about their attack. It was ruthless in its efficiency, though. Bins clattered and rolled as the speaker tripped, sending one of the lids rolling away across the tarmac, until it spun on its rim and clattered like a symbol.

The back door of the hotel opened. Someone stuck their head out to see what the commotion was, and yelled, assuming it was kids, for them to "Get out of it!" Sabine ducked out of sight. Then, seeing the speaker sprawled out in the old empty bins, the man from the restaurant muttered something under his breath and shouted back inside, "It's just some bloody drunk," and closed the door behind him, oblivious to the Carrion.

He was one of the lucky ones.

He didn't see the grey slabs of congealed meat savage the speaker, tearing him apart strip by strip of muscle and blood. Mercifully, he didn't hear the muffled screams either. Or maybe he did, but chose to ignore them. Out of sight, out of mind. That was the motto of survival for the big, cold-hearted city.

When the Carrion started to move away there was no sign of the speaker.

It was as though he had never been there.

And given the kind of life he had led, the lack of contact with others, the loneliness of London all around him, it was as though he had never existed.

The Carrion turned, moving slowly, guardedly, as they prowled back toward where Sabine hid.

Their feral snouts twitched.

Death burned in their eyes.

He couldn't allow himself to be caught by them.

He wouldn't last the minute until the clean-up team arrived.

He backed up a step, never taking his eyes off the creatures.

The alleyway was only wide enough to take one of them at a time.

He backed up another step, knowing that retreating too far would bring him to the wider street and leave him open for them to surround. Right now the alleyway itself was his best friend. But that friendship could only ever last a few seconds unless he wanted to suffer the same fate as the speaker, because even one of the creatures would be enough to tear him apart.

Thomas Sabine spun on his heel and took off, racing back through the alleyway, counting the seconds in his head. "Which way are the team coming in, Alpha? Give me a direction. NOW!"

"Coming in from Piccadilly, Four-Five. Rendezvous in thirty."

He pictured it in his head, and knew exactly where the team was.

The street was empty.

That was good, it reduced the chance of collateral damage.

But it was bad, too, because if the street had been busier he would have been able to get in amongst the pedestrians and continue to observe the Carrion creatures with a wall of human shields between them.

There was nowhere to hide.

He contemplated running into the middle of Shepherd's Market, hoping that more people would be there gathered around the fresh produce, sitting at tables sipping their overpriced cappuccinos, talking loudly, but that would take him away from the team.

What he couldn't know was if the things were hunting him now, or if they were simply returning to their nest. If they were after him, then Sabine's seconds were numbered, and that number was down below thirty, but if they weren't, he could simply try and get out of their way and let them move on through the ignorant masses. After all, this couldn't have been the first time they'd been out moving amongst the general public, and he found it hard to believe they *always* stopped to feed… So if they didn't suspect he'd witnessed their murder of the speaker, then what was there to draw their wrath?

It was a risk.

He held his gun to his chest, knowing it was cold comfort, but even that was better than no comfort at all, and stepped into a deep doorway, counting the seconds in his head.

The Carrion came out of the alleyway.

Sabine pressed up against the door. He could hear them coming: the *snicker-snack* of their claws on the paving slabs.

He didn't dare breathe.

The three creatures stalked past his hiding place, their huge meaty heads bobbing from side to side as they moved.

One turned slightly, locking eyes with Sabine.

Its nostrils flared and it seemed to swell, breathing him in.

He started to move the gun, so, so slowly, not risking any sudden movement.

He could put a shot right between its eyes.

That might slow it down.

Or it might not.

He started to ease down on the trigger, overcome by the rancid stench of them. Up close it was obvious the Carrion were made up from all manner of dead things—anything and everything dredged up from the sewers: rats, stray dogs, cats, brittle bones of birds with black tufts of feather clinging to their meat, but not just animals, either. There were huge slabs of meat that could only be human. Some of the speaker was in there, slowly being broken down and digested into the monstrous creature. Sabine saw the speaker's blood smeared across the creature's chest, but couldn't focus on it because the stain was swirling and shifting with each motion as the remains of the man were absorbed into the walking masses of putrefaction.

Sabine struggled not to gag at the overpowering stench. Waves came off the dead things. Why had they come out from the Underground *now*? Why risk walking amongst the living? Was it hunger? Was it fear? Had they been driven above ground by something *worse*? Had they emerged because the ample food walking these streets was too much for them to resist? Or was there something more going on? Some central, tainted purpose that caused them to break cover from the Underground? He could think of dozens of questions and no answers. His mind raced.

Fifteen seconds, maximum.

More than enough for the Carrion to flense every ounce of fat from his bones.

He leveled the gun, drawing a bead on the huge, meaty slab of gristle across the Carrion's brow.

And the dead thing moved on.

He stepped out of the doorway, onto the street again. He watched the bloody backs of the Carrion creatures, already almost fifty yards away.

"Where's that bloody clean-up team, Alpha? The street's getting a little too hot for comfort."

CHAPTER 15

THE WOLF GUARD

Alice Ho took strange pleasure in the pain.

It wasn't sadistic or masochistic pleasure; on the contrary, it was the pure, unadulterated pleasure of being alive.

The fall had hurt like hell, but even as her bones had screamed from the impact damage, she'd been able to drag herself out of view of the window, and then she had laid there for a few minutes, trying to gather the strength she needed to stumble to her bike. It was a Ducati Monster. A genuine hell-raiser of a motorcycle. A beast. And she loved it. It took her longer than she would have liked to stand, and even as she took a first step, her shinbones sent a shiver of black pain shooting up into her brain. She reached out for the wall to hold her up, and ended up leaning against it, tears streaming down her face. Something was very wrong with her legs. Very wrong. The bones grated against the joints, each tiny stress from a footstep enough to nearly blind her.

She wished she'd parked the bike closer.

She was in no fit state to ride it, but she wasn't getting out of here otherwise. And there was no way she was leaving the Monster out here. It was recognizable and registered to her. It offered a trail of breadcrumbs all the way back to her door. No, worst case, she would roll it up to the Embankment and ditch it in the river, and report it stolen in the morning.

No one would be surprised at her failing to report the theft at night. Not any more. Even with a bike like the Monster. That was a cost of the new policing policy, or lack of policing policy: everyone and their mother knew that the police would do bugger all to investigate personal theft at night; that was just the way it was. It needed something big to drag the filth out of their warm and cozy offices during the long watches of the night. A missing motorcycle, no matter how gorgeous a piece of machinery it was, wasn't big enough.

Alice hobbled along the perimeter of the museum building, barely able to take any weight on her right ankle and knee. She suspected the bones were broken. And if not the bones, there was some serious cartilage damage in there. Her pelvic floor felt as though it had been split in two, and her right arm hung awkwardly, the ball-joint and rotator cuff of her shoulder popped out by the impact for the fall.

She didn't have any choice but to limp and lurch, gritting her teeth through the tears back to where she'd hidden the Monster.

She could hear her drunk still making a nuisance of himself, pelting the windows with stones. She smiled despite the pain. She'd picked the right drunk.

Maneuvering the Monster around was torture. The tubular steel trellis weighed 390 lbs., more than three times her bodyweight, and had a wheelbase of 57 inches, making it a beast to turn when she wasn't out on the open road, but what the Monster lacked in "pushability" the superbike more than made up for when given her head. Top speed was throttled to 120 mph, but Alice had taken it up to 186 mph, where the speedometer ran out of numbers, and she was still accelerating.

Looking over her shoulder, she saw the two guards bursting out of the building, and knew she was going to need every single one of those mph as they came bounding toward her.

She gunned the engine.

Then, she got lucky.

The same couldn't be said for the poor sap she'd bribed into causing the distraction, though. The guards skidded on the gravel, heads up, howling, as the tramp waved his empty bottle at them. The idiot was singing at the top of his lungs. It was hardly *yo-ho-ho and lay the man down* stuff, but he was belting it out and brandishing the bottle like a good old-fashioned nautical pisshead. The guards were caught for a moment, between charging her down and tearing the drunk apart.

Anyone with half a brain could have realized the drunk was nothing more than a dupe, but the guards didn't seem to differentiate. He was there. He was part of the crime. He was going down.

Alice *screamed* as she pushed herself up out of the seat, and came down hard, kick-starting the bike. She almost blacked out from the pain as it chased through the entire right side of her body. Bones were broken, but that was the least of it. Blood vessels had burst, tendons torn, and who knew what other damage had been done to her internal organs. She was weakening by the minute. If she did not get out of there quickly, she knew, she'd be stuck out here, helpless, as things started to go seriously wrong.

She revved the engine and surged forward, tires spitting gravel.

The guards didn't pay her the least bit of attention as she brought the back wheel spinning around, pointing the Monster toward the road out toward Deptford. They only had eyes for the drunk. He'd stopped singing. He cowered away from them, still brandishing the bottle, but this time as though trying to ward them off.

She wanted to help, but there was nothing she could do. She could barely help herself.

But she couldn't just leave him.

Alice brought the Monster around, the huge V-Twin engine roaring, and drove straight at them.

The Monster was capable of nought to sixty in two seconds.

That wasn't fast enough to save the drunk.

Before the bike reached them, the two guards fell on the drunk—who had stumbled to the ground and waved his arms above his head and kicked his legs out and couldn't remember a single coherent note of his song now—like a pair of wild animals. They tore and bit and clawed at the drunk. He found his voice again. His last song was a scream.

Alice leaned down hard on the handlebars and dropped her broken right foot, using it as a pivot-point to swing the Monster around. Her ankle gave out beneath the bike's weight, and even as the studs of the rear wheel churned in the gravel and the cartilage around her ankle slipped, bone grating on bone, she accelerated, tearing away from the murder scene.

In the mirror she saw one of the beasts break away from the slaughter, its jaws slavering, blood slick on its jowls, fur stained red, as it started to bound toward her.

She throttled the Monster, the tires spun, not biting on the gravel, and then they caught and the bike lurched forward. It was *almost* too late. The guard lunged at her, slashing out with barbed claws, and barely missed her midriff, slicing into the leather jacket she wore, and deep into the tubular frame of the bike. The Monster fishtailed. It took every ounce of strength and control that she had to stop it from going spinning out from under her. But, fighting the blinding agony coming up from her ruined ankle, Alice kept it upright.

The claws had missed the petrol tank.

Just.

But they'd cut one of the cables back there.

Fluid dripped out of it as it flapped uselessly at the side of the wheel.

Alice regained control, accelerating away, and willing the Monster to just keep going. She saw the wolf guard in the mirror, dropping back onto all fours and bounding after her.

She gunned the engine, pulling back hard on the throttle to give the Monster its head, and really let the bike roar as it screamed out for the gear change. She was deaf to it.

Thirty.

Forty.

Fifty.

The needle on the speedometer raced toward the red.

And still the creature was in the rearview mirror, gaining on her.

Sixty.

Seventy.

Eighty.

Less than four seconds. That was all it took. Finally the guard receded into the distance. She was clear. The beast rose up onto its hind legs and howled out its frustration as it gave up its pursuit.

CHAPTER 16

THE EYE

Jack Callaghan had the distinct impression that he wasn't welcome at the National Maritime Museum.

The security guards were still on the premises, but were being particularly defensive, not offering much in the way of a situation report, and seemed intent on making his job as difficult as possible. He'd had similar issues before, security guards who hadn't quite made the grade as real cops. They either went out of their way to prove they were better, often beyond helpful to the point of always getting in the way, or they shut up shop and decided their entire *raison d'être* was to be as big a pain in the arse for law enforcement as they could be. And they could be.

Callaghan was already in a stinking mood because he was getting the run around. They were trying to fob him off with a pair of guards who hadn't even been on duty through the night. They'd just come on half an hour before he arrived on the scene.

He tried to make allowances. He'd been on the receiving end of a severe reprimand after mistakes, but it wasn't as though he intended to criticize their failings. It wasn't his job to ream them out for screwing up; they had bosses for that. He just wanted to know what had happened. But he was beating his head against a brick wall. Which only increased his frustration, which meant he was coming across like he wanted to break a few heads. And to be honest, he did. But that was just tough. They were being paid to do a job, and that job was to keep the place secure. No matter how they tried to cut it, they had failed.

"So do you have any idea what's been taken?" he asked one of the administrators who was busy making copious notes on a clipboard.

She looked up at him over librarian-like glasses.

She might have been pretty if she didn't have a stick wedged up her backside.

She grunted. "As far as I can tell, the Drake Jewel is the only thing that has been taken." She shrugged slightly, and turned away from him, indicating the rows of glass cabinets. "There are other things in this room equally valuable, more so actually, but it doesn't look as though anything else was touched."

"So maybe the thief was disturbed?" He looked at the shards of glass all over the floor and at the discarded fire extinguisher. It was clumsy. Amateurish, actually. Smashing a fire extinguisher through the glass cabinet ranked all the way up at the top of the thuggery scale. It lacked any finesse or subtlety. Actually the entire job did. It was like a bad episode of the *Pink Panther*. He had no intention of being Inspector Clouseau, no matter how alluring this particular panther may be. "Is it possible someone found her before she had the chance to take anything else?" Callaghan said to himself without even realizing that he had spoken it out loud.

"She?"

"Sorry?"

"You said 'she.' 'Before *she* had the chance to take anything else.' You have a suspect?"

"Did I? Huh." Callaghan had no idea why he would have said such a thing. He always assumed that a thief was a man and ninety nine times out of a hundred he was right. He could only think that the robbery at the private bank had gotten under his skin, the way the woman had turned to look at the camera but the camera couldn't seem to hold her, and now it was an itch he just could not scratch away. He was seeing her everywhere. And besides, it was fairly unusual to have two jewelry thefts so relatively close together both in terms of time and location, so his subconscious—the part of him that made a good copper—was beginning to try and stitch the two together, looking for connections between them already. Even though he had nothing to go on, he'd learned to trust that inner voice. It had a habit of being two steps ahead of him.

"Okay, tell me about this Drake Jewel," he said, changing the subject.

He could just as easily have read the plaque inside the shattered cabinet, but he wanted to hear it from her.

"The Drake Jewel was a token presented by Queen Elizabeth I to Sir Francis Drake after he circumnavigated the globe." She said it as though she'd said it a thousand times before. She probably had. "On one side, there's a miniature portrait of the queen herself, and on the other, a cameo of an African man superimposed over the face of a European."

That was not what he'd been expecting to hear. "Right. So. Not a whopping great diamond then?" Maybe he was wrong; maybe the thefts weren't related. His mind turned over all kinds of possibilities, and all of them contradicted each other. "Obvious question: Valuable?"

"Impossible to say, really. As with everything, it's down to what someone would be prepared to pay for it, and if they wanted it badly enough. Its provenance makes it an interesting piece. It was incredibly rare for a woman like Elizabeth to bestow her portrait upon a commoner, obviously, and Drake really was her favorite, so it's a unique part of our cultural history."

"Best guess?"

She shook her head. "We're not in the habit of guessing. I can, however, tell you that it's insured for well into seven figures. Well into. We have a portrait of Drake wearing the jewel downstairs in the gallery, if that helps."

"Thanks, but I'm assuming you have some actual photographs of it that we can take away with us? Brochure images. Insurance snaps. That'd be a little more convenient than lugging a painting around with us." He couldn't help but let a little sarcasm creep in, despite the fact that he knew her only interest in him was as a means of preparing for a hefty insurance claim.

Callaghan moved away from the broken case. He walked across

to the window that the thief had obviously used to enter and exit the building. It was raining outside. A weirdly shaped puddle was already beginning to form in a series of indentations in the grass below. It was fairly obvious she'd hit the ground hard and rolled. He shook his head, struggling to wrap his mind around it.

"She just jumped?" The question was directed at the guard who was lurking by the door. He didn't look at him. He was gazing down at the puddle, trying to think how desperate someone would have to be to throw themselves out of a window thirty feet above the ground.

"That's what I was told, sir."

He shook his head again.

"She must have been bloody desperate to risk breaking her neck in a drop like that."

"Drugs maybe?" the woman suggested. He couldn't tell if she was serious.

"I'm pretty sure we can discount your average junkie being able to scale the side of the museum wall without using any ropes, just happening to break into the very room where a million-plus insured state treasure just happens to be lying in a barely protected glass cabinet, does the job in what, a matter of minutes, and out, whilst under the influence of drugs? Performance-enhancing ones, maybe. Class A's, hard to imagine."

"Now, I'd say that sounds exactly like the kind of thing someone stoned out of their mind might attempt," she countered. "It's the getting away with it that's harder to imagine."

And while in theory she was right, it was easy to imagine someone *attempting* it under the influence; it was the getting away with it that made it doubtful. More than doubtful. He checked the window. The fastenings were all still intact. There was no sign that they'd been tampered with. That meant that it had either been left open, been opened from the inside, or somehow it had been opened from the outside without leaving any trace of interference.

That brought him back to the woman at the bank who had appeared to be able to open the vault by doing no more than touching the door.

But the shattered display case contradicted the grace with which the entry had been secured both times.

It didn't make sense.

He looked around the room, scanning the wall-to-ceiling joins, looking for cameras. There was one above the far door, and its red light was on, meaning it was recording.

"What about CCTV images? Is there somewhere we can check them out?" That, at least, would confirm if he was dealing with the same thief. If he was, then resources could be pooled on both cases, rather than having to be split across two separate investigations.

"Sorry, not in here," the security guard said.

"Really? What's that then?" Callaghan jabbed a finger at the camera above the door.

"It wasn't recording," the guard said.

"Of course it wasn't," Callaghan muttered, "because that would have made my life too easy, wouldn't it?" He seemed to think about it for a moment, then raised a finger as though to say *hold on a moment.*

Or maybe it was on, he thought. *Maybe it captured everything and the reason you won't let me near the duty guards or the damned tape is because I'd see something I'm not supposed to see? How's that grab you? Rent-a-cops being overzealous in their policing? It's not unheard of. In fact, I'm starting to wonder if maybe they* threw *her out of the window?* But he didn't say any of that because he knew that if he opened his mouth, he was going to dig a hole for himself no amount of shit-shoveling would get him back out of. Quite simply, he really didn't like the guy. He had no rational reason for it. He was just a security guard. But something about him just rubbed Callaghan the wrong way.

"So what about outside?" he asked, meaning was there any outdoor surveillance that might have captured her fall.

The guard pursed his lips and shook his head. "Nothing. Sorry."

"For some reason I didn't think there would be."

Callaghan pulled the window closed, checking the lock close up. The orange glow of a streetlight sent fractured light through the rain-streaked glass. He was sure that he saw movement in the rain. Something that shouldn't be there.

In the distance, far out over the grimy streets of the slowly waking city, he heard the sound of a sports car's engine gunning into life, the drop of the clutch and the roar of sheer power that accompanied it peeling away from the curb and racing through the empty street, nought to sixty in a heartbeat.

Then, somewhere in the back of his mind, he heard another noise—so familiar to him… He had heard it so many times… And yet, he was sure that he had never heard it before.

It vibrated inside his head…it resonated…as though it had always been there and always belonged there…

It was something between the heartbeat of a great beast and the sound of breathing…beating…rising…

The light shifted in the rain. Swirled through the streaks on the glass.

And he stared into a great orange eye…

CHAPTER 17

SCORCHED EARTH

*F*ear in the air.
   Panic.
   Men's voices rise in terror. Women screaming.
   They stoop to gather their young. They snatch their most valued possessions, anything they can carry. They honestly think there is somewhere safe for them... Hope is the last thing to die.
   The sky is full of huge black shapes...wings beating...wisps of steam venting between razor teeth... They are coming in from the south...and in a matter of moments will block out the sun and plunge the world into darkness.
   They are moving impossibly fast, streaking toward the villagers... These great, winged creatures are like him...but...not. They are different... What do they want? Why have they come? Terror? Do they feed off terror? He knows them... They find succor in fear... They drain the magic of the land in a feast of gluttony, turning it and everything sour. They will dive out of the sun, he knows. They will tuck back their wings to increase their velocity as they swoop down out of the sky to rain dread down from on high. He knows this because it's what he would do in their position...bring their nightmares to life...then end their miserable existence in fire and flame.

That cannot be allowed...

These are good people...

Innocent.

If the horde are not stopped here...now...then where? Who can stand against them?

There must be a line in the sky that cannot be crossed...a line that must be held at all costs.

He could abandon them... It would be easy... Just leave this place...find a new home to bleed dry... Leave Albion to the lifeless...magic-less...pitiful breed...just go...

But that is not their way.

They do not flee.

This is their land. Their skies.... They will not gift it to invaders.

The need to unfurl his wings, to stretch and take to the skies bites deep... The sky is his real home. He was not built to skulk about like a worm on the ground when...the sky offers freedom...

For as far as he can see others like him wait...bristling...eager to launch into the air... He recognizes some of their colors... knows them like kin...others he has never seen before. They have all responded to the silent call...to the threat...drawn to the defense of this strip of dirt... They are part of a cause...each willing to die if that is what it takes to drive the enemy from the sky...

He hears a sound...

Tries to focus on it...and feels himself falling...as though on a thermal in the sky... It is something between a heartbeat and the sound of breathing...but weak...and then a sudden roar rips out of the world all around him and he is looking into a great orange eye.

There is so much power...

A great gout of flame erupts...

Vast leathery wings unfurl to fan the flames...

It is time...

He takes to the sky.

CHAPTER 18

WHERE THE BODIES ARE BURIED

The stitched-together Carrion continued to walk purposefully.
A few pedestrians stepped into doorways to let them pass,
while others felt the urge to cross to the other side of the road,
drawn by something pretty in one of the shop windows. And on
and on it went, with the people of London doing everything they
could conceivably do to avoid the Carrion without ever realizing
they were there.

Thomas Sabine knew they were clueless to the Carrion's presence. None of them had so much as a crease in their brow, and
they weren't that good when it came to hiding fear—humans
never were.

"Moving west on Curzon, toward Clarges," he spoke into the
wire, giving revised directions. The Carrion were moving away
from the disued Underground station on Down Street. He'd banked
on the fact that they'd be drawn back underground as soon as their
blood lust was satisfied, which meant he could only assume it wasn't
satisfied yet. There was no doubting these things were dangerous and
needed to be dealt with. The only reason he hadn't given the signal
to lock and load was because there might—just might—be more of
them and he wanted to be sure they burned every last one of them all
the way back to Hell. "Where the hell is the clean-up team, Alpha?"

They cut across the corner of Green Park, prowling through the grounds of Spencer House and down the Mall toward the waterfront.

Sabine pictured the layout of the city in his mind. Like most Londoners, two versions of London existed in there at once: the London of the Underground, with it's Central, Circle, District and other lines making a schematic map that bore no resemblance to the landscape above, and the London of street level. If they carried on westerly, they'd reach Birdcage Walk and have a clear path all the way down to Westminster and the Embankment.

And there was only one place they'd go from there.

Sabine thought like a soldier: there *would* be more of their kind somewhere. If not already, then as more carcasses and rotting flesh were dredged up.

Someone was using the taint to create them.

To end their threat meant putting an end to the man binding them together.

That unknown man was the operation's linchpin; creatures like the Carrion were appearing with alarming frequency. It wasn't random. Since that first burst of karma leaking back into the world, things had started to change. And not slowly. It was as though the dam that had arrested generations of transformation had been torn asunder and as the backwash of karmic forces poured in to fill the void, every crazy thing that *could* happen was happening. Creatures stitched together from the rotten corpses of stray dogs was just one of them. The fact that they moved around in broad daylight was deeply disturbing to Sabine. It smacked of gathering power. And that, in turn, reeked of trouble.

The fact that they could move through the streets unchecked, unseen, was beyond frightening. The repercussions of such invisibility didn't bear thinking about.

Sabine kept himself close to the wall, moving slowly along the street. The temptation was to run after them, but he didn't want to draw the beasts' attention. He knew where they were going. There was only one place down by the river a tainted thing like them would go.

He was no longer worried about hiding in doorways. The

Carrion didn't even *see* him, which was a curious reversal of their own invisibility.

They didn't consider him a threat.

How little they knew.

He had just become the bane of their existence.

Sabine watched them move, wondering whether they were acting under orders or moving of their own volition. They had no interest in anyone else now that the speaker was dead. And he was dead because he had been a threat. Not because he could harm them, Sabine realized, but because he was drawing attention to them. His rants at Speaker's Corner put their anonymity in jeopardy. How do you hide when someone is permanently shouting, "There! There they are!"

The Carrion stepped into the junction with a side street without checking for traffic, causing a delivery van to screech to a halt as the driver stood on the brakes. Sabine looked at him through the windscreen. He had no idea why he had stopped. Perhaps he had imagined a red light? But then, he was more likely to just blast through a red light because there were so few cars and vans driving around this part of the city now. The chances of hitting someone coming the other way were low. Since the dark cloud over London, all drivers wanted to do was keep moving. Sabine could hardly blame them.

He crossed the road after the van had pulled away again.

The Carrion had put a surprising amount of distance between them. He had to hurry to close the gap once. There was no doubt where they were heading now: the Tower.

He shouldn't have been surprised.

It was a locus for the taint.

If the tainted weren't drawn toward it, the tainted stuff was leaking out *from* it.

"They're heading for the White Tower, Alpha," he said into the wire. "Time to cut them down in their tracks. So anytime the pretty boys with the flamethrowers want to turn up, that'd be great."

"Got that, Four-Five," said the voice on the other end. It was a voice he knew every bit as well as he knew his own, better in fact, and yet he had never been able to put a face to it. Alpha was based somewhere outside the city, away from the worst of it. The distance was a sensible precaution. "Maintain eye contact until further notice."

"Roger that. But that's as close as I'm getting, Alpha. You know me. I'm not one for unnecessary roughness. We've got boys who like to get their hands dirty. Speaking of, what's the ETA on the clean-up squad?"

"Unavoidably detained," she said. There was something in the way she said it that his mind translated immediately to *worst-case scenario*. "They had to deal with a problem that was somewhat bigger, and more pressing, than your spot of difficulty."

"Am I going to be hearing about it on the news?"

"Not if we're doing our job right, Four-Five," Alpha said. "Just maintain eye contact. Do not attempt to detain. I've dispatched a second team. They'll look to cut the Carrion off before they arrive at the White Tower."

"Who's running the show?"

"Three-Seven."

"Then God help us all," Sabine said in mock horror.

Alpha laughed. "I'll pass on your compliments, shall I, Four-Five?"

"You do that, Alpha."

"My pleasure. And try not to get into trouble, Four-Five."

"I'll do my best."

He followed the Carrion, keeping his distance. It did not seem so important now. Something had changed in the way they moved. It was less predatory. Over the next half a dozen streets down to the Embankment they began to lope steadily faster, their eyes— or whatever passed for them—fixed on the Tower in the distance. They didn't seem to pose any genuine threat to the populace. At least not in the immediate future. Ignorance, again, was bliss.

He had no qualms about destroying them. They were abominations. It wasn't his place to worry about studying the enemy. There was nothing to be gained by capturing them. What kind of stuff could the boffins at GCHQ learn from experiments on dead meat that they didn't already know?

He was interested in pragmatics: Did they communicate with each other, and if so, how, because they appeared to act in unison, which suggested some sort of core intelligence.

Sabine drew close to the Carrion—as close as his stomach would willingly allow, given the putrid stench—and saw a pigeon lying dead on the ground ahead of them.

A dead bird wasn't such an unusual sight in this part of the city.

And now, with the taint in the air, it was more common than ever.

He had seen the effects of things coming into contact with the taint, even as tangentially as simply breathing air that had been touched by it. Death was the best of what happened to them. Judging by the state of the corpse, the parasites writhing around beneath its tattered feathers, by the thickening black pall that filled the sky above their heads, and by the proximity to the White Tower, he wouldn't have been surprised if the same fate had befallen the bird. They were vermin, he knew, just like the rats in the sewers, scavengers that fed on the filth of civilization, or what passed for civilization in London. But there was something deeply wrong about death when it came dressed this way.

He had seen too many things die in abject pain, their bodies torn and twisted, because of the taint. The thing was every bit as vile as its name, bleeding into everything, twisting it, destroying it. Or worse, corrupting it.

The Carrion creatures didn't break their stride. One of them trod on the carcass, blind to its presence. The dead bird caught on the stump that served as the Carrion's foot.

Sabine was mesmerized by what happened next.

He watched each clumsy stride.

The Carrion made no attempt to shake the dead bird free. Rather, it *absorbed* the remains into it, step by step, so that the brittle bones and bloody feathers and writhing maggots all became part of it. In a matter of seconds there was no trace of the bird ever having flown. It was part of the Carrion.

He felt a shiver run down his spine.

It might have been the temperature drop, it might have been the fact he'd suddenly stepped into the aura of the Tower, or it might simply have been disgust at what he had just witnessed.

He suspected that it was a combination of the three.

Sabine held back, scanning the hill for signs of Three-Seven and his team. The Tower dominated the skyline now. The grey metal of the four towers' rooftops was slick with evening dew. Some of the windows in the White Tower had been bricked up. The Keep beneath it was dark. The water of the Thames churned and bubbled and broiled around it as it flowed beneath Traitor's Gate.

Sabine felt the surge of revulsion swelling inside his gut; it was his body urging him to keep his distance.

He didn't listen to it.

"Alpha! Where the hell is Three-Seven? We're about to lose them inside the Tower!"

"On site, Four-Five," Alpha reported.

Sabine scanned the hill, the waterline, and the three streets that opened out onto Tower Hill, back up toward the Underground station. He couldn't see hide nor hair of Three-Seven and his team.

"No they're bloody not!" he barked.

And then he saw them, six men, moving fast, weapons leveled as they swept down the hill from the station side.

For a moment he thought they were going to open fire from a distance, but there was no way in hell that their flamethrowers would come close to the Carrion from there, and even as Three-Seven loosed a staccato-rattle of gunfire from his submachine gun, the bullets tore into the hindquarters of the Carrion, but the creatures only slowed, and in doing so, seemed to *grow* as they approached the iron-bound door.

They waited.

Three-Seven and his team didn't open fire again. The leader had emptied an entire mag into the dead things—thirty rounds from the high capacity magazine. They'd not put the Carrion down; they'd not so much as scratched the thing. That answered Sabine's question about how useful bullets would be against dead meat.

Three-Seven gave the signal to engage, charging down the hill with reckless abandon.

Long before the team was at the bottom, the iron-bound door swung open for the Carrion. One by one the Carrion stepped through the huge door and it was closed firmly behind them. Not one of the creatures offered so much as a backward glance as a second clip was emptied in their direction.

"What's happening down there, Four-Five?"

"A whole lot of nothing, Alpha. The Carrion are in the Tower. That was one mighty cock up. And you can pass that on to Three-Seven, too, if you like."

Sabine had caught a glimpse of the doorkeeper in the seconds before he'd bolted the door on the Carrion. He hadn't been dressed in the traditional Tudor State Dress of the Yeoman Guard. He could just as easily have been one of them, Sabine realized. He'd moved with a kind of mechanical detachment, like an automaton. Like slabs of stitched-together dead meat somehow reanimated.

That door served a double purpose: it kept people out, and it kept those things in.

CHAPTER 19

DOWN TIME

Alice had no idea how she had managed to get the bike back to her townhouse on Curzon. She'd stopped thinking about anything long before she'd crossed back over onto the north bank.

The rain had started in earnest as she had crossed the Thames at Waterloo. It had come down thick and fast in a sheet—nine-inch tall soldiers of rain splashing back to attention on the blacktop—but had stopped before she'd gone more than a mile. The shower had made the road greasy, and forced her to take the last couple of miles back to the townhouse much more carefully.

The tortures inflicted on her body had begun to catch up with Alice by the mile. Mercifully there were no other signs of pursuit. She couldn't have defended herself. She had expected to hear sirens wailing, though. That made the silence all the more eerie.

But given what the guards had done to the vagrant, she shouldn't have been surprised. Why would they call in the law and risk bringing attention to the murder? The rain would have washed away the blood, but it would be much more difficult to disguise the guards, and the fact that they were inhuman. That would lead to questions. Questions that didn't have *good* answers. So the lack of sirens shouldn't have come as a surprise.

The day had begun by the time she'd abandoned the Monster at the side of the building. She was in far too much pain to secure it. She had to get inside and give her body the chance to heal.

There were things she could do, charms she could work, but they wouldn't work instantly. They'd take *some* of the pain away, but she knew the damage was serious. It was a miracle she'd walked away from the fall. That she'd made it all the way back to Curzon went beyond miracles. But there was a limit to what her body would take before it started to fail, and she was over that limit.

Through the door, the first thing she did was chain it behind her and fire the deadbolts, not that they would have kept anything unnatural out. It didn't matter; it gave her the illusion of peace of mind. The second was to set the bath running and fill it with salts.

She sat on the side of the tub, waiting for it to fill.

Steam wreathed up quickly to blind the room's mirrors. She was grateful. She didn't want to see the mess.

The bath itself stood on pedestal legs in the center of the room. The legs' feet were dragon's claws. She shut off the water only when it was on the verge of spilling over the top of the bathtub, then limped across to where a slim-line Bang and Olufsen stereo was mounted to the wall. It responded to the proximity of her hand as she waved it across the sensors, and a moment later the sultry voice of Nina Simone was promising that it was a new dawn, a new day, and she felt good. Alice didn't. Alice felt like crap.

She lowered herself into the steaming hot bath, the water sloshing over the side to stain the hardwood floor. She didn't care. She closed her eyes. The smell of eucalyptus was captured in the steam. The heat was uncomfortable. It seared into her skin, but even as it stung it soothed, too, taking some of the pain away even as it broiled her skin an angry red.

She leaned back and closed her eyes, letting the suds lap up around her throat.

And then she began the incantation.

It was a simple enough charm, certainly not powerful enough to save the dying or raise the dead. It merely accelerated the work of the white cells and healing platelets in her body, causing them to do their work so much faster than would naturally be the case.

She felt the warmth steal through her body, and became aware of her pulse, and each and every agony at once, her mind concentrating on the wounds as slowly the incantation began the work that would help her body put itself back together again.

She had no idea if the words themselves were the magic or if the healing was being done by something already inside her, but either way, they gave her comfort. She let herself drift, slipping below the water, bubbles of breath floating to the surface one at a time as she thought about other times, other places.

By the time the water had started to cool around her, the bruises on her side had deepened and darkened to a violent purple. She raised her right arm, testing out the rotator cuff as she worked her fingers across the bone, feeling out the tenderness. She could raise it above her head, which was a huge improvement on even an hour before. But it would be a while before she'd be strong enough to go down to take care of the Monster. It would just have to wait for a few hours at least. She needed to gather her strength. Her next job would be by far the most dangerous—and potentially stupid—thing she had ever attempted. So the longer she could put it off, the better.

She soaked in the water until it was cold, long after her skin had begun to shrink and wrinkle up.

And twice she ran the hot water to infuse some minimal warmth back into the bathwater.

But finally she had to get out.

She winced at the residual pain as she lifted herself up out of the water. Gingerly, Alice wrapped herself in a towel. She savored the feel of its softness against her skin.

She had felt this way before. It was part of the charm. The spell it wove around her body heightened every sensation, making every inch of skin so much more sensitive, to the point that it thrilled to the slightest movement in the air.

The swelling around her ankle looked terrible, but she could tell that it was already starting to subside. Even so, it was difficult to walk. She knew she should rest up for at least a couple of days, but she didn't have the luxury. Alice hobbled carefully through to the bedroom, where her jacket lay discarded on the bed where she had thrown it when she'd staggered home.

She winced as she sat down on the mattress. The contents of the jacket pocket could so easily have cost Alice her life, but she'd never had a choice. She had had to do the job.

She propped herself up with a pillow and unzipped the pocket, pulling out the prize. For one horrible second she thought it might have been damaged in the fall.

She could barely bring herself to look.

She opened her hand.

The Drake Jewel lay in her palm.

There was no stopping the smile as it spread across her face; it was undamaged. She looked at it for the first time, properly, only just beginning to appreciate its unique beauty.

Looking at it, she could understand why someone would want this *so* badly that they would do anything—give anything—to possess it.

In their place, she would have, too.

But it wasn't for her; it never had been. It belonged to the one that she had been bound to forever.

He went by the name *El Draco*.

CHAPTER 20

IT'S COMING TOGETHER

Jack Callaghan was glad to be out in the rain.

He was running on fumes. He'd been up all night and the tank was empty. He wanted to sleep. Not just sleep. Crash. There was nothing left to keep him going, but he didn't have a choice. Things were just getting interesting again.

He trusted his gut. There was something *wrong* about the whole setup at the Maritime building. He didn't know what; it didn't matter. Something was off. That was enough. Now the alarm bells were ringing, it meant it changed the way he looked at everything. When you know someone's lying to you, it affects the way you process what they tell you—or more tellingly what they *don't*. Callaghan had insisted on checking the CCTV system himself, for a start. They hadn't exactly lied, but they'd been economical with the truth, which amounted to the same thing.

Contrary to what they'd said, the camera in the exhibit room had been working when she had entered the room. He watched the tape, fascinated. The supple litheness of her entry through the window, the way she only seemed to need to move her hand across the glass to slip the lock, and then the way she dropped down into the near-darkness of the room like some incredibly toned Eastern European circus acrobat had convinced him that it had to be the same woman.

He should have been surprised but he wasn't.

He'd known it was her even before he'd found any sort of evidence to support the hunch.

He spooled the image back, watched it through again, admiring the way she was always so in control of her body as she moved, and then spooled it back again. Even though he'd only seen perhaps two minutes' worth of footage, total, he'd seen it so often he was sure he'd be able to recognize her movements without ever needing to see her face.

He couldn't help himself. He watched it again. It was mesmeric. The way that outfit of hers clung to every curve and contour as she moved, like hot black wax poured down a lover's back in the throes of passion. Callaghan thought guiltily that he knew her body every bit as intimately as a lover might.

His mouth was dry, he realized, watching her intently as she played the torch across the room in search of the Drake Jewel. He licked his lips, trying to work some moisture into his mouth. He watched her move from display case to display case, looking for the jewel, certain that she was looking specifically for it. She hadn't come here to ransack the place. She took her time locating the right cabinet. She refused to be rushed. Callaghan watched her almost longingly. There wasn't enough light to be able to make out her face, but it was almost better not to see it. It added a level of mystery that went beyond any simple breaking and entering.

The tech boys could no doubt enhance the resolution and brighten it up, but he suspected that even if they did they would find that her features would be blurred just as they had been at the bank.

He'd come to think that she was too good at what she did to make careless mistakes, and showing her face now, after everything, would have been beyond careless.

But none of this meshed with the chaos he'd walked in on at the crime scene.

The last thing the screen showed him was the thief smashing the glass display cabinet housing the Drake Jewel with the fire extinguisher.

And then the screen went black.

He had nothing to go on after that. She'd smashed the case, and then looked up toward the door, seeming to look straight at the camera, and then nothing.

That couldn't have been a coincidence.

The guard protested that he had been told that there had been no footage at all, but Callaghan wasn't an idiot. He could tell when he was being lied to. Something was off. Way off. That was why he had insisted on checking for himself. There was another reason they'd held back on showing him the footage: the timer on it indicated they'd waited over an hour before putting the call through to 999 to report the theft. It was one thing not bothering to report a broken window, or some petty B&E, but the theft of what appeared to be a national treasure warranted a much greater level of urgency than that, meaning that hour had been used to do *something*. His first thought was the time had been needed to doctor the surveillance footage. It wasn't a thought he was comfortable with, which meant it was probably the truth. That just made it worse.

Now, out in the rain, he walked the perimeter, coming back to the open window.

The rain had eased slightly. It was one of those on again, off again mornings, with a wet dawn for once not being down to the glistening pearly dewdrops. The light film of rain was enough to soak through his suit jacket in moments, even though it barely appeared to be raining at all. He wished that he'd carried a raincoat in the car.

He knelt beside the weird indentations the woman's fall had left.

And it was a fall; there was no doubt about it. There was nothing controlled about the way she'd exited the building, which, like the fire extinguisher through the display case, went against everything else he'd seen her do up until then.

He felt out the deepest of the indentations with his fingers, like some Native American tracker capable of reading not only what had happened, where, and when, but what the single blade of broken grass bent the wrong way signified, and what the thief had had for breakfast, all in one fell swoop. Alas, he had no such talent.

The hollow was almost full of water. It wasn't an exact match for the outline of a woman's body, but it didn't take a huge leap of imagination to see that the imprints were down to the hands, knees and, possibly, hip, and very definitely the result of the woman's fall.

The question was: Did she survive it?

He looked up at the window, then back down at the grass, looking for some sort of indication that she'd stumbled away.

It didn't look good.

And a dead body was exactly the sort of thing it would take an hour to cover up, so until he really knew what was happening, it was best to assume she hadn't.

He was still crouched down beside the indentations when the SOCO's van pulled up. Callaghan was a million miles away with his own thoughts as he looked into the water that had pooled there. The surface was so dull it offered no reflection. Doors slammed. Feet crunched on gravel.

He stood slowly and walked to meet them halfway.

The driver still hadn't got out of the van by the time Callaghan reached it, but his two fellow techs were stretching their legs. They shook hands. Callaghan saw Harry Peters juggling a coffee and a grease-dripping bacon sandwich on his knee as he wound the window down.

"No rest for the wicked, eh, Jack?"

Callaghan rolled his shoulders back and then forward. It was as energetic as he was going to get on zero sleep.

"So, what's the score?"

Callaghan shrugged. "I can't see you having much joy, mate," he said. "What we've got is the same woman from the bank job yesterday. Nowhere near as smooth a job, though. Do me a favor: make sure that you get the recording from the CCTV. It won't tell us anything we don't already know, but they don't know that, and right now I want to make them sweat."

Harry raised an eyebrow at that. "Oh really? I love a good conspiracy, Jack. You know that."

"I'll fill you in, not here, though."

"Pint down at the Green Man later?"

"Sounds like a plan."

Harry sniffed his bacon sandwich and set it aside. "It'll keep. So, reading between the lines," he said, switching back to work mode, "you don't reckon we're likely to turn much up in there?"

It was more of a statement than question.

"Hard to say. No prints. She was gloved up. She's a pro. Fibers on the glass case, maybe, from her gloves. But she didn't touch anything with her bare hands. You don't need me to tell you how to do your job, Harry. If it's there, you'll find it, but I'm not holding my breath." He scratched at his nose, lowering his voice slightly. His hand obscured any view of his lips from a distance as he said, "They've had an hour to clean up in there. Place stinks of Domestos, if you catch my drift."

That earned a second raised eyebrow from the SOCO, and a brief nod of understanding.

"My guess is that if you're going to find anything at all it will be around here." He nodded in the direction of the puddle. "She either jumped, fell, or was pushed from that window up there. If she fell, she ought to have landed closer to the building."

"Yes, Detective," Harry said, laboring over each of the three syllables. "Would you like to write the crime scene report up for me while you're at it? It'd sure make my job a hell of a lot easier, and I could get back to this delightful bacon sandwich." The SOCO laughed, obviously enjoying himself. He wound the window up, leaving Callaghan standing in the rain. A minute later the three-man SOCO team were inside the museum sharing a joke. If experience was anything to go by, he didn't want to know what it was. They had a grim sense of humor at the best of times. Laughing in the face of death, they called it. Gallows humor. Normally he would have yucked it up with the best of them, but anything he had to say would have been lost in the rain.

Callaghan walked back to his car.

A pile of sand had been dumped on the grass close to the museum wall. It was a fair distance from the open window so he hadn't paid it a lot of attention the first time he'd walked past it, but with two and two beginning to make somewhere between four and five in his head, he was suspicious about every little thing. A pile of sand was worthy of suspicion.

As far as he could tell there were no other signs of on-going building work or repairs. Nothing that would require sand.

Callaghan knelt down beside it.

He dipped his fingers into it.

It was damp on the surface, because of the rain, but it was bone dry no more than half an inch down, meaning it hadn't been out in the rain all that long. An hour? He found himself looking up at the window again. A lot of things seemed to revolve around a fixed point in time one hour ago. He thought about the thief lying there on the ground after being thrown out of the window. He imagined her injuries as the rain came down, streaking his face like tears. *What would you cover with sand?* he wondered. The truth was, it could hide a whole array of sins. He brushed some of it aside, digging out a small hole. There was nothing but wet mud underneath.

That was just one more thing that didn't quite make sense.

It the sand was dry half an inch down, surely the ground beneath it should have been dry, too?

Maybe there was some kind of seepage going on? Or something to do with the water table? He wasn't a geologist. He didn't have a clue how soil worked. If it got wet it turned to mud—that was about the sum total of his knowledge.

He walked up to the door of the museum, hammering on the glass until someone came down to open up. It was the librarian with the slightly sexy black-framed glasses. "Could you get Harry Peters to come down, please?"

"Sure."

Two minutes later the SOCO was wiping his hands in the doorway. "Jack? Something wrong?"

"Do me a favor, Harry, don't make a big thing about it, but could you take a look at the sand over there for me while you're at?"

"Will do."

"Thanks. First impressions?"

"That I wish I'd taken five minutes to finish my breakfast before I went up there."

"In other words you haven't had a chance to look yet?"

"In other words I haven't had a chance to look yet. If I find anything you'll be the first to know."

Callaghan nodded.

He walked away, leaving Harry and his team to get on with what they did. The answers would come if they were there to be found. All it required of him was just a little patience. He could do that. It wasn't like he had a choice in the matter, though. He kept thinking about the sand. Someone had gone to a lot of effort to hide something. That couldn't be good.

His mobile phone rang as he reached the car.

"Callaghan," he said, rummaging in his pocket for the keys.

"Guv? It's Lawson. We've got another break-in reported if you want to check it out when you're done there."

"I was rather looking forward to going home, Lawson. I vaguely remember where I live. I'm just imagining twenty winks. I'm not greedy, I don't need forty."

"Yeah, well, that's not going to happen."

"What do I need to know?"

"Well, for one thing, this time it's the British Library."

"Someone not wanting to pay their fine?"

Jenny Lawson chuckled at that. It wasn't funny. It was cringeworthy. He made a mental note to stop trying to be funny when he was tired.

"Someone walk out with a jewel-encrusted book?"

"Not exactly, Guv."

"I'm spreading myself thinner than *Flora* here, Lawson. Can't someone else take it? I've got two on-goings as it is."

"I think you want to take it, Guv."

"You're saying they're linked?"

"Nailed it."

"Okay, I'll bite: What makes you so sure?"

"How's this for starters, Guv? Among the things stolen was a map of the National Maritime Museum."

"Okay, I'll give you that, Lawson; it sure as shit sounds like they're connected. I'm on my way."

He hung up and clambered into his car. Callaghan slammed the door and stuffed the keys into the ignition.

Something, a flicker of movement in the rearview mirror, caught his eye, but when he turned, there was nothing to see.

Again, off to the right, down toward the water, he caught a flicker of movement. Low. Moving fast. It looked like a dog. It probably was. The city was plagued with strays. Callaghan didn't give it a second thought.

He gunned the engine and peeled away, tires crunching the

gravel as he drove toward the gate.

His young lady friend had been having herself quite the night, it seemed, which conversely meant that he was going to have quite the day ahead of him.

He could have done without all of the excitement.

But if she was dead, as he was beginning to fear, then it was quite probably the last place she'd been before coming here. He didn't exactly owe her, but he couldn't help but feel that their paths had crossed for a reason and now, inexplicably, inextricably, their fates were intertwined.

"Star-crossed lovers," he joked, looking at his reflection in the mirror.

He looked like hell.

CHAPTER 21

GOING UNDERGROUND

Thomas Sabine was waiting outside of the disused tube station on Down Street when the black-paneled van pulled up onto the curb. It came into the narrow street fast and braked hard. The driver left it half-on half-off the curb. There were some advantages to life in the city now, and one of them was a complete absence of traffic wardens. The trees provided some shelter from the rain, but he still felt chilled to the bone.

The leader, Three-Seven, jumped down out of the passenger-side door. He slammed the door behind him.

"Nice day for it, Three-Seven," Sabine said, nodding.

"Every day's a nice day for it," Three-Seven replied, then banged the palm of his hand on the side of the van hard, twice. "Let's move it guys," he called, and the double doors at the back of the van were flung open. The rest of his team jumped down. Two broke away from the others, left and right, moving quickly. They hit the wall either side of the boarded up entrance, taking up position, and providing cover as the others began to remove equipment from the back of the van. They carried it to the entrance to Down Street's non-existent Underground station.

"So, you saw this stuff. What are we dealing with?" Three-Seven asked.

"Honestly, I'm not entirely sure. I can hazard a guess, insomuch as they're not natural. But it's easier to just tell you what I saw: three of them. They appeared to be constructs, stitched together from dead men. They moved awkwardly, sometimes like beasts prowling on all fours, sometimes walking on two legs. But they weren't really legs, they were just stumps. Their skin was a patchwork of whatever they'd absorbed into them, so there was fur and feather and raw meat. While I followed them I saw them absorb a dead pigeon and I'm pretty sure that they did the same to a grown man."

"Absorb?"

"Yeah. Absorb. Not pretty. They're Carrion creatures. Anything dead winds up inside them."

"Good to know. That's sure as hell not a way I intend to go out."

"I can think of better deaths."

"No death's a good death when it's happening to one of our boys, Four-Five." He turned toward his team. "All right, boys, let's get this show on the road, shall we?" And to Sabine, "You coming?"

"Wouldn't miss it for the world, big man," Sabine said, though in truth he would have quite happily sat this one out. It wasn't his kind of thing. Three-Seven knew that. He wasn't a "hands dirty" operative. He was Intel. Recon. A scout. He found out truths. They had goons to do the killing. But he couldn't lose face in front of the guys now. It was all macho posturing BS, but Sabine knew people, and knew that to the guys on the ground, knowing he was willing to mix it up and get his hands dirty for once was a big thing. Him walking away was out of the question.

Three-Seven gave a sharp downward signal, then indicated eyes-forward, and the two men with the equipment went to work. They'd brought a jackhammer out of the back of the van and a blunt-force ram. They had flamethrowers strapped to their backs and torches on their helmets. They looked like they would be at home on the streets of Fallujah or Helmand Province. Of course, they had all done their time there, too. But if he were to ask any one of them, he was in no doubt that they'd tell him this was the toughest war they'd ever fought, right here in their hometown.

They hit the door hard.

It swung open far easier than Sabine had expected it to.

The clean-up team took the lack of resistance in their stride. All it meant was that the door was in use.

The first of them entered, the beam of his torch on his helmet sending the floodlight of a million candles into the darkness. The light followed his gaze as he panned from right to left across the black interior. The second, third, and fourth went in behind him, taking up positions on either side of the old station entrance hall. "After you," Three-Seven said, handing Sabine a helmeted torch to wear.

Sabine went inside.

The six of them lit up the Down Street interior like bonfire night. There wasn't a patch of shadow left. Torch beams roved left and right, constantly on the move as they looked every which way.

They didn't make a sound.

They took up positions along the wall.

There weren't any barriers now. The old ticket kiosks were little more than rotten wood and broken glass. There were beautiful hand-painted signs indicating the direction of the trains, tiles that were covered thick with grime, but once must have been the most vivid undersea-green, and faded advertising posters for products that hadn't been for sale for the best part of a century. It was as though they'd stepped back in time.

Sabine couldn't hear anything coming from down the old wooden escalator, but that didn't mean that there was nothing lurking down there.

The clean-up crew had residual trace meters clipped to their belts that picked up any trace of the taint in the atmosphere. They were already vibrating off the scale. Sabine nodded to Three-Seven. This was a search and destroy mission. Whatever they found down there, they would incinerate. These things didn't have rights. They didn't get appeals or trials or any other basic inalienable right afforded to a human being.

Three-Seven gave the signal to lock and load, and as one his team slung their weapons around to their chests, powering up the gas tanks on their flamethrowers. It wasn't about subtlety now, it was all about cleaning house.

"Go, go, go!" He motioned one and two forward. They set off fast, keeping low as they hit the escalator and started down. Three and four followed thirty seconds later.

Sabine was last down. He gripped his pistol hard, leading with it as he descended.

Their footsteps swelled to fill the escalator shaft. It plunged down more than three hundred feet, making it one of the deeper descents. The old leather handrail was dry beneath his hands, but immaculate, and the wooden steps were damned near pristine. This place had quite simply never been opened to the public, despite everything being ready to go. It was like a living museum exhibit.

He was breathing hard by the time he hit the bottom of the first escalator. There were more than likely several more to go, along with a series of long and winding tunnels, before they reached the platform. They built these things deep.

Sabine had been involved in operations before, but he really *hated* going underground. It didn't matter if it was the rejuvenated post-Olympics Tottenham Court Road, or the seedy confines of Covent Garden with its rattling cages of elevators, or this kind of ghost station. He treated them all with equal dislike.

It had been a long time since Sabine had actually traveled on the tube. Now that the roads were rarely gridlocked and the Congestion Charge hadn't raised a penny for the Lord Mayor in forever, it just made more sense to use a car.

If people ever saw—really saw—the kinds of things they shared those carriages with, then maybe a few more of them would walk.

They hit the second escalator, moving more cautiously now.

The tunnel smelled rank.

Torch beams speared the claustrophobic darkness, but no matter how bright they were, there were always shadows clinging to the walls, lurking on corners, and some of them stayed there, even when the full force of the searchlights were pointed at them.

Sabine's gun—a Browning 9mm—suddenly felt quite inadequate in his hand.

These were the places where all manner of creatures could hide.

The cracks in the tiles and weeping dust-filled crevices were spaces burrowed out by them to hide their presence from even the most inquisitive of prying eyes. No amount of hiding would save them from the flames when they came.

The isolation of the tunnels offered a false sense of safety for the dwellers of the dark. Sabine wondered how many years it had been since a maintenance crew had even set foot down here. Years.

"No spiders," one of the front two commented. His voice sounded horribly loud in the tunnel, amplified by the ceramics. Somewhere in the distance, Sabine heard the rumble of a train, reminding him that this old station was of course still hooked up into the labyrinth of tunnels that ran beneath every inch of the city. From down here, the Carrion could conceivably reach any part of London. The lack of spiders was a telltale sign of a predator's presence. Spiders always made a home in places like this, always, even if at first glance it seemed unlikely that they would find food of their own. There were webs and strings of spider silk aplenty, Sabine noticed, but they were hanging loose, detached from the tiled walls and corners, abandoned long ago.

"Definite signs of infestation," Three-Seven said, gesturing at a rime of bilious crust clinging to one of the walls. There were bloody streaks across the tiled floor up ahead.

Three-Seven followed the streaks of blood with his torch until they disappeared into the darkness.

The six of them moved deeper into the Underground.

Sabine didn't know the crew, beyond Three-Seven, who he'd run with a couple of times, but he knew they were all good men. The kind of men you'd want side-by-side with you when the shit went down. They had all come from a program that identified men from the armed services with the right instincts: the right *stuff*. Some could see in the way that Sabine could, others just *knew* when there was something odd going on, instinctively, and could sense whether it was friend or foe behind it. The clean-up teams were always made up of a mixture of these talents, those who could see, those who could feel, and in Three-Seven's case, those who could *act*. They stuck together. Brothers in arms, trusting each other absolutely, each man putting his life in the hands of the next.

They reached a third escalator. The smell was almost over-powering now. The ceiling, Sabine saw, was limed with ichor and slime and mold. Filth streaked down the walls like putrid sta-lactites. The floor was coated in waste. Not just mulch and mud and muck but things that he wouldn't have expected to find their way down here—signs of civilization: burger boxes, newspapers, sweet wrappers, and such, but they were wrappers of sweets that hadn't sold in London for more than a decade, and news stories that had been old news even longer ago than that.

This escalator was shorter than the others. Forty feet down to the platform.

Forty feet down to whatever it was that was stinking the place out.

Forty feet down to the hot zone.

Three-Seven nodded to his number two.

The man gave the signal and the team divided themselves be-tween the up and down escalators, giving themselves more room to operate in.

Sabine had expected them to storm down the last flight, going for shock-and-awe tactics over stealth, but they moved cautiously down, their lights playing over every inch of the tunnel, illuminat-ing the cracks. He saw why immediately. There was a huge gap-ing wound in the ceiling at the bottom of the escalator.

The front pair stopped, one of them raising a hand for the rest to follow suit, then sent a huge funnel of flame scorching up into the hole.

Nothing could have survived that.

Nothing living, at least.

Sabine hung back, letting them burn their way to the platform. He followed Three-Seven down the left hand side. He really didn't like being the last man.

CHAPTER 22

THE VILLAIN KINGS

Callaghan didn't get out of the car park.

He saw the big brute of a man with a Neanderthal's forehead and biceps that strained the stitches of his designer suit step in front of the car and barely managed to slam down on the brake before he plowed into the guy. He looked like trouble. Capital T trouble. The kind of brain-dead knuckle dragger that he didn't want to mix it up with in a car park in London. He really could have done without the grief. For a split-second he thought about flooring the accelerator and just driving and to hell with the consequences. The knuckle-dragging Neanderthal man walked around to the side of the car and tapped on the window.

Callaghan wound the window down, just enough to be able to speak to the man, not enough for him to be able to reach in and do any serious damage.

"Would you mind getting out of the car, please, sir?"

Callaghan looked at him.

He shook his head. "I think you're reading my lines, not yours. You should probably move along, sunshine. I'm not the droid you're looking for. Honestly."

"I'll ask you again nicely, sir: Would you mind getting out of the car? Next time I won't be so polite."

Callaghan reached slowly for his jacket, which was lying on the passenger seat, and his ID, which was in the pocket.

"This really doesn't need to be a thing," Callaghan tried again.

When he looked up again he found himself staring into the barrel of a handgun. It wasn't one of those new chunkier Desert Eagles and the like that the criminal fraternity had taken a liking to over the last decade or so—the kind of thing that could open a hole in a guy's head bigger than your fist—but rather an old war-issue Mauser P38. It wasn't the kind of gun he expected to have thrust in his face.

"It probably does. Now, if you'd like to get out of the car."

"That thing's a bloody antique; pull the trigger and it's liable to blow up in your face, you know that, right?" Callaghan said, but he had no intention of playing the hero. Heroes ended up well-ventilated. If a man with a gun was telling him to get out of the car, he was going to get out of the car. It was as simple as that. He reached across and grabbed his jacket and opened the driver's door. He swung his legs out, expecting the knuckle dragger to slam the door on his kneecaps or something equally charming. He didn't, he just waited beside the car for Callaghan to clamber out.

He closed the door behind him, then in a curiously polite moment, all things considered, fished the keys out of his pocket, said, "Do you mind?" and locked up when the big man said, "Go ahead."

As Callaghan turned back around, a black stretch limousine with blacked out rear windows pulled up alongside him.

The knuckle dragger motioned Callaghan toward the car with his antique pistol. He relieved him of his phone, then pushed him down into the back seat and forced him to slide along. The door was slammed behind him. He heard the solid *clunk* of the locks dropping into place. He didn't need to try the handle; he knew the child-locks were on.

The knuckle dragger slid into the front beside the driver. He didn't so much as glance Callaghan's way as he pulled his seatbelt into place.

"Clunk, click on every trip," Callaghan said, quoting the old public safety advert. The two men up front ignored him. He tried a more direct attempt to engage them in conversation, asking, "So, guys, want to tell me where we're going? Or is it a surprise?" The driver took a quick glance at him through the rearview mirror, but neither man answered him.

The limousine pulled away, easing out of the Maritime Museum's car park to join the traffic heading north, toward the river.

"A surprise, then," Callaghan said, as a smoked black glass partition rose to separate the front seat from the back. He settled in for the ride. He wasn't going anywhere. Despite the fact he could no longer see them, he was fairly certain they would be able to hear him. Not that they'd answer.

Without being able to see out of the tinted glass it was hard to keep track of the twists and turns that the car made as it drove through London. For all he knew, they could have been driving the same five blocks in circles, mixing the lefts and the rights up just to disorient him before they left the maze for their real destination.

To be honest, he was more concerned about whether he would make it home again, ever, rather than be able to retrace the path. Stuff like this had a habit of not ending well. His chances of ending up propping up an underpass had increased exponentially since getting into the limousine. He tried to run through a list of villains he'd run up against over the last couple of months. It was a long list and everyone on it would have quite happily wished him harm.

But, the thought occurred to him after more than ten minutes of silence, it could just as easily have something to do with the current case. A private bank gets turned over, he's the man given the job of finding out the who, where, what, and how of it. And those places were all about secrets and people who didn't want their secrets out in the public domain. It was quite possible the owners of the safety deposit box were reaching out to him of their own accord.

He wasn't sure if that was a good thing or not.

All things considered, probably not, but if it delayed the whole buried in wet cement thing, he could live with it.

Sudden darkness triggered an interior light, illuminating the back of the car. All around him, the sound changed too. He knew instantly that they had entered a tunnel, which meant either the Dartford tunnel, Rotherhithe, or Blackwall tunnel. He tried to orient himself, thinking of the city and where the various tunnels went under the river. Either way, they were still heading north, this time north of the river. That opened up all kinds of possible destinations.

Ten minutes out of the other side of the tunnel, the car stopped. The engine idled for a few minutes. Callaghan waited. There was nothing else he could do. He listened for anything that might help prepare him for what would be waiting for him when they finally opened the door, but it was quiet. Disturbingly so.

He heard one of the front doors open, then moments later his door was opened. The knuckle dragger beckoned him out of the car.

Callaghan blinked against the light as he emerged, even though the day was far from actually bright.

He felt the muzzle of the Mauser jab into the base of his spine, right up against the bone. All traces of politeness disappeared as he pushed Callaghan forward. He didn't say a word. Callaghan got the distinct impression he was putting on a show for his unseen employers. They were watching. Callaghan could *feel* their eyes on him.

The driver stayed in the car. Callaghan hoped that was a good sign, and that the limousine was going to be his ride back into town. Given the fact the car had a fairly large boot, it didn't necessarily mean he'd be riding in one of the passenger seats, though. It could just as easily dump his body somewhere out of the way, where he wouldn't be found for a while.

He looked around him.

The car had stopped outside one of the old bonded warehouses. It was on a patch of old industrial land, but there were very few signs of industry there now. The knuckle dragger pushed him ahead, giving Callaghan little time to look around to see if he could recognize a landmark—a tower block, a church spire, anything that would help him identify whereabouts he was. There was nothing to go on. That in itself might even help, given time to think about it. London was a city of landmarks. There was always something to see, something marking the skyline, something to draw the eye. But there was nothing, not even the skeleton of an old crane or a gas tower. No water towers. No tenements or high-rise blocks. Just scrubland. He tried to make out some of the writing in the faded paint brickwork on the side of the warehouse itself, but whatever it said about the previous occupants had long since flaked away to become nothing more than a jigsaw puzzle with too many missing pieces to make sense.

Another stab in the back propelled Callaghan through an open door and into the semidarkness of the warehouse itself.

He stopped trying to look around.

There was nothing to see now.

Just shadows.

The only light came from the doorway behind them.

"Mr. Callaghan," said a voice from deep inside the darkness. "It is Jack Callaghan, isn't it?"

Callaghan found his voice. "It depends. Who's asking?"

"Who's asking? That would be me. I'm asking."

The voice was odd somehow, almost as though it didn't belong there... Perhaps it was a trick of the weird acoustics given the vast emptiness of the warehouse floor. It was arrogant. Confident. It was the voice of someone who was used to getting his own way without question.

"That really doesn't tell me very much, Mr....?" Callaghan let it hang, knowing bravado was stupid, but he couldn't help himself. They knew who he was. They'd brought him out to a warehouse somewhere along the banks of the Thames, probably out in the East End, given the fact they'd come through one of the tunnels instead of taking one of the many bridges. Added to that, whoever it was, they were doing their level best to come across as one hard bastard with this little piece of shadow theater they'd organized for his benefit. He didn't want to let on that he was impressed. Or intimidated, for that matter.

He waited for whoever it was to reveal themselves.

They didn't.

Callaghan could vaguely make out two darker shapes within

the shadows.

The gunman still stood by the door.

He wasn't going to be allowed to go anywhere until they'd had their fun. Trying to make a run for it would be futile. Even if he could get out of the warehouse, where was he going to go? And there was still the driver to contend with.

He waited.

It took a lot to simply stay calm.

Waiting was hard.

He fought the urge to look back over his shoulder. He resisted the need to say something. He kept his eyes forward, his hands by his sides, and simply waited.

The two men stepped forward, not coming all of the way out of the shadows, but far enough for Callaghan to see the first man sufficiently to recognize him—though seeing him, and knowing who he was, made no sense at all. It couldn't. It just couldn't. But Callaghan had seen that face so many times it was imprinted on his brain—a black and white image locked into London's consciousness.

He stared at the man, but now the only urge he fought was the one screaming through every muscle, nerve, and fiber in his body demanding that he run.

Callaghan had never heard the voice before, so he had no idea if the thick East End cockney accent was authentic. It was so thick it was almost mockney—too fake to be the real thing—but he'd never forget it now.

Even before the second man made himself visible he knew exactly what he would look like standing behind his brother's shoulder. Instead of stepping directly out of the shadows, he circled around him, coming up behind Callaghan.

Callaghan could sense the movement but it took him a moment, the long empty silence between heartbeats, to realize that there were no sounds of footsteps to go with it.

When the man finally stepped out of the shadows, he was swinging a cricket bat.

The length of wood caught Callaghan on the side of his knee.

He cried out in agony as the pain shot through his body. A second blow, delivered with clinical precision, sent him crumpling to the ground on all fours. A second pain passed through his body like a sizzling bolt of electricity when he hit the ground.

The cry turned to a scream as the bat came down again. Callaghan rolled onto his side, trying to blink away the tears and cover up, bracing himself for the next brutal blow. He couldn't see what was going on around him, only the dark shape of the man's shadow looming over him. He slapped the blade of his bat on the palm of his free hand, savoring the meaty *smack* it made.

Callaghan drew his legs up, dreading the next crushing blow.

He just wanted to make himself small.

To hide.

But there was nowhere to go.

The villain sniffed, hawked, and spat.

Callaghan closed his eyes.

"Leave him, Ronnie," the speaker said calmly. There was no trace of emotion in his voice. "We don't want to hurt the poor bastard so badly that he won't be able to help us now do we, brother mine?"

"No. That would be a most unfortunate turn of events, Reggie. Most unfortunate."

Callaghan opened his eyes again.

"Glad we agree on that." And to Callaghan he said, "Let's see if we can't avoid some unpleasantness, shall we? There's no need for this to get ugly, after all. All you've got to do is agree to work for us. You can do that, can't you, Mr. Callaghan?"

"It's that or lose the use of your legs, if you're wondering, Jack. My brother's too polite to say it. I'm not," Ronnie said. He swung the bat by his side as he walked back to stand slightly behind his brother.

If there was any doubt as to who they were, that uncertainty disappeared in the moment when Callaghan saw them standing together. Side by side, two of the most infamous brothers the city had ever given birth to. Two of the biggest villains, the kings of London, Britain's Godfathers: Ronnie and Reggie Kray. The Kray Twins—the most notorious gangsters the city had ever known.

The only problem was, they were dead, the pair of them six feet under in Chingford cemetery.

Callaghan looked up at the two men, or rather looked up at their *shades*.

"I know who you are," he said.

And the brothers laughed in his face.

CHAPTER 23

DOWN IN THE TUBE STATION AT MIDNIGHT

They purged the ceiling chasm above the escalator and moved on down to the platform.

The distant sound of a train rumbled through the subterranean labyrinth.

It was getting closer.

Quickly.

Although Down Street was no longer a stop on the line, the rails were still live. Trains ran behind the boarded up section of the station so no one on the train ever saw the abandoned platforms of the ghost station. The barriers had been erected for their safety: what you didn't see you didn't think about, and the last thing London Transport wanted was hundreds of adventurous souls trying to train surf so they could bail out at one of the ghost stops along the line, or kids stumbling accidentally onto the abandoned platform and getting stranded there. It happened, of course. People knew about the disused stations on the Strand, for instance, and wanted to go exploring. That's just what people did. They went out of their way to satisfy their curiosity.

Thomas Sabine felt the air being sucked out of the tunnel like a tsunami drawing the water up from the beach before the wave hit.

And then the train charged past and brought with it a surge of heat.

Something moved in the air above their heads. It swung, just out of eye line, the motion caused by the sudden wave of hot air from the train.

The men at the front looked up, sending their beams of light straight up at the ceiling.

Great grey sacs hung up there.

The torches emphasized the veiny quality of the skin. It was slick. Gelatinous. Ichor dripped from the closest to Sabine, adding to the streaks on the wall tiles.

They pulsed as though they were breathing.

Three-Seven made the sign of the cross.

"What in the—?" The LN-7 operative ahead of Sabine didn't get to complete the sentence.

Three-Seven cut him off, raising his fist for silence.

Discipline kicked in.

The tunnel was silent.

All eyes were on the gelatinous sacs as they pulsed in rhythm with each other. In. Out. In. Out. In. Out.

He couldn't see through the membrane to the thing inside it, but Sabine knew of dozens of creatures that birthed their young outside of the body, normally in the form of eggs that were kept warm, allowing the young to gestate somewhere safe and eventually hatch. He had never seen anything quite like these sacs, but didn't for a minute doubt that that was exactly what was happening here. The Carrion's offspring were in those birthing sacs, gestating, however it was that they did that.

Three-Seven gestured to the lead man. "Take them down."

"Don't you want to see what's happening inside one of those things before you purge the nest?" Sabine asked quietly. His voice carried in the tunnel, sounding horribly loud in his ears. He really didn't want to draw their mother's attention.

"Not particularly, Four-Five. We're not here to gather intel, we're here to eliminate a threat."

"And the best way to do that is to understand it."

"I'm not going to stand here and argue with you, Four-Five. This isn't the time or the place. We're doing what we came here to do, then we're going home. You're a guest, this is our party, understand?"

He wanted to yell that they didn't know what they were dealing with, that they might never get a better chance to understand, because the nest was unprotected. It wouldn't stay that way. The Carrion creatures would return. Especially if these were their eggs...

"Don't you want to know what's inside?" he asked again.

"Not particularly, no." But even as he denied any interest, Three-Seven pulled a knife from his belt and reached up.

"You might want to stand back—wouldn't want to get your fancy suit covered in gunk, would we?" Three-Seven said as he held the knife poised for the thrust. Sabine was mesmerized by the grey translucent membrane. With the helmet torches all pointed toward it now, he could see its contents moving inside, squirming at the touch of cold steel, as though it was aware of what was about to happen and was desperately trying to free itself before it died.

He almost felt sorry for it.

Three-Seven's serrated blade slid in through the membrane with no resistance. He worked it in deeper with a savage twist, tearing the hole wide open. And then it ripped, the weight of the thing inside too much for the sac to hold, and the birthing fluid gushed out, splashing the ground and splattering Sabine's trousers.

He battled the urge to vomit, barely keeping it down as the bile rose in his throat. The torch revealed something...a mass of flesh the size of a child, but this thing was far from human. It was attached by some sick umbilicus that snaked up into the cracks in the ceiling above the sacs.

A desperate keening sound wailed out of the thing's mouth.

Heat rose from the stinking mess.

It was a fusion of rotten flesh; meat and fish tangled together with a white fibrous tendon than stitched the parts into a whole.

There was no mistaking what this would grow into.

This was one of the Carrion, not yet fully grown, but very much *alive*, as peculiar as it was to think of a creature stitched together from the meat of dead things as being alive.

Three-Seven cut the umbilicus.

It fell, writhing on the ground, while they stood over it. Again it let out a strange mewling sound. It wasn't quite the cry of a newborn coming into the world. It was more like a cry for help. A call to arms.

Up above them, a chittering and scratching and keening intensified until every single sac pulsed and writhed in response to the Carrion's cry.

It wasn't one or two or even twenty voices. It was hundreds. Upon hundreds.

Thomas Sabine played his torch all the way along the ceiling as far as the beam would go. Carrion birthing sacs hung from every inch of it.

There were thousands of them writhing and pushing against the membranous tissue, trying to claw their way out before the clean-up team did what it had come here to do.

"Curiosity satisfied, Four-Five?" Three-Seven asked.

Sabine nodded.

"Good, then let's get on with the job." Three-Seven clapped his hands.

As one, the LN-7 clean-up team vented their weapons, and with a hiss of gas and a roar of flame, the nozzles at the end of their flamethrowers burned.

A great gout of flame billowed like dragon's breath, scorching the underwater-green tiles, charring the drips of ichor black as they adjusted the gas flow.

Three-Seven pulled Sabine back toward the stairwell as the cleaners unleashed the fire and the fury.

He heard the screams of the Carrion above the spit and roar of the flamethrowers as they scorched the sacs hanging from the ceiling, setting the abominations alight.

There was no mercy.

This wasn't killing.

It was like taking a car through the carwash, the flamethrowers doing the same work as the high-pressure hoses, scouring the filth away.

Some of the Carrion kin fell to the ground. Sabine could see them twisting and writhing desperately, kicking and clawing out even as the flames stripped away their dead flesh, blistering and shriveling back on their white fibrous tendons. There were no bones beneath the meat. The cleaners stood over the creatures, venting flames until the Carrion stopped screaming.

It was quick.

It was efficient.

It was brutal.

It was thorough.

They didn't leave a single birthing sac untouched, sending gouts of flame all the way up into the broken ceiling to scour the walls clean. Every single damned one of the Carrion kin was burned to a crisp. Nothing could survive that sort of scorched earth treatment.

Even after the last desperate scream had dried up in their seared throats, Sabine could still hear them echoing through the endless tunnels.

It took him forever to realize that it was the shriek of brakes on one of the trains, and then the wave of hot air hit. It was almost gentle relief after the blistering heat of the flamethrowers.

The whole nest was purged in the time it took for one train to leave and the next to arrive at the disused station. Less than two minutes.

The clean-up team took the time to check out the rest of the tunnels, to be sure there were no more sacs or anything else lurking down here.

They worked their magic, keeping the world above safe.

When they were sure the nest was clean, Three-Seven gave the signal to pull out, job done.

It was a long walk back to the surface.

"I don't know about you," Three-Seven said as they emerged from the station, "but I've worked up one hell of a thirst."

"I could murder a pint," one of the others agreed.

And like that, the world returned to normal.

Sabine didn't want to think what normal would have been like if those Carrion had been carried to term and come crawling up out of the world below to creep and crawl through the streets in broad daylight, unseen by all but the gifted few.

CHAPTER 24

A MADE MAN

Jack Callaghan wrestled with the pain even as his brain refused to come to terms with what was happening to him.

He pulled himself along the ground. There were puddles of black water where the old warehouse roof leaked. He couldn't rise.

The Kray Twins.

Ronnie and Reggie.

They had ruled the East End by fear. The constant threat of violence had pervaded everything. It had seeped into the streets, the pubs, and everything they'd touched. They'd been the Midases of organized crime. Except that everything they'd touched turned to blood.

And somehow...impossibly...somehow...they had been brought back and were staking their ghostly claims on the turf once again.

The pair stared down at him, unblinking, unspeaking.

They walked around him.

Their feet didn't make a sound on the wet concrete.

Callaghan felt something wet hit his cheek.

He touched his face, wiping it away.

He fully expected it to be a drop of water. He could hear raindrops drumming on the corrugated roof, and the constant drip of water falling inside, but even without looking at it, he knew that it was not rain. The consistency was wrong. He rubbed it between his fingers. Only one thing really felt like that. Slick. Oily. Warm. He raised his head. Even in the dim light he could see that it was blood on his fingers. The dark stain on the concrete floor that he'd thought was the rain was no doubt the same.

He tried to push himself up. It was agonizing. He could barely muster the strength to go up onto his hands and knees, and even then he had to keep his weight off the knee that Ronnie Kray's cricket bat had done for.

He looked up, craning his neck to see if he could locate the source of the blood.

Somewhere in the darkness of the rafters up above him he could just make out movement. It was a strange, twisting motion, first one way, then back the other. When he strained to listen he could just hear the faint metallic creaking that accompanied each change of direction.

It didn't matter that he couldn't see it properly, he knew what he was looking at: a body suspended on a chain.

If he hadn't been afraid for his life before, he was now.

Still the gangsters said nothing.

Their silence was an effective torture.

A motor started up, followed by a metallic slithering as the winch suspending the body started to lower it.

He didn't care about the pain anymore.

Callaghan scrambled away, kicking through the water and the blood, hands slapping on the hard stone as he scrabbled away from the descending hook. He pressed his back up against a pile of packing cases. He could see both of the shades standing there, the light filtering eerily through their bodies as they watched the body come down with grim satisfaction.

Each movement caused more pain to shoot through his body, but he couldn't just lie there, not with the body coming down, not knowing what was going to happen to it.

He couldn't take his eyes off the macabre scene or the two shades as the body descended between them. The man writhed like a worm on a gruesome hook. The twins remained absolutely motionless. Reggie's face was a blank canvas waiting for some

cruel artist to paint an expression on it. He wasn't taking any pleasure out of what was about to happen. But then, it was never about
pleasure with the Krays, it was all about control. Ronnie was enjoying himself, though; there was no doubt about that. There was
a brutal sadistic glee in his eyes. He was getting off on the shock
and fear that Callaghan couldn't hide. That was the difference between the two brothers: control over gratification.

The body spun around on the chain. Callaghan could just
make out the mess that was the man's face. He had been battered into a bloody pulp. His nose was gone. There was only
a bloody hole in the middle of his face. His eyes were swollen
with huge blood blisters and bloody gashes that left him looking
like the Elephant Man.

Callaghan breathed deeply, trying to steady himself.

He was shaking.

He was frightened.

Properly frightened.

It wasn't hard to guess who had been doing the hitting and with
what. It was a vivid demonstration of what they were capable of.
And in the old school manner it was a message to Callaghan: *This
is what happens to people who cross us.* He got the message loud
and clear.

"Not a pretty sight, is he, Mr. Callaghan?"

The man lashed about, struggling for a full twenty seconds before, breathless, he subsided, gasping, crying, begging.

And then he stopped moving.

He'd passed through all of the stages of denial. He knew there
was no getting out of this. No getting off the hook, so to speak.
Acceptance was the last stage.

He just hung there, waiting for the bat to fall.

"I've seen worse," Callaghan said, his smart mouth trying to
land him six feet under. He looked at the poor man's misshapen
features. There was something incredibly familiar about him.
But not. He was so battered it could have been Callaghan's own
brother and he wouldn't have recognized the man. He tried to
see past the blood and the mangled features, like Oscar Goldman
rebuilding the bionic man.

Ronnie finished him off, up close and personal. He gutted the man with a shiv.

Callaghan didn't look away.

He knew he was being tested.

He wasn't about to be found wanting. Not when his own life depended upon it.

In the stillness of death the man was more familiar, but Callaghan couldn't place him. He knew it was fear screwing up with his recollection.

"No doubt you are wondering what we could possibly want with a burned out copper like you, no?"

Callaghan said nothing.

"Well, as you can see, we tried it the other way, but Mr. Hannon here rather let us down. Not once. Twice. No one lets us down twice. So, I'm rather hoping that you'll be able to help us where he couldn't. You do know who Mr. Hannon is, don't you, Mr. Callaghan?"

The body twisted again, this time because Ronnie's shade turned it to be sure Callaghan could see the dead man's battered face clearly. "Take a good look, Mr. Callaghan." Callaghan didn't have a choice in the matter. He couldn't look away. He stared at the poor unfortunate whose corpse Ronnie was manhandling as he might a ragdoll. The truth was, even his own mother wouldn't recognize him after the beating he'd taken. It was the name he recognized. Hannon. The blood-soaked suit was the final piece of the puzzle. Callaghan knew who he was. It was the less-than-helpful manager from the bank; the man who had gone out of his way to protect the anonymity of his clients.

Callaghan was looking at the price of failure where the bank manager's clientele were concerned.

It was all starting to make sense—or at least sense in a world where dead men could torture and abuse working stiffs. Callaghan had to stifle a mad giggle at the thought. Shades of gangsters, thieves with faces that cameras couldn't focus on, like vampires not casting reflections…it was a mad, mad world.

"What do you want from me?" he asked eventually.

"We want you to help us get our property back. That's not too much to ask, is it? We only want what's ours, don't we, brother mine?"

"Only want what's coming to us," Ronnie agreed. He sniffed.

Callaghan didn't want to ask what could be so important the ghosts of two dead mobsters had come back to claim it, but it was the only way he was going to get out of this mess. He felt the cold comfort of the packing cases against his back. At least no one could come around behind him and cut his throat while he stared at the dead bank manager trussed up like a turkey on the winch. "And what would that be, given that an early grave's been taken off the table?" Callaghan asked.

"Got a smart mouth for a dumb copper, ain't you?" Ronnie said.

Callaghan said nothing. He couldn't really argue with that.

Reggie moved toward him, stepping into the light.

The effect was disturbing—like a photographic negative being held up to the light. Beams of rainy sunlight speared down through cracks in the roof, and on through him, scattering like gold coins at his feet.

"Some things were stolen from our safety deposit box and we would rather like to have them returned."

Things, plural, so not the jewel from the necklace, Callaghan reasoned, thinking fast.

"Things?"

"Two coins. They are precious to us, Mr. Callaghan."

"What makes you think I can get them back for you?" It was a reasonable question.

"Don't worry, Mr. Callaghan, we don't need you to get the coins for us; we're quite capable of that. All we want is for you to do your job to the best of your ability, find out who robbed our bank, and when you know, tell us their name before you fill in any official reports or try to make any arrests. We can take care of the rest. All we're asking for is a name. That's not so unreasonable is it? A name in return for your life?"

"You didn't have to drag me down here at gunpoint and damn near kneecap me just to ask me that."

"Maybe not, but it's the way we like to do business. It helps us get our message across. We wanted you to know the severity of the situation." Reggie nodded toward the banker's corpse.

"I understand it."

"We thought you might. Visual aids can be very compelling, can't they?"

Callaghan drew in a deep breath. "How do I get in touch with you?"

"Oh, don't worry yourself, we'll be in touch. We know where you work. We know where you live. We know everything there is to know about you, Jack Callaghan. We like to know about people who work for us."

Callaghan needed the packing crates to help him stand.

"Okay, well, I guess I'll be seeing you around."

"Perhaps Charlie can give you a lift back into town?"

Callaghan nodded.

He wasn't about to look a gift gunman in the muzzle.

"Thank you."

"Don't thank us. Everything comes at a price, especially kindness."

The knuckle dragger stepped away from the door, offering Callaghan his arm to lean on. Callaghan shook his head and started to limp toward the door, knowing just how lucky he was to be alive.

And hoping fervently it stayed that way for a while longer.

CHAPTER 25

LONDON CALLING TO THE UNDERWORLD

A lice had slept. Not well. But she had slept.
Unfortunately, she still felt like she could sleep for a week. Her body felt like it had been used as a punching bag by a Mixed Martial Arts team. She didn't just *ache*. Ache didn't come close to covering it. But she was healing. Give it a week and she'd be fine. Unfortunately, she didn't have a week. She had an hour. Not even long enough to move tenderly downstairs to see Franco and carry on her caffeinated love affair.

She eased herself out of bed and stretched, working her muscles gently but thoroughly, getting the blood circulating to them as she tested every joint. There was still plenty of tenderness down her right side, especially around her ribs, but that was only to be expected. You didn't break your ankle, collarbone, and at least a handful of ribs and not feel it the next morning, no matter how powerful the *juju* that fixed you up. On top of the bones, there was no telling what sort of internal damage had been done. She was just lucky she'd been able to get herself back to the townhouse before she lost consciousness. If she hadn't, there was no telling what sort of state she'd be in now.

Alice looked at her naked body in the full-length dress mirror in the corner of the room. Her skin was a map of red and blue-black bruises, but they would fade soon. The pain had lessened already. She continued with the stretches for a few more minutes, gingerly extending herself until she felt almost supple. She couldn't touch her toes without wincing, though.

She spread the plans she'd taken from the British Library vaults out on the bed. She looked at them, licking her lips as her eyes ran over the blue lines, knowing that what she intended to do wasn't just crazy, it was downright ridiculous…and yet ridiculous or not, it was pivotal to the success of everything. It was the final piece in the jigsaw. One last job, and then everything would fall into place.

She shook her head.

How many crooks had she heard utter those self-same words and then end up in Holloway or the Scrubs within days? Last jobs had a bad habit of going wrong. She knew that. But at least she knew Hampton Court. She knew the grounds fairly well and she had visited the palace itself a couple of times, unlike the Maritime Museum, meaning she'd been able to walk the route, go over the plans in her head, and think it through in-situ, everything coming together in her mind's eye like some giant jigsaw puzzle.

The advantage, and disadvantage, of it lay in the fact that it was just far enough outside of the city—and the ever-present pall of black cloud that hung over it like a shroud—that it still attracted visitors. The numbers were down, of course, but the fact that it was still something of a tourist attraction meant that Alice could come and go without drawing undue attention to herself.

Rufus Shadwell had offered to help her, which was out of character for him. The offer had surprised her. Everything Shadwell did served his own purpose. There was nothing altruistic about the man. If he wanted to help her, it was because it helped himself. She couldn't imagine it was because he wanted to get back into her good graces; he'd had everything off her, and of her, he could possibly want. So that meant it was all about his own amusement or personal gain.

What Rufus didn't know was that she was just as capable of using people as he was.

It would be a fun lesson to teach him.

Payback.

It was a bitch.

And that bitch was called Alice Ho.

She grinned. The thought of getting one over on him felt good, but she knew herself well enough to know that going through with it would be hard; Rufus Shadwell had that thing, when he looked at her he seemed to see right through her, into the deepest, darkest places where she kept everything hidden. And there was nothing she could do to stop him. No lead lining she could put up around her soul to fend off his gaze.

Getting him involved, letting him anywhere near what she was doing, was playing a very dangerous game. But...

There was *always* a "but."

Alice took the plans of Hampton Court, rolling them carefully, and slid them into the protective tube. She replaced them on the bed beside the plans of the final building she planned to rob.

Her last job.

If it came off, then all would be right with the world in every possible way. But if she failed, then she lost everything, and not just material possessions, *everything*, every shred of her being, every ounce of her spirit, her soul. Everything. But...

There it was again.

But...

She'd never have another chance like this.

Alice traced her fingers along the route she planned to take, imagining it in her mind's eye: the stairs she would have to climb, the doors she would have to breach, once she was done, and, assuming the best, the escape she would have to make.

Without the escape then any robbery, no matter how grand, how impossible, or conversely, how simple, was worth nothing.

There was no room for doubt. If she was going to do this, she had to do it right. After all, the Tower of London was the most heavily protected building in the city, and in so many more complex and dangerous ways than just lock and key.

CHAPTER 26

MAZE MONSTERS

Alice traveled upriver along the Thames in a sleek-bodied speedboat, skipping over the spume and churning up the black water in its wake.

It was hard to believe the water had ever been clean, let alone fresh.

The small boat was more than powerful enough for her needs. She enjoyed the feeling of raw power beneath her as she surged through the water.

She'd already made the trip by road a dozen times over the last month, running through the various permutations of highway, backstreet, and alley that the streets offered, leaving nothing to chance. None of those routes was faster, or offered such a minimal chance of detection as going in by water.

It also offered her the best chance of escape.

She eased up on the throttle, coming to a stop beside an old jetty on the riverbank, overgrown weeds and tall grasses having reclaimed it. She tied the boat to one of the mooring posts and hopped out. She waited on the jetty for a few minutes in case some officious little man came waddling down the hill toward her, demanding that she should buy a ticket. Stranger things had happened. No one came. She hadn't really thought they would, but it was better to be safe than sorry. So few staff remained on site that it was hardly surprising they didn't bother with collecting mooring fees when they had to maintain the grounds, and care for the exhibits, keeping inquisitive and sticky-fingered guests in line. Collecting a couple of pounds for a boat on the slip was quite reasonably well down their list of priorities.

On her last visit she'd ascertained that parts of the grounds were sealed off from the general public, and had marked those out-of-bounds areas on the plans. There was a *chance* that she might have to venture off the beaten track when it came to making good her escape, but that all depended on exactly how the next hour or so played out.

It was the only part of her plan that she hadn't been able to map out meticulously because it involved a certain amount of variance, depending very much on how the guards reacted or if they reacted at all. It was very much the fall back option, though. If things went well she'd be back on the speedboat and churning up Thames long before anyone noticed. That was the plan. Anything outside of that would involve a little extemporizing.

Hampton Court lay far enough away from the city that they no doubt hoped it was safe from the strange happenings elsewhere, just because it was out of the shadow of the dark clouds. That was a naïve way of thinking. Naïve and misguided. There were things here, she knew, that rivaled many of the monstrosities she had encountered within the Square Mile.

The difference was they kept themselves hidden, lurking in places where they wouldn't be recognized for what they were, or for some, hiding out in plain sight precisely because they weren't recognizable. Alice knew where they lurked.

She took a path that wound through the grounds rather than a more direct route that would have taken her into an area where the very air tasted of tainted danger. Judging by the lack of staff, it was more than likely that she would have the luxury of taking the leisurely path when she left the dead queen's apartments, too.

The Tudor palace's main doors were open.

She walked in through the front door as bold as brass—after all, she belonged there every bit as much as every other tourist. Nothing about her appearance would raise an eye.

There were a few other people wandering through the building, so she mixed with them, joining the guided tour they'd paid for. The guide offered them little snippets of the building's history, how it had been built as a gift around the same time as another stately home just outside of the city, Nonsuch, not that the original palace out in Ewell survived. Alice listened intently as he talked about the comings and goings of the great and the good of the Tudor age. There was such a rich history to the city, from the Tudors and the Stuarts all the way back to the Plantagenet kings and before them. England was steeped in history. And so much of that history was steeped in blood. But unlike so many other countries of the world, the English were very much aware of it. It was their heritage. The tour guide talked about beheadings, boar hunts, plagues, never-ending wars with the French, the dissolution of the monasteries, the creation of a new Church of England, and of course, at the center of it all, the fat king himself, Henry VIII.

The guide smiled, weaving his story with an actor's charm, knowing when to pause a beat to allow something to sink in, knowing how to bring a chuckle with a seemingly innocent *double entendre*, and generally keeping them entertained. It was a pity his performance was wasted on only a handful of listeners.

She slipped away from the tour as it came toward an end. Having been on it twice before with the same guide, she recognized some of his jokes, and knew he was perhaps ten minutes from wrapping everything up. That was just long enough for her to do what she'd come here to do.

A few of the staff were decked out in medieval dress in an ill-conceived attempt to turn the visit into an experience. Costumes didn't do that; they made people not dressed up either self-conscious or suddenly aware that it was all make-believe. The idea was that they would move through the building pretending to be housekeepers, servants, or even nobility, acting just as they would have done in their day. That, at least, was the theory. Tourists stopped them every few minutes asking for directions to the nearest bathroom or the gift shop or one of the exhibit rooms, despite them all being clearly signposted. Alice didn't need directions. She knew exactly where she was going.

Anne Boleyn's apartments were locked.

That wasn't a problem; despite her weakened state, a Tudor-era lock was hardly going to be taxing. But there was another way in, and this one would pretty much guarantee she wouldn't be disturbed.

A tired-faced guard sat on a narrow stool outside the door. He looked up at Alice as she approached. The apartments had long been known as the Anne Boleyn Gate because of their construction and location within the palace. She smiled when she saw him. It was the same man she had seen on previous visits. She was banking on him remembering her, which for a thief come to rob the place was rather arse-backward, but there was more than one way to skin a cat.

"Sorry, you can't go in there, Miss," the guard said as she approached the door, then gave a slightly puzzled look as he obviously remembered her and was trying to work out from where. And then he placed her, right back at the same door. "Ah, back again are we?"

"Couldn't keep away," Alice said with a grin. "You know what it's like, addicted to this stuff. Born in the wrong time, I guess. I thought I'd come back for one last look before I head off."

"Ah," he said again, obviously slightly uncomfortable in her presence. She had that effect on some men. And some women. "You've missed the last tour of the day, I'm afraid." He pointed to the board on the white-washed wall that showed the viewing times for the rooms.

"Damn," she said, and then made a moue, knowing the slight pout would wrap him around her little finger. Some magic didn't require incantations or charms; it was all about flirtation. But she wasn't about to rely solely upon her feminine wiles when she had a charm that would seal the deal. "That's a major pain in the arse."

He smiled sympathetically. "I don't make the rules, Miss, I just follow them."

She pretended to think about it for a moment, and then smiled—a small, hopeful, please-save-this-damsel-in-disappointment smile. She breathed a word beneath her breath, triggering the charm, and his eyes lit up. "And there's no way that you could,

I don't know, let me sneak in just for a couple of minutes to have one last look on my own? I know it's a lot to ask, but it would mean so much."

He shrugged, a fish wriggling on her hook. "I wish I could."

She smiled, this time a little sadly. "Then I guess this is good-bye," she said, like a lover reluctant to leave. She pitched it note perfect. "Thank you so much for showing me 'round the other day. I can't begin to tell you what a joy it was to hear about her from someone who is obviously passionate about the subject, in-stead of some boy being paid to act like he is."

She held out a hand, sure that he wouldn't be able to resist. She was so far out of his league she was playing an entirely different sport, never mind different division, and she'd chosen some of her words carefully, knowing that he wouldn't be able to resist touching her skin, and that was all she needed to make the bind-ing complete.

He took her hand and her smile broadened into the first genuine smile since she'd entered the gate.

His grip was a little on the limp side. What was it with men not knowing how to shake hands with a woman? She closed her fingers around his hand, then placed her other hand over them. Skin on skin—the suggestion was irresistible. Alice maintained eye contact. She didn't blink. That was all it took.

She released her grip. The seed was planted. And what's more, he would always think that the idea had been his.

She leaned in and kissed his cheek. "You're a wonderful man."

Alice turned to walk away. She had barely taken two steps before she heard him cough awkwardly, and then say, "I sup-pose I could always make an exception, couldn't I?" She had thought it might take half a dozen steps before he called her back. Two, she hoped, was a good indication of how susceptible his mind was.

Alice turned around.

He was already opening the door for her.

She said nothing.

She didn't need to. A spell woven, when in place, needed no more words.

The man was enthralled. He would do anything in his power to help her. All she had to do was ask. But that commitment to her would always be stronger if he was allowed to lead.

Alice gave him a second peck on the cheek as she walked past him and into the room, reinforcing the contact.

"Just knock when you're ready, Miss, and I'll let you out."

She heard the door lock as he closed it, but rather than feeling locked in, she felt that anyone who might have tried to stop her had just been locked out.

She had all the time in the world to find everything she needed without fear of interruption.

In her head she had a checklist of things she was going to need from the obvious dress and jewelry to the less obvious powders and perfumes. It did not take her long to find what she was looking for.

None of the display cabinets were locked. She did love the kind of place that thought a lock on the door and a guard in front of it was deterrent enough.

They really hadn't counted on a persistent and ingenious thief with a mission.

She had seen enough period dramas to know that the dress was going to be far too bulky with its underskirts and ruffles and whalebone bodice for her to carry, so she unhooked the eyelets and stepped into it, pulling it up over her own clothes. She couldn't fasten it up properly, but there were some willing hands right outside the door.

She moved about in it. It was going to make running difficult, so she was going to have to hope she didn't have to. Wearing the dress out of there was the best method of stealing it she'd been able to come up with. The jewelry was a different matter. That was still locked in secure cabinets. She slipped on a dark wig that had been placed on a mannequin and knocked twice, softly, on the door.

Alice stepped back and waited for the door to open.

The guard was neither shocked nor surprised to see her dressed up like the dead queen. He took it in his stride. That was a happy side effect of the enchantment.

"So," Alice asked, giving him a twirl, "what do you think? Will Cinders go to the ball?"

"Oh, Miss, you shouldn't have you know."

He closed the door, and as he stepped into the room, she started to worry that perhaps she'd gone a little too far with the enchantment. The last thing she needed was to be fending off his amorous advances.

"It's just a little bit of fun. I saw it and thought, *I wonder if we are the same size?* Button me up, would you?" If anything, the dress was a little tight, but then, she had a second layer of clothing on beneath it, and she hadn't done up the corset yet, which would reduce her waist significantly—at the cost of her not being able to breathe.

He came up behind her, and one by one, fastened the hook-and-eye clasps. "Breathe in," he joked. She could feel his breath on the nape of her neck, pricking. He kept his hands to himself. Almost—smoothing the lay of the dress on her hips as he turned her around to face him.

His expression was rapturous.

There was no thought about having his trust abused; instead he was absolutely complicit. This was their secret game. "There's just one thing missing," he said, and fumbled with his bunch of keys. He smiled like the cat that had just got the cream as he opened up one of the jewelry display cabinets. "Take your pick, my queen."

She selected a few items from the tray, including an array of pearls to weave into the wig, matching the period fashion.

Alice stepped back to admire herself in a mirror, well aware that the guard had not taken his eyes off her since entering the room. He was like a little boy, lost.

"Now," she said, offering the last little mischievous suggestion, "if only someone could forget that I was in here, that would be wonderful. I wouldn't be able to go anywhere now would I? I could stay in here all night. Sleep in the queen's bed. Sit at the queen's dressing table. I could be queen for a day. Isn't that what every little girl dreams of? Being queen for a day?" She said it to herself, swaying her hips from side to side and swishing the folds of skirts around her ankles.

"Why don't you stay in here all night?" he said, as though the idea had just occurred to him. "I'm sure no one would mind. After all, what they don't know won't hurt them, will it? I can lock you up all safe and sound. I'm on duty first thing in the morning and can let you sneak out. That is…unless you want me to stay with you? I wouldn't mind."

"What a marvelous idea," Alice said, then seeing the sudden blush of hope on his cheeks, added softly, "Ah, but, Henry never slept in here, did he? She'd always have to go and join him, so if we were going to do it properly, really be Anne for a day, you'd have to sleep elsewhere and I'd sneak up to your chamber when everyone was gone?"

He stepped closer, eager.

She placed a finger on his lips.

"Not until later, my liege. Anticipation only heightens the longing, after all, and a queen is worth waiting for, isn't she?"

He understood.

He left her alone in the room.

* * *

Alice lay on the dead queen's bed listening to the comings and goings of the palace, imagining what it must have been like to live back then, to be a woman like Anne Boleyn in the man's world of court.

The last time she had set foot in this room, the guard had told her stories of how the Venetian Ambassador had described the queen as "not one of the handsomest women in the world…" But then, Anne was the opposite of the pale, blond-haired, blue-eyed image of beauty of the time. She'd had a long, elegant neck and small breasts, as well as dark, olive-colored skin, thick, dark brown hair, and dark brown eyes that often appeared black. Some even claimed she had a sixth finger and a goiter on her neck, but Alice couldn't see how a woman with numerous moles and warts and physical deformities could have stolen the heart of the king.

She felt a deep affinity for the woman.

It wasn't that they had a lot in common—how possible was it to have that much in common with a woman five centuries dead?—but rather that, lying here in her bed, wearing her clothes and her jewels, even her wig, she felt a bond.

Alice closed her eyes.

Anne was different. She was surrounded by people like Thomas Cromwell looking to bring her down and using the king's affection for Jane Seymour to do it. Her friends had been taken and tortured into making revelations about her—adultery, incest, and even plotting regicide. The men accused of sleeping with her were not allowed to defend themselves, as the charge was treason. They were found guilty and hanged at Tyburn, cut down while still living and drawn and quartered. Anne herself was tried in the Great Hall of the Tower of London, her sentence handed down by her own uncle, either to be burned at the stake, which was the punishment for incest, or beheaded, at the discretion of the king. On May 19, 1536, with one swift stroke she lost her head on Tower Green—though given the fact her marriage to Henry was dissolved and declared invalid, it made little sense as to how she could have committed adultery if she'd never actually been married.

What must it have felt like to lie here, thinking you were the love of the king's life, knowing you'd come second to the royal bed, but not knowing there were four more wives waiting to follow you, and all that really awaited you was a sword shipped in especially from Calais to take your head?

All of these thoughts went through Alice's mind, almost like memories because she had heard the stories so often.

Finally, after the last of the staff had left for the day, and the light had started to fade, Alice pushed herself up off the bed and prepared to make her exit. Under ideal conditions, she would have liked a clearer night so that she would have been able to see her way to the river, but a few clouds made her more difficult to see from the main house, so it was a case of swings and roundabouts.

Actually, she would have preferred to wait until dawn.

She really didn't like the dark.

She had known all of her life that things *lurked* in it. She could have faced down any one of them in the daylight, but the dark gave them added strength—at least over her.

And she knew they were out there in the grounds because she'd seen them before when she had staked out the place to chart the night watchman's habits. Like the song said, they only came out at night, lean and hungry.

The night watchman made three incomplete tours of the grounds, checking for signs of anything unusual. He never ventured away from the perimeter of the house. And, to be honest, given the strange happenings she'd witnessed that night, even if he did see her she wouldn't have been surprised if he ignored her, thinking that a dead queen was just one more of those peculiarities of Hampton Court to be ignored, rather than identifying her as a thief.

She waited until he had completed a circuit before she opened the window and slipped out. It wasn't an easy climb given the incredible weight and awkwardness of the dress, but she found comfortable handholds, her fingers sticking as though glued to the wall as she scaled her way down hand-over-hand. She kept her body pressed as close to the wall as she could, working her way around to a trellis that in turn gave way to a low roof that allowed her to make her way around to the last short drop to the ground out of sight of the main gate. She landed lightly on her feet, crouching as the gravel crunched, and listened, not moving off before she was sure the guard wasn't heading her way. Satisfied, Alice started to make her way down toward the river.

Her footsteps seemed so loud to her as she walked, trying to keep her bearing regal.

What little moonlight managed to creep though the cloud cover set weird shadows playing across the grass lawn in front of her.

The wind picked up.

She heard a rustling in the hedgerows off to her right.

Her breath frosted in front of her face as she exhaled.

More rustling.

She caught a flicker of movement out of the corner of her eye, but when she turned, there was nothing but the leaves of the maze and the topiary shapes so carefully crafted into the hedges. She had no desire to walk too close to the maze.

Alice started to walk just a little faster, finding a few extra inches for each footstep. She glanced over her shoulder, sure that something was following her.

There was nothing there.

She was alone on the path.

The wind swirled around her, bullying her skirts.

Alice walked as quickly as the dress would allow. She gathered the skirts up, lifting the hem off the gravel so that it didn't drag. She double-checked, then cut across the lawn, not wanting to spend a second longer out here in the dark than she had to. She wished dearly that she could have found a way to carry the dress instead of having to wear it. It slowed her down terribly, and there was something dreadfully macabre about walking through the dead queen's gardens dressed up to look like the dead queen's ghost.

Again she heard movement in the maze, but as quickly as she could turn to see, the shapes had settled back into the thick leaves of the hedgerows, though she got the distinct impression the huge figures of leaf and twig had twisted and turned to face her.

She refused to look at them.

Alice kept her distance, almost running now as the rustling intensified. She felt the ground beneath her feet heave, and heard the sound of roots being torn up. And in that second, with the frantic swirl of the wind and the churning soil, Alice started to run, almost stumbling over the hem of the dress as she did. She had thought, naïvely, that with their roots being planted deep into the earth and having so many years to burrow down deeper and deeper, they would have been trapped in place, rooted to the spot.

They had been when she'd watched them from the safety of the riverbank on her previous nocturnal visit.

But that wasn't so now.

The only difference was then she hadn't looked like the dead queen who had no doubt planted much of them five centuries before, and tended them, and walked through them even as her life was drawing to an end. How much of her psyche still stained them? How much of her pain was still tangled up with their roots? Could plants hold echoes of grief like stone was supposed to absorb grief and reflect it as ghosts?

Alice was breathing hard, chest heaving as she ran, the dress tangling around her legs. The grass was wet beneath her feet. She didn't slow down. She couldn't. She ran. She stumbled. She almost fell, slipping and sliding in the muddy grass, but kept on running. All she could hear was the one sound she really, really didn't want to: the sound of rustling leaves and shrubs that had uprooted themselves following her.

She ran, wishing that she had thought to leave a light on the boat.

She ran, hating the dark.

She ran, because if she didn't, she might never get to leave.

CHAPTER 27

TOPIARY OR NOT TOPIARY

The LN-7 clean-up team was loading the last of their equipment back into the van when the call came through.

The agency had certain resources and uncertain responsibilities as the self-appointed guardians of the nation. There was nothing democratic about protecting the country from uncommon foes. What the normal people didn't understand, what the everyday Joes walked around oblivious to, they not only knew but these few good men stood as the last line of defense against them. As karma pooled back into the world, so too did creatures of magic: primordial spirits of land, sea, and air, the fae's reopened portals between worlds, demons, angels, things summoned and bound, they'd all found their way back; even the blood of the wolf was awake, and the men and women who carried it in their veins listened to the call of the moon once more.

The city had changed.

The world had changed.

And LN-7 stood against those changes.

Daily they faced down the abominations created by the taint, things like the Carrion dead of Down Street's abandoned Underground station, foes of supernatural origin sometimes, or more mundane but no less dangerous men driven mad with the power of magic that flowed through them since the return of karma. They were out-gunned, out-numbered, and often out-foxed by an enemy which grew stronger day by day, but they never shied away from the fight. They simply locked and loaded and threw themselves back into the fray.

The clean-up team were armed tactical response soldiers. Officially Three-Seven's unit was known as "cyphers." There were others, "Thelema," who were different. Less like *real* soldiers, though equally skilled in covert ops, they were a lot more like the enemy in many ways, fighting fire with fire, but then, given that Alestair Crowley had christened them, their nature should hardly have been surprising.

It had taken a long time to scour the disused station, down every line, into every tunnel, deep into the darkest embrasures, checking every nook and cranny to root out every last Carrion birthed abomination hiding there. It had all been done in stages, the first wave involving the flamethrowers burning the sacs from the ceiling and incinerating the corpses. The second was chemical, ensuring that the last of the membranes were absolutely dissolved, every last trace of the Carrion gone, and then they'd used high-pressure hoses to sluice the muck away. It had to be done like that, otherwise they'd come back. That was their nature. The Carrion were the undead equivalent of cockroaches.

They'd worked up one hell of a thirst, but they could read Three-Seven's face. The call that had come in wasn't good news.

It was work.

They weren't going to get that beer or get to head home to wives, partners, or cats. Work came first. Always. Without question. It was only the men with feline companions who could share their day's work. The others had to lie. Some of the cypher teams would simply claim to have spent the day behind a desk pushing paper; others would say they were doing runs "up north" with lorries full of consumer goods, electronics, refrigeration units, and frozen food. A few would simply say they were out on maneuvers, and one or two would admit that they couldn't talk about it.

Too many of them went home to empty houses, unable to maintain a meaningful relationship.

It was the nature of the job.

Thomas Sabine didn't have cats.

He didn't have a partner, either.

He was one of the many agents with an empty house waiting for him.

But he always had the job. That never changed.

And now, by the look on Three-Seven's face, they had another one.

"Who fancies a little trip south of the river, boys?" Three-Seven asked, shutting off the call to his headset. It was a rhetorical question. He hefted the last of the chemical drums up into the back of the van's flatbed. "The Thames Barrier Warning System's playing up. Readings are coming in from sensors. They're reading off the charts. Alpha's tried to use the Eye in the Sky, but cloud cover's bollocksing up any sort of visual confirmation. Judging by the readings, though, something's seriously kicking off around the Hampton Court area. Alpha's dispatched a scout. We're the cavalry." Three-Seven paused, waiting for the groans. None came. The absolute unquestioning, unswerving loyalty he got out of his men was impressive. Not a word of dissent. Not a single sigh. These guys just dug deeper and found whatever last wellspring of strength they needed to tap to keep on going. And, Sabine knew, they'd be every bit as deadly in the last moments of a skirmish in the grounds of Hampton Court as they had been in the first moments of the decontamination deep under Down Street.

They were special, each and every one of them. That was why they had been recruited.

Three-Seven turned to him. "There's room if you're up for it."

Thomas Sabine thought about bed, about food, about the empty house waiting for him, and knew that they wouldn't judge him if he walked away. He'd done his stint down in the tube station—he wasn't a cypher—but equally there was no way he was going to send them off into God-alone-knew-what if there was even the slightest chance he could make the difference. Not that he thought for a minute that he could. He'd done precious little more than stand and watch them do their thing all day, but that was beside the point. There was a new incident to deal with. This one could be different. His particular skills might be the difference between the operation's success or failure this time.

Besides, if he stood toe-to-toe with them in the trenches, the next time he needed them—and there would always be a next time—they would know he was every bit as committed to the cause as they were, willing to risk his life every bit as selflessly as they did. It took guts to do what they did. They knew that. Standing with them would earn him far more than just respect. Conversely, if he walked, he'd lose a lot more than just respect.

But he was exhausted. Tired people made mistakes. He wasn't like these guys. He wasn't powered with Duracell batteries. He couldn't just keep on keeping on. At some point he'd screw up or stumble, and with the whole leave-no-man-behind thing he could become a very literal burden for them. Would his presence increase the risk to the team?

He was wavering.

"We'll be taking a boat up the river," Three-Seven said, as though sensing his indecision. "A fast one. You did good down there, Four-Five. Chances are you'll do just fine second time of asking. Put it this way: I trust you. I wouldn't invite you along for the ride if I didn't. Now, I'm not about to say we *need* you— that's way too chick flick for guys like us—but who knows, you might just come in handy. There's no telling. I mean, miracles do happen, we see 'em every freaking day." Three-Seven grinned, having made Sabine's mind up for him.

And he hadn't been lying. It was a *fast* boat.

It was waiting for them when they arrived at the police launch, already fitted out with fresh supplies. They abandoned the van. It would be replenished while they sped up the river in the dark.

It was night, the roads *should* have been clear, but there was no telling what might happen between Green Park and Hampton Court. There was always the chance of something kicking off on the Thames as they crossed it, too, but the boat reduced the likelihood of unforeseen happenings, save perhaps for the water rising up itself to overturn the boat and drown them all. Given the fact the sensors were out on the Thames barrier and had relay beacons along the Embankment, anything was possible.

Who knew what lurked amid the silt on the river bottom?

Who could guess what creatures stirred and swam with the eddies where salmon had once swum?

The river was deserted. Given the hour, this was not a great surprise; what traffic still used it rarely traveled farther upriver than the city. Nothing really went beyond the barriers.

Three-Seven opened up the throttle.

Sabine sat back as the spray kicked up. The engine roared, splashing and spraying them all as the boat skipped across the top of the river.

There was next to no moonlight, just a pale shimmer on the surface of the water up ahead.

Sabine heard the wail of another engine out there, but thought it was an echo of their own boat coming back to them off the warehouse walls from the disused shipyard. It was only when he saw the two wave patterns merging that Sabine realized it wasn't an echo he was hearing at all. "Incoming!" he shouted. "There!" he said, pointing to the dark outline of a second speedboat cutting right across their path.

It came out of nowhere, surging through the river, barely missing their boat by a matter of feet as it cut away, churning up a huge backwash as it changed direction.

Without his shouted warning there was no telling what would have happened.

Sabine only got the briefest glimpse of the woman behind the wheel, the lights of her instrumentation panel revealing her features, but it was enough to know that he had never seen her before. He would have recognized someone so heart-achingly beautiful if he had. But that wasn't why he knew he'd never seen her before. It was because she had been taint-touched in some way. No, it was more than that. She was more than just touched.

She was *different*.

It was a feeling he had experienced before, though in her case he had no idea what it meant to be *different*. This was what had attracted the LN-7 recruiters: they'd seen this gift in him—his ability to instinctively identify wrongness in things, in people, but he had no real control over the strange feelings when they occurred. It was rather like a cop saying they had a gut instinct, following a hunch. It wasn't always helpful, and he rarely knew exactly what the sensations meant, but they never failed him. If something was *off* in any way, he knew. He could just *tell*.

There was no *good* reason why a woman would be out on the

Thames in the middle of the night—and coming from the direction of the trouble they were off to quash. He really didn't like coincidences. But she was gone and they had work to do.

He put her out of his mind.

Which was no easy thing to do.

They moored the boat on an old wooden jetty and disembarked. The wooden boards creaked and groaned beneath their weight. The only sound was the gentle slosh of the wake washing up against the riverbank.

Sabine stared into the darkness.

He strained to hear *anything* at all.

He could see a couple of dim security lights in the main building; they lit up several of the windows, but did nothing to illuminate the grounds.

Three-Seven gave a silent signal that sent two of his men onto the riverbank. Within thirty seconds they'd planted a couple of spotlights that would be seen a couple of miles away. They'd work as a beacon for their withdrawal, and would serve to light up the undergrowth around the boat. The last thing they needed was some straggler springing a surprise. That was how they lost men.

Three-Seven prepped his weapons. He didn't need light to do it. No doubt he could strip and reassemble them blindfolded. Men like him could do stuff like that. "Catch," he said, and tossed Sabine a pistol. It was a Heckler and Koch VP70. He under-armed a second clip of ammunition. "Nine rounds a clip. Just point and click if you need to. If you don't, well, keep back and try not to shoot one of us."

The instructions were clear enough. "Keep back" wasn't quite "stay the hell out of the way." He hefted the pistol. It was surprisingly heavy. But then it was weighted down with enough ammunition to end nine lives; it shouldn't have been light.

As soon as they were all out of the boat and standing on the damp grass, one of the men tripped a switch and the grounds were flooded with light.

Sabine felt a sudden scream rise inside his head.

He gripped the pistol so fiercely he thought he might crush the grip.

It was worse than anything he could have expected, and the

VP70 in his hand was going to be about as much use as a pea-shooter. He couldn't tear his eyes off the things to look at Three-Seven. He didn't need to; he heard the roar from one of the team, and then they were all charging at the giant topiary figures that were tearing themselves free of the hedge maze. They ripped their roots up from the ground, shaking earth free as they clumped toward them.

Sabine let off a shot. The 9mm round ripped through the leaves. It didn't stop the giant leafy Tudor lion that came toward him.

He could feel the taint all around him, bleeding up from the ground into the roots of the trees and bushes, up through the stems and stamen and into each and every leaf, bringing them to tainted life. Just standing on the grass was enough to make Sabine feel as though he was on fire inside.

His shot was the signal.

All hell broke loose.

One of the cyphers let rip with fire and flame as tendrils of ivy snaked toward him.

The hedge monster loosed a shriek and that shriek resonated through all of the leaves and branches of the other topiaries, all of them joined as one living entity. It didn't matter that they were a hundred different genera of plant species, now, taint-risen, they were all the same beast.

Branches entwined with thorn and bramble swung down, lashing at them, slashing at the air around them, and as they whip-lashed out, they snatched at the soldier who had burned them up. The huge branches swept him up into the air, and even as he kicked and screamed, trying to wrestle himself free of the suffocating bonds, they let him fall.

He hit the ground with a sickening thud.

Sabine could see from the way he lay unmoving in a sprawl that his neck had been broken in the fall.

Two more men broke rank, moving forward while the others laid down cover fire. They moved fast, crouching low as they covered the ground between them and the broken body of their fallen comrade.

There was a *chance* he was still alive, but even if he wasn't, they'd have done the same thing because they knew what happened to flesh caught by the taint. There was no way they were going to leave him there a second longer than they had to. They would grieve for him later. Right now it was all about making sure he didn't come back to haunt them.

Three-Seven launched a huge tongue of flame at the nearest of the hedge creatures. The monstrosity reared up, casting weird shadows all over them, and then it came down, tendrils snaking out across the grass to snare the fallen cypher's ankle, and growing vine-like up his leg, enveloping him.

Before anyone could reach him, the leaves of the tallest topiary began to knit into a canopy over them, joining with the high branches of two of the trees and weaving into a solid structure all around them.

Three-Seven barked instructions at the men. Sabine's head spun. He didn't know whether to go right, left, forward, or back, about the only thing he knew for sure was he couldn't stand still.

One of the men beside him grabbed his arm and hauled him back in response to Three-Seven's shout. Then the soldier turned and raced back to the boat. Three-Seven strode forward. He didn't hesitate. He opened fire again, his flamethrower scorching grass and hedge alike. He sprayed the flame around indiscriminately. It tore into the things, shriveling leaves, charring twigs and branches, and leaving more flame in its wake as the living wood ignited.

The maze creature screamed—though it wasn't any human kind of scream, it was a shrill, almost supersonic wail that vibrated right the way through Sabine's skin and played his bones. There was no mouth, or so Sabine thought, until it twisted and turned in agony revealing a great knotted maw in the bole of its ancient trunk. As much as it looked like a rotten mouth, that wasn't the source of the cries. Trapped inside the branches and tendrils of bramble a man screamed. And those screams were everything. They were the core of all of the pain the living wood felt, given voice. The wooden mouth opened wider than it had any right to and Sabine *felt* as much as heard the next desperate cry.

And he started to understand; the cypher's neck was broken, but he wasn't dead. Not quite. Some desperate survival instinct refused to die and that only made what was happening to him so much worse. Branches pushed through the man's chest, open-

ing him wide. Brambles burst out of his mouth. Ivy crawled up
his legs and wrapped itself around him. Thick ropy vines wove a
crown around his forehead. Thorns made a necklace at his throat,
cutting in so that blood dribbled down his chest into the cavity
left by the branches. And still the stuff grew out of him—and into
him—until there was nothing to show he had ever been there, but
Sabine knew that he was still in there.

He had eight shots left. He couldn't think of a better way to
use one.

He raised the gun and aimed it squarely at the tangle of foliage.
He knew exactly where the man's head had been. It was marked
by a ring of roses. He stared down the barrel of the gun. And then
he pulled the trigger. Once, twice, three times. The bullets tore
through the scrub and brush, finding their mark.

And then the flames reached it, and as the undergrowth burned
away Sabine saw him, like Guy Fawkes trapped inside the bonfire. Burning.

The two men who'd broken rank to recover their fallen comrade were still fighting with the undergrowth to drag him free, and
the plant life showed no sign of relinquishing its prize. Flames
raged all around them. The heat battered them back, but they kept
trying to get back to the body.

The last man returned from the boat.

Three-Seven killed the flames as the man waded past them.
He now wore an asbestos suit that shielded against both heat and
flame, at least temporarily, and carried a large container on his
back that acted as a reservoir for a pressure spray.

At first Sabine thought that he was trying to dowse the flame,
but then he saw the reaction the fine spray had when it hit the
hedge creature's foliage.

"Stay back!" Three-Seven yelled as Sabine started instinctively to follow him. It wasn't a sudden urge of bravery, and it
wasn't foolishness. He saw the other men in trouble and moved
to help them. If Three-Seven hadn't pulled him back, he would
have stepped straight into the path of the receding tendrils as they
whipped through the air. The soldier soaked the patches of veg-
etation that weren't already ablaze, causing them to turn brown
and shrivel, transforming them into ripe tinder for the flames.

186

And this time when Three-Seven unleashed the fury, the fires raged, streaking high into the night.

The dissolution set in. Leaf by leaf the plants withered, shriveled, blistered, burned and sent sparks rising into the night.

Standing there, watching the flames rising, Sabine felt a change in the creature; it had been abandoned.

The taint had shrunk away, leaving nothing behind but burnt, brittle wood and slashing, lashing, trailing vines filled with the last vestiges of consciousness trying desperately to stay alive. Slowly roots found their way back into the disturbed earth. They dug down for nourishment. Dirt was life. But not now. There was nothing left in the dead earth. They could dig down as far as Australia and it wouldn't help; the stuff that Three-Seven's man had sprayed was relentless. Once it came into contact with the leaves it was absorbed into them and spread along the small netted veins in to the midrib and down the petiole to the branches, working its poisonous way all the way down to the roots, leaving everything brown, shriveled, and dead in its wake.

Slowly the dying hedgerows shrank back far enough and the thorns and brambles fell away so that the fallen man was exposed to the air. His clothes smoldered, smoke rising up off his corpse. The spray had turned his skin a jaundiced yellow. The smell was awful, but it didn't matter—the leave-no-man-behind imperative was far stronger than any rancid odor. Three-Seven ran to his side despite the fact there was nothing he could do for the dead man apart from take him home.

Sometimes that was enough.

It had to be.

Sabine understood them now. He knew how they functioned as a unit.

They needed to know that when it was their turn, they'd be taken home, too.

There was never any question that one day it would be their turn.

CHAPTER 28

THE BROTHERHOOD OF CERNUNNOS

The huge towers of glass and steel that made up most of Canary Wharf were all but deserted.

There were some apartments within what was mostly an abandoned business district; a few of them were actually occupied, but only a few, and at this time of night those were swathed in darkness just like the empty offices.

Emergency lights burned in one window, or perhaps it was an insomniac gripped by a book they just couldn't put down. It happened. It wasn't a television, she could tell that much; the backlight from a screen was different. It rippled constantly. This was static. Gentle.

Alice eased the Monster to a halt at the curbside and kicked down the stand.

The stairwell lights in her apartment building were triggered by movement—without any, they dimmed to low light and eventually went out, waiting for the sensors to trip and bring them back on. No one ever took the stairwell. The building was too high and the lift was never out of order. It wasn't that kind of place. There was no trace of squalor. This was how the other half lived. Literally. They were luxury apartments, where the word luxury actually meant dictionary definition, not some real estate agent's bending of the truth to tack on a zero.

Some of the neighboring towers had been converted into hotels, but they had even less people staying in them than the apartment blocks.

London had changed since Canary Wharf had been erected. The original intention had been to serve the high-powered businessmen with their Challengers and Falcons, Gulfstreams and Learjets, and helipads at the nearby city airport, but now that London was shunned by so many, the hotels were all but empty and the apartments unoccupied, waiting for their owners to return at some uncertain date in the future. Those who could do their business elsewhere did. Paris thrived. Manchester had become the true second city it had always wanted to be. Birmingham might have been more central but the rail and air networks, once London was taken out of the equation, only served to isolate it.

Alice took the glass elevator. As ever she found herself thinking about the Roald Dahl story as it rose and rose. At least she didn't look like the dead queen anymore. She'd made a detour to the townhouse to stash the dress and jewelry. Unlike Charlie's great glass elevator, sixty floors up, the lift stopped. She exited it.

She owned the entire floor, though ownership was something of a loose interpretation of the definition as she'd never actually paid a red penny for it. But it was hers. She walked up to the door and placed her palm against the security panel. Her pressure triggered the retinal key, and a moment later the image scanner had processed the veins and capillaries on the back of her eye and recognized them as her own. The bolts fired back and the door swung silently open. The bolts were overkill, perhaps, four-inch circumference titanium sunk twelve inches deep into the brickwork of the doorframe. They weren't the only protection she had in place. Infrared beams criss-crossed the entrance hall. They were keyed to her biometrics. She waited for the scan to complete itself. If it hadn't been her standing there, the building would have gone into lockdown. And getting out of her workshop was a lot more difficult than getting in. Deliberately so.

The beams disengaged.

In terms of real estate, this place was probably worth upward of two million, but she only used it for planning jobs. It was large enough, and essentially abandoned, meaning she had all the room she needed to construct scale replicas of the buildings she intended to break into. These weren't the old balsa wood models she'd made as a child. They were computer-generated representations projected by multiple lenses to give them a pseudo-3D feel. Being scalable, they allowed her to walk around within the designs, allowing her to familiarize herself with the layout of any building without ever having to set foot into it. That was the beauty of technology.

No one ever visited her here; the few visitors she entertained only knew about the townhouse. This place was "the office." And because possession was nine tenths of the law, there was no paper trail to put her name on it either. She was careful about things like that. She called it Sanctuary. It was the one place she could hide out during the day knowing she'd be undisturbed.

But she never visited at night.

And for good reason.

But there was something she needed to do now. She needed to strike up a deal with the king of Canary Wharf. The area was part of the city still known, somewhat affectionately, by the locals as the Isle of Dogs. Only they weren't dogs at all.

The Isle belonged to the Brotherhood of Cernunnos.

And she had just run from two of their kind the day before, in Greenwich at the Maritime Museum.

It felt like walking into the jaws of a rabid werewolf, but she couldn't wait until morning. The clock was ticking. El Draco wouldn't wait. Not forever. Not when the prize was so close. She could sense his impatience even when he was nowhere to be seen. So she'd come back here, knowing it would draw the werewolves out. She would apologize, clear the air, ask the king to forgive her trespass and promise to make amends. She hoped it would be enough. And then, if she was still breathing, she'd finish what she had started.

Alice walked through to what would have been the bedroom. It had been converted into an armory. It was stocked with a small arsenal of weapons for every situation, from submachine guns, to pistols, sniper rifles, ceramic knives, stun grenades, smoke bombs, CS gas, and even blocks of C4. And yet she never carried a gun. Other weapons, yes, but never a gun. Her philosophy was: if a job came down to shooting, then it was a job done badly; and she didn't do jobs badly.

Alice pulled the ceramic knife from the ankle sheath she wore, and put it back in its place on the racks.

She went through to the main living area.

It was white and utterly devoid of any furnishings—but it wasn't empty. In the middle of the hardwood floor was a huge, eerily blue image of the White Tower. She walked right through the middle of it. Later she'd feed the schematics in so she could literally walk "inside" the Tower. Right now it was only a scaleable shell. The image lit up her back as she walked across to the huge plate glass balcony doors. She opened them up, letting some air in.

She looked out across the night.

London, even now, truly was spectacular.

The juxtaposition of new and old, the rooftops of the Victorian and Edwardian houses side by side with the sleek lines of the modern malls and offices, the gargoyles and green men set in stone to glower down over the streets, the intricate details of Wren's masterpieces, all of it stretching out as far as the eye could see, and always offering *something* to see. There wasn't another city like it in the world. She loved it. It was hers every bit as much as she belonged to it. It had shaped the woman she was, everpresent in every experience she'd ever had.

She breathed it in.

She was at home here.

Alice heard a low, throaty growl behind her.

She knew exactly what it was, the only surprise was that they had come for her quite so quickly. She didn't know whether to be relieved or terrified. Logically, of course, the creature had had her scent all the way from the museum.

She didn't turn.

There was nowhere for her to go—she had no intention of jumping from the balcony this time. Sixty stories was too far for her to fall and running away didn't solve anything. She needed to clean the slate.

So she waited.

And she listened.

It took her a moment to differentiate the sounds. There were at least two of them. She could hear the subtle difference between the rumbles growling around in their throats: one sounded like sharp-edged rocks grinding together, the other more like the rasp of a percolating coffee brewer. They moved to either side of her.

"Well, hello, boys," Alice said, finally turning around.

There were three of them, not two. The largest of the three stood in the middle of the holographic White Tower. He towered over her, naked and muscular, his pelt blacker than black save for a single white slash right across his heart.

The other two still wore the remnants of their guard's uniforms, though they were ripped and torn from the shift between forms.

They dropped to all fours, more comfortable now.

"So what happens now?" Alice asked.

"You come with us," the alpha male said.

"It doesn't look like I have much of a choice, does it?"

He shook his head. "None."

"You really know how to make a girl feel wanted."

* * *

They led her through the streets.

She heard dogs howling. She heard the distant sounds of a fog-horn calling out forlornly on the river. They didn't say a word.

She thought about running, she knew these streets, but she also knew that no matter how fast she was, they were faster.

She allowed them to push her along.

They took a path that eventually led beneath the Docklands Light Railway platform, where, standing in the shadows beneath the underpass, a man waited for them.

She knew who he was.

How could she not? This was his kingdom.

The Wolf-King stepped out of the shadows. His face and naked, furred body were smeared with the dried blood of a night's hunting and killing.

"So, young Alice, I must say, I wasn't expecting to see you so soon. Actually, I thought you would have stayed as far from here as possible after your *adventures* in Greenwich. You must have known my brothers had your scent; after all, you're not a stupid girl, are you?"

He knew. Of course he did. The minute she'd seen the lupine features of the guards she'd known the Brotherhood's paws were firmly meddling in the whole thing. The only surprise was that he already knew it was *her*. She'd thought it would take them longer to isolate her scent and identify it. "How did you know it was me?"

He barked out an abrasive laugh. "How did I know?" His lips curled back to bare white teeth stained red from the night's entertainment. "Alice, Alice, Alice. Do you really think we're all idiots? Do you think we walk around this place blind to your comings and goings? You are *tolerated*. But every single one of my brothers knows your scent, girl. You can't live amongst us and expect to be a mystery to us. We see you come and go. We *smell* you come and go. We observe. But you ask how I could know, specifically? No one else would dare, girl. No one else would throw themselves out of a window to escape and crawl away broken. And of course, there's that Monster of yours. No one else rides a motorcycle like that at night."

"I had intended to tell you myself," she said. "To explain. I had no idea the place was under your protection. I didn't want there to be any…repercussions."

He came in close. She could smell the unmistakeable odor of drying blood, his stale sweat, and his fetid breath. Her stomach churned, a mixture of revulsion and fear. She tried to hide it.

The wolf guards behind her pushed her down to her knees.

Alice winced as she hit the gravel.

She looked up at the Wolf-King. He stood over her. Menacing.

"What you took meant nothing to me, Alice. Nothing. All you had to do was *ask* and I would have given it freely. I have other reasons for safeguarding those walls, not that it is any of your business. First my guards sniff you out in the library—oh yes, we know that was you—and then you cause us so much trouble at the museum. It can't go on, Alice. It can't. Too much is at stake."

"I didn't know…"

"Of course you didn't, that was the whole point. No one knows we are there. No one knows because I don't *want* them to know. But you brought the police to my door. You have caused me a lot of grief, girl. I don't like problems. And I find myself left with a dilemma. By rights I ought to dispose of *everyone* connected to the place." He weighted the word *everyone,* leaving her in no doubt who he meant. "But right now that would create more problems than it will solve. The situation can always change, though."

"I am sorry."

He shrugged. "As you should be, but it's done now. It would have been remiss of me not to warn you that if you should fail to keep our secret there will be a world of hurt waiting for you."

She said nothing.

There was nothing she could say, and anything she did would only make things worse. Silence was a virtue. Besides, she knew that if she didn't speak, he would. It was a weakness amongst his kind. The change in their bodies gave them a feeling of superiority. To reinforce that strength they postured. It was a relic of the wolf gene. The pack leaders weren't humble. They roared their achievements, using them to cow their packmates. In their own minds they were invincible. That was how they rose up the pack. There was no room for weakness. Weakness was exploited.

Alice could feel the cold of the silver bullet she wore on the chain around her neck as a lucky charm; the bullet had already killed one of his kind.

She thought about offering it to him as a gift, a show of good faith, but then the Wolf-King began talking again.

"We only need to use the place at night. By moonlight. And soon we won't need it at all, so all you need to do is keep quiet while we complete the serum. The world is about to change, Alice, again, but this time it will be changing for the better. We need the optics from the Royal Observatory, but in two more cycles we will be done. Soon," he said, tossing back his head and shaking out his mane. He looked at her. Smiled. "Soon."

"You've found a cure?" Alice said. The notion that the Brotherhood might have even been looking for a way to dampen the blood of the wolf, cleansing their veins of its demonic stain, surprised her. They were so comfortable in their wolf skin that it was hard to imagine them willingly surrendering it.

"A cure?" He didn't laugh. He seemed genuinely perplexed by the suggestion. "What is there to cure? We are not *sick*. This is not some affliction. The blood of the wolf is a blessing. We are closer to our god than any of our kind have ever been. When we step out under the moon we feel the thrill of blood and magic course through our veins. We have it within us to find Cernunnos. This little island around you is ours, the beginnings of a brand new kingdom; the kingdom of the wolf!" And as the Wolf-King said those last few words, he let out a howl, baying up at the sky. The cry was taken up all across the Isle of Dogs as one by one his subjects answered. "No, Alice, you couldn't be further from the truth. We aren't looking to *cure* the blood, we're looking to *enhance* it…to harness the moon. Imagine. In our true forms we have the kind of freedom, the kind of power, that those without our blessing can't hope to comprehend…yet."

"Yet?" One of the most powerful words in the English language. *Yet.* It sent a cold thrill of fear down the ladder of Alice's spine.

"We are so close… Imagine, this could be a way of sharing our gift with the rest of mankind."

She was still awestruck by the ramifications of what he was suggesting when a challenge roared through the underpass. Claws scratched along the tiled wall.

Alice's heart froze.

She could see another wolfman at the far end of the tunnel. It was huge. It dropped to all fours and started to bound toward them, it's huge gait eating up the distance between them.

"Get out! Now!" the Wolf-King bellowed at her, then turned to face the newcomer, letting out a roar to match his challenge.

The newcomer rose up onto his hind legs a few feet from the Wolf-King and beat on his own chest with his clawed fists. Blood was smeared into the fur that still covered his body. His eyes blazed red. The blood frenzy was upon him.

She stood up, moving so slowly it almost seemed as though she were frozen. It was impossible to say if the creature saw her as its next meal, or if it was here to challenge the Wolf-King.

"I said go!" the Wolf-King raged. She didn't need telling twice. The challenger came on.

"Come on then!" the Wolf-King barked. "If you *really* want to die!"

The Wolf-King stood tall, putting himself between Alice and the frenzied wolf as it dropped back onto all fours and charged the last few feet between them. It snapped and snarled, tearing at the king. He met the challenge tooth and claw. The creature was monstrous. The blood frenzy had turned it rabid. Saliva drooled from its lower jaw. It slashed at the Wolf-King with bloody claws, tearing open a gash in the king's already matted fur.

The Wolf-King howled his agony. The underpass transformed it into a maddening chorus.

The challenger took the king down, tearing at his throat.

Alice reacted without thinking.

Despite every screaming instinct of her body, she didn't run.

She pulled the bullet from its chain, wrapping her fist tight around it.

She didn't think about what she was doing.

She just did it.

Alice ran the six strides back to where the beast was killing the Wolf-King, and as his head came up, madness blazing in his eyes, she rammed her fist into his mouth, screaming as the werewolf bit down on her arm.

As its teeth closed around her flesh she tried to open her hand.

Tears of agony streamed down Alice's face.

The werewolf's fangs tore into her forearm.

She couldn't pull her hand free.

She couldn't open her fist.

The Wolf-King summoned some last ounce of strength, and bit back, sinking his teeth into the challenger's throat.

He saved Alice's life.

In turn, she saved his.

Her hand came open.

The silver bullet spilled out of her palm, and as she pulled her hand back, the creature's mouth exploded with blood. It couldn't purge the silver from its system. It clenched its jaws, writhing on the grubby floor of the underpass, its body jerking and twisting in uncontrollable spasms, every muscle shuddering and juddering.

Blood dripped down her arm.

It had broken the skin.

She didn't know what that meant for her...if it was like the stuff of legend and that bitten, she was cursed, or if she needed to take it's blood into her, and merge, her blood and the blood of the wolf, for the curse to spread...

Alice felt no pity for the creature as the silver went to work. It was anathema to the beast. And once inside, there was no way it could fight it, save to claw its own guts open and tear it out.

Half changed back to its human form, the werewolf tried desperately to haul itself up onto its feet.

The Wolf-King roared, slashing at the half-creature, claws ripping at skin, opening deep gashes that bubbled and frothed blood. A second vicious slash tore out the challenger's throat.

More blood gouted from severed arteries, the arterial spray splashing great bloody arcs across the wall of the underpass.

In the distance, dogs bayed.

The howls were taken up by the Brotherhood patrolling the streets.

Blood was in the air.

The blood of the wolf.

The challenger stumbled and staggered, legs buckling as he twisted and fell, clutching at his ruined neck.

The Wolf-King looked up at her.

There was something in his eyes.

Something that frightened her to the very core.

"I said *run*...," he growled, deep in his throat.

And this time she didn't hesitate. She ran. And she ran. Arms pumping. Legs pumping. Heart pumping. Racing breathlessly through the Isle of Dogs back toward the sanctuary of her workshop, back toward the Monster and a way out of this place.

In the distance, the sky began to lighten.

Dawn was almost upon them.

Alice ran, her lungs burning, every muscle on fire, driving herself on as though, like Cinderella, she needed to be back home and hidden away before the time the sun came up.

She heard the frantic sounds of the dogs fighting over something—and knew it was the challenger's corpse. That was all it could be. The Wolf-King would let them have their fill; it sent a message to the wolf brothers within the Brotherhood of Cernunnos: He was their alpha.

With her apartment building in sight, Alice slipped and sprawled across the pavement as she trod on something. She picked herself up. She didn't feel a thing. The adrenaline was pumping through her system. She looked down at what had tripped her. It was a dead raven. A certain omen of trouble ahead, for sure, but more than that, it reminded her of something…

CHAPTER 29

FEATHERS

*B*lack feathers spin in the air... They brush against her skin with the lightest of touches...they tease...they caress...they love...but they are not the only things carried by the air. There is death on the breeze.

In the distance she hears the sound of battle joined...the clash of metal on metal...sword striking sword, striking shield... She hears the babble of voices, of panic...of fear...of courage...of warriors urging comrades on, and of the dying... They are in a language she does not know, and yet she understands so much of what is being shouted...but then, death is the universal language of battle and it is as old as life... Death is not just an ancient tongue...it still exists...it is more brutal and more ugly, more guttural and violent than it ever was, or so they would believe...those men out there dying...but so much death has been lost to history, lost in the midst of time...it has always been brutal.

But this is more than just the language of the dying...it is a language that has crossed Europe, changing and evolving as its people took it to new lands.

She knows that this is a battle she can change the course of... but it is not her battle to fight; this is a war between men...and men should be left to decide for themselves. Let them die. Once *her kind starts to intervene, there will only ever be more death, more devastation...*

The feathers have stopped falling...

She looks down at her feet to see one of the saddest sights in the world: a dead bird.

But not just any bird.

A raven.

She feels a tear start to form and she cannot hold it back; this is a time for sadness.

And despite the sounds of battle and death, she hears a single word that fills the whole world: lladratwr.

She knows the word and the word is thief.

CHAPTER 30

THE BIRDMAN OF
CAMDEN TOWN

Someone was inside the apartment.

The Wolf-King's lackeys hadn't given her a chance to set the alarms or even lock the door. So, for all that security, her workshop was vulnerable and it had been breached. She wasn't in any shape to fight. She needed to tend to her arm, disinfect the wound, stitch it, and dress it. She couldn't use the enchantment twice, not so soon after she'd already used it. It was still working on her system; it would accelerate her healing regardless of how many fresh wounds she picked up. It didn't discriminate.

She knew who it was even before she pushed the door open.

The workshop was in darkness, the illuminated White Tower put out, but the balcony doors were still open, letting the cold night air in. She could feel his presence. It quickened her pulse. She felt her body responding to his nearness. Alice thought long and hard about closing the door and walking away. There had been more than enough trouble tonight; she hardly needed to invite more into her life in the form of Rufus Shadwell. It was hard to believe that until a few hours ago this place had been her secret sanctuary sixty floors above the city. Now it was like Kings Cross with everyone coming and going.

"Good evening, Alice," he said from the shadows. He always

liked to play his games, to try and keep her off balance. She was wise to him. She didn't say a word. "I was just watching the sunrise. It really is quite beautiful up here. You could almost forget the whole place has gone to shit."

"You always did have such a way with words," Alice said, turning on the light. She wasn't about to let on just how angry she was at this invasion of her privacy. It was Shadwell, he had no concept of the word. "And now you've seen it, why don't you just toddle off and leave me alone. I'm dead on my feet. I just want to curl up and go to sleep. Alone," she added, before he could make any lascivious suggestions. "Besides, if you leave now, you might get lucky and find that the dogs have saved you something."

Shadwell smiled at that. It was barely warm enough to thaw an ice cube. "Oh, I must admit I did rather enjoy that little confrontation of yours down there. You and wolfie really were quite ruthless. The way you plunged your hand into the animal's mouth, though, that, my dear, was pure theater. I thought you were going to rip his heart out. And then I remembered that little lucky charm of yours. Clever. You're a dangerous little fox, aren't you?"

"Yes. And yet you break into my apartment, so either you've developed something of a death wish, or you want something? So how about you tell me what you want, and get the hell out of my life?"

"You wouldn't want that now, would you, Alice?" he asked, feigning being wounded. "It's me. It's always been me. Our fates are written in the stars, yours and mine. You wouldn't be able to stand the thought of never seeing me again, surely?"

"Try me," she said.

He pressed a hand to his heart, as though her words were barbed arrows and the truth had just pierced it. "Now *that* hurt, but," he said, brushing it off, "I'll forgive you. Just this once. Besides, I've come to offer you my assistance once again because you're obviously going to need my help."

"Am I?"

The holographic reconstruction might have gone, but the leaflets, the plans, and the notes she had made for the other jobs were all still scattered around the room. "Oh yes. Like it or not, you need me on this job. You can't get in alone. You need someone to help you, and I've decided that it has to be me." He made it sound quite reasonable.

She wanted to claw his eyes out. Instead she said, "What makes you think I want you involved?"

"Oh, I'm quite sure you *don't*. But given the undertaking, I don't think you really have a choice, do you? Not now that I know."

"And dare I ask what's in it for you?"

"What makes you think I wouldn't just help you out of the goodness of my heart? Women, always so suspicious."

"I know you, Rufus. I lived with you for the best part of two years. I know you better than you know yourself. And I know that you *never* do anything unless you're going to get something out of it."

"Quite right," he nodded. "But don't concern yourself with it. It doesn't affect your scheme. If it helps, just think of me as a silent partner."

"We are *not* in business together."

"Okay, look, aside from the thrill, there could well be a little trinket in there that's got my name on it. Satisfied?"

"Not remotely."

"Besides, Joseph will enjoy the experience."

"Joseph? What the hell has it got to do with him?"

"Oh, didn't I mention? The enigmatic Mr. Pennington will be coming along for the ride."

"This isn't a bloody day trip to Alton Towers, Rufus."

"You need someone who can get inside without having to go in through the front door, so just think about that. Joseph and I have the means. You know that. And you know how to get ahold of us. Think about it."

He pointed to the open window and offered her a single black feather.

She remembered the dead bird she had nearly broken her neck tripping over and shuddered. Rufus stepped out onto the balcony and turned to face her.

With the sun at his back he held out his arms and started to shake them, gently at first, as though working the kinks out of tired muscles, and then faster, and faster, until they started to move so quickly, the fluctuations too fast for the eye to see, that they eventually blurred into a single black shape. The shape became a mass of feathers, wings, beak, claws, and the wings continued to beat faster and faster, agitating the eddies of air around it as it seemed to shrink. And it kept on shrinking until it was no more than a large bird—a black-winged raven—that took to flight from the balcony.

Alice watched the raven as it flew toward the rising sun.

CHAPTER 31

OTHER THINGS ON HEAVEN AND EARTH

This was becoming something of a habit.

Callaghan really didn't like habits.

Habits were predictable.

They got you into trouble.

The car had been waiting when Callaghan returned to the office that morning. He had barely slept. He'd tried. He was so bone dead tired that by rights he ought to have gone off like a light, but all he'd managed to do was toss and turn restlessly all night. He felt worse now than he did before he'd climbed into bed.

The paperwork mountain would be reaching the dizzy heights of K2, if not quite Everest proportions, if he didn't deal with it soon, but as long as his favorite thief kept causing him grief that wasn't going to happen. He'd actually come to think of her that way, too: his thief. Like they were joined.

He hadn't had time to visit the British Library, but had called. The call had turned up nothing. Well, nothing other than the fact that it was her, again, given the signature mangled lock, but he'd already decided it had to be her.

The two men waiting for him this morning were much less polite than Charlie, the gunman the Krays had sent to collect him. The car was a lot less elegant, too. But Callaghan took comfort from that. Villain kings drove fancy cars. This kind of beat-up tin can spoke of an entirely different kind of authority.

The pain in his knee had subsided but it still hurt like a bastard, and it had swollen up to the size of a grapefruit.

When he was offered medical attention upon arrival, it was hard to refuse.

Callaghan had not expected it to be provided in the old Admiralty Building, though. Engraved into the archway were the letters D.I.S.—Defense Intelligence Staff. He had no idea what was going on, or why some government Big Wig would want to drag him in. All he could think was that his thief had trodden on some toes, and now he was treading on the same ones. But the Kray Twins wouldn't ever have fallen under the auspices of Defense of the Realm stuff.

There was something off about the building, Callaghan realized, with that same copper's instinct that had served him so well over the years.

He didn't see any clerks bustling through the corridors. He didn't hear telephones ringing. There was no water cooler chat. But it *looked* the part, with its rich mahogany panelling on the walls and granite stairs worn down in the middle by the shuffling feet of centuries of civil servants. It was only when he really looked, thinking about what he saw—or didn't see—that Jack Callaghan began to suspect this was all a front for something else. And by then a man was already leading him away from the nurse's station toward one of the dusty offices upstairs.

And looking at him, he didn't seem like your average civil servant either. There was something about him. He had the haunted look of a man who had seen things. Callaghan would have guessed undercover cop, maybe out in Ireland or dealing with terrorist threats. It was in his eyes. He'd seen things you couldn't un-see and done things you couldn't undo. Like Callaghan. It was a case of it took one to know one.

"You look like crap," the man said. No sugar coating it. Callaghan appreciated that. The nurse had given him a painkilling injection, which she'd said would also help reduce the swelling, but that there wouldn't be any lasting damage. Just bruising. She had tried to tell him what he would need to do to improve his recovery, but the man had come for him then and cut the whole doctors and nurses thing short.

"You could say that it's been one of those days…for the last week."

"Hah! Sounds familiar." The man seated himself across from Callaghan and pushed a coffee toward him; he accepted it willingly. The coffee sealed the deal; this wasn't some low-level civil servant pen pusher. The stuff tasted like manna from heaven.

"So," Callaghan said, figuring that the guy would appreciate the same cut-to-the-chase attitude from him. "What is this place? Because it sure isn't like any government office I've ever been in."

The man smiled. He planted his elbows on the table between them and knotted his fingers as though he was about to say grace. "You noticed? Good. I thought you might. Actually, I rather hoped you would. Technically we're part of the D.I.S.—the Defense Intelligence Service. You'll have seen the moniker above the door when you came in? But our particular wing, Librum Niger 7, or LN-7, is a little different. We're all about the things that the government would rather that people didn't know about."

"Dirty tricks?" Callaghan had heard plenty of rumors about such things, but he'd always just put that down to the usual newspaper-fed bull. Then again, there was no denying the fact that even over the relatively short span of his life, the people of Britain had given up almost every freedom they'd ever held dear, all of those freedoms their grandparents had fought for, and all in the name of security, so it was hardly surprising that when the Red Tops talked about dirty tricks and smear campaigns and heightened terror threats and all of the rest of it, people couldn't stop listening—they needed to believe there was a war on the streets, be it against drugs or crime or terror or anything else that could reasonably excuse the State taking absolute control over their lives. Callaghan had never thought of himself as much of a socialist, but his dad had been a working-class man through and through, proud of the fact that he used his hands and made something, while his granddad had been a miner who saw his livelihood effectively ended by Thatcher during the closures of the 1980s. He'd just grown up skeptical. Governments on the whole, and shady men in long trench coats with trilby hats in particular, were not to be trusted.

The man smiled. Callaghan couldn't read him. Instinctively he wanted to think friend as opposed to foe, but… "We do get our hands dirty, yes, but not in the way you might think. We are the ones who clean up the mess."

"And what kind of mess would that be?"

"The sort you keep coming surprisingly close to stumbling into. You're either blessed or cursed, Mr. Callaghan. I'm not sure which."

"I'd say cursed, but then I live my life, so I would, wouldn't I?"

"Quite. You do seem to have the devil's own luck. And yes, we've been keeping an eye on you ever since you started turning up on the fringes of our investigations. Once could be considered bad luck, twice puts us in the realm of dangerous coincidence, but three times? That's all the way into the realm of uncomfortable. At least as far as we are concerned. You understand how it is, I'm sure, given your line of work? When the same face keeps turning up around investigations, it's only natural to wonder if they're involved."

"I would say that I'm flattered, but it's not like you're the only ones. You're not even the most frightening."

"I take it that's a reference to your little trip into the East End?"

"How do you know that's where I was? *I* don't even bloody know where I was." Callaghan's first thought, like a knife in the back, was that this joker was behind it all, and that he'd been dragged from the frying pan to the gas hob.

The man tilted his head to one side and looked at him. "I'm really not sure if you're very clever or very stupid, Mr. Callaghan."

He stared at the man.

"I'd go for a mix of both, always the safest to assume you're not the cleverest man in the room, but then I would think that, because the one thing I am, for sure, is very cautious."

"A very cautious man wouldn't be in the mess you're in, though, would he, Mr. Callaghan?"

"Call me Jack."

"I don't think so. We're not friends. Now, I am very curious about your trip to that warehouse. Would you care to tell me what happened there?"

"Not really. Like you said, we're not friends. I don't even know you're name. If this was a film script, you'd be Government Heavy Number One. Hell, for all I know you're behind the whole thing."

"I take your point. Let's try this a little differently, shall we? I've got no interest in us getting off on the wrong foot. Really don't have the time for that. First, believe me when I say I have nothing to do with your kidnapping." The man reached into his pocket for his wallet and pushed his ID across the table to Callaghan. The photo matched, but that meant nothing. He hadn't heard of Librum Niger 7 nor seen an ID like this before, so he had absolutely no idea if it was genuine. He could have bought it from Hamleys for all he knew. The only thing that made him think it was genuine was where they were, but even then, he wasn't sure the old Admiralty Building was even in commission, despite the whole charade being mimed out around him downstairs.

He made a face.

"Librum Niger 7? The Library Police?" Callaghan shrugged. "I genuinely haven't got a clue who you are, or what that ID is supposed to prove."

"Might I suggest you call your boss?" Sabine nodded toward the telephone. "A smart man knows the trick to asking questions is asking them of the right people. LN-7 operations are strictly Need-to-Know. Until today you haven't needed to know. Ask him. I'm sure that he'll be able to verify who we are."

Callaghan made the call.

"Central Robbery Squad," the voice on the other end of the line said. The name had been in place since 1981, but people still knew it by one of its two nicknames: the Flying Squad or the Sweeney, from the cockney rhyming slang "*Sweeney Todd, Flying Squad*."

"It's Callaghan, I need to talk to Challinor," he said into the phone, and waited to be put through. Marcus Challinor, the top man.

"Challinor."

"Guv, it's Jack Callaghan, I seem to have got myself into a spot of bother with some crew calling themselves Librum Niger 7. They've got me in an office down by Admiralty Arch. This joker seems to think you'll know who they are."

"Oh, I know who they are, Jack. I suppose I should be grateful you haven't gone over to the Dark Side."

"Been working a case."

"And now you're on LN-7's radar?"

"Looks like. So how do I proceed, Guv?"

"You look at the nice man across the table from you, you smile, you say, 'Yes, sir, no, sir, three bags bloody full, sir.' Got that?"

"Loud and clear."

"Don't dick around with these boys, Jack. They're serious in ways you really don't want to know about. Do something for me, Jack: try and stay out of trouble."

"Can't promise anything, Guv."

"I know," Challinor said.

The line went dead.

He looked at Sabine, who didn't seem all that surprised by the way the conversation had gone.

"It seems that you have my full cooperation whether I like it or not, so I guess I can tell you what you want to know. But, before I do, I'd really like to know just what the hell it is you think I'm involved in, and how it relates to your investigation. Mr...." Callaghan glanced down at the man's ID again before pushing it back across the table. "Sabine."

"I'm not cleared to tell you everything, but I can offer you a few answers. Just bear in mind whatever I say is only the tip of the iceberg. The world is different. Seven million people may live in London and think to themselves, *Oh my, isn't this all a little...curious...how that little bit of good fortune just seemed to save the day, how that bit of bad luck just keeps on recurring...* Things might seem like they're just the same as ever; the East End stalls still flog their jellied eels, the economy is still in the crapper, the politicians are on the telly trying to one up each other, prisons are still overcrowded, and the Lord Mayor's still an idiot. Same old same old."

Callaghan nodded. He lived in London. He didn't need the guided tour.

"You don't need me to tell you London's become a city of contrasts: fear and faith. Fear of violence, with crime figures at an all-time high; fear of gangs who are waging wars in the southern slums of Brixton and the surrounds. Fear of destitution as debts are coming back to haunt people, interest rates and over-inflated house prices and negative equity coming home to roost. But there's another kind of fear that's crept into the psyche of the city, Jack," Sabine said, using Callaghan's first name for the first time. Callaghan knew it was a deliberate gambit. He'd done the same sort of thing in interrogations before. "Fear's an insidious evil. It manifests itself in so many ways, in whispers of government conspiracies, in talk of cults and devil worshippers snatching people from the streets to offer as sacrifices; people are seeing the ghosts of loved ones and enemies and even listening to the End of the World prophets who stand around evangelizing on street corners as though they actually know something. We clean up that sort of mess. The mess caused by fear."

That didn't make a whole lot of sense to Callaghan, but he didn't interrupt the man as he continued. "You've seen the newspapers, I take it? Hard not to, without living in a bubble. They're full of sensationalist rubbish of course—supernatural outbreaks, grisly murders, that sort of thing."

"I've seen them."

"Well, what if I told you there was a grain of truth to what they were saying?"

"I'd say you were barking. Or I would have until a few days ago."

"When you stumbled into one of our investigations."

"If you say so."

"I say so, Jack. Now, I said contrasts: fear and faith. You can't have missed the fact that the mosques, the churches, the temples, they're all having something of a renaissance; people are desperate to believe all over again. That's one kind of faith right there, but others, the disenfranchised, have found a different kind of faith—they're believing in older things, finding their way to those beliefs in drugs and magic, or a debauched combination of the two. And yes, I did say *magic*, Jack. That's the kind of mess we deal with."

Callaghan didn't know what to say to that.

"Like I said, if the world at large knew our business, there would be the risk of panic, and that's the one thing we are trying to avoid. There are new powerbrokers on the streets of our city. A new kind of turf war is happening. And we're in the middle of it. The weird stuff that people are seeing around the city is just the tip of a very deep iceberg; it's straining, pushing at society's weak points, and the strain's beginning to show, so the fewer people who know about us and what we're doing, for now, the better. But believe me when I tell you that right now, out there, battles are being waged between ancient cabals of sorcerers and malign spirits made flesh. All of these villains gather their forces beneath banners stained dark with blood. And many of the gangs and criminal fraternities in London are unwittingly serving the diabolical plans of insidious masters; others are knowingly subscribing to their vile plots, seeing them as a road to wealth and power. It's not just the bogeymen anymore, Jack. It's a full on war."

"You are aware just how mental that sounds, right?"

Sabine raised an eyebrow. "But?"

"But I've seen enough weird shit over the last couple of days to know that you're not full of it."

"That's a good place to start. How about you tell me about what happened at the Sidney Street Bank?"

"You know about that?" Callaghan couldn't keep the surprise out of his voice. On the face of it, the bank job was nothing more than a straightforward robbery. There was no reason anyone should link it to anything *outré*.

"Let's just assume I know about most things; it'll save time," Sabine replied, sipping at his coffee. He put the mug down on the table between them. "So, tell me about it."

Callaghan explained how the door seemed to have been opened without any trouble, the lock mechanism melted as opposed to picked, and that the most curious thing about the whole job was that despite the entirety being on CCTV, they couldn't identify the thief because her face was blurred in the footage. Only her face.

"Curious," Sabine admitted. "Some sort of glamour, perhaps. And you've identified what was stolen?"

"A gemstone. It was pried out of a necklace."

"Again, curious. Why not just take the whole necklace, I wonder?"

"Who knows?"

"Anything else taken?"

He thought for a moment about telling him about the Kray's treasure, but for some reason held back, despite Challinor's orders. He'd already told Sabine he was a cautious man. The LN-7 agent ought to factor that admission into everything that passed between them. In his place, Callaghan would.

"Not that we've been able to ascertain. But there are links to other robberies. First, there was a break-in at the Maritime Museum in Greenwich, which by itself wouldn't have raised any eyebrows, except for the fact that CCTV footage suggests it was the same thief. She was also responsible for a robbery at the British Library."

"A busy girl."

"You're not kidding. She's got her fingers in more pies than Little Jack Horner."

"Tell me something: When you were studying the footage from Greenwich, did you happen to see anything else that was ah, out of the ordinary?"

"Such as?"

Callaghan's decision not to say anything about his own weird experiences meant he was walking a bit of a mental tightrope. He wanted to be as straight as he could be, and tell Sabine about the sand and his suspicion it was covering up blood, and how he had a bad feeling that his thief hadn't actually walked away from the scene of the crime this time, but it was difficult. Anything he did say could easily implicate himself in a deeper, more elaborate lie. And as Sabine had said, the chances were he already knew…but Callaghan was still wary of the man. So, the best course of action was probably to just offer what he most likely already knew unless Sabine asked him a direct question. Then he had to decide if he wanted to lie or not.

"You tell me."

"Well, honestly, it was all a bit peculiar. I got the distinct impression they were covering something up. They took an hour to make the call. The guards weren't around to answer any questions. They weren't exactly helpful."

"What was stolen?"

"The Drake Jewel—some trinket the queen gave to Francis Drake. And no, it's not an actual jewel, before you ask, so there's not a link there. Or at least not the obvious one."

"Okay. So can you think of any reason they'd want to keep you away from the guards?"

"No."

"This is going to sound a little out there, but, just to satisfy my curiosity: You didn't see any sign of big dogs or wolves when you were there, did you?"

Callaghan thought about it, trying to remember, but so much had happened since then it was more difficult than it probably ought to have been. Then he remembered that flicker of movement, the dark shape, moving fast, running. He'd been sure it was a dog. A big dog. Could it have been a wolf? It was possible.

"Wolves?" he said, partially repeating the question instead of answering it. "Why would there be wolves?"

"Never mind, it was just a thought; we've been having reports of a large number of strays," Sabine said, waving away the question. Callaghan knew right then and there that the man was lying to him. It hadn't been just a thought at all, it had been the entire purpose behind this line of questioning. And the fact that he had seen something, well, that made that flicker of movement all the more curious, but he wasn't really sure what to do with the information beyond file it away. "Now, tell me about the warehouse. What *really* happened inside?"

How could he skirt the truth? He was hardly about to say, *Oh, the ghosts of Ronnie and Reggie Kray beat the crap out of me.* The secret of a good lie was keeping it close to the truth. He hadn't made his official report, so he gambled that Sabine had nothing to go on, so giving him some of the truth shouldn't hurt. He rubbed at his jaw. The stubble had started to grow through. He sniffed. "It was a disagreement about lost property."

"Theft? Related to the Sidney Street job?"

He was good.

Callaghan nodded. "Seems that someone was a bit annoyed about their property going missing."

"So they dragged you to a disused warehouse in the East End
and busted your knee for you?" Again that set an alarm bell off
in Callaghan's mind. How could this guy know he'd busted his
knee in the warehouse? They'd obviously been watching him for
a while. Long enough to realize one day he was fine, the next he
was hobbling around like a cripple.

"Something like that."

"So they think you're involved?"

He shook his head. "No, they just want the name from me before I arrest the thief."

"And will you give it to them?"

"What do you think?"

"I think it would go against every instinct you have as an officer of the law."

"But you're not saying whether you think I'll hand her over
when I catch her."

"Because I don't know if you will. I'd like to think I've got the
measure of you, Jack, and that you'll do no such thing, but my
mother always said I liked to think the best of people."

"I'll catch the thief and, if possible, recover the stolen property.
It will be returned to the rightful owner in due course."

"The rightful owner is an interesting choice of words. One
might read between the lines and think that the people in possession of said stolen property might not actually be the rightful
owners?"

"Thankfully that's someone else's problem, not mine. I just take
down the thieves. I leave the rest to colleagues better equipped to
handle it."

Sabine looked at him without speaking for a moment, seeming
to weigh up his words. Callaghan felt the same sort of discomfort
that countless people on the receiving end of his interrogations
must have felt.

At least he knew the game. He distracted himself by drinking
the coffee. "I can tell you're not civil service," he said, offering
a lopsided grin. "This stuff is really good. Nothing like the swill
they serve us in Scotland Yard."

"Nothing else you want to tell me?" Sabine said, not distracted
by the coffee talk.

Callaghan shrugged. "Nothing else to tell."

"Then I guess we're done here. Thank you for your candor, Jack, and your time. We'll be keeping an eye on you, because trouble seems to be following you around."

"I think it's more like I'm the one who's following the trouble around, you know, given that it's my job."

"You keep on believing that, Jack," Sabine said, pushing back his chair. He led Callaghan out of the office, and out through the maze of corridors toward the main door and Admiralty Arch.

In one of the rooms they passed he overheard a group of men talking about something that had happened the night before. He heard the words "Hampton Court," but couldn't catch anything else before Sabine closed the door. He knew better than to ask what it was all about. The fact that the LN-7 man had closed the door was indication aplenty he didn't want to talk about it, which using a sort of reverse logic meant it was exactly the kind of thing Callaghan wanted to know about. If there was some overlap between their investigations, maybe Sabine's lot were a step ahead? It sure as hell seemed like it back there. So maybe, just maybe, Hampton Court was linked into the Maritime job, or the Sidney Street Bank job? There was only one way of finding out.

"Something I should know?"

Sabine shook his head. "Different investigation, nothing for you to worry about."

"You sure? *Quid pro quo*, right? I've told you about the warehouse. If this in any way pertains to my investigation, I have a right to know."

"We'll speak again, when you are ready to tell us everything. Then, perhaps, we'll tell you everything. Until then..." Sabine held out a hand for Callaghan to shake—a very formal gesture. It was a good firm shake, though; Sabine held on for just a moment longer than was comfortable, as though he was testing him. Callaghan just smiled at him. Sabine nodded. And them something changed in his face. He didn't just let go—he pulled his hand away. Callaghan felt it too. It was like his hand had suddenly caught fire. The heat between them was incredible.

He looked down at his hand. It looked just like it had always looked. When he looked up again, Sabine had opened the door.

Outside the world seemed suddenly fresh and so much more vibrant than it had even a few moments before. The air felt alive compared to the stale interior of the old Admiralty Building. He breathed it in, savoring it, glad to be outside.

Whatever those people were, there was no denying there was something odd about them.

His car was waiting for him outside, the keys in the ignition.

In the last twenty-four hours the shades of the Kray Twins and some covert arm of the British government had kidnapped him. These people frightened him more than any ghosts.

"I ain't afraid of no ghost," he said, grinning at his reflection in the passenger side window.

He walked around to the driver's side door. The broken body of a dead bird lay in the gutter, a single bead of blood on its beak…

CHAPTER 32

DEATH AND THE DRAGON MAIDEN

They are on the hunt.

He can feel the thrill of flight...the air full of the sound of beating wings.

At last they have El Draco on the run... He has been forced into hiding, licking his wounds.

This is war...

A war they are winning...

El Draco's brood will be with him, offering him protection. They will fly with him...at his side...putting themselves at risk to save his worthless hide... He pities them the fate that is going to befall them... That pity burns inside him... He does not pity the humans who chose to stand beside them...they deserve what is coming to them.

In the Welsh Marches the rebel who would lead a nation stands strong; the Raven King, Bran the Blessed, has gathered forces loyal to him to guard against those who would put down his rebellion. Bran and El Draco are about to become bound to each other in a pact that will assure their mutual protection...or perhaps it is their mutual destruction?

They fly hard...

The mountains are already in view. He knows that El Draco

will be in there somewhere. He can smell him. It has to come to an end this time...for peace. The ritual that will bind those two together must be prevented...but he can feel the energy surging up out of the earth, the earth magic swirling and churning all around them... The ley lines are bleeding magic...that magic sings in his veins...it flows through him...it is the wind that raises him up... it is everything...and it has led them like a beacon to where the apostate and his faction have gathered.

He breaks away from the pack, streaking down, determined to be the one first to attack...the first to kill.

Even before the gathering comes into sight, a dragon rises from the ground, foolish enough to face him. It is a female. He can smell the blood on her. There will be more blood. He will show no mercy. In his stead, she would show none to him.

He is too strong for her.

It is over before it has begun.

The first breath of fire sends her reeling.

He swipes one great, clawed wing at the beast, crippling her. Her wing tears...sending her spiraling toward the ground.

Far below he sees other dragons start to take to the air, too late to save her, too late to save their master... His dragon kin streak down toward them, flame and fury, scorching the air and the earth.

He follows her down as she spirals out of control...

He is above her with claws extended when she hits the ground.

There is no mercy.

He lifts her broken body into the air again, rising high, and dashes her against the side of the mountain, her bones broken on the jagged shards of rock. She tumbles and rolls and cries out as she comes to rest amongst the Raven King's followers. She is not dead, but he is certain that she will never fly again.

That is worse than death.

And that is his gift to her.

CHAPTER 33

ENTER THE DRAGON

Callaghan had no idea how he had managed to get behind the wheel of his car, or how long he had been lost to the world, caught up in that…what was it? A dream? A waking nightmare?

He shook his head, trying to free his mind of the last remnants of the vision, and turned the key to fire up the engine.

He didn't like the fact that they had brought his car here. It smacked of the sort of government arrogance that he instinctively rebelled against. Better to let him walk back to the Dacre Street Entrance of New Scotland Yard. This was just a way of letting him know they really were watching him, that they knew which car was his, and let him extrapolate everything else they knew about him in the process. It was all mind games. Well, screw them.

He pulled out into traffic, following the flow on the Strand, around Nelson's Column in the middle of Trafalgar Square, and down Whitehall all the way to Victoria.

He had plenty of time to think as he drove.

There had been something odd about the way Sabine had acted when they had shook hands, that last moment before they'd broken contact. He'd felt it. The thing was, it wasn't the first time he had had a reaction like that.

Who?

He tried to retrace his steps in his mind, visualizing the people he had come into contact with over the last few days, linking them to the crimes and crime scenes, but no matter how many times he went over them in his mind, none of them offered up the answer he was looking for.

Meaning it hadn't had to do with the crimes at all. Not really. Once he arrived at that conclusion, it whittled down the list of possible people to one.

Callaghan looked in the rearview. No one was behind him. Without a moment's hesitation, he pulled down hard on the wheel and up on the handbrake, pulling off a rubber-burning handbrake turn. Tires laying down a thick black coat of rubber, he accelerated away.

There might have been seven million people still tied to the city, but the traffic through the center of London was nothing like it had been. Even so, he ran two red lights on the way to Art Mortimer's flat in The Gaitskell. No one really cared about lights, not the way they had when the streets were so congested to ignore them would have invited chaos. Now, as long as there was no collision, speed cameras were ignored for the most part and one-way signs had become something of an optional extra.

He left the car directly outside the Tower block, locking it. There were a couple of potential twoccers hanging around the concrete bollards in their hoodies looking like rebels without the slightest clue. He nodded to them. They ignored him. They knew he was filth; he had the stink.

He wasn't surprised to discover the lift was still out of order.

The stench in the stairwell was, if anything, worse than it had been on his previous visit. He wasn't going to let it slow him down. Taking a deep breath, he tackled the stairs two and three at a time, using the handrail to haul him up as his legs started to burn. He reached the landing with the broken window and paused for a minute, just to breathe some clean air, and then he was off again. He was light-headed and out of breath by the time he made it to Morty's floor. He leaned against the wall for a minute, breathing hard. The plywood was still there with its anti-Semitic scrawl. He couldn't understand why Morty didn't wash it off. Or maybe he did. Maybe it kept coming back, and every time he scrubbed it away it just made it all the more sickening to see it return? That made more sense.

Callaghan banged on Morty's door. As before, there was no immediate response as the old man skulked in the darkness, afraid of who might have come calling.

"Morty, it's me, Jack Callaghan. Let me in."

Nothing. He tried again, banging on the side of the frame.

"Come on, Morty. How long have we known each other? It's me, Jack. Let's just sit down and have a drink, eh?"

Still there was no reply.

He crouched down and flipped open the letterbox flap, then called again. "Morty! I'll huff and I'll puff. Come on, mate, open up."

This time he saw movement, but the old man was not coming toward the door.

"Go away!" Morty yelled down the hallway at the closed door.

"Come on, Morty, I need to talk to you. Just for a minute."

"Well, I don't need to talk to you. Just leave me alone."

"Morty! What the hell is wrong with you? I need to talk to you. Just for a minute. Please!" Callaghan could feel a rage starting to grow inside him. He'd never felt anything like it before; it was a burning that filled his very being.

He took a step backward, rocked on his heel, and kicked at the door. The blow broke the feeble lock, sending the door flying inward. "Morty!" Callaghan bellowed, walking inside.

The old man cowered in a corner of the living room. He was on his knees, making himself as small as he possibly could.

Callaghan could *smell* his fear.

"What did you see? Tell me," Callaghan demanded. "When I was here before, what did you see? Why wouldn't you answer the door now? What was it?"

The old man struggled to his feet. He kept his back pressed up against the wall. He was trembling violently. He was terrified. Callaghan hated himself, but even as that moment of awareness surfaced, the fire in his soul crushed it. The old jeweler looked at him then. Met his eyes. Held them. "I saw what you *really* are, Mr. C. I've seen it before. I've always known it was there, but this time it'd woken up."

222   STEVEN SAVILE

"What do you mean?"

"There's something dark and ugly inside you, Mr. C. You might not know that it is there, or maybe you did, once, a long time ago, but have forgotten, but you're starting to remember it, aren't you?" Morty stepped away from the wall. It took him a moment to realize the old man didn't look scared anymore. "Are you starting to have dreams, Mr. C? Nightmares? You are, aren't you? Do you dream of killing people? Do you wake up in the middle of the night bathed in cold sweat? Do you?"

Callaghan said nothing.

"These aren't dreams, Mr. C, oh no. Not dreams. These are past lives being remembered. This is your true self being revealed." Morty shoved him in the chest, pushing him back. "This is who you are!"

Callaghan was taken aback at the old man's outburst, surprised by Morty's strength as he pushed him. "Get out of my home. There is no place for you here. Go!"

The old man pushed Callaghan again, even more forcefully this time. Callaghan stumbled backward, almost losing his balance. He reached out, trying to grab ahold of something to stop him from falling. "Get out!" the old man raged, shoving Callaghan again and again until he was almost back to the door, when the old man's hand slammed against his ribs and something broke—not the bones, but the dam that had been barely holding his rage in check. He lashed out, pushing Morty back. He wasn't going to take this! He was not going to be pushed around by an old man who hid away in a piss-stinking flat with junkies living outside his door! He was not going to take this from a two-bit jewel thief!

The rage overwhelmed him. It pounded through his veins. It beat against his eardrums. It hammered against the walls of his skull and tore at his heart, trying to rip it clean out of his chest.

He grabbed the old man by the scruff of his neck and threw him backward.

Art Mortimer fell to the ground with his hands covering his ears, mumbling the same words over and over again.

They were words that Callaghan simply couldn't understand.

CHAPTER 34

RAGE

Sabine reached the doorway just in time to see Callaghan completely lose all control of his emotions.

The last seconds of their handshake at HQ had been enough for him to know that there was something unusual about him, and by unusual, he meant *wrong*. It wasn't the first time he had felt that same sensation. It wasn't even the first time that day he'd felt it.

The woman—even now he could remember how incredibly beautiful she was, but he couldn't for the life of him recall her face, which was disconcerting—that he had caught a glimpse of in the other boat had given off the same vibe, though with her it had been so strong it hadn't even required contact for him to pick it up. Whatever she was or whatever she carried, it was stronger in her than it was in Callaghan. But it was the same. There was no doubt about that. And that bothered Thomas Sabine. He didn't like being bothered by things. Hence, he'd decided to follow the cop and see just where the trouble took him.

In point of fact the entire place reeked of that peculiar vibe.

It was burning off Callaghan, infesting anything and everything all around him. Even the old man, apparently having beaten down on him that furiously.

The old man was mumbling something. His lips were moving

fast, but the movement itself was barely perceptible. Sabine assumed he was offering a prayer to whatever god he held dear, but there was always the possibility he was trying to use some sort of magic to stop Callaghan. Sabine had learned a few incantations of his own on the front line in the battle against the *outré*. He had no particular qualms about using the enemy's weapons against them, either. He recalled the lines as though they were his native language, the syllables tripping from his tongue with his lips barely seeming to move. The old man gave him a strange look, but Sabine was deep into the incantation by then and needed to make sure each vowel was perfect, each syllable shaped exquisitely as his voice rose from a whisper to a scream. He started softy at first, harnessing their power, growing ever louder, sacrificing control for strength.

Callaghan struck the old man again, driving a fist into his chest, and again this time to the jaw. The old man's head flew back, the bones in his neck cracking even as Callaghan hit him again. Sabine knew he had to intervene, but there was no way in hell he was strong enough to stand up to Callaghan while this rage was upon him.

He had to calm him, and the Siren's Song was the only charm he could think of in his bag of tricks that could possibly do that. He placed both hands flat on Callaghan's back, feeling the fire blazing through his muscles, and let the song of magic sing higher, louder, right into his ear. He felt the big man begin to crumble, the rage flooding out of him. It was only a temporary measure, Sabine's hands cooling the anger, but it worked. Callaghan stopped hitting the old man, who cowered on the ground, his knees tucked up to his chest, hands covering his head as best he could. When Callaghan stopped whaling on him, the old man still didn't look up, as though he didn't trust the pain was over.

"What's happened here?" Callaghan asked, kneeling down beside the old man and trying to cradle him. "Who did this to you, Morty?"

It was as though he was a completely different man, a different personality, and this one had no idea it had almost killed the old man with his bare hands.

The old man's words were unintelligible, his lips were still moving, and Sabine could tell it wasn't any sort of spell now—he was begging, only it was drowned out by the pain and the tears.

Sabine placed a hand on Callaghan's shoulder and without the cooling charm to protect him, almost cried out in pain himself as he felt the searing heat coming off the man.

It hurt. *Really* hurt. But he refused to let it show.

"*You* happened to him, Callaghan," he said.

The policeman looked down at his hands. He turned them over as if trying to grasp the fact that they were bloody and cut, and that the blood was his, not someone else's. He looked at the old man. He looked back at Sabine. The rage was gone, utterly. His eyes were haunted. He was spent.

The Siren's Song switched one emotion for another, equally potent—in this case grief—but wouldn't last forever. The rage would return. In truth, given the strength of it, the switch might barely last long enough to get Callaghan out of this place.

CHAPTER 35

HISTORY BOYS

Callaghan woke in darkness.

It took him a few moments to gather his bearings. The memories came back much slower. He didn't want them. The last thing he could recollect with any clarity was banging on Morty's door demanding to be let in. Everything after that was a blank.

He tried to move.

Every muscle in his body complained. He felt fire all the way from his hocks to his head, running along the nerves. It was as though he'd lain absolutely still, in the same position, for hours, and they'd set rigid. Like rigor mortis had set in while he was still alive. Callaghan flexed his fingers. The broken skin around his knuckles cracked, causing him to wince. He felt around in the darkness, coming into contact with cold metal panels, and realized that he had to be in the back of a van. The rear windows had been blacked out so he couldn't see where he was. He sat up. The world reeled around him, the cramped darkness just making it worse. On his hands and knees, Callaghan banged on the doors, shouting at the top of his voice, "Let me out of here! Let me out! I'm a police officer! Let me out!"

He heard sounds coming from outside the van.

Footsteps.

And then the doors swung open. He tried to scramble out, but someone stood in the way, preventing him from leaving. It took him a moment, squinting through the sudden brightness of the weak sun to realize it was Sabine, the LN-7 agent.

"I don't know what you did to me back there, but you'll pay for it. I swear to God you'll pay for it."

"Very melodramatic, Jack," Sabine said. "Now shut the hell up and stay where you are. First, I didn't do anything to you apart from calm you down."

"You gave me a sedative? You drugged me?"

"Something like that. Don't look so shocked. You nearly killed that old guy. I wasn't about to get beaten senseless just because I was in the line of fire. Now, listen to me, Jack: I don't know what's happening to you, but it's not good. I'm not doing this for the good of my health. I've got orders, just like you. Mine are to stay with you and try to work out what the problem is. And, if needs be, see that you are quarantined. Now, look at me, Jack. Look me in the eye. There's something you're not telling me and I need to know what it is if I'm going to help you."

"Who says I need any help?" Callaghan said stubbornly.

"I do, for one. If I hadn't arrived when I did you would have killed that poor old sod."

"Poor old…" Callaghan looked at his damaged knuckles, then back at Sabine, finally holding his gaze. "Morty? How? Is he all right?" And suddenly he had more questions, dozens of them demanding to come tumbling out of his mouth, but he bit back on them.

"I called an ambulance after I got you out of there, but, amazingly, I don't think you did any serious damage, even if you did give him one hell of a seeing to. Want to tell me why you went to see him in the first place? I assume it wasn't to kick seven shades out of him."

"We had a falling out," Callaghan said, knowing that it was almost the truth, but not quite. He still couldn't bring himself to share what was happening to him with Sabine, even if it seemed like the LN-7 agent already had an idea what was going on. "I wanted to try to put things right."

"Well, from what I saw, it didn't look like you were making

a good job of it, if you don't mind me saying? Now, we're both men of action, Jack. Lies are unbecoming. I'm going to ask you a question I asked you earlier, one that you didn't answer truthfully; I'd like you to tell me the truth this time, okay?"

"I didn't lie to you."

"We both know that's not true. So, take your time, think about it, and in your own words, I'd like you to tell me what *really* happened in that warehouse, okay?"

Callaghan didn't even have to think about it. If he was going to admit to seeing ghosts, he wanted something in return, and the only thing he could think to ask was: "Okay, but only if you'll tell me why you wanted to know if I saw any wolves on the CCTV."

"That seems quite fair," Sabine said. "I'll even go first. I have my suspicions about the nature of the two overnight guards you didn't quite manage to encounter at the Maritime Museum. And by suspicions I mean that I have reason to believe that they are, in point of fact, packmates from the Brotherhood of Cernunnos, operating out of the Isle of Dogs."

"The Brotherhood of what the hell are you talking about?"

"Cernunnos. The Horned God. I take it you aren't familiar with the mythology?"

"Err. No."

"And you've never encountered the term 'The Mythic Age'?"

"Again, err, no."

Sabine rubbed his jaw as though trying to decide where to begin. "I might as well say once upon a time." He grinned wryly. "Because I suspect you're going to have some difficulty swallowing what I'm about to tell you."

"Try me."

Sabine took a deep breath. "Europe hasn't always been like this…the world hasn't. Long before any sort of industrialization it was called Erebea, and was essentially a vast forest. That forest was home to the people of Cernunnos, the Horned God. A dragon of the Mythic Age."

"Okay…dragon. Right. Yeah. Okay. Completely. Dragon. You wanna let me out of the van now, please?"

"This is your history, Jack; you might want to listen. Who knows, you might even learn something. Cernunnos gave his people a blessing that allowed them to fuse their spirits with the physical forms of wild animals. The world was turning bleak. The Horned God had realized that the future would be devoid of magic; the wellspring of karma was all but bled dry, so by doing this, the dragon hoped that his people might survive in a land where there was no more magic. And they did."

"You do realize this sounds like a fairy bloody tale, right?"

"I am aware of that. How do you think such tales come to be? Cernunnos misjudged his people. In the terrible years following the cataclysm, they degenerated, the animal aspect becoming far stronger than the man, and they turned on each other. They hunted and killed their own until only the strongest remained. And so it was until they found that by taking the blasphemous form of half-man half-beast, they could mate with humans and continue their bloodline."

"What are you saying?"

"The Brotherhood are descended from those tribes. They carry the blood of the wolf in them. It has awoken. That is why I asked you if you had seen any wolves."

"Half-man half-wolf? You think they're *werewolves*? You think the guards at the Maritime Museum were *werewolves*? Do you have any idea how insane you sound right now?" Callaghan stared at Sabine in absolute disbelief. The guy had to be pulling his leg. It was a wind up. It had to be. *Werewolves?* He shook his head. "You can't be serious."

"You asked. I told you what we do. I told you that there are things out there it's best no one ever finds out about. You assumed I meant terrorists or more mundane threats. Now you know the truth."

"The truth…"

"I'm not hiding anything from you, Jack. This is where our paths cross. The thief you are hunting, well, I believe that Brotherhood packmates may have set upon her. Maybe she got away, maybe she didn't. Did you happen to notice the pile of sand?"

Callaghan nodded. "Yes, I asked SOCO to look into it. You found something?"

"We did. After we cleared it away, we found the body of a homeless man buried underneath it."

"That's interfering with a crime scene."

"The body had been torn apart. Forensic examination proved conclusively the wounds were caused by tooth and claw."

Callaghan was having trouble taking in what he was being told. But not being able to comprehend it didn't make it a lie. He had seen enough to believe that in this new world, anything was possible.

"I saw something," he admitted. "Nothing more than a shadow, really. It was moving fast. I caught it out of the corner of my eye. I thought it was a dog."

"Thank you. Now, tell me about the warehouse."

"I told you the truth about what happened in the warehouse…" He paused, not quite sure how to tell Sabine what he had seen, despite the fact that it was no more fantastical or ludicrous than the idea of werewolves in London.

"No, you didn't, Jack, you told me a part of the truth. I'm asking you to tell me *all* of it."

"Okay. Well. Right. So. The owners who so desperately wanted the return of their property? They had me collected by their driver, Charlie, who took me out to the abandoned warehouse. I saw them beat the bank manager from the Sidney Street Bank to death while he hung by a chain from the ceiling." Sabine nodded. "It was Ronnie and Reggie Kray. I swear to God. But that can't be right, can it? They are both dead."

"Ahh," was all that Sabine said. Callaghan looked at him, trying to see if he was either shocked or surprised by the news that the ghosts of long-dead gangsters were once more terrorizing the East End.

"So it *is* possible?"

"Oh that it wasn't. There've been sightings. We'd heard rumors that their shades had been seen in some of their old haunts. A lot has changed since their days, of course, but it would seem that they are doing their damnedest to regain control, and judging from your experience with them, I'd say they have nothing to lose. Who will stand in their way? Our only hope is that their movement is restricted to the part of London they frequented in life. I do not want to think about what will happen to my city if they aren't satisfied with what they had, and try to carve out an even larger empire built on blood and hate."

It was hard to believe everything he was hearing. It was hard to believe even *part* of what he was hearing, despite the fact he had experienced some of it with his own eyes and was carrying the wounds in terms of a busted knee. If what the man was telling him was true, then Callaghan had to believe that there was more to all of it... Werewolves. Ghosts. Dragons... And that what he was experiencing—the dreams-nightmares-hallucinations or whatever they were, and the rage, the burning contact when he touched someone—all of them were more than just stress or exhaustion.

He needed time to think.

And the best place to think was drunk, occupying seat number one at the end of the bar.

CHAPTER 36

CARDS ON THE TABLE

At last Callaghan had some time to himself.

He had occupied the last barstool for three hours, wishing the world away. There was no salvation at the bottom of any of the glasses he drank, though the warm, distinctly pleasant bite of the single malt did take the edge off. Drinking alone was dangerous. It left him craving company and a man that much in need of *not* being alone was liable to do something stupid. So he went home.

That didn't help, because it wasn't home anymore, it was just a house.

It was too large for one man, and rattling around inside it only served to remind him that the job was all he had.

Evening was already fast approaching. He wasn't confident of sleeping tonight, either. Callaghan drew the curtains to shut out the night. He turned on a small desk lamp. His house was in a leafy suburb just beyond the reach of the Underground, which meant he could afford it. That was right around the turn of 2001 when he'd bought it with Anna. It had been six years since his ex-wife had set foot in their house. He'd thought about selling up, moving to something smaller that didn't have a spare room painted as a nursery for the son they'd never had, but the suburb was just a little too close to the city to be considered desirable.

How times had changed.

Callaghan poured himself a whisky, dropped a single ice cube into it, and settled down at the dining table with a pack of index cards.

He was a creature of habit, and this one dated all the way back to the training academy. He liked to write facts down on index cards then shuffle them around on a big empty table to see what possibilities could be thrown up by chance arrangements. Sometimes it offered nothing he hadn't already considered a thousand times and dismissed; other times it sent his brain off thinking tangentially, and that could result in what all those management consultants liked to call "thinking outside of the box."

He uncapped a pen and started by writing down every individual fact he could recall about the Sidney Street Bank job and then the Maritime Museum and lastly the British Library on separate cards, keeping them grouped by crime scene to start hoping he'd be able to see more than just the obvious similarities. Of course it wasn't just about the overlaps—sometimes the differences were every bit as important to the investigation.

He started out with the premise that the mystery woman was responsible for each of the crimes, and therefore the catalyst for his meeting with the Krays.

Any way he looked at it she seemed to be at the fulcrum.

He had been reluctant to include the ghostly meeting to begin with, but one thing he'd learned in the years of reading the cards—he smiled at the thought, it made him seem like some sort of Gypsy Rose Lee fortune teller—was that it was better to include something and then discard it if it didn't fit rather than setting it aside from the outset only to miss something vital.

Something was nagging at him.

He looked at the cards, then shuffled them and laid them out as fate would have it. They made no sense whatsoever like that.

There was something missing.

Some linchpin that pulled it all together.

He had no idea what it was.

He picked up a couple of cards at random. The first asked the question: *Did thief open two boxes?* The second said: *Something of Krays' stolen from bank.* He amended the card to say two coins. They had been in the second box. People like Ronnie and Reggie weren't the sorts to accept any sort of theft, as it was disrespecting them. If it was a spur of the moment thing, it was quite possibly the worst box she could have broken into; these were not enemies you made out of choice. But…what if it *wasn't* spur of the moment? What if it was the intended target of the robbery all along?

He regrouped the cards into the crime scene groups again.

Two things were stolen from the bank: the stone from the necklace and the coins.

The thief was interrupted before she could have possibly taken anything else from the Maritime Museum other than the Drake Jewel. She may have wanted more, but not been able to finish the job.

So what about the British Library? She'd taken the plans for the Maritime Museum, but was that just another case of showing them something she wanted them to see, to distract them from the real purpose of the break-in?

He checked his watch. It was far too late to get ahold of anyone who would be able to tell him if anything else had been stolen, assuming that they even knew yet. But he knew where he would be going first thing in the morning.

Callaghan wrote the question on another card, then picked up another and wrote: *What happened at Hampton Court?*

The conversation he'd overheard at the LN-7 headquarters might have nothing to do with anything, as Sabine had said at the time, but if that was the case, why close the door? You only did that if there was a chance someone might say something that led to two and two being put together. You couldn't put two and two together if cases weren't in some way related. It was a leap, but it was worth writing it down and adding it to the puzzle.

At worst, Hampton Court had nothing to do with his investigations, but so many things appeared to be connected at the moment he wasn't about to discount anything.

He reached for the whisky and swallowed a mouthful, feeling its fire as it slipped down his throat.

CHAPTER 37

BRAN

Fire burns through him. He releases a great gout of flame.
  And it is glorious.
  This is battle. This is war.
  This is death.
  This is victory.
  He swoops down from the sky as the clouds part, expecting to see El Draco's nest, and the ancient dragon himself, but El Draco is nowhere to be seen. He can smell the enemy. He was here. He isn't now. Instead, the warrior Bran stands alone beside the river Hafren to draw his attention away from the dragon and his fleeing followers. One druid stands close to the water, casting an incantation as the tide rushes up from the sea, sending a great swell upriver.

The druid motions the river as though he is commanding it, rather than the swell being part of nature. Shapes move within the water until they rise flapping out of the tidal flow. Hundreds of fish, thousands of them sucked from the river, thrashing and unable to breathe... They start to cling together in a great mass until they are slowly joined by debris from the silt; their dead and rotting brethren, crabs, shrimps, and eels are all caught together, moving under the druid's command.

The golem towers above Bran and protects him, fighting the
dragons as they attack, beating them away again and again. And
when he streaks toward it, the golem collapses around his tongues
of flame only to reform as though made of nothing more substan-
tial than smoke as he breaks on through to the other side.

Fire and flame bring it to an end when finally the charred remains can no longer hold together.

For the first time, Callaghan knows that this is no dream, that
he isn't trapped in some insane hallucination, but that he has
found a memory.

He is part of this.

He was the dragon tearing at the golem of dead fish risen up
out of the river. He feels the dragon's rage burning inside him. He
feels its fire.

He is the dragon.

He is the dragon.

He is the dragon.

The knowledge fires through his mind, filling him with
strength.

He fights now with renewed vigor, fiery breath burning and
incinerating the fleeing men, but leaving Bran unharmed. He will
need to be made an example of, and now that he is a thing of
magic, he needs to be dealt with accordingly.

Warriors rush from the bushes brandishing spears and axes,
woad-painted faces, gripped by the ríastrad, the berserker's fury,
their muscles twisting and straining and bulging as they seem to
grow physically, the earth magic pounding through their veins
even as they charge the dragons down. This is no easy fight. Not
now. They clash with the dragons. Their axes bite hard, cleaving
scales and spilling the rich, dark, thick blood of the dragon kin
across the soil of the battlefield.

He can see his own broodmate on the ground, skull split open
by Bran's axe. She is dying. Her wings beat desperately at the
earth as she tries to draw some last sustenance in from the ground,
but there is nothing, it is all flowing through the ríastrad-frenzied
warriors. They are draining the world dry, drawing up all of the
karmic strength in the soul of the soil and turning it into fuel for
slaughter.

The rage surfaces within Callaghan's dragon and he surrenders to it, streaking back down toward the berserkers, hating the painted men more than he has ever hated anything in his long, long life.

He tears into them, rending flesh. He burns them, charring bone. Again and again.

Their axes are useless against him. Their spears bite, but not deep enough to prevent him shaking them off.

His claws rip through bare flesh, opening up men, spilling entrails hot and bloody across the battlefield. His teeth take heads clean off shoulders, leaving bodies to stagger on, not realizing they are dead. The rage consumes him. And whenever it feels like it might falter, like he might lose that potency that fires his blood, all he needs to do is look down at where his mate lies bleeding and the rage resurfaces.

They cannot stand against him, no matter how fearsome they are. He is the dragon. He is mighty. His breath is fire, his bite venom, his claws death.

The battle is done.

The dragons rise into the sky again, climbing for the clouds.

He has Bran in his clutches, his claws sunk deep into the man's body so that any amount of resistance only serves to tear himself apart. As Callaghan takes to the air again, the cursed druid casts one final incantation with his dying breath, even as Bran the Raven King is being dragged away. They cannot know what words he is speaking, or what his intentions are, but they will know soon enough. The last of the brood remain on the field, finishing the fight. They cannot afford the luxury of taking prisoners on the long journey back to their homeland, but Bran is no ordinary prisoner.

He needs to be paraded to confirm his capture.

Or, Callaghan thinks, perhaps just his head will be enough to prove his death?

But, as hard as it is, they must not get ahead of themselves...

The battle may be won, but the war is not yet over.

El Draco still lives.

CHAPTER 38

COME TOGETHER

Callaghan woke on the couch just as the sky was starting to brighten. His head hammered, and not just from the aftereffects of one too many glasses of whisky. It wasn't a hangover, it was rooted deep in the stem of his neck and fanned out through every blood vessel in his body. A shower and a handful of paracetamol washed the worst of it away.

He dressed in the same clothes he'd worn all week.

It wasn't a fashion parade.

He locked up and left, stuffing his hands in his pockets.

He'd left his car across the road from the house. He could have parked it in the driveway, but that was where Anna always parked hers, and six years on, he still couldn't bring himself to take her spot. It was stupid really, but somehow it felt as though by doing so it'd be all the more real. Though how it could be any more real than the decree absolute and her first child with another man, he couldn't actually explain. It just would.

He unlocked the car door and clambered inside. The first thing he did was put the radio on. After the news bulletin and the traffic report, the DJ treated London to an eclectic mix of The Pogues, Aztec Camera, and the Gorillaz, and asked callers to find the link. It was an easy one. The Clash: Joe Strummer had, for a time, replaced Shane MacGowan as lead singer of The Pogues for their 1991 *Hell's Ditch* tour; Mick Jones had dueted with Roddy Frame on Aztec Camera's "Good Morning Britain"; and Paul Simonon and Mick Jones played with Damon Albarn's band on *Plastic Beach*.

Feeling quite pleased with himself, Callaghan drove back into the city.

He parked outside the British Library. There was one of those overpriced designer coffee shops across the street. He was blowing on too-hot store-bought coffee before the first member of staff arrived.

He wanted to be sure that his questions were answered before they began their daily routines—mainly because the sooner he broached the possibility of other thefts, the more chance they had of actually discovering them before someone disturbed anything else in the room.

It was all educated guesswork, but if she had stolen anything else it would most likely have been taken from the same place. That was how it had worked before.

The curator of that particular room was one of the first to arrive once the guards had opened the doors, allowing employees to file into the building and begin their daily toil. The curator was only too happy to do whatever he could, grateful for the chance to help. He was obviously the kind of person who loved his job, to the extent that while it wasn't quite an extension of his body, it was his soul. The loss of a single exhibit hurt him, as though one of his own children had been stolen.

"A complete inventory?" He looked at Callaghan as though he'd lost his mind. "Do you have any idea how long it would take *just* to check the contents of this room, never mind the rest of the library?"

"Well, not being funny, but it makes my job easier if we know what has been taken. Look, I get it, it's a needle in a bloody old dusty stack of books, but if I am right, we're only looking for one or maybe two other missing items." He paused for a moment, realizing that he was leading the man. He needed him to think for himself. But it couldn't be helped, it was all about cutting corners and making intuitive leaps. There had to be links between the objects stolen, somehow. The problem was, whilst he knew about the Drake Jewel, he had no idea what kind of coins had been stolen from the Krays, so there was no way of confirming his theory. They could have been quite literally any denomination, their value sentimental or actual. Still, he said, "This is a little random, but try checking for anything to do with buildings where anything that might be considered a national treasure is housed. That might narrow it down a little."

"A little. The definition of national treasure is pretty vague."

"No one said saving the world was going to be easy," Callaghan joked.

Once he had given the curator a purpose, he set about checking the CCTV footage.

The coverage was patchy at best, and unsurprisingly focused on doorways, windows, and the stairwells between exhibits, but not on the actual exhibits themselves. It was almost as though they didn't want to know who damaged things, like they were willfully turning a blind eye. But, at least it was possible to follow her path through the library, even though she frequently slipped out of view of one of the cameras; the time lapse between her disappearing and reappearing was too short for the thief to steal anything *en route*. If she'd taken anything else, it had to be from inside the room, which was what he'd thought from the beginning. The CCTV just confirmed the theory.

"What time was the alarm triggered?" he asked the guard beside him. The guards were surprisingly dedicated, as though they, too, took the theft personally.

He checked the log and handed it to Callaghan.

He looked at it twice. It didn't make sense, but according to the time coding on the footage, the alarm hadn't been triggered until *after* she had taken whatever she had managed to retrieve from the room. It didn't match. She wasn't sloppy. If Sabine was right, the Maritime Museum job had only gone south because of the werewolves. There was nothing here to prevent her walking out into the night, no one any the wiser. Unless she'd deliberately set the alarm off. "Do you know where the alarm was set off?"

"A fire exit on the ground floor. It opens out at the back of the building."

Which made sense, if it was deliberate…she could enter and move around freely without tripping the alarm, so it had to be deliberate. Why would she do that? What could she gain by alerting them to the robbery? He stared at the still-frame of her standing in a corridor, caught in a moment in time, and knew one possible explanation was to make sure that any police on duty that night would respond to the call, meaning they wouldn't be available to pursue her on the other side of the river when she went about the "real" night's work. He couldn't help but admire the woman. She had *chutzpah* that was for sure.

He checked his watch and realized that he had been watching her move along corridors for the best part of an hour. That surprised him. He'd lost himself there. He knew that the more he watched her move, the more familiar she seemed to become. But there was something different about it now. When he watched her he couldn't be sure if the familiarity was down to the time he'd spent staring at her, or if he was tapping some other memory locked deep inside his mind. He hated that he couldn't trust himself. It turned everything he'd ever thought about who he was on its head. But that last flashback that had taken him to the Hafren River, that hadn't been a dream at all. He'd been there. He had been the dragon scorching the land. How, he didn't know. Until a few hours ago, dragons had been make-believe monsters. Now he didn't know what they were. Or, come to that, what *he* was.

In the room, the curator was hunched over a desk checking off items on one of the huge ledgers that recorded the contents of the room. Even Callaghan appreciated just how painstaking a process it was, with the man being methodical to the point of being anal in his work, going box by box, shelf by shelf, in order around the room. It would take him the best part of a week to catalog each and every item in the room. Callaghan did not have that long. Besides, he had a hunch, and now was the time to test it out.

"Do you keep anything here about Hampton Court?"

The man looked up at him and shook his head—not to say no,

but rather to say, *you are joking, right?* "Of course we have. This is the premier collection of maps in the United Kingdom, officer. It wouldn't be much of a collection without one of the finest estates in the country, would it?"

"Show me."

The curator set aside his pen, and put his glasses on the ledger, marking his place. He moved over to the drawers where the plans and schematics were filed. He knew the collection inside out and back to front. He pulled open one of the drawers and thumbed through the blue lines and white lines. The way his brow furrowed and he thumbed back through a few of the schematics was enough to tell Callaghan it wasn't there.

"The plans for Hampton Court should have been in here. They're gone."

Callaghan wanted to punch the air or kiss the guy. He felt that surge of emotion that made the job worthwhile; it wasn't just the thrill of being proven right, it was more of a *vindication*, like guessing the link between three not-so random tunes on the radio. It proved his mind worked in that very unique way a cop's mind needed to. He had another piece of the puzzle now. She had broken in here to steal the plans for both the National Maritime Museum and Hampton Court, and as before, she'd made one theft obvious to hide a second less-obvious one. She wasn't concerned about the theft of the Maritime plans being discovered, but she *was* about Hampton Court. She didn't want people following her to know that she was heading there next. He would have been excited by the discovery, thinking he'd finally got one move ahead of her in this game of cat-and-mouse, but for the fact Sabine's crew had been talking about what had happened at Hampton Court, meaning she was already done there. But he was close. Tantalizingly so. And getting closer. She'd slip up. She would. She had to.

Callaghan tried to think.

Something connected all this, just like the songs. There was something. One thing. It pulled it all together. It had to.

"Do you want me to carry on looking?"

"Please," said Callaghan.

"For anything in particular? More treasures of the realm?"

He shrugged. He didn't have any reason to suspect something else would be missing. She'd only stolen two things from the Sidney Street Bank, so why would she steal three things here? Even so, the fact that she'd gone to lengths to conceal the theft of the Hampton Court plans had to mean something. There had to be a connection. Without really thinking about it, he said, "What connects the National Maritime Museum and Hampton Court?"

The curator gave him that odd look again. This time, though, it had more of a *see how clever I am* air about it, rather than inferring the inquisitor was stupid.

"The Maritime Museum contains several exhibits connected to Sir Francis Drake, if memory serves…"

"The Drake Jewel," Callaghan interrupted.

"Among other things: portraits, nautical charts—"

"No, the jewel was stolen. That's why the thief took the plans from here. They're connected. So what's the Hampton Court connection?"

The curator's face lit up now; he was in his element, imparting knowledge to a hungry audience. "Then, might I hazard that the Tudor connection is a strong one. Queen Elizabeth gave Drake the jewel, and Hampton Court was one of her royal residencies."

He'd been hoping for something a bit more direct. That was a little tenuous. He didn't say it out loud, but the curator obviously saw the disappointment in his face. He shrugged. "You asked what the connection was."

"Anything else? Could there be another link?"

"There could be any number, I'm sure."

"Okay…" Callaghan rubbed at his chin. The stubble was almost thick enough to call a beard now. "So, let's try this: If you had to pick a *third* building that had a connection to both Hampton Court and the Maritime Museum, which would it be?" He was shooting in the dark, but really it was no different to the index cards, which were in his pocket secured with a rubber band. It was all about freethinking and mental associations.

The curator closed the door and turned to lean against the cabinet. "Again, there could be any number of places."

"Just one. Somewhere with something worth stealing."

"A national treasure," the curator said, picking up the train of thought Callaghan had left dangling. "Well that certainly narrows it down a bit. My guess would be the Tower."

"The Tower? As in of London?"

"One and the same. There's no shortage of treasures in there, or at least there was before it was locked up. It's relatively safe to assume they are still there."

"Okay. If I buy that, what's the connection?"

"For one, Elizabeth spent time in the Tower, and of course, her mother was executed there."

"Executed is good... Look, erm, not to wave the ignorance flag or anything, but it's a long time since I was in a classroom, and even then history wasn't really my best subject..."

"Anne Boleyn," the curator said, taking pity on him. "Elizabeth's mother had her head chopped off at the Tower of London, or to be more precise, on Tower Green, outside the White Tower."

"Do you think you could...?" Callaghan started to ask, but the curator was one step ahead of him and had already pulled open a drawer to check, then seemed to remember and went over to the wall where a set of plans hung.

He let out a grunt and took the frame down from the wall.

"Gone," he said. "Replaced with the Imperial War Museum. Clever."

"Then I guess that answers my question."

It was hard to imagine that the thief would have taken plans for more than three buildings, so for the first time since the Sidney Street Bank, Callaghan felt like he might just be one step ahead... But the Tower? Could she really be contemplating breaking into the Tower? The very idea seemed ridiculous, and yet she had stolen the plans. That wasn't random. Nothing she did was random. So, if she hadn't already, she was going to break into the Tower. He didn't know whether to be impressed or horrified at the idea. What he did know was that catching this woman was fast becoming an obsession.

It was an itch that he *needed* to scratch.

Of course, if he knew what had been taken from Hampton Court, then perhaps he'd be in a position to slot another piece of the puzzle into place.

There was only one person he would be able to get that information from.

As much as he hated the idea, it meant he'd have to start sharing with Sabine. And he would have rather chewed glass. But he wanted her. And if that meant swallowing his pride, he could do it.

CHAPTER 39

THE WATCHMEN

Callaghan had no idea what he was hoping to gain by simply looking at the Tower. It was a landmark. And like every other resident of the city, it had been part of his mental image of London for all of his life. But it had become something he took for granted. So he'd come back for another look.

He knew that the chances of catching sight of the woman were remote to say the least, but no matter how slim it was, there *was* a chance that she could be doing the same as him. And she had no reason to hide herself. There was no way that anyone would be able to recognize her or connect her to the robberies. No one should even be looking for her. But Callaghan wasn't *anyone*. He was obsessive. And he knew he would recognize her even if no one else did; the way she moved, the way she walked, it was ingrained on his soul.

"So not all roads lead to Rome," Sabine said as he walked up to him. Callaghan wasn't surprised to find the man here. He hadn't called him. Sabine had said he'd be watching him. Callaghan just hadn't bothered trying to lose him. He'd known the location would draw him out.

"So it would seem."

"Or so it *wouldn't* seem, I suppose," the LN-7 man said. "So,

Jack, what brings you here?"

"You show me yours and I'll show you mine," Callaghan replied, glad to see that Sabine was capable of smiling in response, even if it was a weak effort.

"Just out stretching my legs, getting some air. You know how it is."

"Right. And if I believe that, you've got a bridge to sell me, right? Okay, no bullshit, no beating around the bush: tell me about Hampton Court. Lie to me and I won't tell you what I've found out. Simple as that."

"How much did you overhear?"

"Assume I heard nothing. What I *will* tell you is that the plans for Hampton Court were stolen at the same time as those of the Maritime Museum. Now, I don't believe in coincidences, meaningful or otherwise."

"Interesting," Sabine said.

"So with that in mind, I'm guessing that whatever you went there to look at was down to the same thief that I'm after."

"That seems like a reasonable assumption."

"So are you going to tell me?"

Sabine shrugged. "Honestly, there's not a lot to tell. We had to deal with an incident."

"And that's as clear as mud."

"We lost one of the team and two more were seriously injured."

"I'm sorry." Callaghan fell silent. There wasn't much he could say to that. He didn't know the guy well enough to sympathize. But he did know what it felt like to lose a team member. It had happened to him once, during the riots down in Brixton. It wasn't something he'd wish on anyone. Ever.

Sabine broke the silence. "There's a possibility I might have seen your thief. There was a woman heading downriver as we approached the jetty, but she was there and she was gone before the thought of pursuing her even occurred to me. To be honest, I saw her, but the minute our boat passed hers she was out of my mind, like I'd never seen her. I didn't even remember her, or link her to your investigations, until now."

So close.

He made a decision.

"Look," Callaghan said. "I get it. You and I exist in different worlds. I don't pretend to understand the stuff you deal with, but for whatever reason, it's obvious our worlds have begun to overlap. We've got a choice: we either act like the other doesn't exist, or we put our heads together. I think it's time we put our heads together, myself. But only, and I mean *only*, on the understanding that this is just between me and you, right?"

"Fair enough," said Sabine. "Then I guess both your station and mine are out of the question. You know a decent café?"

"Better than that," he said, and led the way to his car.

CHAPTER 40

WRITTEN IN BLOOD

The front door was wide open when they reached Callaghan's house.

The glass panel beside the lock had been shattered.

It wasn't his thief's work.

Callaghan pushed the door open with one foot, and stepped inside.

His senses were assailed by the unmistakeable stench of death. He'd been in enough death houses to recognize it.

Sabine drew his gun. "Stay back," he whispered, moving past Callaghan. It wasn't the first time in the last couple of days that Callaghan regretted his decision not to carry a handgun. The armed response laws had changed to deal with the new threats, allowing officers to carry, but it remained a matter of choice. There fear of escalation never really went away, the entire British logic being that if the police weren't armed then there was no need for the villains to tool up, either, meaning less fatalities. The world had changed, though. More police chose to carry. Callaghan was just old school. Guns made him uncomfortable. He had never fired one. Not that a gun would help here; he knew without setting a foot in the lounge it was too late for any kind of gun. There was no one alive waiting for them.

Knowing that and seeing *why* were two very different things.

They found the dead banker on his knees in the living room; the only thing that stopped him sprawling onto the carpet was the fact that his hands had been nailed to the coffee table.

It was more than just a sign; it was a trademark.

"I take it this is the handiwork of your friendly East End gangsters," Sabine said.

"I don't think there's any doubt about that," said Callaghan, pointing to the mirror. There, written in what was almost certainly blood, was a two word message: *You're Next*. The consequences of not recovering their property seemed pretty clear.

Sabine ignored the banker's body as though it was of no consequence, moving to the dining room.

"I'll get this taken care of," he said without turning around from the dining table.

"This is my mess," Callaghan replied, realizing that the man was examining the second set of index cards he'd left on the table. "I'll call in, get SOCO out to go through stuff."

"My people are discreet, Jack. Right now I think discretion is important. Let me deal with this."

"Fine."

Sabine shuffled the cards about. Sniffed. "Good. Thorough. I've got a few extra things we can to add to these. Got a pen?"

Callaghan wrote on a couple of extra cards: on one he recorded the theft of the plans to Hampton Court, on the other the plans to the Tower.

Sabine rearranged the cards by crime scene and took some of the blank cards to write on himself; enough to make a duplicate set. Callaghan watched as he recorded details in exactly the same manner that he had: a single fact on each card.

In the column for Hampton Court he added cards recording the death of his colleague, wrote the words "hedge monsters," the theft of one of Anne Boleyn's dresses and some jewelry, and on a final card wrote a single word. It was a word that held no meaning for Callaghan: *taint*.

Sabine started a new column headed with the words "The White Tower" and added a card with the same word beneath that: *taint*.

"I think it's time I improved your education," said Sabine. "But we might want to do it somewhere with fewer corpses?"

CHAPTER 41

DRESSED TO KILL

Alice's police scanner burst into life as they made their way along the river toward the Tower.

Shadwell had arranged for transportation, another boat, not as sleek or fast as the one she'd used the other night, but more than fast enough for the Thames. He insisted on steering, even though it was clear he'd never steered a boat in his life. Under other circumstances it might have been amusing: two men and a woman in a boat. It wasn't quite Jerome K. Jerome.

Joseph Pennington clung onto the side of the boat as though his life depended on it. He looked anything but the suave, debonair Daea of the Summer Court now. He was out of his element. His pallid skin looked decidedly sickly. His raven black hair streamed behind him. The wind tore at his clothes. His fingers dug into the wooden rail behind him. She couldn't remember ever seeing him this ill at ease. He had wanted to make his own way there, but Shadwell had insisted that they stay together. Joseph had argued that the three of them together was inviting trouble, but Rufus was having none of it.

"Do you really have to go so fast?" Pennington asked as the boat bounced through the waves. It hit the corpse of a dead dog floating in the river.

Shadwell laughed. He was enjoying himself. That in itself worried her.

Alice couldn't catch every word on the scanner; it kept crackling and cutting out, but from what she could hear it seemed that football violence was at the heart of it.

It wasn't hard to imagine what was happening. Football had always been tribal. From the sounds of it, rival supporters were standing up to each other and old enmities were resurfacing. Match days had become a show of defiance over the last few years, offering a chance for ordinary people to forget about their fears and behave as though nothing had changed, as though London was exactly the same as it had always been, when football had been more important than matters of life and death. That was the wisdom of Bill Shankly, one of the greatest managers of all time, and back then it had been true for a certain kind of fan.

The psychology of violence wasn't difficult to understand. They'd gone through a short period of freedom from fear which allowed for the release of pent-up frustration and anger. That violence was always going to explode according to the color of the shirts and the affiliations of people who didn't belong to their tribe, be it Tottenham Hotspur, Arsenal, Fulham, Queens Park Rangers, West Ham, Millwall, Palace, or Chelsea. The colors of the shirts replaced the colors of their skin, their religion, or any other segregating factor, and gave them an excuse to beat each other senseless, surrendering to the mob mentality without having to feel like they were subhuman.

But today seemed to be different. If the panic in the voice of the operator was anything to go by, today was *worse*.

Reports came through thick and fast as they piloted the Thames. Violence was breaking out in different parts of the city. Fans gathered at their own grounds and set off, marching through the streets of London toward the grounds of the traditional enemies, taunting them as they smashed shop windows and set light to parked cars. Petrol bombs and Molotov cocktails lit up the sky, detonating one after another. Around the Seven Sisters Road between the Emirates and White Hart Lane it could have been a DMZ.

The furor was working in her favor, providing a layer of distraction.

The police were going to be too caught up in the civil disorder to worry about her and the two men she was traveling with. Even the river police were being called in. It was all hands on deck.

So, knowing that she wasn't going to have to concern herself with the police getting in the way, now all she had to focus on was getting past whatever lay inside the walls; whatever it was that guarded the Tower.

When she'd pushed Shadwell for details, all he'd said was that he had a plan to get her in. She could only assume that he knew how to break down some of the charms that protected the place, but there was a huge element of trust in that assumption and she wasn't a trusting woman. As far as Shadwell was concerned, she trusted him about as far as she could throw him—and that was just over the side of the speedboat into the black water of the Thames.

She was prepared. *Amat Victoria Curam*—victory loves preparation. She was already wearing the dress she had stolen from Hampton Court, ready to play the part, or rather ready to *become* the dead queen. What she intended went beyond playacting.

It wouldn't be long before they reached their destination, and what she hoped would be the easiest way for them to get within the walls of the Tower.

There was something unsettling about entering the Tower through Traitor's Gate wearing Anne Boleyn's dress. After all, that had been how she had entered the Tower herself, and everyone knew how her life had ended there.

Alice hoped the same fate was not about to come her way.

CHAPTER 42

PANIC ON THE STREETS OF LONDON

There was something very wrong about the violence that was erupting in and around the city.

Callaghan listened as the reports came in over the radio. It had been like listening to one of the old Radio Four *Play For Today*s, right up until the mass of fans had come around the corner and surged toward him like a tidal wave. They didn't so much as break their stride as they overturned a police car that had been parked in the middle of the road to try and slow them. It became an opportunity to cause damage, not a deterrent.

It wasn't just football fans, of course. Running along with them were thugs in search of violence and looters ready to take advantage of the cover the fighting provided. There was no one to stop them smashing shop windows and helping themselves to flatscreen TVs and Xboxes and anything else that took their fancy when so many bodies were forcing their way through the street. It was impossible. A tsunami of violence crashing on the shores of London.

He didn't have time for this. Not today.

Sabine had received a call, said nothing beyond, "I understand," and left him alone. The man was infuriating. No sooner had they agreed to join forces than he was off playing the Lone

Ranger. And, of course, he had refused to share whatever it was that required his attention so urgently, fobbing Callaghan off with, "It's not connected to our case, trust me." Callaghan had found that hard to believe. At the moment *everything* seemed to be connected to everything else, and Sabine, despite everything he'd said to the contrary, was only paying lip service to the idea of sharing.

There was no way the crowd was going to stop their inexorable progress, and no way Callaghan could stop it, so he threw the car into reverse and backed up, fast, swinging the car into a hand-brake turn and down a narrow side street that he hoped would take him away from the press of bodies.

The last face he saw in the rearview mirror was a familiar one. One of the fans leading the march, chanting and raising a fist with the rest of them, was Danny Jackson. Detective Constable Danny Jackson. Jackson had gone undercover with N17, one of the football firms, trying to discover just how coordinated the gang violence was. There was just one problem: Danny Jackson had died in the line of duty six months ago. Callaghan had attended his funeral and sat with his kids at the wake.

Callaghan tried to make eye contact with the man, just so that he knew that he was being watched, before he peeled away, full pelt down the alleyway.

He managed to catch Jackson's gaze.

The man stared at him for a moment, but showed no reaction, no emotion. He was utterly dead inside. Callaghan shuddered. He wasn't the only man in the crowd utterly devoid of emotion, shuffling relentlessly forward. Plenty of the other men around Jackson were displaying enough emotion for all of the ones who weren't—a mixture of rage and excitement, of raw anger and hunger for violence—but not the ones like Jackson. They just went through the motions.

There was nothing that Callaghan could do without destroying his cover, even if he didn't understand *how* Jackson could be there, so he did the only thing he could do: he floored the accelerator and left the once dead man there in the middle of the fighting.

Another call came in on the radio reporting another incident.

It was the same everywhere.

Violence was breaking out in pockets all over the city without rhyme or reason. In the space of five minutes, reports came in of fighting in run-down neighborhoods close to Kings Cross, and down by the leafy suburbs of Stamford Bridge and the King's Road, Chelsea.

Callaghan parked and pulled out an A to Z and started marking out each of the flashpoints with a pencil.

Contrary to first impressions, these weren't random acts of violence. They were coordinated and converging on the major transport routes.

Someone was trying to bring London to a complete standstill.

CHAPTER 43

TRAITOR'S GATE

Shadwell cut the boat's engine and it drifted slowly toward Traitor's Gate.

The entrance into the precincts of the Tower was barred by a metal gate which needed to be opened from the inside. Even if they could somehow angle the boat close enough that Alice was able to touch the rusted and pitted surface of the gate, she knew that her gift wouldn't be up to the task. Opening Traitor's Gate was going to take more than a little manipulation of internal mechanisms or melting part of the lock's barrel.

That was why she'd conceded to Shadwell and the pair of Seelie fae were here with her now. As he'd so stubbornly pointed out, she couldn't do it alone.

Pennington looked ill after the trip up the river.

"Well, I guess now's the part where I tell you you're going to owe me for this, right, lovely Alice?"

"I think I've paid you plenty, Rufus. More than plenty."

"Letting me touch you doesn't count as payment. I think I should probably charge you for that. I hear I'm rather good."

"I wouldn't believe everything you hear. Women are notorious liars when it comes to pillow talk. *No, no, it was lovely, yes, I did, the best I ever had, so big.*"

"I do so miss how we used to banter. There was a real spark between us."

"I can't say that I remember it."

"Now, now, do you want me to help you or not, Alice?" Shadwell laughed. He beckoned Alice to take over the wheel, even though the boat was doing no more than drift, bumping up against the portcullis. Shadwell moved adroitly, clambering onto the prow of the boat, his footing sure despite the layer of Thames water that slicked the wooden sides of the speedboat. The boat rocked in the water. Shadwell rode the sudden movement with ease, adjusting his balance as he edged toward the great metal gate, always somehow keeping his footing even as he stretched out. She thought for a moment he was going to grasp the iron gate. He didn't.

Just as he had done on Alice's sky rise balcony, he began his transformation, his body blurring into raven form. This time, though, there was no longer the element of surprise. Alice watched as though it were no more miraculous than any other piece of theater; showmanship that demanded an audience. It would have been preferable if he had been able to carry out the change a little less ostentatiously, but as much as it pained her to admit it, he was right, she needed him. Shadwell took to the air. She watched as his wings outstretched, taking him out across the Thames to start with, allowing him to gain the speed that he needed to maintain flight, and then he rose, climbing as he circled the Tower, just like any other raven might do.

There was something majestic about him as he flew, a natural grace. Eventually he glided out of sight.

Now it was a matter of waiting.

In the silence, Pennington suddenly turned to her, concern in his voice. "Watch out for him. He can't be trusted. I make a habit of staying out of other people's messes, but just this once I'm going to make an exception, mainly because he dragged me into the middle of it. Rufus is a bad man. I'm serious. He'd sell his mother for something shiny if he took a fancy to it. He shouldn't be a raven; he's a jackdaw at heart. And like any hoarder of pretty things, he's just as liable to discard them a week later without a second thought."

"Don't worry, Joseph, I know what he's like. And you know me every bit as well as he does. We've all danced around each other. I know he hates you. I know you hate him. But you both love me, right?" Alice grinned. "Anyway, I've been there, bought the T-shirt, remember, so don't worry about me."

"Of course I worry, you silly girl. It's Rufus. And back then it was *you* who did the discarding, was it not? That changes things. I don't think Rufus likes the word no. I imagine he's just waiting for the opportunity to prove you were wrong, and then break your heart. I can understand the obsession; of course, you really are quite an exquisite creature. Comely." He smiled, the spark of his charming self there in that instant.

"Hush, you," Alice said, shaking her head. She knew exactly what he meant when he talked about *comely*, and she had no intention of falling for his effete charms and giving herself up to become one of his comely ones. She'd almost succumbed to that once before. She didn't think she'd be able to save herself a second time.

They waited for what seemed like forever.

There were spikes set into the brickwork. It wasn't hard to imagine the heads of Enemies of State adorning them. The longer they lingered, the more likely the chance of someone marking their presence and raising the alarm. The sight of a boat moored near the gate was conspicuous enough, but when one of the passengers was dressed as Anne Boleyn, it was nothing short of remarkable. Her only hope was that any observer simply thought they were watching the ghostly procession repeating the queen's last hours.

"Come on," Pennington urged. He was on edge. She watched him. He had a ring on his ring hand, and kept playing with the white-gold band with his thumb, flicking it, polishing the underside of it, twisting it around his finger. He was growing more and more agitated the longer they waited.

She didn't say anything.

She felt curiously calm.

She closed her eyes, soaking in the bloody history of the watery tunnel into the Tower. She touched the wall beside her, wondering if the dead queen had done the same thing on the way to meet her maker, or if she had simply sat in the small boat, calmly awaiting the gate opening?

Eventually the sound of rusty metal straining filled the air.

It seemed impossible that everyone inside the Tower grounds, or even beyond, wouldn't hear the noise. But no one came running. No alarms split the dark day—the huge cloud made it feel like permanent night this close to the Tower. At last the huge iron gate juddered and started to rise inch by inch into the ceiling of the tunnel until it was high enough for the boat to sail beneath.

Alice started the engine, giving it just enough throttle to build the momentum it needed to sail through the gate before she cut it again.

On the other side, she and Pennington clambered out. They pushed the boat back through Traitor's Gate, hoping that it would remain out of sight at least long enough for her to get into the Tower itself. After that, it wouldn't make a lot of difference if it was discovered. The gate came down hard, splashing into the water. The boat was on the other side. She wasn't going to be able to leave the way she'd come in, but that had never been part of the plan.

Shadwell was waiting for them as they clambered up the dead man's steps from the water's edge. He did not offer an outstretched hand to make it easier.

This was always going to be the easiest part of the plan, but only because of her ex-lover. Without Rufus, she'd still have been on the outside looking in. From here on in, things got difficult.

Alice adjusted her dress, setting the corset properly on her hips and straightening the wig, in an attempt to make herself look less like someone who had just taken a wild water ride along the Thames and more like a dead queen.

She took a deep breath.

It was time to become Anne Boleyn.

CHAPTER 44

CROWD CONTROL

Thomas Sabine had seen plenty of strange things in his life, but this was quite unlike anything he had come across.

He had taken up a vantage point to watch one of the mobs of football supporters as it grew to take on a life of its own. He recognized the colors of the InterCity Firm, the firm associated with the claret and blue of West Ham. He saw one skinhead with a T-shirt declaring: *These colors don't run!* The ICF were amongst the worst of the football firms, having earned their name terrorizing the InterCity train lines on match days during the 1980s. They were thugs of the worst sort.

He ignored the looters; they were using the mob as cover and weren't part of its angry heart. And he discounted the obvious hangers-on who had just come along for the fight. Instead he concentrated his attention on those in the replica shirts and the scarves. The claret and the blue colors that didn't run. These were the things that separated the tribes. The colors. He had heard people talk about football as being tribal before, but he had never experienced it for himself before today. Here, now, on the streets of London, the tribes were going to war.

The mob grew, gathering smaller clusters of fans into it as it raged down the street.

Devastation trailed in its wake. Smashed windows, cars overturned, lampposts bent, bulbs shattered, street signs torn down, garbage bins torched.

They were chanting.

The chants grew louder and louder with thousands of voices singing the same thing in time until they became a single voice, chanting: *"I'm forever blowing bubbles!"* They marched in time to it, their feet sounding a militaristic beat to accompany the inane words, as the chanting took on a life of its own.

Behind them, though, more men shuffled in eerie silence. They were like some tidal swell of humanity…only…there was something about the way they moved. It took him a moment to realize what was wrong about it: their feet dragged and their knees didn't bend, making them lurch awkwardly. He stared at this part of the mob, looking for details, clues. They were so much better dressed than the rest, wearing suits and ties, their hair slicked down. And then he saw the rot that had begun to set into some of them and realized what he was seeing: the dead risen from the cemeteries of London to join the riot.

"Not good," Sabine said to himself. It was one of those delicious British understatements. He crossed himself. He wasn't a religious man. The motion was ingrained in the psyche, as though divinity might help. It never seemed to.

He saw another firm coming in the other direction, chanting to the tune of "Que Sera Sera," their words more vicious, promising: *"When I was just a little boy, I asked my mother what will I be? Will I be Arsenal? Will I be Spurs? And here's what she said to me: Go wash out your mouth son, and go get your father's gun. Shoot some Tottenham Scum!"*

The living and the dead marched on.

He looked back at the ICF crew as the grunts at the front stopped still, almost as though there was an invisible barrier holding them back. He expected them to bellow some sort of challenge and charge the rival firm, but they didn't. The row behind them pushed into the front men, knocking them to the ground and stumbling themselves. There was an eerie moment when none of the skinheads made a sound, they just continued to surge forward, running over each other, grinding their fellow hooligans into the road. And then people screamed, but that did not stop them surging forward. All that it succeeded in doing was bringing an end to the beat. At the back, people still chanted as the bodies piled up, claret and blue shirts clawing at claret and blue bodies as the dead marched over the living.

Sabine watched in horror as the mound of bodies grew higher and higher, men and women becoming entangled as the mountain rose. It took him a moment to grasp what, in truth, was happening. It was the birth of a very different kind of Carrion. The dead scrambled and clawed their way up the piles of bodies, crushing skulls and arms and legs beneath frantic feet as they clambered higher up the stacks, until the mass of writhing bodies began to take on a cohesive shape: they came together in the shape of a man. A giant man made up of dead men and women that kept on rising, bodies piling upon bodies, until it towered above many of the buildings in the area. And, instead of chanting its triumphant song, the Carrion golem rose in eerie silence.

Then it began to walk.

The giant flesh golem was unsteady at first, lurching from side to side as it moved. But soon it was crushing bystanders and looters underfoot. And even as it did, it left no man behind, absorbing their crushed corpses into the vast human golem. It grew taller and taller until its head dragged the black clouds above the city.

The living ran from it.

It wouldn't be difficult to track the giant's progress across the city, but there were so many people moving around down there on the ground, small clusters of hooligans either trying to scramble away from the Carrion golem or looking to join in the fight, opportunists looking to capitalize on the chaos. Either way, Sabine couldn't risk getting swept up into it. Instead he made for the best vantage point he could think of: the river.

The boat that the Three-Seven's cypher team had used for the trip to Hampton Court wasn't in use. A quick call in to Alpha managed to secure it and the services of a pilot. He told them exactly what he was following and requested backup. Looking at the sheer size of the giant creature, it was going to take more than just a few flame-throwers to bring it down—not that they *could* burn it, he thought, imagining the "innocents" who had been swept up inside it.

It was hard to tell for sure. Most of the golem appeared to be risen dead, responding to the unseen magician's call, but there *had* to be some living men trapped in there, too. It was impossible for there not to be.

By the time he was on-board he saw a second golem, this one swathed in the blue and white of Tottenham's N17 firm. The claret and blue golem had crushed the resistance of the Arsenal fans before they could even begin to form their giant. But now these two behemoths of writhing bodies were coming together on a collision course to meet somewhere in the middle.

It took Sabine a moment to realize where the tribes would clash. He should have known.

"All roads lead to the Tower," he said to himself as the boat surged away from the Embankment.

The pilot didn't argue with him. His eyes were fixed intently on the Tower.

* * *

It was impossible to look at anything other than the inexorable march of the golems, but as they approached the Tower, Sabine caught sight of another boat approaching Traitor's Gate.

For a moment he thought he could see three people on-board, but it was difficult to tell with the black pall of cloud covering the daylight over the Tower. A moment later there were only two people and a raven flew across the water, skimming lower than he had seen one fly before, the beat of its wings raising a spume of white water in its wake. It wheeled around and turned back toward the Tower before landing somewhere behind the walls.

It was no surprise that there were ravens around the Tower, of course. The pair were inextricably bound together in mythology. The superstition was that the Tower would fall when the last raven left, and when the Tower fell, so too would the city, and when the city fell, that was the death knell of the country. Given the changes since the return of magic, the old superstition seemed more and more plausible and possible. That couldn't be allowed to happen. If the Tower fell, then whatever was bound within those walls and worse, whatever was down below in the Chamber of Sorrows, would be set free.

And while he didn't *know* what was down there, Sabine was in no doubt it was better for everyone if it stayed down there. The old white stone was like a well cap on the worst nightmares of the entire populace. Every reading they'd picked up, every occurrence of the taint, appeared to link back to the Tower in some way.

"Can you get me a clear view of Traitor's Gate?" he shouted across the engine noise. The man nodded, not even attempting to speak. He angled the boat toward Tower Hill and the Embankment.

Sabine knew that the golems must be part of some great plan that was somehow wrapped up with the problems that Callaghan was trying to unravel. Once and for all they proved the man was in way over his head. The ordinary forces of law and order might have been able to deal with a single thief, even one capable of using magic to help her in her work, but not this. Not golems of crushed corpses clashing like mythical titans over the rooftops of the city, fists of dead men clashing together. No, even the men and women of LN-7 were going to struggle with this. The Thelema would need to find some way to unbind the creatures.

The police would respond, of course. They had to. But all it was going to do was tie up resources and manpower in a battle against an unbeatable foe.

Sabine put in another call to Alpha as the boat picked up speed. He tried to make himself heard as the spray hit him in the face. "How's that backup looking, Alpha?"

"I thought you'd appreciate a visit from Three-Seven."

"That's my girl. I really hope he's bringing the big guns. I've got a bad feeling about this."

"Don't you always, Four-Five?"

"Doesn't mean I'm wrong, though, does it, Alpha?"

She laughed at that.

"Looks like we're crashing a party in the Tower."

She didn't laugh this time.

The boat swung out toward the center of the river, kicking up more spray in its wake. There were no other birds in the air, Sabine realized, as the boat turned in again, cutting across its own wake.

He could see Traitor's Gate clearly.

It was open.

There was no sign of the boat.

Then he saw it come bobbing back into view, empty. And the metal portcullis came down to bar their way.

They were inside.

There was nothing good about this.

Nothing.

The pilot took their boat up toward the gate, coasting on the churning river, but made no attempt to get close.

The other boat drifted toward them.

Sabine reached out to snag it, and as his hand came into contact with the wooden hull, he had that strange feeling again, the one he had experienced when he shook hands with Callaghan, and again on the river on the way to Hampton Court. Sabine was certain he had just seen Callaghan's thief disappear into the Tower.

CHAPTER 45

GOING TO THE CHAPEL

There was more than just the White Tower within the walls of the Tower of London.

Alice felt a lingering regret that she had never managed to make a return visit before it had been locked and the public barred. It would have been nice to walk the place again. It had been a long time since she last had. But she had studied the plans in detail. She had seen the aerial photographs, some in books, others on archive film footage that had been made for visitors in the dim and distant past. She knew the layout intimately, knew exactly where the Chapel of St. Peter ad Vincula was within the general layout, down to the number of paces from the river jetty to the door, but she still felt vaguely disoriented as she adjusted her dress again.

Pennington and Shadwell were nowhere to be seen, but she could sense their presence close by. They were unique creatures, even here in the Tower.

On the open grass, a few of the Tower's ravens pulled and pecked at the ground in search of grubs and worms venturing too close to the surface. She wondered if the Seelies were hidden amongst them? She doubted it. Shadwell had some reason for coming along and it wouldn't be to hide out among some ravens.

Alice was torn.

Her every instinct was to be secretive; to try to stay out of sight and reach the chapel without being seen by anyone, because anyone who might see her had to be a threat. The place was protected by more than just charms or wardings. It was the most protected building in the city, with security far above and beyond surveillance cameras and motion sensors. But it was all guesswork on her behalf. She assumed there were charms, talismans, geegaws, and wardings, but had no way of knowing if there was anything of the sort. The magic of some places was simply down to reputation; if enough people claimed it was impenetrable, it became impenetrable simply because of those whispers. They acted as their own form of defense. But the Tower was different. It had to be. When they said it was defended they meant it was *defended*.

But by who, or what?

Who would guard the one place in the city everyone seemed afraid to go?

It was a question she didn't have an answer for.

Alice's plan relied on her being confident, on her being able to stride to the chapel as though she belonged there, so that any eyes that happened to catch even a brief glance of her would let her pass unquestioningly.

If the Seelies had walked at her side, the ruse would not have been as effective. This was not like Hampton Court. This was not a tourist attraction that still tried to function as a visitor's center; this was a place with death ingrained in the fabric of each and every stone.

Alice stood at the chapel door. She had thought about this moment for most of her adult life. Planned for it. She was prepared to have to use her gift to unlock the door to the Chapel of St. Peter ad Vincula—St. Peter in Chains—but she didn't have to. It was unlocked. She was relieved. She hated the idea of using her touch to manipulate something so ancient, ruining it. This was the final resting place of dead queens and saints, regardless of the fact that they had met their end here on the executioner's block. Inside these walls were the bones of Thomas More and John Fisher, executed for refusing to support Henry VIII's creation of the Church of England and its separation from Rome. Here also lay Anne Boleyn and Catherine Howard, queens who were guilty of that heinous crime of failing to provide their husband with a male heir, along with Lady Jane Grey, the original nine-day wonder, made *de facto* queen of England for that length of time but never crowned.

Alice respected the history of the chapel and the echoes it left behind; she could almost feel its sorrow as she placed one hand on the door.

CHAPTER 46

GIANT

Callaghan tried to put a call through to control to share his suspicions about the transportation hubs, hoping that might at least make deployment smoother, but the whole of the city was already snarled up. The radio was down and the landlines were all engaged.

He was not surprised.

People panicked. Panicked people called 999.

Football firms running riot would jam the switchboards up.

The dead rising up from the cemeteries of London would do a lot worse than that.

Callaghan slipped out of his car and started to jog back to the main length of the Seven Sisters, where the Spurs fans were moving along like a relentless tide of pent-up rage. He was looking for Danny Jackson, but it was like looking for a needle in an angry haystack. He didn't know what he was going to do if he found him. The dead didn't just rise up again and decide to riot their way through Holloway. That didn't happen. But…

The Seven Sisters Road was a solid mass of people. He couldn't see any way that he would be able to push his way through them to reach Jackson at the front of the mob. It would have been easier to drive right through the middle of them, or try to work his way through the side streets and get ahead of the mob, rather than this. He cursed that one moment of decision-making, and turned.

As he did so, he came face to staring face with of one of the Spurs mob, who yelled: *"Jambo! Paxo! Deptford! Get here! Now! Tiffers! Shubes! Archie! Get this bastard! Orps! Come on you slag! Tomst! Get in here! And you, Foof! Roberto, you muppet!"* The guy's mouth was ringed with spittle as he reamed off the list of names right into Callaghan's face. His mob seemed to respond, chants of *"Yiddo! Yiddo!"* rising above the chaos. *"Oasis! Eggsy, lad, come on! Mutters!"*

For the moment at least, there was no way that Callaghan could return to his car. Instead he found himself being swept up into the crowd to become part of the tide of humanity flowing along the Seven Sisters Road toward Arsenal.

The chanting rose in volume and urgency now that he was part of it. He was forced into step with the others; a regular *thump, thump, thump* jackboot march to provide the backbeat. He couldn't turn back and he couldn't move forward. The mob filled every inch of space across the width of the road. People clambered over parked cars because there was no room to go around them. A uniformed police officer tried to hold them back, like Canute trying to stem the tide. He called into his radio for assistance but no one was listening. Even if they had been, there was nothing they could do to help him.

And then the mob was on him.

For some reason the people at the front of the queue stopped suddenly, making it seem as though the lone policeman really had managed to hold back the rioters all by himself.

The mob was claustrophobic. Dizzying.

The constant press of bodies increased each moment, threatening to crush the breath out of Callaghan. He was trying to walk forward, the momentum of people behind him forcing himself on, even though no one was moving in front of him. He could hear chanting and yelling from the front of the crowd, but beyond it, it was eerily silent. He kept trying to see over the top of them as the tide of humanity pushed mercilessly at him.

He tried to crane his neck to get a better view, using the man in front's shoulders to lift himself up high enough, and as he turned, looking back the way the crowd had come, he saw a couple of tall people. Then he realized they weren't tall, at all, but standing on something. There was something about them…like Danny… He saw one of them fall, and then someone took their place.

He knew what they were standing on now. He didn't have to see the huddled up bodies of the fallen curled up in the middle of the road being trampled.

And it was all done silently.

The sheer mass of bodies continued to push at him, and in moments was reduced to a mass of limbs. People ought to have been crying out in pain. The fact that they weren't told him more about the nature of the monster forming in front of him than he could ever want to know. Behind him, the pile of dead men was almost fifteen feet high when he felt himself being swept up into it. The men in front of him, Tomst and Orps and Jambo and all the others, fell badly, making a ramp that Callaghan couldn't stop himself from being swept up, his feet walking on their backs and chests and faces.

He looked down and caught a glimpse of a bloody face as a boot came down on it.

Callaghan rose with the others, climbing and staggering and slipping on the broken backs of dead men and trapped Spurs fans, but somehow kept his feet and kept on rising up the man mountain, finally able to breathe. The sudden sweet relief of the air came at the expense of the others beneath him, but this was one of those occasions where there had been no choice. His fate had been sealed the moment he had taken that first step into the street. After that there was no way that he could have turned back.

But what now?

He felt the pushing again as more bodies clambered onto the pile, self-preservation driving them on to get to the air, others seemingly moving without any sense of free will at all, like zombies.

That's what they were, of course, like something out of a Romero movie.

It was all impossible.

Callaghan wanted to scream, but no one else was.

He just wanted to hear *something*. The silence was freaking him out.

Callaghan leaned forward, trying to reach for the rooftop of a house across the street, thinking he might be able to drag himself free of the madness, but lost his footing, and even as he tried to save himself, fell.

He landed on the man below him. Callaghan did everything he could to avoid what happened next. He kicked and yelled and screamed and grabbed at the shirts and belts of men above him; he tried to drag himself across the top of the bodies, but it was useless. The weight of bodies piling down on him grew heavier and heavier by the moment. It was irresistible. Inescapable. Each move was agony. It tore at his busted knee. It pulled at the cartilage and sent daggers of black agony through the ball joint, firing his nerves off, but he had to ignore it, or at least best it. It was that or die.

The mountain of bodies started to heave and sway all around him.

Callaghan was convinced that it was about to topple to the ground as the thing that he had somehow become a part of began to walk.

In the distance he saw the Tower.

He knew that he was no longer a bystander in the strange events that had been touching his life. He couldn't move. Not so much as an inch. Bodies pressed in on all sides, crushing the life out of him remorselessly.

In the sky he saw a small black shape circling the Tower before it swooped down to land beyond the wall.

And he screamed…

CHAPTER 47

TAKE FLIGHT

The men carried the head of the traitor Bran all the way from the Welsh Marches.

A single sword stroke had severed it from the rebel's shoulders as he kneeled like a supplicant...but it would not be silenced! It profaned, it cursed, it damned his enemies for all time. On and on.

At first the warriors tasked with the burden had been in awe of this miracle, but as the journey wore on, it had become tiresome.

They tried to silence him.

For the long walk, the head had been followed by black birds who refused to be frightened away; this was just another reason why he was called the Raven King.

At last, though, with the head wrapped in sackcloth, they have reached home and they will be able to silence his curses once and forever.

Callaghan circles above them, watching as the men begin to dig the hole that will be the final resting place of the Raven King's head. The head lies on the ground unattended while the ravens respond to his muffled shouts with caws and cries as though they can communicate with each other.

And perhaps they can, the dragon thinks.

This is an important moment.

This hole will contain whatever lingering magic Bran's head possesses. It will be used for good, as part of the city built around it, and as part of its defenses.

Callaghan feels a surge flow up through the ground, sparking through the air like lightning reaching up for the sky, and in that surge, he feels the heady joy of battle again, reliving the victory once more. But more than just the battle, this moment is key; it is the anchor, a fixed point in time. It had to happen. Always. It is more important than any single moment the dragon has lived through.

The ravens take to the air and form a great black cloud as they bank and flock; so vast is their number that even whilst constantly in motion they seem utterly still, hovering in the air with their wings outstretched over the Raven King's head.

Behind them there is another shadow, blocking out the sun.

Dragons flying toward them fast.

At the head of them is the unmistakeable shape of the dragon that was once the greatest of them all: El Draco. Set in his skull is the biggest diamond Callaghan has ever seen.

It is the gem that will one day be called the Koh-i-Noor.

CHAPTER 48

IN HER SHOES

Alice left the chapel door open, letting the dimmed daylight flood in.

The light cut like an arrow through the gloom, but it fell a long way short of the altar, barely making it halfway down the aisle.

She took a deep breath before stepping inside.

This was something new; this was more unnerving than any of the robberies, any of the fights or confrontations, even the one with the Wolf-King in the shadow of the DLR. She had no idea if this would work, or why it even should, but if it did, she almost certainly wouldn't be the same when this was all over. If she was going to turn back, now was the time. She smiled. She was never going to turn back. If her plan worked then *any* price was worth paying.

Alice had learned the incantations by rote. She already knew that they worked. She'd been playing a long game, and her plan was too intricate and important to allow an element of chance in, so she had tapped into the taint and used it to raise the spirit of someone likewise closely ingrained with a certain place, like Anne. She had called to him and he had answered. This time the task could well be harder, if time factored into the equation. She was raising the shade of a woman who had been dead much longer. The last time she had summoned a man, but he had not come alone. He had brought someone with him. His brother. They were so closely bound that death had reunited them, not divided them.

She had only meant to bring back one of the Kray brothers, but as the old song went, you can't always get what you want. Instead she had actually succeeded in returning both of them to the East End. It had taught her something about the process, though. She had found herself privy to secrets they had wanted to keep to themselves, reading them like an open book.

That was how she had learned about the coins and why, when she'd felt them calling to her, she had been unable to resist. The fact that they were the same coins Rufus had wanted was just an added bonus; what the Seelie didn't realize was that she'd played him. She'd wanted him to come after them. Him or Joseph. They had gifts she needed to breach the Tower walls. Sure, it made things so much more complicated. But, it also meant she was here, now, inside, so complicated wasn't necessarily a bad thing if you planned for it.

In the near-darkness of the chapel, there was precious little light apart from the sliver of dull sunlight spearing in through the door. What little there was came through dirty stained glass windows that had been left neglected for years.

A shadow passed in front of the door.

Her heart leapt into her throat.

But when she turned, she saw the figures of Pennington and Shadwell, both returned to human form, watching her.

Alice knew where the dead queen's burial was commemorated, but that was not important; her spirit was linked to this place, and not to the bones that lay beneath the ground.

She steadied herself and then knelt on the cold stones, focusing on the chill. She hadn't expected to have an audience while she carried out the ceremony. She closed her eyes and tuned the two Seelies out. They were irrelevant. As far as she was concerned their job was done. They had opened the gate. They could go now. She didn't need them. She had a job to do. Of course, Rufus had some other reason for accompanying her. And Joseph hadn't helped with opening the door, so she wasn't sure quite why Rufus had insisted on his presence. She pushed the rogue thoughts from her mind. She needed to keep a clear head.

She held her arms out wide, concentrating on her fingertips as she whispered the dead queen's name, urging her to make herself known.

Alice felt the echoes in the room stir. She felt the reverberations that ran through the stones, the traces of things that had happened within these walls being woken. She licked her lips. A cold chill ran down her back. She shivered. She listened to all the voices as they called to her across the years, each of them hoping that they would be the one who was being called, praying that it was their turn to live again, to breathe and taste and touch and feel, that she was offering them a way out of purgatory.

But there was only one spirit she sought.

She called again, naming the shade. The spirit resisted. The dead queen was challenging her, testing her strength, to see if she was worthy. Alice imagined her, summoning the pain and the doubt she must have felt in her final days, drawing upon the grief of the old stones and the sorrow that had bled into the dirt outside, drawing it all into her. Again she called her name. The fine hairs along her forearms and nape of her neck bristled. The chill grew in the chapel, turning the cold stones icy. And finally, Alice felt her entering the room.

She opened her eyes to see the beheaded queen, restored in death.

They had a connection.

The shade moved slowly toward her, ghosting over the stone floor, each step against her will as Alice drew her in.

She felt the queen pushing against her, straining to break the spell. She heard her in her head, cursing and spitting, nothing regal about the words spitting from her tongue.

But Pennington and Shadwell only saw the dead queen walking one step at a time toward their girl. It was a battle of wills not of physical strength. Alice stood slowly. She did not merely need to have the dead queen in the room, did not just need Anne to leave the chapel with her, she needed the shade of Anne Boleyn to be *part* of her.

They had to be one body, one entity, if she was going to fool the protections placed on the White Tower.

After all, the dead queen was one of the few truly at home in the Tower, meaning she could come and go as she pleased.

That was what Alice's entire plan hinged upon.

The shade of Anne Boleyn moved closer, inch-by-inch, as Alice concentrated harder and harder on drawing her near. She wanted to move, just to close the gap between them so she didn't have to fight so hard; every step of the way drained Alice, but she knew that moving would break the connection. Right now it was that fragile. She had to remain still.

Behind her, Pennington spoke, but Alice could not spare the attention to listen to what he was saying; she focused intently on the sound of her own voice. Nothing existed beyond that. She blocked out every other sound.

She suspected that Pennington had guessed what she was trying to do.

She prayed he wouldn't try and stop her.

"Come to me," she breathed, reaching out. At last the shade was within touching distance. Alice touched the dead queen's hand. A spark leaped between them, arcing from one fingertip to the other as the connection sealed between this world and the next.

Alice twined her fingers between Anne's and the queen moved closer. The touch thrilled her. It was more than just electric. It reached across five centuries, fueled with the raw energy of all that history, the countless sorrows, the denials, and the innocent blood, and it only intensified as they came together, nose to nose, brow to brow, breast to breast, until the two of them occupied the same space at the same moment in time.

Alice turned slowly to face Pennington. Joseph had taken a few tentative steps toward her, but Shadwell hadn't moved. Anne's face slid across hers, not yet fixed in place. She could feel the shade accepting the comfort of her heartbeat, the one thing the dead could never have. And at last the shade was one with her, complete. For the first time Alice wondered about what would happen now. She'd never really believed in her heart of hearts that the scheme would work, that she could raise the dead queen and force her to take a sort of vacant possession of her bones…

In that moment she knew the first glimmering of fear: Would she even be able to release the shade and reclaim her body as her own when she was through?

Alice started to walk toward the door, slowly at first, needing to be sure that the shade did not slip away, finding a way out of her skin. She need not have worried. The ghost had no desire to leave Alice's body. Alice could feel the sense of euphoria, like an adrenaline kick, that the shade released, but beneath that, behind it, between all the firing synapses and neurons, there was something else…a shared *recognition*…another link.

There was no time to think about it now, but later she would need to understand.

For now, at least as far as the Tower and its defenses were concerned, she was Anne Boleyn made flesh once more, not some outsider who did not belong. Alice had every right to move freely wherever she chose.

And she chose to enter the White Tower.

Joseph Pennington stepped out of her way as she walked past him. He had a look somewhere between avarice and admiration on his pale face, and half a smile. She had always suspected the Seelie was drawn to the dead in ways she couldn't really grasp and didn't want to contemplate. She had heard stories of the comely and the coarse.

Alice stepped out of the chapel, and Anne took her first deep breath of air, fresh after the staleness of death for five hundred years. It was intoxicating. Overwhelming. Alice didn't know how long the bind would remain, especially as each new sensation, even one as simple as taking a breath of air, threatened it. She could not afford to delay even a moment longer than absolutely necessary.

She headed for the Tower, all too aware of the swish of fabric against her legs and the thrill of simply *feeling* again.

The ravens watched her intently.

CHAPTER 49

Two Princes

A lice raised her hand to the door.

It started to swing open before she had even touched it.

There was only darkness inside. Not so much as a chink of daylight crept in as the door opened wider. The daylight shunned these corridors. The cold stone embraced the shadow and the night and the dark places. Even when the door swung open fully, the sunlight barely turned a few feet of stone floor grey. Everything beyond it was black.

From inside she heard a voice, an old voice that spat curses and called people to take arms, to rise up against the enemy. *"Fight! Fight! Take flight! Fight!"* Only it wasn't English. It was Welsh. The old tongue. She knew the words well. She had lived in that part of the world for a long time in another life…an old life…

Her skin bristled.

She stepped inside, instantly wary of the voice, but still determined.

Her prize was close.

"Get inside!" Shadwell barked, pushing her through the door. His manner had changed completely. He was no longer encouraging; that natural arrogance that seemed to be part of his kind's character was gone, replaced by cold, ruthless efficiency.

"Whatever I say, you do it. You don't question me. You don't hesitate. You do it. Understood?"

She nodded.

"Good."

Shadwell descended into the blackness. She followed him. Each step taking her closer to the voice still spitting its curses. Alice's eyes adjusted slowly to the gloom. There was some feeble light that filtered in through the windows on the stairs. The staircase curled around three complete turns, taking them under the earth. She could feel the change in the air. The voice was louder now, barking commands and challenges. She saw what was talking. It wasn't a man. There was an iron cage suspended by chains that hung from the ceiling.

It swung on the chains the more violent the epithets became.

There were other passageways beyond the chamber, fresh excavations deep into the earth, down into the Chamber of Sorrows, through the bedrock and silt and dirt, to the entrance of a narrow stair so clearly not crafted by human hands. She was within fifty feet of the entrance into the Black Cathedral below, and all of the horrors of that vile place, but ignorance, and Shadwell, saved her.

He wasn't remotely interested in what was deeper down below.

He walked slowly toward the center of the chamber, and stood before the cage almost reverentially. He placed his hands either side of it, on the chains, and breathed in deeply. "Forgive me, my old friend," he whispered, which seemed the strangest thing in the world for him to say, and grunted as he lifted it down.

Alice saw at last that the voice was coming from a severed head that was held within the confines of the iron cage. It had a ragged beard and empty sockets where eyes should have been. Shadwell worked the couplings that secured the cage, and pulled the grille back. The head shouted its triumph. Shadwell tangled his fingers in the long, matted locks of raven black hair and lifted out the head.

"Do you know who this is?" he asked Alice.

She shook her head, but for one sickening second she lost her grip on the shade inside. Anne did not turn her head. Alice felt her face blur, reminding her just how tenuous her hold on the dead queen was.

STEVEN SAVILE

"This is the head of Bran the Blessed, the Raven King."

The voice continued to talk, becoming more and more impassioned, and while Alice could grasp the tone, and recalled some Welsh enough to grasp the underlying meaning, this time she did not know any of the words. They spilled from the Raven King in a rage. She thought she didn't know, but then a memory stirred, something long buried. She could no longer be sure if it was hers or Anne's.

Shadwell looked at her. "You have minutes. I would stop wasting them if I were you, lovely Alice. Run along, find whatever it is you're looking for, and for the love of…well for the love of Bran here, do so quickly so we can get out of here," he said, starting back up the stairs.

She had to rush to follow him as he climbed, taking the old stone steps two and three at a time. He moved with a purpose. She couldn't remember ever seeing him like this. Not ever.

"Where's Joseph?" she called after his back as he disappeared into the darkness above.

He didn't reply.

He didn't slow even half a step.

She felt the sudden temperature drop all around her. Her breath frosted before her face. She reached out, but it wasn't her hand reaching, it was Anne's, touching the vapors.

She stopped dead in her tracks, halfway between one step and the next, as something moved in the shadows above her. Two figures seemed to have stepped out of the very stones. They were small, the shades of two young boys, and they walked hand-in-hand down the stairs toward her.

She took a step up, onto the next stair, and then another, but too quickly, and her shoe caught in the hem of the old dress, tearing through the lace. The bustle was too unwieldy, the dress too heavy; as she tried to stop herself from falling she only made it worse. Alice fell, hitting the stairs hard. She tried to scramble away as the children descended.

She couldn't imagine a sadder sight.

She knew, or rather the shade inside her did, who the poor boys had been. The Princes in the Tower, imprisoned by their uncle, Richard the Third, who had then had them murdered in secret so that he could claim the throne for himself. The boys who should have been kings, but never grew up to be men.

They moved toward Alice.

As they stepped into the light, she saw the malice in their faces.

It was impossible to tell if she was their intended victim, or if it was the ghost of Anne they had come for.

CHAPTER 50

ETON RIFLES

Sabine stood in the shadow of Tower Hill, in almost exactly the same place he had been when he'd met Callaghan on the hill. The boatman had returned to Traitor's Gate to make sure that the thief would be unable to make her escape by water if that was her plan, while Sabine lurked outside the walls, keeping a vigilant eye on the main gate.

He really didn't like this place. The permanent swathe of shadows, the storm clouds churning in the sky above, the eerie silence that surrounded everything. It was sinister. He couldn't shake the feeling that some nameless evil watched through the darkened windows of the Keep, staring at him even now.

He knew a little of its history—how William the Conqueror had built his tower on the Cornhill the ravens had already been resident in for millennia, guarding some deep, dark secret. What drew them to the Tower in the first place, no one knew, or at least no one remembered. Some of Crowley's old texts claimed the Guardians of Athoth had placed them there after the cataclysm, knowing there was some great well of evil there, and had set the seven ravens, Hugin, Munin, Garmin, Cedric, Gwyllum, Hardey, and Incantatious to stand vigil. *If those birds could talk,* he thought idly, *what secrets would they tell?*

He checked his watch.

"ETA on Three-Seven, Alpha?"

"One minute, Four-Five."

And true to her word, a black van screeched to a halt only a few yards from him within sixty seconds. The back doors were flung open and a squad of armed men tumbled out.

He recognized some of the men now. Trusted them. They were used to combat in every kind of condition, armed with equipment capable of dealing with *any* situation. And it wasn't just a case of automatic weapons; they had everything imaginable at their disposal, including one man, dressed in a simple T-shirt and jeans, who looked nothing like a solider. He had a plain face, shocking blue eyes, and thin blond hair that was balding. Sabine knew what he was: a Thelema, an adept in magic, capable of dealing with those taint-raised things. He looked at Sabine. "Pulsford," he said, giving his name, but the way he said it, it might just as easily have been his rank, or a defensive warding against the waves of tainted air pulsing from the Tower. "Are you running the show?"

Sabine nodded.

"Situation report?"

He told them the little he was sure of, resisting the temptation to fill in the blanks. "No offense," he said to Pulsford, "but I really hope we don't need you."

"We should wait until this thief of yours emerges," Pulsford said. "Minimize the risk to our people, not put them in danger simply by entering the Tower. We shouldn't go in unless we absolutely have to. This is about containment. Who knows what's in there?"

"We can't let her slip between our fingers this time," Sabine said, shaking his head in disagreement. "We should go in after her, try to stop her before she gets what she's come for." He had an inkling of what she might actually be, if not who. She was certainly no ordinary thief, not even one who had been touched by the taint. She was unlike anything he had ever come across—apart from Callaghan. The two of them seemed inextricably linked. And that was a whole other problem.

The ground shook all around them. Echoes of giant footsteps rolled down Tower Hill and bounced back from the far side of the river, rolling over them. Sabine explained what he'd seen, how it had started as the press of rival football firms, but the dead had joined them and come together to form the towering Carrion golems. "It's like a manifestation of their tribal spirits," Sabine said. "I don't know what's holding them together, but it's powerful, whatever it is, and sure, it's different in terms of size and the actual dead things they're composed of, but they're fundamentally the same as the Carrion we encountered down in the Underground. So the odds are it's the same man behind it. I assume you've been briefed?"

The Thelema nodded.

"Good, that makes things easier. There's no other discernible difference. The Carrion came together as an amalgam of dead flesh and bone. These are flesh and bone." Sabine shrugged. It was an eloquent gesture. It spoke volumes.

Again, the Thelema nodded.

"I'm good at what I do," Pulsford said matter-of-factly. "Trust me. I can control the forces I channel. If needs be, I will tear the golems apart person by person."

"I don't even want to think about it…but some of them may still be alive in there."

"That's not my problem," Pulsford said, turning to watch the giants approach.

The claret and blue ICF golem was only a matter of streets away, while the blue and white N17 giant was towering over the buildings of the financial district as more and more men were absorbed into them.

"Maybe they'll take a few bankers with them," one of the cyphers joked.

Gallows humor.

Sabine knew it could only be a matter of moments before the two clashed.

"Fancy seeing you here," Three-Seven said, joining them. "You've got an uncanny habit of turning up in the most interesting places, Four-Five."

"I was going to say the same thing."

"Great minds and all that."

"Fools seldom differ, I think you mean."

"That's the one. Okay, boys, hate to break up the party, but…" He jabbed the muzzle of his submachine gun in the direction of the entrance to the Tower. "Duty calls."

CHAPTER 51

TAINTED LOVE

A lice lay transfixed, unable to tear her gaze away from the shades of the young princes.

They stopped two steps above her, all the while still holding hands as though over time they had become inseparable. Anne knew their story, and their horror. Alice imagined them reaching out to comfort each other in their fear, finding strength in the simple act of being together, but now it was different. They were stronger together than they could ever be apart.

While they seemed fascinated by her presence, there was an element of confusion between them. They traded glances. They hesitated. And Alice knew that the shade inside her was proving sufficient to negate at least one of the Tower's spiritual defenses.

The eye contact was broken by the sound of someone rattling at the door that had closed behind her when Shadwell had pushed her inside.

But they were alone, surely? No one could have entered the confines of the Tower. It was impossible.

And yet there was someone outside.

She breathed in, resisting the urge to panic, and on that breath she recognized the scent of at least one of the men out there. She didn't know where from, but it was distressingly familiar. They had crossed paths recently.

Blue fire crackled across the door and someone cried in pain. She could smell the sudden acrid reek of burned flesh. It was sickly sweet. The princes turned their attention to the door. Something shifted in their demeanor. They no longer cared about her intrusion, or had somehow been reassured that she posed no threat to the Tower itself; or more likely, thought that the men outside were a greater threat and they could deal with her later. She wasn't about to stand on the stairs and argue just how dangerous she really was.

Alice started up the stairs in search of the Treasure Room, the Jewel House that contained the Crown Jewels and an incomparable collection of orbs, swords, crowns, scepters, and state regalia, and amongst them, the prize she had come for: *the Koh-i-Noor* diamond. The Mountain of Light, as its name translated, was what every single step of this journey had been leading up to. This was the culmination of everything. She felt her pulse quicken and took a moment to calm herself. She couldn't wait long, though, not if she intended to finish what she had started. And she would not leave this place without it; it would be better to become one of the Tower's ghosts than to disappoint the stone's true owner.

Shadwell lurked in a deep-seated window on the stairwell.

He emerged behind her as she tried to find the right room, the turns of the spiral stair having turned and turned her about. He watched her every move. She was uncomfortable beneath his scrutiny, and the presence of the shade within her and the sudden urgency caused by the men battering down the Tower door all served to confuse her memory of the layout. The hours she had spent poring over the plans felt absolutely wasted at that moment.

"We don't have forever, you know," Shadwell said. "Get a move on or I will be leaving without you."

The head in his hands let out another stream of vitriol, babbling words that meant absolutely nothing, and yet struck some deep, resonating note within Alice's bones. She knew what it was doing: speaking an enchantment.

"Oh, do shut up for a moment, Bran. Please, you're giving me a headache." He swung the head like a miner's lantern.

"Do you think it was wise to move it?" Alice asked.

Shadwell was not concerned.

Something occurred to her...no, to the shade inside her...a memory...linking the head to the Tower's fall?

She started to ask, "Isn't there something in the mythology here that if the head is taken away—"

"The Tower will stand as long as there is a raven left in the Tower," Shadwell assured her. "That's the myth."

But Anne remembered now. "The ravens are only here because of him. He was the Raven King!"

"Don't fret, my pretty little one, you'll get wrinkles. And besides, we'll be long gone before anything responds to this thing." He held up the head, ignoring its cries. "Or the lack of it. Now chop-chop, time's a-wasting."

Alice reached the door—and even in the semidarkness she knew it was the right one. She closed her eyes. She could almost feel the gem inside, calling out to the master that had once worn it. So strong was the link between the gem and the dragon. They had been one.

The door offered little resistance when she pushed it open. For years this room had been the most secure in the kingdom, home of trophies like the Confessor's sword and the Black Prince's ruby, but now it was as though the doors were throwing themselves open, the treasures begging to be stolen.

As the door opened, the head let out a single, sustained shriek that started a vibration that rose in pitch and intensity until it threatened to shatter every piece of glass in the building.

This was not the cry to battle, nor was it the cursing of enemies or the attempts at incantations it had released; this was a cry of fear and pain, the like of which Bran, alive or dead, had never made before.

Shadwell stepped in behind her and the head of the Raven King unleashed another harrowing shriek. He slapped it just as he would a hysterical woman. The head lashed about in his grip, its cries only worsening. Something in the room was causing it genuine torment despite the fact that the head itself was a part of the fabric of the building; it had lain here so long.

And that, more than anything, convinced Alice that she was in the right place, and that the jewel she was looking for was there. Because just like her, and just like the dragon, El Draco, Bran's life—and his death—was intrinsically linked to the stone.

The floor moved beneath her feet as she strode across it. And with every step she took, the tremors worsened. She refused to stop. The tower had accepted her as Anne Boleyn. She was inside the Jewel House. The *Koh-i-Noor* was within reach. If the reverberations were the defenses stirring, then so be it; they were not attacking.

It crossed her mind that it could be Shadwell's presence drawing new dangers to them.

"Stay outside," she urged, but he was having none of it. "Please. Can't you feel it?"

"I'll go wherever I want, Alice," he said. The delivery was sweet, but the meaning might as well have been snarled. "And I take whatever I want."

His arrogance was short-lived. He shrieked in sudden pain as the floor shifted and splintered beneath his feet.

He slipped a few inches then cried out again as his foot was dragged down between splintered floorboards.

"Take this," he yelled, no sweetness in his voice now. He held the head out for her.

"I'm not holding that!"

"If you want to get out of here you will. Do it!"

Reluctantly she took the head from him. She held it at arm's length, repulsed by what it was and what it had once been. Shadwell struggled to free himself from the splinters, which had begun to rip and tear at his skin, puncturing the flesh around his ankles. In moments he would be caught completely, as though this had been a trap set to catch vermin. And at that moment that was exactly how Alice thought of him. Vermin. She watched as he started to move his arms in that now familiar motion, trying to force the transformation so that he might take to the air and free himself.

There were more noises coming from the bottom of the stairwell. Alice could smell the distinct, overpowering reek of sulfur.

Something was coming up the stairs.

They had to move quickly.

She ignored Shadwell and moved around the room. She found the cabinet she was looking for. The agitation from Bran's head drew her toward it. She had been right; the ancient diamond was behind the Raven King's fear and discomfort.

The cabinet was locked. Of course it was, but not because it needed to be kept secure, but because no one had needed to open it. She could have touched the mechanism, fused it, but every time she tapped the magic a little of her strength was sapped, and not knowing what other trials awaited on the way out, it was just easier to break the glass. The only thing she had to hand was the head of the Raven King. She didn't even think about it. Gripping the fistful of hair tighter, she swung, smashing the dead man's head through the glass. It shattered into a million pieces while Bran's tormented scream could have easily shattered them into a million more.

She reached inside and snatched the *Koh-i-Noor* up, knowing that she was another step closer, but as she held the diamond in her hand, she felt a memory that was not hers sweep up, threatening to undo everything… She'd remembered it all before, but not like this—she seemed to tap into the eyes of another, recalling the Mythic Age from the wrong perspective. She didn't know how it was possible that she could share a vision.

The intensity of it frightened her as…

CHAPTER 52

THE LAST DANCE

The sky fills with dragons.

They cast great shadows across the land. Gouts of flame and smoke flavor the air with the unmistakeable tang of sulfur. This could be the last great battle between the dragons of Albion, the war to end all wars on this soil at least... It is hard to imagine many—if any—surviving the day. Here, today, it ends, and with it, so easily could their mighty race. Callaghan is caught up in the fever of battle... He roars... Rages... He is not concerned with survival; his only thought is to kill the enemy.

His name is not Callaghan.

His name is Callagh'an.

He is the dragon.

The thrill of speed rushes through him...all around him...his wings...the scaled spines along his back, and his tail. He knows exactly who he is, who he was, what he was. He knows it all. He is awake. He is a dragon here, now, in this time and place, Callagh'an, from the Isle of the Mighty, and Callaghan in the world where he is a policeman, but the two are connected, one a scion of the other. The two are the same. The two are awake!

In his head he hears a voice. It is a voice he knows... And it cries: Thief!

Callagh'an looks around to find his nemesis and he sees the great dragon El Draco approaching, his wings outstretched, claws reaching toward him... The diamond in his skull glints in the sunlight.

You robbed me of my mate!

The words boom in his mind and Callagh'an knows that El Draco means the dragon that he dashed against the hillside, the wretched creature he crippled in their last encounter. He takes no satisfaction in it. That fight is gone. Now they fight anew. And El Draco is stronger now, recovered and fueled by the need for vengeance.

El Draco slashes at Callagh'an...

The dragon beats the blow away with a wing, feeling the searing pain as a claw slashes through the leathery membrane, tearing him open.

He backs away, beating his ruined wing harder, desperately trying to rise, to climb higher, drawing his enemy away in the hope that he can gain some sort of advantage... But only now is he beginning to realize just how powerful the other dragon might be.

He may be older, but that does not make him weaker.

On the contrary...it makes him immortal.

Callagh'an swoops down as El Draco streaks upward, the vortices of wind tearing at them, downdrafts bullying them... He tucks his wings in tight beside his body, gaining precious extra speed as he dives...and snatches at the other dragon as they come close, desperately hoping to break a wing...

He fails.

Worse...

El Draco catches hold of him, wraps both of his huge leathery wings around him and bites deep into Callagh'an's neck, tearing through scale and meat with great teeth as they both plummet down toward the earth.

He feels the absolute black agony of muscle and sinew being ripped away from his neck, the excruciating pain of bones straining and cracking in the grip of the great beast.

El Draco releases him at last, climbing back to watch Callagh'an's fall... Callagh'an's wings are useless...every joint screams as he tries so desperately to move them...there is nothing...he is done... He falls and falls and although he lands in the sea instead of broken on the rocks and hard-packed land, it makes no difference.

The last breath of life has left him and his body sinks slowly beneath the waves.

CHAPTER 53

REVELATIONS

Callaghan strained for breath. It wasn't water that he was trying to suck into his lungs, but air. The golem still strode across London, moving ever closer to the other monster, the mass of humanity clothed in the other tribe's colors.

He couldn't move.

He couldn't fight it.

He so desperately wanted to find an ounce of strength, enough just to tear his lips free of the latticework of bodies so that he could breathe.

But he couldn't.

That last vision had been the worst of them all. He could still feel every blow from the battering, every cut and bite from the dragon. He could still feel the fire smoldering in his gut, and he knew it was burning out. He knew his nature even if he didn't understand it. His name was Callaghan, he was a policeman, he existed here and now. His name was Callagh'an, and he soared in the skies above the Isle of the Mighty.

Not that it mattered. He was going to die here.

CHAPTER 54

SUFFER THE CHILDREN

Waiting wasn't an option.

Something was happening inside the Tower.

The Thelema led them across the green to the gates.

The presence of taint was unmistakeable.

The skies churned, a vortex of black cloud boiling and bubbling as it coiled serpentine around the Tower of London.

There were a dozen charms bound into the metal bands that needed disabling, but they were little problem for Pulsford, who stood beneath the gateway arch with his hands outstretched and began to unravel the strands of magic with quick words and quicker wits. Sabine saw sparks of electric blue light crackle around the frame, chasing along the bare metal as the Thelema caught hold of one of the aspects of the defensive charm and teased it free. Sabine saw it as a color, a green band of light, but as Pulsford got at it, it turned a virulent, sickly black. And then it snapped. He repeated the process over and over, teasing out each filament of color and unweaving the charm that bound it to the gate, and then, with one colossal surge of will, he spoke the word of opening.

Done, the thin-haired, pale-faced man turned to Sabine and Three-Seven. "Over to you, gentlemen."

They took the men inside.

Seven ravens watched from the grass. Other creatures lurked in the shadows. "If they aren't a threat, move on. We're not here to purge the nest," Three-Seven told his men. Still, they broke away in pairs, chasing down the shadows. The staccato bursts of gunfire were enough to scare all but the most stubborn ravens away. When the first burst of flame scorched the earth, even they scattered.

The door to the White Tower was more challenging, even though it was not clear what was stopping them; the door was unlocked and the handle turned, but try as they might, the cyphers could not open it. They tried pushing against it but there was no give in the wood at all, which would have been the case had the door been braced from the inside. Three-Seven pounded on it. In response, a sizzle of blue fire cracked across it.

He pulled his hand back, howling in pain as he staggered away. What was left of his right hand was a charred and blackened stump. Curls of smoke and the reek of burned flesh filled the air.

"Get that thing open!" Three-Seven barked at the Thelema.

The wood changed as Sabine looked at it. The knots in the old timber became eyes. The rich grain gradually took on the outline of two small figures. Boys. They didn't emerge from the wood. They were like carvings of nymphs, but for the sheer malice in their faces.

The team backed away. Pulsford looked at the figures in the wood, unsure of what they were dealing with, until the two child-like guardians began to push their way out of the door.

"Break the bloody thing down if you have to!" Three-Seven barked, and immediately his men sprang into action.

"No," Sabine said. He didn't shout. Sometimes quiet words contain the most power. Every single one of Three-Seven's cypher team stopped, including Pulsford. The Thelema turned to him. Just being this close to the Tower caused a stabbing pain that drove deep inside him. There was magic holding the door closed. But not in the way they thought… "It doesn't feel right… I don't know why but…can't you feel it?"

"You have an idea?"

He shook his head. No, he didn't have an idea, but…he felt the most incredible sadness looking at the two children as they met his gaze. Tears glistened in their eyes. Looking at them hurt his soul.

The team waited for the word. It was only a few seconds coming, but it felt like forever to him.

And then the two children began to cry. Their sobs affected everyone who could hear them, even the coldest of the men. There are few sadder sounds than the cries of a child in torment. The men in the team who had children, grown men who had fought the most terrifying foes, were reduced to tears, choking back the sobs that the two princes drew out of them. Their grief was contagious.

Sabine was caught, tears streaming down his cheeks. He had no idea how much longer he could bear to look at the children, or how much longer it would take for the grief to cripple him.

With a supreme effort of will, he broke eye contact.

It lessened the effect of their tears, but only a little.

He didn't want to break the door down, but they couldn't stand here, exposed. Even these few seconds had put the team at desperate risk.

"I'm so sorry. I'm so very sorry," Sabine said, knowing what the cost of this one little victory over the taint would be. "Do it! NOW!"

The weeping worsened. Beside him, Three-Seven succumbed to gut-wrenching sobs. Sabine felt his own sorrows being drawn out by the two princes, and wondered what sorrows the cypher commando was being forced to recall.

There was movement above, high on the roof.

He stepped back farther, trying to get a better view.

Tears stung his eyes, making it difficult to see clearly.

There was a man perched there.

No.

Not a man.

"Get the damn door open!" Sabine could barely focus on the figure up there, but he could see that there was something wrong with him; he was half man, half bird, trapped in the midst of transformation, so he was both and yet neither. "Whatever you've got, C4, magic flaming missiles, just get that door open!"

CHAPTER 55

THE LAST RAVEN

Still carrying the head, Alice followed Shadwell as a raven up toward the roof.

He'd completed the shift into raven form, but blood oozed from a wound around one of his legs, a very visual reminder of the dangers that the Tower itself still posed to them.

She closed her fist tight around the *Koh-i-Noor*. She knew the legends of the gem: any man who claimed it would suffer only misfortune, while a woman who bore it would rule the world. She had no desire to rule the world, only to serve her mate. She was still shaken from that last vision—the vision seen through another dragon's eyes. Callagh'an. The one who'd dashed her against the rocks and left her for dead. The one who was killed by her mate in revenge.

Her mate. The emptiness inside her threatened to consume Alice, but she had to remember that he was alive, here, now.

She had found him, El Draco, even if he didn't know his own nature yet. That was why she had needed to find things to wake him. Only a few hours ago she had pressed the Drake Jewel into his hand, and watched as the consciousness behind his eyes changed. The gem from the necklace had started the awakening, but the Drake Jewel had done a lot more, she could tell. That had been the most incredible moment, him coming back to her. But still, he was only waking, not awake. That was why she needed the *Koh-i-Noor.* To finish what she had started.

"The things we do for love," Alice said to herself.

As they were about to emerge into daylight, Shadwell's raven shimmered, the blur of wings thickening. He stepped out of the shadow-black circle, returned to his human form. He stretched his arms, rolled his shoulders, and then tossed his head back, shaking his long hair out so that it whipped at his face. Alice wondered how easy these changes were, and if there was a price to pay for each transformation. That was the way of every magic she'd ever encountered—and the price was always punishing. She couldn't believe that he could really keep changing back and forth at will without causing some sort of physical damage.

She gripped the head tighter. Bran hadn't stopped talking for a moment. She was getting used to it. It was background noise now, like a radio tuned to a foreign station. She held the diamond in the other hand. There was nowhere in the dead queen's dress to safely secrete the gem.

"Where is Joseph?"

"He is waiting for us on the roof," Shadwell said, pushing open the door. In doing so, he let the daylight in.

Alice closed her eyes against the sudden brightness.

Shadwell moved in close, she thought in a show of gallantry, to help her negotiate the threshold, but instead he snatched the head from her, ripping it from her grip. She was left clutching a handful of bedraggled ratty hair in her fingers.

He stepped out into the light, and turned in a circle, holding up Bran's head, first seeming to show it the world, and then to get a closer look at it.

The head spat and finally stopped cursing Shadwell as it felt the fresh air touch the remains of desiccated, enchanted flesh that still clung to its skull.

"Better," Shadwell said.

"Where?" Alice asked. She couldn't see Joseph, and there was something uncomfortable about Rufus's grin. What she *could* see were the gigantic flesh golems staggering and lurching toward the Tower. The sight of all of those bodies, all of those men and women crushed together in their football shirts in with the vile scum of dead risen from the cemeteries shocked her. She had known what to expect, but knowing couldn't have prepared her for the reality of it.

Alice was at Shadwell's mercy now and she knew it. She had entrusted him with the task of creating diversions in the city to keep the police occupied, but she hadn't believed him capable of such wanton carnage. She should have known. She should have known there wasn't a shred of morality or humanity in him, that he was utterly misanthropic, a sociopath in its purest form. It was a horrible lesson to learn about someone you'd once shared a bed with.

Again she heard the sounds of commotion at the bottom of the stairwell. There was no going back down there.

A cry distracted her from thoughts of panic; it was agonizing, and it was close by.

She spun around, trying to locate it. The cry came again, half man, half raven's caw. She saw Pennington lying on the ground. He writhed in brutal torment. She saw feathers where there should have been skin and realized that he was trapped, caught between human and raven. More slick, black feathers lay on the ground beside him. They were soaked in blood.

"Joe!" Alice cried, doubling up in empathic pain as soon as they made eye contact. She rushed to his side, and knelt down beside him. He reached out for her with one feathered hand. She clasped it.

"I…warned…you." He barely managed the three words, and the last ended in a raucous caw that split the blackened sky.

She let go of his hand. Her palm was streaked with blood. She eased him upright, looking for the wound. What she found was barbaric; his arm-wings had been clipped and were utterly useless. He couldn't lift them, never mind move them with anything like the speed needed to complete the transformation. She looked Joseph in the eye. She said one word. "Rufus?"

He barely had the strength to nod.

"Shadwell!" she yelled. A storm was gathering. It whipped away her words. "You did this to him didn't you?" She wiped the blood on the dead queen's dress. The other Seelie had disappeared. She laid Pennington down gently on the shingled rooftop, promising she wouldn't leave him.

And then she saw the raven peering at her with beady black eyes from the battlements. She rushed toward the bird, but only succeeded in startling it into flight. The raven carried Bran's head in its clawed feet.

"SHADWELL! Come back!" she shouted, leaning out over the wall.

As her voice echoed off the Tower walls, the thing she—and the city—most feared, happened. The seven ravens that had been scouring for food on the stretch of grass known as Cornhill took to the air, joining Shadwell.

No. Not joining Shadwell. Following the head and the voice of the Raven King.

How could she have been so stupid?

She knew…

She knew she couldn't trust him…

And yet she had.

And he had betrayed her.

Alice screamed.

The sound of booted feet and more screams from down below shook her out of the stupor. She ran back to Pennington's ruined body. Both of them were covered in his blood now. It looked worse on her dress than on his dark suit, but so much more real there.

"We have to stop him," she said, begging Joseph to have a plan, a way to undo her mistakes. He could barely lift his head. He couldn't make a difference. Shadwell had seen to that.

"It's too late…," he wheezed. "This was his plan all along, don't you see? 'Each separate dying ember wrought its ghost upon the floor…'"

"No. You're not dying, Joseph. You're not." A burst of gunfire down below begged to differ.

"He knew that the head had been dug out of the ground when Mathers excavated the Tower. I don't know how he knew, but he knew… And he's snared me in the perfect trap. That bastard always gets what he wants, Alice. Always."

"But…"

"But the legend? The raven? That's the joke, girl."

"I don't understand… The Tower, the country… If the legends are correct, then both will fall…"

"Only when the last raven leaves," he said.

"They've gone," she said, looking up to see the black birds trailing after the Raven King.

"Not all of them, Alice. I'm still here, clipped wings and all. I can't go anywhere. I'm the last raven, you see?" He laughed bitterly. "Not any old black bird. A raven. And I can't leave. The Tower won't let me leave. That was his plan. He wasn't stealing the head for itself, he was stealing it so that I would be trapped here. And now he can claim what he's always coveted."

"I don't understand."

"It's simple. Poe's 'The Raven': 'Each separate dying ember wrought its ghost upon the floor—'" He broke off, cawing. When he found his voice again it was only to say, "'Nameless here forever more…. All my soul within me burning… Quoth the raven, nevermore…'"

She looked at him, not understanding.

"That's the grand joke: me, a ghost upon the Tower's floor. He wants The World's End. He wants the comely ones and the coarse. And now there's no one to stop him."

CHAPTER 56

Burning Down the House

There was no finesse to it. The grief of the children was too much for Pulsford to cope with; he had tried to open himself up to the magic and let the karmic forces flow through him, but the place was so tainted he felt his self-control failing him and had to withdraw, leaving Three-Seven to give the order for the boys to bring the big guns in and burn down the wooden door. As soon as the flames had begun, the shades had disappeared back behind the wood. The flamethrowers were every bit as effective on the haunted door as they had been on the hedge creatures.

At last the metal braces hinging the doors buckled and twisted and the huge doors crashed in. Two of the cyphers came up to the front, moving fast, and sprayed the flames with a burst of extinguisher foam. As the flames were smothered, the rest of the cypher team charged inside.

The shades of the two boys were waiting for them on the other side. They grabbed the first man across the threshold before anyone was able to fire on them. It was Three-Seven with his ruined hand. The ghostly boys hugged him like a long-lost father returning home after so long away. But this was no happy homecoming. There was raw agony written all over the man's face. Every last trace of happiness was stolen from him in that "loving" embrace. He was left with only the pain of sadness, infinite sorrow. And finally even that wasn't enough to sustain him. The last spark of life was taken away.

His gun discharged as he fell, the bullets seeming to disperse the ectoplasmic matter the nearest child was made of, perhaps, Sabine hoped, giving him peace at last after centuries of being trapped in that place.

Pulsford stepped in. The taint flowed through him. It was written on his flesh, black lines where veins lay were picked out starkly. They covered every inch of his face as he crouched beside the second boy. "Join your brother, little man," he said, almost sympathetically, as he embraced the ghostly child.

The child's screams as he was banished went beyond anything they had been subjected to thus far.

Sabine heard movement from a floor above.

Done, Pulsford stood. He took over from Three-Seven, issuing instructions as to who should be where without a moment's pause, but having seen the taint flowing through him, his men refused to obey him. Sabine offered the same instructions and they moved instinctively. He knelt beside his fallen comrade—a man whose name he didn't even know—and knew immediately there was no helping him. He stepped over Three-Seven's corpse. There was no time for sentimentality. Death couldn't be changed. Three-Seven would still be there when they had completed their task. He told himself he'd remember to ask Alpha for Three-Seven's name; it seemed important to him now.

Something had changed inside Sabine with the death of Three-Seven. There was a fatalistic confidence there that he had not felt before. He climbed the stairs in the midst of the men rather than following on behind them.

His objectives were simple: apprehend the thief, and gather all the information they could about the taint while they were here. They weren't going to be able to secure the Tower on a permanent basis—quite simply they didn't have the resources for that—but every piece of information would be vital in their fight for the future.

The men in front veered off to a room with an open door.

Sabine stood in the doorway. The Treasure Room. The Jewel House. The thief was long gone, having claimed her prize from amid the Crown Jewels.

He had seen the strange half-creature on the roof. It had to be part of the thief's plan.

He didn't wait for the rest of the team; he charged up the final flight of stairs to the roof. Sabine burst out of the door, oblivious to the potential danger that could have been waiting for him, and stopped dead in his tracks.

A woman—a stunningly beautiful Asian woman—in a blood-stained medieval dress looked up at him. She cradled the half-man in her arms. Tar black feathers and blood surrounded them. It took Sabine a moment, but suddenly it was all blindingly clear: this was why she'd broken into Hampton Court. It had never been about the jewels. Looking up at him, she bore a striking resemblance to the woman she was pretending to be.

He couldn't imagine why she thought she needed the fancy dress costume to break into the Tower until she looked up at him, and for just a second, her face didn't follow… No, that wasn't quite right, it was a blur, like an afterimage, as though her soul trailed just a fraction of a second behind her body and was suddenly visible. The features were that similar, but there were differences too: the ghostly thief was not beautiful, not in the same way, despite sharing almost identical bone structure. She was plainer, and yet somehow more authentic…the word regal sprang to mind, and suddenly he was left thinking that in that momentary blur he'd witnessed the impossible: a past life peering out through the eyes of the current one.

And seeing her in the dress, knowing where it was stolen from, knowing that tragic woman's ties to this place, he knew what life was looking out at him.

"Oh, what have you done?" Sabine said, but there was no way the words would carry to the woman. He looked at her. He looked at the broken man-bird cradled in her arms. He didn't have a weapon. She didn't know that. He moved as though reaching for a gun at his hip, easing his hand slowly inside his jacket.

"Don't do anything stupid," he said. The woman's features

blurred constantly, the two faces struggling to occupy the same space. It was the continuously changing expressions that confirmed his suspicion.

The thief lay the bird-man down on the rooftop, then stood. She was at once ugly and beautiful. He felt that same momentary frisson he'd felt as they passed on the river, the same sudden intense heat he'd felt grasping Callaghan's hand.

"Don't make any sudden moves. Put your hands above your head," he said, knowing she wouldn't.

She turned her back on him, looking out toward the giant golems. The two colossuses were engaged in battle, swinging huge, lumbering blows at each other, and as each connected, dead supporters were hurled from the body of one to the other. The city beneath them was stained with death. Broken bodies lay sprawled out like discarded rag dolls where they'd fallen from the towering men. He could make out the shapes of men within the golems, locked arm in arm, legs entwined, a solid wall of flesh and blood so impossibly compacted by the sheer weight of bodies there was no way anyone within those huge limbs could ever walk away.

Each movement made the ground tremble.

They came closer and closer, those that could, screaming, those that couldn't, already dead.

They were just like the Carrion they'd encountered, in every way. The man who had raised these had almost certainly been practicing his dark arts down in the Underground...

He reached for the woman, to pull her back, as one of the colossal figures staggered and stepped over the Tower Wall, planting a huge foot in the ground where centuries before the executioner's axe had swung. The proportions of the golem's body were wrong. It was top heavy, too many corpses crammed together in the upper chest like some idealized warrior built to intimidate and not negotiate city streets. Those huge muscles had displaced its center of gravity, moving it dangerously high up the mountain of corpses, and making it almost impossible for the golem to stop if it started to fall.

Sabine watched in horror as it blotted the sky out above him completely. It teetered, half-in and half-out of the Tower, threatening to come crashing down as the second golem struck, landing a juddering blow to its chin.

The golem reeled.

The woman didn't hesitate; she threw herself over the edge.

CHAPTER 57

LOSS

A lice fell.
    She had no idea if it would work; she hadn't had time to think it through. She sent out a desperate prayer to the diamond she clutched in her hand. She didn't ask for much, only that she wouldn't simply fall to her death.

She *had* to return the diamond to its rightful owner. She had to. Without it, she'd never be able to reawaken her lover. Not fully. That would mean life alone, knowing he was there, so close, but so far away. She couldn't let that happen, even if she had to crawl to him on broken bones.

She did not crash to the ground.

She made the jump with feet to spare, coming down in the huge cupped hand of the lily-white and blue N17 golem as it steadied itself, clumsily trying to regain its balance.

Alice lay on entwined corpses, with limbs bent into positions that they were never intended to take digging into her spine and side.

But she was out.

She let out a huge sigh of relief, unable to believe that she'd done it, broken into the Tower *and* escaped with the *Koh-i-Noor*. For a nanosecond she was thankful for Shadwell's disgusting creatures of distraction, as he'd ended up not only getting her into the Tower, but out as well. He'd helped her without even meaning to. A huge hysterical laugh bubbled up inside her, but before she could let it out, something broke inside her. Snapped. She doubled up in agony as the towering golem took a single precarious stride *away* from the Tower.

That was when it happened.

It was pain like no other. It was as though her liver, kidney, and lungs had been torn out of her chest in one vicious wrench, but that wasn't it at all. It was Anne. The shade was being torn from her; still grounded to the Tower, it couldn't leave the confines of its walls, even as a passenger in another body.

Alice felt the loss immediately; it went beyond pain. It was the loss of separation, of losing a part of herself, being diminished. She was less than she had been while Anne had walked with her.

And it was unbearable.

All she could think was that death would have been preferable to this. She couldn't understand it. The bond shouldn't have been so *complete*. It was as though they were a single soul, divided now in a way that they had never been divided before.

The golem strode away from the Tower, drawn down toward the river.

Was it following its maker?

One huge foot of corpses splashed into the water.

Every lumbering step crushed hundreds of cemetery dead, the shockwaves compacting ever higher up the huge thighs, the dead submerging in the mud and silt in the riverbed, sinking in deep.

It was hard to hear anything above the crush and snap of bones and the wrenching of muscle being torn from bone, but there was one sound quite unlike any other: gunshots. They were hardwired into the human psyche. Rooted down deep with the primal fears. There was no sound quite like them. Bullets strafed the sky, tearing into the bodies of the Londoners long, long, long dead—and while they might not have caused any more hurt to the corpses, they were a very real problem for Alice. She rolled over, pressing herself flat against the woman beneath her, her face less than an inch from the dead woman's blue lips. Rot and ruin was all around her.

Armed men lined the rooftop of the Tower; every one of them, save for the man who had tried to stop her jumping, emptied their weapons into the Carrion golem.

Bullets met dull wet thuds all around her, burying into dead meat.

And even though they couldn't kill something that wasn't really alive, each shot was doing damage. An entire cartridge of submachine gunfire tore into the upper arm above Alice, the bullets scything through the lattice of contortions the dead men and women had put themselves through to bind the golem. Parts of bodies fell away, each fresh burst of fire weakening the golem's construction.

It wouldn't hold together forever.

It couldn't.

One of the shoulders exploded with fire as something struck. It took Alice a moment to realize it was some sort of Molotov cocktail, filled with oil that soaked into the bodies. The "lucky" few, hooligans who had been swept up into the Carrion creature but had somehow managed to scramble away from the crush of bodies before they were absorbed, clung desperately. One man screamed as he fell toward the water. His luck had run out.

A few others, still very much alive, found themselves trapped within the framework of its chest, protected from the worst of the crushing weight by the corpses around them forming a kind of grotesque skeleton. They couldn't scream. It was all eerily silent.

The corpse creature strode out toward the middle of the river, diminishing with each step as it lumbered out of range of the weapons.

The golem was undeniably weakened, each new step dangerously unbalanced as it splashed down the river, but there was no way she could bail out. She had to see the ride through to the end, and just pray that the man of corpses clung together long enough to get her to her destination.

She had the diamond; all that remained was to put it in the right hands as soon as she could.

CHAPTER 58

ENTER THE DRAGON

Callaghan was painfully aware of the fact that he was surrounded by the dead. It was impossible not to be. But somehow he clung to life, even as those around him had long since stopped struggling, and whatever enchantment that had raised them failed. There was one small mercy in their second deaths: their bodies relaxed, creating a little more space within what he now thought of as the creature's ribcage, meaning he could breathe.

Some of the bodies slipped and fell whenever the creature stumbled, making survival a lottery. So far Callaghan had a winning ticket. It had been touch and go when the golem had stepped over the wall of the Tower of London, a tidal crush of bodies moving suddenly, teetering forward as it appeared to snatch something out of the air that fell from the top of the Tower.

Callaghan scrambled over those around him to find any precious space, just an extra couple of inches where dead meat wasn't crushing against his ribs. All he wanted to do was to breathe.

As the golem lurched away from the wall, the bodies parted, and through the gaps in the wall of dead flesh he saw someone lying on the palm of its hand; he knew her in her dress covered in blood...but he didn't know her. Bodies shifted, stealing her from view and driving the wind out of him. Callaghan fought desperately to extricate himself from the tangle of bodies, trying to wriggle between a woman and a man, both long gone. The bodies parted again, and this time the gaps revealed a new nightmare: this was not the only towering man of corpses.

He caught a fleeting glimpse of the woman again. It wasn't just any dress. It was like something out of a period drama. She moved in the golem's hand, rising to stand. Her balance was perfect.

He knew her.

It was the way she moved. It was *her*. His thief. It had to be. But what the hell was she doing here?

As if she sensed him, she turned in his direction.

Her face seemed to blur as he looked at her, but something passed between them in that instant, a sense of recognition. She knew he was there. He was *sure* she knew, despite the bodies between them. The connection was different this time, stronger than he expected. They'd shared that last "vision"—he had felt her there as he'd found his name—but more than that…he could *feel* something else…something deeper. The change. She'd gone through it too, though many years before. The awakening. He felt a sudden surge of energy spark through every body that lay between them, conducted by the dead, their arms and legs jerking and twitching and twisting as current passed through them.

The contact completed, the connection absolute, something inside Callaghan started to burn. He could feel it kindling, the fire rising, fueled by the change that had started that first rage within him—the one that had almost cost Morty his life. His clothes began to smoke and smolder. The heat coming off him ignited the clothes of the corpses around him. His senses were overwhelmed by the smell of burning flesh.

The dreams and nightmares were not visions of some impossible time; they were echoes. Memories of his past long suppressed. But not anymore. There could be no holding them back now.

His rage burned bright as the dragon inside him awoke at last.

In that glorious moment, as Callaghan surrendered to the ancient beast Callagh'an, who once soared through the skies above the Isle of the Mighty, his full power opened up to him, feeling every nerve and fiber of his being.

He blazed.

Brilliantly and brightly.

He burned.

Purging his flesh.

And in that searing heat more and more of the corpses around him caught light, joining in the inferno that slowly burned a hole in the fabric of the golem. Bodies plunged down to the river. And still there were no screams. The dead couldn't scream.

Callaghan loosed a huge elemental roar, tearing free of the bodies that moments before had crushed his legs and trapped his arms. He could see the riverbank through the gaping wound in the collapsing Carrion golem. He didn't hesitate. He hurled himself out in one huge leap of faith, kicking, arms windmilling, as he sailed through the air toward the shore. It was a fall that only hours earlier would have killed him. Not now.

The golem staggered back toward the shore, battling the current as its body slowly crumbled. His fire accelerated the rot started by the LN-7 bullets. The thing had no chance. It crumbled and fell, crashing backward. The corpses of its head hit the bank.

Callaghan hit the ground hard, the impact bone-jarring, but somehow not bone-breaking. He saw armed men running toward him. No, he realized, they weren't interested in him; it was the girl they wanted. She stood on a raft of bodies in the shallow water.

She stood absolutely stock-still. He did not blame her. It was hard to see what choices were left to her: death, capture, or the river. He knew what he would have done in her place.

His fire may have burned itself out, but the charred remnants of his clothes were still worthy of someone's attention. He scanned the crowd of faces to see if anyone was looking his way. He saw Sabine, but his attention was focused solely on the girl, as though nothing else mattered. He wasn't the only one watching the girl. Callaghan saw another intent spectator. A man he recognized; one he had not expected to see here.

Art Mortimer.

The jewel thief.

Unlike everyone else that had gathered, though, Morty was able to tear his gaze from the grotesque carnage of the collapsed golem and the dead, and turn his back on the beautiful Asian girl in the middle of the river, and stare straight at Callaghan.

What was Morty doing here? When he realized that he'd been seen, Morty started to run toward him.

The old man was moving faster than he had any right to.

Callaghan knew why.

They'd had this fight before.

They went back. Way back. The three of them. The thief, the old man, him. They are all part of the same bloody history.

Morty roared a challenge at him.

Callaghan straightened, ready to fight for his life.

But they were not the only players in the final clash; in that instant he'd forgot about the woman. There was nothing he could do to stop her as she ran to Morty's side even as he erupted in flame, releasing his own dragon. Callaghan knew the beast he faced. He had died at his hands once before.

El Draco; Drake's Dragon.

In that instant of recognition, Callaghan made the final connection, the last piece of the puzzle slotting into place. The thief was part of El Draco's brood; more than that, she was the great beast's mate—the dragon he had once dashed against a hillside in the Marches of Wales and left crippled.

He knew her.

She knew him.

She ran to El Draco's side, pushing something toward his clawed hands as his huge leathery wings beat in slow rhythm. She knelt, subservient. It was an offering. She was talking fast but he couldn't hear a word she said above the roar of the blood pounding through his skull. The dragon lowered his head to her, allowing the woman who had once been his mate to place the *Koh-i-Noor* diamond into his forehead. She kissed him before he let out a roar and a tongue of flame licked the ripples across the surface of the Thames.

Callaghan stood alone against the two of them.

Helpless.

He had no conception of what he was capable of, what his past meant…he didn't even have a bloody gun.

Impotent rage welled up inside of him.

He was going to die here.

After everything.

And that rage burned.

Burned.

Burned.

It was all consuming.

He saw fire behind his eyes.

Flames engulfing the city and all of the dead.

Fire.

A raging inferno he dared not release.

A huge conflagration he could not contain.

He was the fire.

He was the flame.

The fire was him.

The flame was him.

And he was the fury of both.

He opened his mouth to scream and the fire thundered out.

He raised his arms to the heavens and they weren't arms at all.

Callaghan felt the rush of heat, the churning air, and the beating of wings as he took to the sky, every memory eclipsed by the battle rage surging beneath his scales as he soared upward.

CHAPTER 59

BROKEN WINGS

Alice watched them rise into the sky.

Every instinct, every nerve and every fiber of her being cried out for her to join the fray, to shuck her mortal form and become once more the dragon she had been…but it wasn't that easy. She hadn't given herself over to the metamorphosis once since she had awoken. It would have been so much easier if she could. She wouldn't have needed to make her Faustian pact with Shadwell, Joseph wouldn't have been caught between heaven and hell like that, and the filth, Callagh'an as she recognized him now, would be dead between them. She didn't know if it was psychological, some sort of mental block, some last barrier blocking her way from complete transformation, or if it was physical, but she couldn't draw on that power. She couldn't become what she had once been. It was still inside her, but it wasn't…not truly… not liberated. Whenever she tried to tap the strength of the great dragon she was a scion of, all she found, ever, was the memory of Callagh'an dashing her body against the mountains, and all she ever felt was the agony of each and every bone in her body breaking.

It was worse than death. Death was an end. It was finite. Agony was infinite.

She stood on the banks of the Thames, and watched her master, her love, her mate, rage and roar as he shucked his mortal form becoming truly majestic once more, the *Koh-i-Noor* blazing in the center of his great skull. She wanted so desperately to fight at his side but knew that she would have only lessened El Draco. She had done her part. She had brought him back. This was his fight, not hers, and he had won it once before. He would do so again. And then they could rebuild their lives. They could be what they had always been destined to be. Their brood would rule the skies of London, bringing about the Dragon Age.

CHAPTER 60

THE DEATH OF SELF

Callaghan knew the ancient beast had beaten him with strength, guile, and force of will last time. He wouldn't allow himself to fall into making the same mistakes now.

He had to find a way to gain an advantage, to use the city, the black clouds, the river, anything that might give him the upper hand.

El Draco gave out a roar as he took to the air. The *Koh-i-Noor* set in the huge plate of bone above his eyes blazed the sun.

Callaghan held his ground. To attack now was suicide. He had to buy himself some time to test himself, to learn how agile he was, how fast he could fly—*how to fly!*—and the only way to do that was to flee. To fly out west across the city.

He rose higher into the sky, flying now. Awkwardly. There was nothing smooth or graceful about his ascent. But this was natural. He was born for this. Callaghan came down low over the river, almost skimming the surface as he streaked beneath the arch of Tower Bridge. His talons skimmed the churning water. El Draco banked and dived, settling into the airstream made by his tail. The ancient beast tried to follow him beneath the lower platform of the cantilever bridge, but at the last minute rose, tucking his wings in, and bulleting through the larger gap above the bridge's road section.

They rose, circling the city. St. Paul's, the Old Bailey, St. Martin-in-the-Fields, Covent Garden all swept by beneath them. Callaghan's wings swept tiles from roofs as he flew over them. The spines of his tail caught on Wren's ornamental masonry, sending the leering body of a gargoyle crashing to the street far below.

And El Draco gained on him remorselessly, so much more adept in the air.

El Draco snagged Callaghan's tail, and he knew that the older dragon had him. He couldn't shake him loose. He tried. He twisted and writhed desperately, the added weight dragging him down. Far below him he saw the tower of Big Ben, and behind it, Parliament House. He felt himself being dragged down, and loosed an almighty breath of fire. The heat took him up, giving him the precious altitude he needed to reach the old clock tower.

He twisted, tucking his left wing in, swiveling to slam El Draco into the spire of Big Ben. The impact was vicious, tearing the dragon from his tail as debris scattered in every direction.

Callaghan used the moment's respite to *fly*. As far and as fast as he could.

The last of the golems, wearing the claret and blue of West Ham, stood motionless beside the river.

Callaghan streaked through the air, heading straight for it.

There was movement within its battered and broken musculature, but the enchantment binding it was failing. He saw it crumbling apart as he banked low, coming in fast. Callaghan flew toward it, turning quickly as it passed, and *breathed*, bathing it in fire.

The golem caught light, burning like a giant Guy Fawkes over the Parliament the old malcontent would have burned down. Callaghan banked again, coming back for another run at the blazing golem as El Draco reached it.

The ancient dragon fought to maintain his momentum, shaking off the blazing corpses as they fell on him. But that moment was all Callaghan needed to fall on him. Callaghan...Callagh'an... there was no difference now...sank his talons into the ridges of El Draco's spine, digging deep between the scales into the soft meat beneath. He rose, unleashing a huge tongue of fire to take him up, his wings beating powerfully against the currents of air, riding the thermals as he climbed. They tore at each other. Talons sank beneath scales, digging into the meat of the dragon. They bit and burned, searing ridges and spines of dragonhide. They clawed at eyes and roared, spinning and spinning as they climbed. Huge jaws snapped around throats, teeth sinking in, piercing, puncturing, opening. And still they fought, rising ever higher. Over and over, tearing and rending and ripping. Higher and higher, lacerating, slashing, and shredding. Faster and faster, burning, biting, and battering. And then, somewhere during the ascent, El Draco's wings no longer beat at the air.

Callaghan strained to carry the dragon higher still, gouging and biting as he did, until the once majestic El Draco was little more than a lump of lifeless meat in his grip.

And still he rose, until he could climb no more. Black clouds churned all around him. Every muscle in his powerful body blazed against the strain of his burden weighing down on him, against the tainted air and the sheer agony of the battering his body had taken, and knew that he could carry El Draco no further.

Smoke billowed out of his nostrils as he breathed hard, each huge intake of air requiring a supreme effort.

Callaghan vented one final tongue of flame, burning away the black cloud so that he could watch his enemy fall, and released his grip. One of his talons tore away as it snagged in the tatters of El Draco's wing. It was a small price to pay for victory. He let out a roar of victory that rumbled across the rooftops of London as the ancient beast fell to the river, its lifeless body not resisting the pull of the water as it sank beneath the waves.

Callaghan's moment of victory was short-lived, though, as exhaustion overtook him, every last ounce of energy suddenly spent. The fire in his heart burned out. His wings felt unbearably heavy. He was barely able to use them to slow his descent.

He fell the last few feet to the ground in human form.

CHAPTER 61

UNFINISHED BUSINESS

Sabine was the first to come to his aid, pressing water to his lips.

"That was some show," the LN-7 man said. "I'm thinking of calling you the Red Arrow."

Callaghan didn't feel up to laughing. He coughed, every spasm that raked his body was agonizing.

"What about the girl?" he asked finally, taking another sip of the water gratefully. "I saw her there... I saw her set the stone in his head... Tell me you got her."

"No such luck. She gave us the slip while you were doing your thing up there."

"Then it's all been for nothing," he said, but Sabine shook his head.

"Not at all. Her name's Alice Ho. She's got a place on Curzon Street, and a workshop on the Isle of Dogs. And she's racking up enemies like they're going out of fashion. There's a certain follower of Cernunnos who is none too happy with her, for a start. But my guess is you'll find her at The World's End. We're in no hurry to pick her up. She's all yours."

Callaghan tried to sit up. "How did you manage to identify her? Did you already know?"

Sabine shook his head. "One of her accomplices was left behind and he's singing like a bird." Sabine laughed, but Callaghan didn't get the joke. "Meeting you has been an experience, Jack. I had heard about men with your, ahh, unexpected talents, but never met one. A dragon scion!" He shook his head again. It took Callaghan a moment to realize it was in admiration. "I must say, I'm rather hoping we get to do this again. If you're interested, that is?"

Callaghan resisted laughing; he felt like he had been only a moment from death and yet here Sabine was offering him a job with LN-7.

He looked at the man, trying to gauge if he was reading him right.

Sabine handed him a set of the team's coveralls. That was when Callaghan realized he was naked, his body blackened with soot.

"We'll take care of cleaning this lot up," Sabine said. "No need for you to hang around. Go home. Clean yourself up. Then go get the girl, hero."

* * *

Sabine had done a good job of getting the living room cleaned up; the corpse had been removed, the bloodstains scrubbed clean out of the carpet, and the mirror cleaned of the bloody message.

The only obvious signs that remained were the two nail holes in the coffee table.

Callaghan poured himself a whisky and looked at the index cards still spread on the dining table. He pushed them around with one hand. Every word written on them looked so prosaic, while the truth was anything but. These had not just been a series of audacious thefts; they were an incredible and complex route to resurrection. It was something that no amount of studying could have revealed. He could have scattered the cards any which way and never come within a hundred miles of the truth. He looked at them one last time for the day. He could see the critical path that joined them all now, from the first theft, the gem in the necklace that Alice had needed to stir El Draco from the depths of Morty's unconscious to the *Koh-i-Noor* which gave him his wings back. The maps charted the crimes one by one, taking her from the library to the museum and the Drake Jewel all the way to the Tower by way of Hampton Court, the home of the dead queen, Anne Boleyn. It was all there, even if it didn't make any sort of rational sense.

He hadn't noticed it before, but on the card with the words *Drake Jewel*, Sabine had scrawled the name *Francis Drake*, and beneath it: *Nickname: El Draco, the dragon*, and scratched under it in red ink. He hadn't seen Sabine write it down. He had no idea what had set the LN-7 man thinking in that direction.

No. That wasn't true. He knew. It had to have been that moment in Morty's place…the rage inside him…the way it had spilled over into everything. Morty had recognized what Callaghan was even before he himself knew. It wasn't just that he'd masked it. Alice, the thief, had started to wake him in between those meetings. She must have pressed the stolen gem into his hand and watched as he began to understand. And that was why, when Callaghan returned, Morty had been so off with him. He *knew*. Not at the beginning, but at the end.

There was a lot to think about, but it was all there.

He ran a steaming hot bath and sat in it with another full glass, enjoying the touch of water on his skin, feeling its restorative properties ease away the aches and pains he had been able to ignore until now. He'd put men on the Curzon Street townhouse and the Docklands apartment; both had been empty when the cars arrived. He'd find her, though. He knew who she was. He sank beneath the water, slowly letting bubbles leak from his mouth to pop on the surface.

He still didn't understand his connection to Alice Ho. Not completely. How much of a link did they share? Why were they even linked? Surely any link that existed should have been to Morty, not him…but why had she been able to share his flashback? Was it simply because he had killed her? Did being her murderer mean they were joined forever in some metaphysical manner? Was it that in killing her, he had sealed his own death at the hands of her mate, El Draco, forming an impenetrable Ouroboros of cause and effect all around them?

Anger bristled inside him at the thought of his mortal enemy feigning human helplessness like that, the water around him bubbling as it heated to a rapid boil, but before it could blaze out of control, he mastered it, focusing on thoughts of Alice... and their bond.

Was it still there, now?

Could she sense him?

Could he reach out to her?

What did it mean?

So much had happened to him, so many things that radically altered the way he thought, that the idea of carrying on as he had been was out of the question. Perhaps he could help Sabine. It was worth thinking about. LN-7. Was he that sort of man? Yes. That was exactly the sort of man LN-7 he was. Questions plagued him. Answers were the only things that gave him rest, and it had *always* been in his blood to protect this place. What else was he going to do?

He didn't notice that the water never went cold, despite him being in the bath for more than three hours.

Wrapped in a robe, Callaghan took his glass downstairs for a final top-up before he turned in for the night.

"Mr. Callaghan," a voice said from the shadows. "We've heard that the thief slipped through your fingers today. Say it isn't so?"

There was no question who the voice belonged to. The twins didn't have to reveal themselves to talk to him. They couldn't know about his change, though; if they did, then surely they wouldn't be bothering him now. Or maybe they would. He had power, but what was that fire against the dead? Did he hold any sway over the dead? Not in his present state, he thought.

"Not through mine," he said. It was the truth, if not the whole truth.

"We hear you've put guards on two places, a posh townhouse in Mayfair and some flashy apartments over in the Isle of Dogs." He sniffed. "They linked to our thief?"

"Yes," Callaghan said. There was no point in lying; they would get the truth from him eventually no matter what he said.

"Good man. Reggie reckoned you'd try and blag us. I didn't. I had faith in you, Mr. Callaghan," said Ronnie. "But it's a good job you didn't try to lie to us. We already paid our girl a visit. Lucky for her, she wasn't there; unlucky for us, neither was our property."

"That's as much as I know. Sorry. You asked me to get you a name. That's it. Alice Ho."

"Word is she weren't working alone." Again that sniff. It was the punctuation of intimidation. "Would you happen to know anything about that?"

Callaghan knew what would happen if he told them where Sabine had said he'd find Alice.

"Don't hold back, Mr. Callaghan."

"Yeah, you don't wanna do that," Ronnie agreed.

"We just want our property back."

"Of course you do." Callaghan didn't believe him, but it was nothing to him now. "Try The World's End," he suggested, knowing he was damning Alice in the process. Ghosts of gangsters versus the shadow of a dragon: who would win? "You know it?"

"Thank you for being so cooperative. We really do appreciate it. In fact, we appreciate it so much, Ronnie and me, that we hope that we won't be seeing you again, if you know what I mean?" The threat was obvious even if it was unspoken. They would be back if the information proved incorrect or insufficient.

Epilogue

The quiet of The World's End was shattered by the sound of breaking glass.

Shadwell had been half asleep. He came alert immediately. He rushed into the pub, baseball bat in hand. The long mirror behind the bar had been splintered and the optics torn from their mounts.

"What the…?" he demanded.

Alice lurked in the shadows waiting to see how this played out. She had come here to kill him. Or at least, she thought she had. Grief twisted her thoughts around so much she couldn't focus on anything. Joseph. El Draco. Friends, lovers, stolen from her. And at the root of that loss, Rufus Shadwell. She hated him. He was a cancer in her life. A destroyer.

She closed her eyes, wrestling for control of her emotions. Grief was overwhelming, but if she allowed it to worm its way into every inch of her soul it would lead to mistakes…and mistakes would lead to death. But then, being dead wouldn't be so bad, would it? Not if that's where her beloved waited?

Two hours ago she had been under the filthy water of the Thames, cradling the corpse of El Draco, reduced to the ruin of an old man once again, and clutching the *Koh-i-Noor*, which hadn't been enough to save him.

An hour ago she had burned his body, building a pyre for him, the dragon to flames returned.

Without him she was nothing. That was all she could think. But she was determined that wouldn't be so. She had the gems, including the *Koh-i-Noor,* and she had the Drake Jewel... She would find him again, if he was there to be found. In the meantime, she would become something else: vengeance. It started with Shadwell, now, but this was only the appetizer; the policeman, Callagh'an, was the main course. She would find a way to overcome that block and release her dragon, and then nothing in this world or any other would help him.

She knew that Shadwell wasn't even aware that she was there; she had a gift for hiding in the shadows. Unfortunately, she couldn't be sure that the same went for the two men and the shades they had taken their orders from. They hadn't paid her the slightest bit of attention as they'd shattered the bottles, but that did not mean that they were unaware of her presence.

"Mr. Pennington, I presume?" the man asked, then smiled coldly as Rufus was about to set them straight with his usual smooth talk. They weren't about to be charmed. "Oh no, he's sort of tied up in the Tower, isn't he? We know what it's like in there, don't we, Ronnie? You might say we had a bit of holiday in there a while ago." The man laughed at his own joke, but didn't expect anyone else to laugh along with him. "So I guess you must be Mr. Shadwell? We've been hearing your name a *lot* lately."

"What do you want? Money? Is that it? Are you expecting me to pay for protection? You and Joe have some sort of deal in place? We can honor it, I'm sure. No need for this to get nasty."

"Once upon a time, maybe," the shade said, "but not anymore. We just want what's ours. We believe that you either have it or know where it is."

"I don't have anything of yours."

"I think that you do, Mr. Shadwell. We're not patient men, you understand? So when I say something of ours was stolen in a bank robbery recently, I expect you can appreciate that we are a little vexed, yes?" He didn't wait for Rufus to answer. "To make matters worse, it seems that these items may have found their way into your possession. Now, I'm willing to believe this was an honest mistake on your part, Mr. Shadwell, and that you didn't intentionally plan to rob us, because that would be, well, rude. What we are looking for, Mr. Shadwell, if I really have to spell it out to you, are two coins. Two gold coins."

"Those are mine," Shadwell said. "They have always been mine."

"Our mum gave us those coins, Mr. Shadwell. They mean a lot to us."

"They are *mine*!"

"No, Mr. Shadwell, see, they can't be yours, because they are ours. Mum found them in the mud of the Thames and kept them for us."

Alice slipped out of the pub and into the office. It was going to get ugly. She smiled. Shadwell wouldn't back down. She hated him. But he was hers to kill, not theirs.

The safe offered no real challenge.

She felt the metal of the tumblers as they fell into place, guiding them until she heard the reassuring click of the lock open.

Words tumbled out.

Bran.

The head raged, the Raven King's voice threatening to betray her. She clapped a hand over his mouth and said forcefully, "Soon. I'm going to take you back to the Tower. I swear. I'm going to bring my friend back from the hell this bastard trapped him in there, but I can't without you. I need you to bring the ravens with you. But if you don't *shut up*, none of that's going to happen."

The head seemed to understand, at least that was how she interpreted its sudden silence.

She found the coins inside a small velvet pouch. There were other coins and gems in there, secured in great bound volumes. He hadn't been slow in bringing his possessions with him.

She took the bag, but left the rest untouched, closing the safe behind her, just in case Bran took it into his head to issue some sort of war cry.

Alice returned to the pub, seeing Shadwell beginning his transformation, but the men were ready for him and cast a net over his head, sending Shadwell thrashing to the ground unable to escape its snare.

"I don't think you quite understand the gravity of your situation, Mr. Shadwell. We've done a bit of digging. You're not very popular, Mr. Shadwell. In fact, it's safe to say that there are a lot of people out there who would love to have a nice quiet chat with you. Face-to-face, so to speak. We don't want to be the ones who tell them where to find you. Like I said, all we want is our property back."

Shadwell tried to free himself from the net, but the more he struggled, the tighter he seemed to become entangled. One of the thugs walked up to him, shaking a can. There was enough petrol to soak him.

Shadwell froze as the second thug struck a match.

"If you get your property back, will you just walk away?" Alice asked. Every eye turned to look at her standing in the doorway.

"You have my word as a gentleman and a scholar, my dear," the shade said. He gave absolutely no reaction to her appearance. "We have no interest in hurting your friend, just maintaining our reputation, you understand?"

"I understand," she said, tossing the bag to the nearest thug. "But he's not my friend."

The man tipped the contents into his open palm, showing the two golden coins to the shade. "Thank you, Alice. You are a lady of many talents," Ronnie Kray said with admiration. "We're done here."

"Not quite." She turned to the man with the match. "Give me that."

The thug turned to the shade, looking for permission. Ronnie Kray nodded.

Alice lit the match and flicked it at Shadwell.

He screamed as his body was engulfed in flames, the cries quickly becoming desperate caws as the ropes of the net burned through. He writhed, contorting on the floor, the flames scorching the beer-stained carpet, and blurred, desperately trying to transform.

Alice watched him pitilessly. "That's for Joseph. For my love. For me."

The shades looked on approvingly.

And blazing like a phoenix, Rufus Shadwell completed the shift, becoming a raven and trailing the ghosts of embers as he flew through the window into the night.

She didn't care if he lived or died, only that he was out of her life.

THE END

ACKNOWLEDGEMENTS:

A lot of hardworking people do their best
to make me look good and I love them for
it. Again, Darren, hope you enjoy your guest
appearance, Adele for the cheerleading, Pat
for the Fantasy Football, Nate for steering
me this way, Jordan for being an awesome
wingman, Mathias for the amazing art, and
of course, Patricia, who invited me to play
with her toys...

ABOUT THE AUTHOR:

Over the last decade Steven Savile has written twenty novels, beginning in the popular *Warhammer Fantasy* universe, then adapting the cult *2000AD* comic strip *Sláine* into a series of novels. He's written for TV shows including *Doctor Who, Torchwood, Primeval,* and *Stargate,* as well as his own worlds, including the UK bestseller *Silver,* and his first YA original *Traitor's Heir.* Most recently he wrote the official novelization of the computer game *Risen 2: Dark Waters* and *Black Chalice,* an extension of the King Arthur legends. He also wrote the storyline for the massive bestselling computer game *Battlefield 3*, and Sony Entertainment in the United States recently bought the rights to turn one of his stories, *Monster Town,* into an exciting new big-budget television show.

His books have been published all across the world, becoming bestsellers in the United Kingdom, Italy, and Germany. He has also won the Best Young Adult Novel category in the 2010 Scribe Awards given out by the International Association of Media Tie-In Writers for his *Primeval* novel, *Shadow of the Jaguar,* the Writers of the Future Award, and was runner-up in the British Fantasy Award.

Basically, he's a gaming nerd who loves TV and books and music, and refuses to grow up.